Saw the Sea

PJ Flynn

TO DAD

THIS IS BASED ON A TRUE STORY

CONTENTS

PART ONE

We are the pilgrims, master: we shall go
Always a little farther: it may be
Beyond that last blue mountain barred with snow,
Across that angry or that glimmering sea.
- James Elroy Flecker,
The Golden Journey to Samarkand

INTRODUCTION

My Father, the Sea, and the Tapes He Left Behind

You don't know what a hero is until you're old enough to hear what his silence left behind.

My dad was my hero. He wasn't some storybook hero or high-ranking officer with a wall of medals. He was no officer at all. Just a Navy man through and through, who served aboard an LST in the sweltering gut of the Pacific Theater during the Second World War. The kind of man who once patched a cracked radiator hose with an old belt and kept driving. Who drank his Pabst Blue Ribbon straight from the can and wore white undershirts year-round, though by July, the sleeves were always gone.

I remember those summer nights. Crickets sawed in the tall grass, dry and metallic. The hum of someone mowing two blocks over even though the sun was already sinking. We'd be out front, him in one of those old aluminum-framed lawn chairs with the plastic webbing that stuck to your thighs, and me on the porch step, or the cooler, or just in the grass, waiting for that voice I trusted.

And he always had stories.

Most veterans don't like to talk about the war. Not Dad. He'd tilt his head back, stare up at the stars, maybe seeing the Pacific in that black sky, and out would come the stories. Kamikazes and typhoons. Diesel fumes and salt spray. Days so hot you could fry an egg on the deck. He talked with the ease of a man remembering old friends more than old fears. I asked too many questions. He never told me to hush. He liked that I cared.

But being a hero didn't always look the way you expect.

It looked quieter. Simpler.

It was my dad waving at every damn car that passed us on a two-lane road, grinning at strangers with the warmth most men saved for old friends. It was him talking to strangers in the hardware aisle, treating them as cousins he hadn't seen since the war. Didn't matter who they were. Man, woman, kid, gas station clerk or guy with a neck tattoo and a 12-pack of Natural Light. Dad talked to them as though they mattered. As though they had already been counted in.

And as a kid, that used to mortify me. I'd shrink behind him in line at the store, praying he'd just pay for the milk and bread and keep walking. But he never did. He'd make a joke or ask the clerk where they were from. I'd tug his shirt and whisper, can we go now, and he'd wink and say, relax, Paddy. This here's just life happening.

It took me years to understand how few people carried themselves that way.

Because even though Dad was warm and good-natured, one of those rare people who made the world feel a little less cold, there was a line you didn't cross with him. And God help you if you did.

I saw it once. Just once.

Some cookout in the park. Fourth of July, probably. Paper plates, lawn chairs, hot dogs burned on one side. Everyone drinking and laughing the way people do when there's sun on their shoulders and Monday's far away. Some guy, friend of a friend, slapped my dad on the back and said, ain't that right, you old son of a bitch?

Most people would've laughed it off.

Not Dad.

He always said his mother wasn't a bitch, and if someone called him a son of one, joking or not, that was crossing a line.

I saw it happen in a blink. His posture shifted. Shoulders back. Fists clenched at his sides, old wrenches of bone and scar. The air dropped ten degrees. His eyes narrowed. The hand holding his beer went so still the condensation stopped running. No yelling. No bluster. Just that look.

The other guy, Murray I think, barrel-chested, loud all afternoon, went ghost pale. Stammered, tried to laugh, offered an apology that came out as a cough. But his feet were already backing him away.

Then the moment passed. The air reset. Dad sat back down, took a sip of his beer, and went back to talking about outboard motors or fishing lures or whatever it was. As though nothing had happened.

But it had happened. And I never forgot it.

Dad was the friendliest man I ever knew. But he came from a time and a place where respect mattered. Where words meant something. And if you insulted his mother, even by accident, you'd better mean it. Because he sure as hell did.

Years passed. Life came in like tidewater. Steady, unstoppable, and a little indifferent. I moved out. Got a job. Got distracted. But the itch never left me. I wanted to preserve those stories.

One day I asked him. Dad, you gotta record those. Put them on tape. I wanna have them forever.

He waved me off. Said his voice wasn't what it used to be, not since the cancer. But I kept at it.

Then one day, by some small miracle, he handed me a little bundle wrapped in a rubber band. Five dusty cassette tapes. His handwriting on the labels was shaky but clear.

Navy Stories - Dad

That night I sat cross-legged on the floor of my old bedroom. Popped the first tape into my Walkman. Pressed play.

His voice filled my ears. Raspy, slower, thinner than I remembered. And for a moment he was sitting right beside me again. Beer in hand. Stars above. The cicadas rising and falling, wave after wave, on some distant, invisible shore.

A few years later I moved to Australia. He passed not long after. The cancer finally won. Or maybe it just wore him down.

All that's left now are those five tapes.

What follows is my attempt to share what he gave me. Some names have been changed. A few scenes rearranged or trimmed, the shape adjusted so the story could move under its own wind. But the heart of it, the truth of it, is untouched.

This is a recollection, a testimony of memory: of men, of places, of days that never made it into textbooks or muster rolls. It is a human story, told through the eyes of a young man on an old ship, sailing into war and whatever came after, not a catalog of specs or ordnance.

This is what remains of his voice, thin on old tape and carried forward as best I can. From here, the story belongs to him, though the telling has passed through me.

1932 – The Great Depression

The year the corn failed I turned ten. The wind came down off the prairie like it meant to take something from us. We kept a bucket by the door to catch rain but there was no rain. Just dust in the pail and dust in the bedclothes. My sister coughed in her sleep and sometimes woke with her mouth black and dry as chalk.

Mom soaked rags and hung them over the windows, but it made no difference. The dust came through nailholes, floorboards, the chimney throat. It settled in the coffee tin and in our ears and under our nails. It got in the bread dough and we ate it anyway. I remember picking grit from between my teeth and swallowing it, proof we had anything at all to chew.

We lived on the edge of Wagner, South Dakota, in a shack with three rooms and no insulation but the quilts we sewed from what we couldn't sell. Tarpaper walls held down by old tires. Boards that moaned when the wind rose. The stove was an old iron Franklin with one cracked leg. The cold came up through the floor and fed on us from beneath. Nights we slept piled together in the big bed. Me and my brothers and my sister, elbows tucked and knees drawn up, her fists pressed to her ribs to hold back the ache.

Mom made coffee from burnt wheat and told us it was close enough. We told her it was good, even when it wasn't.

Dad was rough stock. Irish blood. Big in the shoulders. Scar on his brow from a barroom glass. He could not read and he could not write, and the shame of it lived deep in him. You could see it when paper came out, when names were called for, when the talk turned to things written down and settled by men with softer hands. Something would darken in him then. He fought because fighting asked nothing of letters. He could whip a man twice his size and once laid out six in a row, if the telling was true. He taught us boys to hold our ground, chin down, fists up. When we dropped our hands he cuffed us hard across the ears. He said the world would put you down fast enough without you leaning into it.

He worked when work could be found and when it could not he went to liquor. Once the bottle had him the days quit keeping count. He would go off down the road and come back days later with blood on his shirt and whiskey rising off him before he reached the door.

He hid jars of corn liquor in the floorboards, mean and clear. Called it his lightning and held it up in the lamplight, the only friend he had left. Some evenings I came home from school to find him and his buddies slouched on the porch steps, passing those jars between them, their talk getting louder and meaner as the dark came on. Mom kept us inside and we learned how to stay small.

I don't remember when the fighting started. Only that it never really stopped. He taught us the way he'd been taught. No words, no warning. Just Get your hands up. Then he came at us slow, studying us the way a buyer studies stock, watching how we moved, where we flinched, how long our anger took to rise.

One morning the sky went black at noon. We'd seen storms before but this one rolled like judgment. A wall of wind and grit that ate the horizon. Mom screamed for us to get inside. She wet the sheets and nailed them over the windows. The dust hit with the sound of iron running through the walls. The lamps burned by midday and you couldn't see your own hand. I heard the porch groan and knew he was out there, cursing at the sky trying to shame it into giving.

After it passed, we dug out the front step with tin bowls and our bare hands. The yard was gone, just a dune now, and silence. Inside, dust had found every seam and laid its gray hand over the table and bedclothes. Mom sat on the kitchen floor with a bowl of dough collapsed in her lap, sobbing without sound. Dad stood at the door with his arms folded, his face gone still. He did not curse the sky. He just stood there.

Next morning he came out with work gloves and dropped them in the dirt.

Get your hands up, he said. The world don't care if you cry.

We fought in turns. Me and Dan and Orville, our arms heavy, our breath short, the sun already hot on the backs of our necks. He took our measure in silence, his eyes gathering us in without mercy. When I caught his wrist he grinned, then knocked me back so hard I bit my tongue.

That's the only truth, he said. What you carry in your blood.

I nodded with my eyes on him, wanting only to be seen.

When the dust eased, the locusts came. They rode the wind in dark masses, devouring whatever green remained. They rattled across the roof by the thousands, a hard dry clicking that never stopped. By nightfall they had taken the fields clean down to sticks. The corn was gone. Beans vanished. The county stood shorn to stalk and stem. We swung sticks through the swarm and shouted ourselves empty, and still they rose and settled and fed. The sky blackened with them and the whole county took on the sour stink of a green world being eaten alive.

We lived lean. Lard on dry bread. Potato skins boiled in ditch water. Sometimes just silence at the table. My sister whimpered in the night, too tired to cry proper. I rested my hand on her belly, wanting to give comfort and knowing only the shape of my own helplessness.

Once we salted a hog. It turned in the barrel before we could cook it. That night half the town was doubled over in the grass and the women spewed bile into the ditch. Dad kicked the barrel till the staves broke and the slop spilled into the dirt. The dogs whined and would not go near it. The whole place stank for days, a sour living sickness, and folks talked about it for months.

That night he sat up by the stove while Mom lay in the bed, a wet rag on her neck, and every time she stirred he looked over but did not say her name.

A man came up the road one afternoon in a long coat and fedora, his boots clean, hands like he'd never lifted a shovel. Said there was land out west. Programs. Camps. Said California had water and trees that kept their green all year. Said oranges. He said that more than once. Oranges.

I asked what California looked like.

He said the air was sweet with fruit.

Dad stood behind me, arms crossed, unmoving. After the man left, he lit a cigarette and stared at the road awhile. Then he turned to me.

Ask again and I'll tan your hide.

I didn't ask again. But for days I watched the wind for some answer, some faint map written in grit and sky.

The years went long. Wagner withered. The feed store boarded up. You could walk down the road and count more panes gone than left whole. The church mice outnumbered the congregation. The trains passed but never slowed, and the rails stayed bright with absence.

We stayed. Each day we woke and waited for something to give. By then the world had narrowed to hunger, storm, and the sound of his fists beating us tough as leather.

I used to think we were waiting on rain.

But it wasn't the rain.

It was the fight.

I didn't know when or where, only that somewhere it already carried my name.

1932 – The Fight

We walked the road to school each morning, four of us in a crooked line against the wind. Dust moved in low spirals across the prairie. The land stretched flat and empty, offering nowhere to hide. Nothing between us and the sky but our own breath.

Some mornings the frost clung to the barbed wire in thin lacework. Our breath froze in our collars. In summer the heat rose off the dirt in wavering sheets. We walked in every weather. The road only ran one way.

Flo counted fenceposts. Orville chased grasshoppers until his nose ran. Dan kicked at stones with punishment in every swing of his boot. I walked at the front because I was the oldest and Dad said that meant something.

Once we passed a mule half-buried in the dirt, its hide cracked and drawn tight, old leather over bone. Another time a hawk followed us nearly a mile. Dan said it was waiting for Orville to fall over. Flo told him to hush. Orville cried anyway. The wind carried it off behind us.

I was ten. Dan was nine, Flo seven, Orville five, and Leo still home with Mom. We wore thin coats and hand-me-down boots and carried the cold in our bones. I carried the weight of being first whether I wanted to or not. Dad said the oldest takes the blows first, and if he falls, the rest fall harder. Said if a man would not

"asa

hold his line then those behind him were lost. I was only a boy, but I believed him.

The schoolhouse was one room with cracked windows that rattled in their frames and a stove that smoked more than it burned. The floor groaned when you walked on it. Desks were carved with names of boys who had gone east or under. Inside, the heat lay close with coal smoke and ink and the faint steam of boiled potatoes from lunches wrapped in wax paper. Some kids had nothing but lard on a biscuit. Some had nothing at all and stared straight ahead, hunger carved into their faces. You learned not to ask. Miss Culver was the teacher. Her hair tied close to her head and she was not kind. She kept a willow switch laid across her desk and each morning she tested it with a little flick, the air snapping open.

Flo sat in the front, her hair tied with string, dress patched twice over. She liked school, and she liked Miss Culver. She tried to please her. But girls don't survive on kindness alone.

Dan and Orville sat behind me. Dan was fast with his mouth. Orville couldn't sit still long enough to hold a pencil right. Dad's fire ran in both of them, same as me. We didn't always know what to do with it.

I tried with the reading. I did. Mom said a man who can read walks straighter in the world. I was slow but steady. I liked the numbers better. Numbers didn't lie. They didn't buckle when the wind blew.

At recess the world widened. Just wind and weed stubble and the reach of bare land. We played ball with rags or pushed each other around for the heat of it. The teacher never stopped us. Boys fought. That was just part of the curriculum.

That day the wind was sharp enough to sting. Dan came running, his voice already broken with urgency. He said Tommy Kruger had Flo hemmed up near the fence.

I heard the shouting before I saw anything. Then I saw the ring. Children circled, faces sharp with the old joy of violence. Flo stood in the center, her dress yanked sideways, hands clutched in her lap. Tommy was circling her, bigger than me by a head, soft in the middle but loud. He called her patch-girl, rag-princess, said maybe he'd buy her braid for a nickel. One of the older girls looked on and said nothing.

Flo kept her eyes on the ground. She didn't cry loud. She never did.

The Krugers lived across the road in a weathered house with a crooked porch and a lean in its bones. Their yard was bare dirt and twisted wire and old rust. Their chimney smoke came out darker than anyone else's. On Sundays you could see folks cross the street rather than walk past their yard.

The Krugers had children everywhere, some born to them, some kin, some simply taken in because no one else would have them. They spilled off the porch like beetles from a stump, all elbows and open mouths. People said they were feral. That nothing good could grow in that house. Even the dog was mean. A half coyote mutt they called Pup, missing half a tail and limping from a bullet in his leg, ready to bite anyone dumb enough to get close.

Nobody stopped the Kruger boys. Neither teachers nor deacons. Not the sheriff. You gave them space and hoped they turned their rage on someone else.

I pushed through the ring. Shoved Tommy back.

Try that on me, I said.

He looked surprised, but not scared. He spat in the dirt and pulled a wood chip from his pocket. Balanced it on his shoulder, a poor boy's crown.

The others closed in tighter. They started to chant, low and sharp. That sound cut through me harder than the wind.

I knocked it off.

He came at me quick. No stance, just fists and fury. I stepped aside and caught him in the nose. Felt the pop in my hand. He staggered, swung wide, caught the edge of my chin, but I didn't move. I hit him in the ribs and he dropped.

The dust kicked up around us. The crowd screamed, high and wild, and the yard filled with the sound of weather breaking loose.

Get up, Kruger, I said.

He blinked. Blood and snot on his face. He looked small in a way no boy should look, emptied by fear. He crawled to his feet and ran.

Dan whooped. Orville laughed till he hiccupped. Flo wiped her face. She didn't smile, but she looked at me like I'd done something that mattered.

That night, before bed, she whispered, You didn't have to. I could've handled it.

I didn't answer.

I wasn't proud. I was shaking.

I heard Dad in my head, hard as ever. A man stands his ground.

We walked home under a low red sun that hung in the dust, tired and hungry. Flo held my hand the whole way. Dan and Orville chased each other, kicking rocks into the ditch. I didn't say much. My knuckles stung. I kept clenching and unclenching my fist just to be sure it was mine.

I expected trouble. The Krugers didn't forget. I thought they'd be waiting. But when we reached the shack it stood the same as we left it. Three rooms against the wind. The chimney leaning. The windows blinking with dust.

That night the sky burned yellow, thin and fevered, with a firelight cast. The wind came back strong. Boards shook. The walls moaned. Mom tucked us close and tried to hum a hymn, but her voice cracked and ended in silence.

I lay awake beside Flo. She didn't sleep. Just stared at the ceiling like she was watching something crawl across it. I kept thinking about Tommy. How he had looked when he turned to run. Seen through at last. His bluff called, fear plain in his face.

I didn't feel bigger for it. I felt older.

In my dream I stood in the ring again. The children screaming. My hand bloody. The sky roaring. But nobody moved.

I was only ten. But the world looked different after. And it didn't change back.

The blood dried. The bruises faded. But the ground felt different under my boots. Like it had seen what I'd done. Like it would remember.

1939 – CCC

— • —

I was seventeen when I signed on with the Civilian Conservation Corps. They called it the CCC. A cleaner name. Easier to speak than what it stood for. Land and boys both, two fields left fallow too long. One to be plowed, the other broken in.

I had quit school three years earlier, just past the eighth grade. I could read well enough, write my name, tally a few numbers. Enough to know we were always behind. There wasn't much left in that schoolhouse for a boy who could swing a hammer straighter than a pencil.

Mom didn't argue. She just stood at the sink and nodded. The water was running and I don't know if she heard me or just didn't want to answer. Her hands stilled in the dishwater like she meant to speak, but she didn't.

The CCC recruiter sat behind a card table in the county building with a flag pinned behind him and a stack of forms he barely read. I signed with a stub pencil and didn't look back. That part's true. But the road between signing and leaving felt longer than it ought to.

They sent me west into the Black Hills. The land there looked peeled. Wind worn and mean. Trees stunted by the hard country, punished for trying. The sky hung wide and close. You could hear it listening.

The camp stood in rows, straight and obedient as furrows. Barracks lay flat and tarpapered. A mess hall squatted in the center. The machine sheds stood off to the side. Inside were tractors, graders, and trucks gone half dead with rust, their pans black with old oil.

The boys came from everywhere. Dakota mostly. Some from Minnesota, a few Okies with red dirt baked into their hair. You could see the lean years in hipbones sharp under government wool and wrists loose in their cuffs. You could tell how long a boy had been hungry. You could see it in the teeth.

We slept shoulder to shoulder on narrow cots, so close you could have reached out and touched whatever the other man dreamed. The wool blankets held old sweat and mouse piss. At night the air carried woodsmoke, the sour of old canvas, and the damp rot of boots gone stiff with red dust. You could hear the wind test every seam in the walls. The canvas snapped and bellied in the wind, alive with rough breath.

The bugle cried before sunup. Sharp as a nail driven into sleep. We dressed fast, teeth chattering, and lined up outside while the frost cracked underfoot.

Then came work.

We dug earth till our hands blistered and then we dug some more. Planted trees where there had been none. Long rows to break the wind. Shelterbelts, they called them. We strung wire through the frost and hammered posts with hands gone numb. Some days I drove a tractor, the engine rattling in its iron bones. Other days I was bent over a shovel, or sweating over vats in the mess hall, stirring pots heavy with beans and salt pork and lard. By sundown the work hummed in my bones.

There was no space for dreaming. The work ground it out of you. But sometimes at night, with the lamps low and the wind moving across the barracks roof, your mind would slip somewhere else.

I would think of Mom's voice in the kitchen. My sister laughing through her braid. The little creek behind our shack, gone dry two summers back. I carried those sounds in my head and sheltered them there as long as they would last.

The pay was thirty dollars a month. Twenty five of it went home in an envelope I licked shut with spit. That money kept the lamp oil full. Fed the little ones. I kept five dollars. Small money, though it carried me.

Enough for a bottle, if you found the right backroom. Enough for a dancehall ticket and a half stale roll in someone's barn. We weren't of age, but the war was coming and no one had the stomach to chase us off a stool. We drank whatever we could steal or buy. Corn whiskey. Something called panther sweat that burned hot going down and sat like gasoline in your gut.

There was a boy called Cully from Rapid City. He was long and plain and upright, with hands too large for the rest of him. Could fix anything with a wrench. Didn't know the alphabet past G. Another named Breece who swore he had ridden the rails clean to Amarillo and back. And Blue, the quiet one, singing old sorrowful songs when the wind moved through camp.

On Saturdays we huddled around a barrel fire behind the shed, bottle passed hand to hand. The cold sharp enough to make your spit freeze. Blue would sing, the fire snapping with a bone-dry crack. We talked about girls and Chevrolets and towns we only knew from roadmaps. There was one girl I kept circling back to. Annie. Red shoes, coiled-rope hair, and eyes too sharp to be fooled. I'd seen her at the grange hall twice. Said maybe four words to her. But in the cold, with the bottle warm in my hand, she came back to me and would not leave.

But the drink and the girls and the heat of it never ended clean. There was fighting. Always fighting. Boys full of pride and corn liquor, ready to bleed over nothing. A word. A grin. A hand on the wrong girl's waist. We fought behind barns and in alleys and out in the fields under a white moon. Fists landed. Teeth broke. Blood went dark in the dust. I had been raised for it. Dad had put hardness into us the only way he knew, and by then my body understood before my mind did. I struck to end the matter. A man I hit hard usually stayed where he fell. The ones who crawled off talking vengeance never found their way back.

The nights stank of liquor, sweat, and blood. Boys came back to the barracks broken-nosed and bruised, shirts torn, knuckles split. Some laughed, spitting teeth into the dirt. Some lay quiet on their bunks, staring at the ceiling, their eyes dark with ghosts only they could see.

There was a fight behind the bunkhouse one night. A boy from Belle Fourche. Tall. Blond. The kind that always looked sunburnt. He said I had cheated him at cards. We had been playing on a crate with a deck worn soft as cloth. He was drunk enough to believe it.

Then he called me a son of a bitch.

I was up before the others could move.

He came at me wild and wide. I hit him once in the ribs, again in the mouth. He dropped fast. Blood on his teeth, knees in the dirt.

His head hit the frozen ground with the sound of iron splitting wood.

But he didn't get back up.

That was the part I hadn't planned for.

He just lay there. Breathing shallow. Face turned to the side, refusing me even in defeat.

Someone pulled me off him, though I hadn't hit him again. I remember standing there, my breath clouding the dark. My knuckles went numb, then filled with a strange low humming from bone to skin.

We carried him in. He didn't speak to me after. Wouldn't look my way in the mess hall.

The others didn't say much. Just nodded, accepting me by the old law of blood.

But I didn't feel like I'd earned a thing. Just hurt. The kind that didn't show on your face but settled in the meat behind the ribs. I kept waiting for someone to say it had gone too far. But they didn't. So I stopped waiting.

Later that week I saw him again in town, standing alone outside the feed store. His lip split. He looked past my face, cold and empty. Maybe that was worse than a punch.

Annie kissed me once behind the grange hall and laughed into my collar like I'd told a joke I didn't know I'd made. That was the week before the fight. She never came around after. Maybe she heard. Maybe she just had better sense than I did.

The CCC was meant to save us. The land and the boys both. And maybe it did.

The trees we planted remain, and the fences have not given way.

But the boys it made. We came out different.

Harder. Quieter. There was a kind of danger in us we didn't yet have a name for.

I used to think the CCC taught me how to work. But I already knew how to work. What it taught me was how far a man could be pushed. And what waited on the other side of that line. You learn a man's shape from the weight he bears in silence.

Years later I went back to the hills. Just passing through. The camp was gone. Nothing left but some stone blocks and two rusted hinges in the dirt. I walked the path we had cut through the timber. The trees we planted now tall enough to speak in the wind.

Halfway through I found a name carved in one. Faded. Hard to read. Might have been mine. Might have been someone else's. I couldn't say.

I stood there as the sun dropped low, the wind moving through the branches like breath through a body. I waited for something to come back to me, but nothing did. I had come looking for the boy I was, and found only the place that had kept him.

December 7, 1941

The morning came slow and ordinary. The kind of Sunday that never meant to be remembered. A light snow had fallen in the night, just enough to soften the yard and cover the ruts. Mom stood at the stove, frying bacon. The window over the sink had gone white from steam. Dad was out stacking the woodpile again, knocking the snow off with the back of his mitt and hauling what he could inside. Said you never trust a fire to keep burning unless you feed it yourself.

I'd been back from the CCC camp a week. The red dust of the Dakotas clung in the seams of my clothes, in the cracks of my hands. Mom had washed what she could but some places it stayed, a second skin that didn't know it was time to come off.

I sat at the table with the paper spread out, though there wasn't much in it. Wheat prices. A picture of the president. Somewhere down at the bottom, a line about Japan and China, the kind of scrap that seemed to belong to another world. Europe felt the same. A far-off nightmare unfolding behind someone else's door. The war had not touched us. Not yet.

I helped Dad mend a gate behind the shed. The wood was hard with cold and split at the screws. The sun came low and pale through a sky the color of tin. After lunch we listened to a music program out of Sioux City. The station buzzed with static and gospel. I remember thinking how quiet everything was. Even the wind seemed to have stepped back from the house.

By late afternoon the sky had turned the color of ash, and the snow clouds pressed low over the horizon. The house was still. No voices. No radio. Just the faint crackle of lard in the skillet, potatoes browning slow at the bottom. Mom stood at the stove with her sleeves rolled, a paring knife in one hand, slicing thin what was left of the sack. Mostly peel and soft centers. Waste to most folks. But not to us.

Then from next door we heard the neighbor woman cry out. A crash followed. The sound of a plate breaking. Mrs. Anderson sobbing. Long and low.

Dad was out of his chair before any of us could move. He ran across the yard without his coat. We watched from the window. A minute later he came back in hard, boots wet, face gone pale.

Turn on the radio, he said.

He knelt beside it and spun the dial with shaking fingers, tuning past music and static till the voice came through. Clipped. Urgent.

Pearl Harbor... aerial attack... American ships struck... many casualties feared...

The voice kept breaking, words lost inside the static. I had heard sermons on that set, weather reports, crop prices, men selling seed and soap and patent tonics. This was different. The voice came thin and far away, carrying smoke, salt water, and fear.

Dad's face went hard. He hit the side of the set with the heel of his hand.

Goddamn bastards, he said.

No one moved. The potatoes burned. Mom leaned against the counter with both hands flat like she was bracing against a wind that wasn't there. The skillet hissed behind her, blackening. Dan and Orville stood in the doorway, bare feet on the floor boards, their faces small and unsure.

Are you gonna go, Pat? Dan asked.

I don't know, I said.

Dad turned then. You'll go. You both will, he said, though only I was old enough. He said it plain, without anger, with the quiet finality of a man closing a gate.

The radio voice went on. Ships burning. Men lost. The words came slow, each one dropping into us and not coming back.

Out in Wagner other radios had come to life the same way. You heard doors opening and screens slap shut, people stepping out in their housecoats and Sunday shirts, standing on porches and gravel roads with their arms folded against the cold, looking up like they expected to see smoke on our sky. Their voices went low and stayed close, vanishing into the evening air. They got us good, you could hear. There'll be hell to pay now. An old man on the corner just stared east and did not say a thing.

I stood by the sink and looked out into the dusk. The yard lay quiet. The wind had died. Nothing moved. The news entered me cold, then burned as it sank.

The world had changed. Outside, the sky looked like it always had.

Perman showed up just after dark. He came up the road in his coat and gloves, breath white in the air. His boots tracked mud from the thawed ruts. He stopped at the fence and raised a hand. His nose was red from the cold. One eye was always half-squinted, doubtful before anything happened.

You heard? he said.

Yeah. We heard.

He came up the steps and took a seat on the porch rail. His cheeks were raw and windbit. We sat a long time without saying much. Inside the house, the radio kept going. A different voice now, reading from a statement. Declaration. Casualty. Every voice carrying the same doom.

It's war, Perman said.

Yeah.

You going to go?

I think I have to.

He nodded. Me too.

We sat with it a while. The cold rising up through the boards. Our breath came out white and thin. Somewhere down the road you could hear a truck door slam. Another neighbor going to check the radio or warm the engine.

I turned back to the window. Mom was still standing in the kitchen. Her hands weren't moving. Just her eyes. Watching the radio, afraid of what it might say next.

What do you think it'll be like? Perman said.

I don't know. But it's coming for us, whatever it is.

He lit a cigarette. We passed it back and forth. The ember flared red between us, burning down slow.

I kept thinking about the paper from that morning. The picture of the president. The quiet snow. All of it already belonging to some other life.

When the broadcast ended, silence held the room. Dead air hissed from the set. Then the wind came back over the prairie, old and familiar against the walls.

That night I couldn't sleep. I lay in bed and watched the frost grow along the inside of the window. I kept seeing ships burning I had never seen. Men calling out names I didn't know. I didn't feel brave. I didn't feel afraid either. It was deeper than both, the sense of being drawn toward a place my life had been aiming at all along.

Whatever peace had lived in the corners of our house was gone. It would not return.

THE COIN TOSS

The morning after the news broke the farm woke as it always had, but nothing in it felt the same. The frost lay hard across the fields, a brittle crust of ice and snow that turned the stubble of the corn to glass and made each fencepost shimmer in the pale light. The trees stood black and stiff against a sky the color of tarnished pewter. Smoke from farm chimneys rose straight and without sway into the stillness. It was winter in Dakota and the fields lay frozen and bare, the whole country gone quiet under the snow.

Perman came up the road at first light with his collar pulled high, his hat low on his brow. He carried the cold with him into the yard, his breath hung in the air, ghostlike. I watched him come through the haze of that frozen dawn, his boots crunching the snow with the rhythm of a clock that could not be wound back. He stopped at the gate and nodded once.

You hear anything new.

Just the same. Ships burning. Thousands dead.

He spat into the snow.

Guess they got what they came for.

Yeah, I said. And now we'll give it back to them.

We did not waste words. There was nothing to say. The thing was already decided though we had not spoken it aloud.

We climbed into my old Model T. The door hinges creaked and the seat springs groaned and the iron of the machine was cold to the touch. I pulled the choke and cranked and the motor came alive reluctant, coughing into the cold morning. We rolled out slow on the rutted track, the tires whispering and singing their thin hymn on the frozen earth. The road east toward Sioux Falls lay white and hard, a ribbon of ice cutting across the empty miles.

Perman rubbed his hands together.

Cold enough to freeze the devil's spit, he said.

You'll get used to it, I told him. We might be heading for colder yet.

He laughed once, no humor in it.

Long as it's somewhere worth the trip.

The land stretched out around us, wide and without end. Cattle huddled black against the drifts, steam rising from their backs in the brittle air. Here and there a lone farmhouse, shutters closed against the season, the people inside bent close to the stove and the news crackling from the radio. A crow crossed the prairie sky, small and black and ill with meaning.

We said little on that drive. Words felt small against the scale of what had come. We knew the count of the dead and the ships burning in that far harbor, and we knew nothing would go back to what it had been. The Ford rattled and shook, its bones old as our fathers, and it carried us onward, eastward, toward the war we had chosen and the war that had already chosen us.

In my head I saw the nickel already.

Perman had always talked Navy. Said his uncle was a machinist's mate out of Bremerton. Said there was a certain peace in ships. A quiet order. You had a rack and a routine. That was his kind of war.

But I had always imagined something else. I wanted to be a Marine. I pictured jungle patrols and boots in the surf. A rifle across the shoulder and nothing behind me but sea. I thought if you had to go, you ought to go all the way.

We were different that way. Maybe that was why we got along.

Two hours of road and we came into Sioux Falls. The town lay crusted with snow, the streets gray with ice turned black beneath wagon wheels and tires. Storefronts stood frosted and dim, windows clouded by breath and heat. We pulled the car to the curb and let the motor die, the sudden silence broken only by the tick and ping of cooling iron.

Perman lit a cigarette, cupping the match against the wind. He looked out at the long line already forming by the federal building.

Guess we ain't the only ones heard the call, he said.

Guess not.

We sat there for a moment. Perman reached into his coat pocket and drew out a nickel. He turned it between his fingers, the faintest grin on his face though there was nothing of humor in it.

Heads for the Marines. Tails for the Navy. That was the pact.

He flipped it into the air and the coin rose spinning into the cold light, silver turning over and over until it came down and the choice with it. It fell and struck his palm and when he showed it, tails.

I cursed.

Shit. I didn't want to be a sailor.

Perman laughed and shook his head.

Well, you're gonna be one now, Pat.

So it was settled. The coin lay dull and final between us, a small piece of metal that would stay with me longer than it ever stayed in his pocket. We climbed out and walked toward the federal building where the flag hung stiff in the winter air. The wind caught the edge of it and it cracked once, sharp as a shot. A line of men already stretched down the block, collars high, hands in pockets, breath white in the cold. Farmers and ranch hands, machinists and clerks, boys not yet grown and men already stooped by work. None spoke much. Each stared forward, each waiting his turn to step across the threshold and sign his name into the ledger of war.

You think we'll make it through, Perman said.

If we don't, at least we'll have tried.

He nodded.

Reckon that's all a man can do.

I remember the faces. A kid no more than seventeen who looked like he'd lied about his age, his hair sticking out from beneath a cap too big for him. He tried to smile at us but his lips quivered in the cold. Ahead of him a broad-shouldered man in overalls, the knees dark with grease, a wrench still in his pocket like he'd come straight from a garage where the tools lay scattered and the job unfinished. An older fellow stood behind us, lines cut deep in his face, his eyes tired yet fixed steady on the door ahead. He could have been someone's father, someone's grandfather, come to give himself though no one would have asked it of him.

The line shuffled forward. The sound of boots on frozen boards, the low murmur of breath, the flag above us rippling slightly though there was no wind. Someone coughed, another spat into the snow. We moved on, step by step, the line itself seeming to drag us forward.

When at last our place came we stepped inside, the heat close and smelling of ink and wet wool. The walls echoed with the scratch of pens, the clatter of typewriters, the dull bark of orders given. A sergeant behind the desk looked at us without expression and slid the papers across. His eyes were hard but tired, as though he had seen this scene before in another war.

You boys come to sign your lives away he said.

Looks that way, Perman said.

The sergeant grunted.

Could be worse. Could've drawn the Marines.

I picked up the pen. My hand was steady.

When the ink touched paper, my hand no longer felt like my own. The name spread dark beneath the nib, and something deep and cold began to move. For a heartbeat I saw Mom at the kitchen table, her hands folded on the oilcloth. Then the name was written and there was no taking it back.

Perman signed beside me, his hand steady. We were sailors. Not by desire. Not by dream. A nickel had seen to that in the winter light.

Outside the cold remained. Nothing moved on the dim, snow-choked streets. The line of men waited, each moving toward the same end, each bearing his own silence. The world had shifted and none of us could turn it back. Perman looked down the street, the coin in his hand again, turning it once more though there was no need.

You ever wonder what'd happen if it landed the other way he said.

I looked out across the frozen town, the flag snapping against the gray.

No, I said. I think it landed the only way it was ever going to.

SAN DIEGO

That night was the last I would spend beneath my father's roof as a civilian. We gathered around the kitchen table in silence. The air in the room didn't move. Chairs creaked, but no one spoke. The lamp burned low. Dad smoked his pipe. The smoke curled and folded into the shadows and was gone. Mom sat with her hands folded in her lap, her apron stained with flour, her eyes dark with sorrow. My brothers shifted in their chairs, unsure of what to say, and my sister leaned against my side trying to hold me there by force of will alone.

Outside, the wind moved over the prairie, long and low and endless. You could hear it in the corners of the house and in the trees beyond the fence line. Nobody said the word war. It hung between us, a ghost no one dared acknowledge.

Dan's hands were streaked with grease from a broken-down Ford he'd spent the afternoon trying to fix, his fingernails black with grease, the kind that never washed out. Orville picked at the crust of his bread. Leo stared into the flame like he saw something there he hadn't before. Mom wiped her eyes with the corner of her apron and didn't look at me. When she finally did her voice was so soft I nearly missed it.

I wish you didn't have to go.

I know, Mom.

But I reckon you do.

Yes ma'am. I do.

Dad smoked in silence, eyes fixed on nothing. Then he cleared his throat.

You'll serve well, he said. You come back whole, you hear.

I'll do my best.

You've always done that, he said. That's enough.

The fire crackled low in the stove. Outside, the wind pressed against the windowpane and rattled it in the frame. My sister reached across the table and touched my arm and I looked down and saw her tears and didn't know what to say.

After supper I sat on the back steps. The frost had crept up the windowpanes and the pump handle in the yard wore a crown of ice. I could see the toolshed standing black against the night, and above it the stars so clear they looked etched into the sky. I thought about the house and the fields and the people sleeping inside them and wondered if I would ever come back to it in the same shape I was leaving.

At dawn I rose and dressed and went about the motions of breakfast though the food lay tasteless in my mouth. The kitchen held coffee and woodsmoke. Dad shook my hand as a man already gone, and Mom clutched me hard enough to wring the life from me if it meant keeping me there.

You be safe, she said into my chest. You come home to me.

I will, I told her. I promise.

I bid them farewell and I bid farewell to the house and the fields and the long reaches of South Dakota where I'd been a boy and was now no longer. The frost clung to the grass. A dog barked somewhere out past the shed. The sun had not yet broken but the sky held that quiet promise of light.

I walked alone to the bus stop at the edge of Wagner. Gravel popped beneath my boots and the cold cut through my coat and found my bones. I carried what I owned in a sack slung over my shoulder and the rest carried in my chest. Perman was already there.

He stood with his hands in his pockets and nodded when he saw me. He nodded once, his face unchanged.

You sleep.

Not much.

Me neither. Just stared at the ceiling and waited for morning.

We didn't speak much after that. The silence was its own kind of knowing. The bus came around the bend in a rattle of steel and smoke and we climbed aboard. The driver gave us a look like he'd seen a hundred boys just like us and would see a hundred more, then swung the door shut without a word.

We rode in silence through backroads and sleeping fields, frost on the windows, our breath fogging the glass. Farmhouses drifted past in the gray light, barns sagging in defeat, mailboxes leaning crooked along the road. Somewhere a rooster crowed, then thought better of it.

At Sioux Falls we stepped down into a station that stank of coal smoke and wet paper. A thin wind pushed scraps of newspaper along the tracks. We waited on the platform till the train pulled in, long and black and breathing steam, its headlamp cutting through the gloom with the force of judgment. We climbed aboard and found a seat near the rear. Perman folded his coat behind his head and leaned back, ready to sleep the whole way to California. I watched the land fall away behind us, fenceposts ticking past the glass. I don't know when I stopped looking.

It was three days to San Diego. We rode through states that barely had time to settle in our minds before they were gone again.

The land opened out before us and rolled away endless. Prairie grass bent low beneath the wind and the sky was vast and pitiless and blue without limit. We crossed into Nebraska where the earth grew flat and the rivers wound dark and sluggish through the bottomlands. In Colorado the ground began to rise and we watched the long backs of mountains rear up against the horizon, their crowns snowbound and cold, ridged and scarred with old weather. The train cut through passes and tunnels and the smoke of it clung to the walls of the world.

You think the war will change us Perman asked one night.

I think it already has.

He nodded, the answer already in him, and didn't speak again for a long time.

Westward, the land gave way to desert. Harsh rock and sand glared in the sun, and little towns lay adrift in the waste, flotsam from some forgotten sea. In Utah and Arizona the country rose into red stone and sand, and the wind carried grit that tasted of rust and salt. The sun hung hard in the sky. Mesas stood in the distance, old altars abandoned to heat. Ghost towns blinked past and were gone again.

At last the hills softened and gave way to the coastal valleys and the air changed. The dry heat yielded to something salt-heavy and strange. The light seemed to sharpen, and the air carried tar and ocean and a sharpness that had nothing of home in it. The train hissed and slowed and the iron wheels screamed against the rails and we rolled at last into San Diego.

The cars shuddered to a halt and the doors were thrown open. Air came in sharp with salt and tar and oil, and with a newness no country home had taught us. We gathered our things and filed out into the daylight. We stepped down onto the platform, and the place burst around me in light and noise. The sun was too bright. The buildings too clean. The people moved with a kind of speed I didn't trust. Around us stood a scatter of other boys from all across the country. Some with crooked teeth. Some with accents rough as gravel. All of them trying not to look lost.

Perman turned and shaded his eyes against the sun.

This the end or the beginning.

Same thing, I said.

On the platform the Navy men barked orders and pointed us toward the line of buses idling at the curb. Their engines rumbled deep, black smoke curling from the stacks and drifting above the depot, the herald of some new order. I saw boys with hands scarred from the plow and the axe and I saw boys pale and soft who'd known only city streets. Some were wide-eyed and eager, some already worn down by the weight of it. A few smoked cigarettes with the affectation of men though their faces had yet to learn the shape of hardness.

Perman and I moved among them and I thought how every man here had left behind a family, a town, a past. Now we were joined together by nothing more than the choice we had made and the uniform we had yet to wear. The buses growled there in the sun, beasts waiting to bear us off. Beyond them the city shimmered, unknown and vast, and beyond that the Pacific lay as some ancient witness that cared nothing for us at all.

We climbed aboard and found our seats. Inside it was leather and gasoline and sweat. The driver ground the gears and the bus lurched forward. I looked back through the window. The train sat there, its smoke unraveling into the sky, already fading from the world. We were carried through the streets toward the Naval Training Center, what they called Camp Paul Jones.

The bus rolled through the city and I sat with my head canted toward the window watching the streets go past. Storefronts and palm trees, the hard lines of stucco buildings, the bright wash of the sun. Civilians walked past us without seeing us. Maybe we were invisible. Maybe we already didn't belong.

A kid across the aisle pointed.

There's the harbor, he said.

Blue water gleamed in the distance. Cranes moved like iron insects. Ships lay at anchor, quiet, indifferent, gray hulks riding in the bay, their masts and guns etched sharp against the sky.

At length the buses turned and the streets gave way to wide roads and open ground. In the distance the gates of the Naval Training Station rose white and stark in the glare. A great sign announced the place. U.S. Naval Training Station. Beyond it lay a world enclosed, a city within a city, its streets lined with barracks and drill fields, with mess halls and machine sheds and the bones of industry. The air hung with the tang of salt and the odor of oil and tar.

The gates swung wide and the buses growled through. Inside the camp men in uniform moved with the precision of a machine. Their boots struck the pavement in unison, a steady hammering beneath the morning glare. Orders were barked in clipped tones and the recruits who had come before us stood rigid at attention, their faces already stripped of softness, their eyes flat and unyielding.

We rolled past long rows of white barracks, each the same as the next, and past fields where men marched in columns, rifles at their shoulders. I thought then of the prairie back home and the silence of it and I knew that place was gone from me. Perman leaned forward in his seat and peered out.

This place looks like it eats people, he said.

Maybe it does, I told him. No turnin back now.

At last the buses came to a halt in a wide gravel lot. The doors clattered open and we were driven out into the sun, cattle under orders. A petty officer in dark shades waited for us, his voice sharp as wire.

Line up. Move it. Faster, goddammit.

And so we stood shoulder to shoulder, a hundred boys from a hundred places, all of us bound now for the same reckoning. I looked down the rows of faces and thought how by the time we left this place we would no longer be what we had been. Beyond the roofs and masts the ocean waited, something that had seen it all before and would see it all again.

Boot Camp

We were taken inside a long low building where the air reeked of bleach and sweat and fear baked into the paint and the brittle scent of paperwork stacked to yellow and curl. Men with clipboards marked us down. Numbers against names. Names against faces soon to be shorn of what little set them apart. One shouted move and we moved. Always forward. Always to the next station.

Fluorescent lights buzzed overhead with a dry insect hum. The floor was scuffed and streaked with boot rubber and with mud and fallen hair ground flat. A corporal sat smoking behind a desk, ash curling off the end of his cigarette, the butt resting on a tin lid stained with nicotine and ink.

Name, he said, not looking up.

Flynn, I told him.

He checked a list with a pencil worn flat at the end. You're in Company C. Next.

The barbers waited for us with their chairs and clippers already warm from the heads they had stripped before. I sat and the man pressed his hand to my crown and tilted me forward and in moments the hair fell in auburn sheaves at my feet. I stared the pile, the last leaves from a felled tree. A boy left in that pile and a raw-headed recruit in his place. I did not recognize the face in the mirror and they gave me no time to study it. Out of the chair and on down the line.

Someone laughed. A kid with jug ears and a buzzed head said, Jesus, we all look like convicts.

A voice from behind replied, We are.

The corpsmen waited next. White coats stained with ink and sweat. They lined us shoulder to shoulder and drove steel into our arms. Typhoid. Tetanus. Smallpox. Yellow fever. Words I had only read before now burned into the flesh. The sting of it left a throb in the bone. The man ahead of me swayed but did not fall. The man behind me cursed under his breath and was told to shut his mouth.

You ain't done till you've bled for your country, the corpsman muttered, sliding another needle home.

We were herded into another hall where uniforms lay stacked in neat piles, every garment marked and measured by hands that had never known us but knew our size all the same. They flung the bundles into our arms and told us, This is yours now. We stripped off the clothes of our youth, and the old skin of civilian life lay at our feet. We put on the new skin of the navy. The fabric stiff with starch. Boots heavy on the floor. Belts cinched tight. We stood in rows and looked to one another and saw men all stamped to the same pattern, the same rough shape, the same colorless fate.

A kid to my left tried to button his jumper and fumbled. You ever wear one of these?

No, I said.

You look like you were born in it, he said.

The drill instructors came then. Two of them. One tall and lean with a hatchet face, the other broad and silent with eyes that never seemed to blink. They stood before us and let the quiet fill the room.

You belong to us now, the tall one said. You will move when we tell you. You will eat when we tell you. You will sleep when we tell you. You are material. We will see what can be made of you. There is no man among you who is free.

The words dropped into the room and settled on us the way prayers do when the body's already in the ground.

We were divided into platoons. The voice called out and we crossed the line into whatever lay next. The men beside me became my brothers in that instant, though I knew nothing of them. Their names spoken quick, their faces pale beneath the fresh cuts of the clippers. We were shown to our barracks, long rows of iron cots, mattresses thin as wafers, the air tinged with oil and leather and a dozen sleeping men's breath. Each man assigned a bed and a footlocker. Order imposed on us with the ease of a hand striking a match.

The rest of the day was given to papers and tests. Questions asked, numbers measured. Height. Weight. Teeth. Eyes. Could you read. Could you count. Could you swim. Could you shoot. They wrote it all down and stamped it with ink. We sat at desks with pencils dull from overuse and answered what we could. The room was silent but for the scratching of lead. I wondered what they thought of me as they read my answers, if they saw me as weak or strong, or if they saw anything at all.

Night took the sun and the lights of the camp rose in defiance, flickering against the dark, stars brought too close to earth. We marched in lines to the mess hall where food was ladled without ceremony onto dented trays. Meat gray and shapeless, bread that tore the roof of your mouth, coffee bitter as ash. We ate because eating was commanded. Around me the men spoke little.

You gonna finish that? a boy asked, nodding at my bread.

You want it, take it, I said.

He grinned with half his teeth. I'll trade you my apple. It's got a worm in it, but he's friendly.

That night in the barracks the sergeants walked the rows and barked at stragglers who had not yet folded their uniforms as instructed. Their voices cracked against the tin walls. At last the lights were killed and we lay in silence staring into the black above us. I heard a man crying softly in his bunk and another cursing under his breath and no one told him to be quiet for we all knew the shape of his sorrow.

I closed my eyes and the hum of the camp filled my ears, the shouts and the marching feet ringing there. I was no longer mine. I was theirs.

The days began in the dark and we rose with the whistle. The barracks rattled with the sound of boots striking deck plank and the breath of three thousand men rising up like steam. They issued us a set of whites for inspection and a set of dungarees for drill and work and they told us which was for what and there was no mistaking it. Each man had a bunk upstairs with a footlocker and a little bucket for washing out his own clothes and you learned quick the worth of soap and elbow and the patience of hanging damp cloth on a line strung across the room.

Before chow we marched out to the blacktop and the morning was cold enough to sting your hands and face. Three thousand of us in lines, rows stretching near to the horizon, all of us bent to calisthenics under the dim electric lights while the sky went from black to gray to the white of dawn. Pushups. Situps. Squat jumps. An hour of it before they'd let us eat. Our stomachs burning with hunger and our limbs quaking.

You ever done this many squats in your life? someone muttered beside me.

I said, Not unless you count all the times I've picked up dropped tools back home.

After breakfast we drilled while the morning burned off and the heat rose in waves off the blacktop. Marching in step with rifles not yet ours, loaned to us the same as the names they called us by. The sun rose hot and unforgiving and the cadence barked at us until it seemed it would drive the marrow from our bones. Chow at midday. Then back to drill again until the shadows ran long. Hours of marching and turning and halting and stepping again, the rhythm of boots drumming across the hardpan. When the day was ended we were cut loose to our bunks and we sank into them with the day itself climbed onto our backs and meaning to stay there.

Perman and I took the drills side by side. We had come in together and somehow we managed to keep our places through the endless shuffling of men, a kind of tether against the anonymity that swallowed you in a camp that size.

It was not long before trouble found its way into the ranks. A Texan named Allen discovered our barracks held black men and he did not like it and he made sure others knew it. A black kid at the far end of the room looked up once from shining his boots, met Allen's eye, then went back to his work. Soon a knot of Texans stood before the commander's office, loud in their drawl. They told him plain they weren't going to stay in the same barracks where the blacks were sleeping.

The commander looked them over without much expression at all. He said: You get your asses back to your barracks or I'm going to court martial you. All of you. Then he said: You are not back in Texas. You are going to eat, work, and live with the blacks whether you like it or not. Do you understand me?

The Texans didn't care for it, but they cared for prison less. They tumbled back into line, shoulders drawn in, eyes on the floor, and you could see the smolder of it there, but they kept their mouths shut. After that they said little, and there was something sour in the room when the lights went out.

The drills went on as they always had and the days did not change. The ground cold in the morning, the sun cruel by noon, the sweat and ache of men remade into sailors.

I woke one morning with a pain in my belly, a tight hard thing low on the right that made me catch my breath, and I knew something was wrong. The barracks held the smell of canvas and boots and men sleeping, but I could not stay. I went to the sick bay folded over, one hand pressed there trying to hold whatever it was in place. The doctor pressed his fingers into me and his face went dark and he said it was the appendix and it had to come out. Right then and there.

They laid me back on a narrow table and swung a white lamp over my face. The needle bit. Then my flesh went dead beneath the sheet, dull and strange, belonging more to the knife than to me. I watched them open me in the reflection of the lamp until a nurse saw my eyes fixed there and she laid a towel over my face. For a moment I saw the meat of myself laid bare, something to be studied. You could taste the iron of blood and bleach in the air, a bitterness that settled in the teeth. I felt the tug and pull of them working inside me.

I was sore for days. The stitches pulled with every breath and I walked bent at the waist. But it freed me from the drills and the endless shouting and I counted that as a small mercy. When I healed I rejoined the line. Three weeks had gone and in that time we had become something other than the boys who'd first stumbled in. We moved in step, spoke as one voice. The boy who'd left his hair on the barbershop floor was gone, and in his place stood something forged.

San Diego Liberty

Three weeks in and we were ground down to gristle. Raw and half-formed. The skin rubbed off our heels. Throats sore from shouting aye sir into the wind. Faces sunburnt in strips where the brim didn't cover. Our hands blistered from rifles and our knees bruised from gravel. Time didn't pass the way it used to. It passed through you, not around you, rain through rotten wood. You woke and drilled and slept and drilled. The days kept piling, each one laid over the last.

They broke us down by inches. Repetition did the breaking. The same commands. The same bell. The same voice calling your name and never quite pronouncing it right. Somewhere in there whatever boy was left in you slipped off without a word.

Then the word came. Quiet. A rumor whispered through a hole in the wall.

Liberty.

They only said it once. Didn't need to say it again. A man beside me laughed and slapped the table. Another stared ahead like he'd just been told the war was over. I didn't move. Just let it settle into my bones, heat after rain. Perman stood behind me, quiet. Then he grinned. That dumb wide grin that came up from somewhere deeper than joy.

We left that afternoon. Stepped through the gates in clean whites and shined shoes, our names tucked inside folded paper, our orders stamped in blue. We poured out from the cracked jar of discipline, briefly uncontained. No longer recruits for a few stolen hours. Just boys again. Or the ghosts of boys.

San Diego unfolded before us with a promise it never meant to keep. The sky was pale and endless. The palm trees black against it. Streetcars clattered past, their wires sparking overhead, lightning chained to steel. Neon flickered, little wounds of color in the dark. Signs buzzed. The sidewalks breathed out the day's heat from the concrete.

We walked side by side, Perman and me, not speaking much. Both of us had changed. I could feel it. I'd wanted to be a Marine. He'd wanted the Navy. Said he didn't care about glory. Said he just wanted a clean rack and a good pair of shoes. I told him I wanted to fight. I told him I needed to.

Now neither of us said a word.

We hit the first bar thirsty enough to drown. Old beer and floorwax and cigarettes hung in the air until you could feel them coat your teeth. Music grinding out of a jukebox somewhere in the rear. The songs were strange, but easy to the ear.

A big man checked IDs at the door. I handed him mine and he looked me over once.

Too young, he said.

I stood there. Nothing to argue. Just nodded.

Margoff stepped out from the shadows and lit a cigarette with the slowness of a man without any rush in him.

They turn you away?

Said I wasn't old enough.

You're not.

He took a drag and watched the smoke climb into the dark.

But maybe tonight you are.

He handed me his ID. Wire-rim glasses too. Slipped them into my shirt pocket with the care of passing a bullet. I looked nothing like him. Didn't matter. The man at the door didn't even glance up the second time. Just waved me through.

Inside it was half hell and half heaven. Lights spun through the smoke, stars caught in grease. The place was more hall than bar, the ceiling swallowed in the dark above us. Sound came from every direction. Brass blared, strings sawed, drums cracked from a raised platform over the floor, the band half hidden in smoke and the violence of its own music. The brass punched the gut. The drums cracked bone. The strings slipped in under the ribs and stayed there. Voices crashed together, rough and white with noise. Men and women and the staggering space between them all lit up and filled with shouting.

I bought a drink. Rye. Poured like it was being punished. It hit my throat with the old clean threat of liquor, and I welcomed it.

The girls danced in circles and lines and none of them touched the ground. Their dresses were stitched with lies and their shoes knew how to lie too. I took a redhead by the hand and spun her once and then again, her hair bright under the hall lights. I asked no name. Some names were better left inside the music.

We moved like we weren't at war. Time gave us room that night, just enough for a handful of boys in white.

She asked where I was from.

South Dakota.

She asked what I did.

I told her I was dying slow and trying to look good doing it.

She laughed and that laugh stayed with me. In the sternum. In the spine. The kind of sound that makes you want to lie more just to keep it going.

Someone shouted for another round. A man fell backward through a set of double doors. The bartender didn't flinch. Just kept pouring. The room swayed and I let it. Let the lights spin and the floor tilt and the redhead press her hand against my chest and ask if I believed in love or only in leave.

I said leave comes quicker.

She smiled and brushed her lips against my cheek and said you ain't wrong.

Later I found myself out on the street. The stars were faint and high. Streetlamps buzzed overhead, hornets trapped in glass. I walked toward the bay. Ships out there blinked their lights across the water, restless and alive. The water black as the spaces between the ship lights. Cold wind through the collar. Someone laughing down an alley. Someone crying. I couldn't tell which was which.

I thought of home for the first time in weeks. The feeling of belonging to a name. That feeling was slipping.

I didn't belong to a place anymore. Only to what waited behind the fence.

A bus idled down the street. Headlights yellowed by grime. Doors folded open with a gasp.

I got on.

The ride back was quiet. Men sat scattered through the seats, some asleep, some staring with eyes full of what they had seen. A fight. A kiss. A betrayal in a rented room. I sat by the window and watched the city fold itself back up. One light at a time.

Someone threw up near the back. No one turned.

The air was ripe with smoke and sweat and perfume long since soured. You could taste the sweat and whiskey in it, sharp and rank as a bar floor at closing.

We reached the gate just before dawn. A thin light bled along the east. MPs waiting with clipboards and pens. Nodding. Checking. Counting us back in like tools being returned to the shed.

The barracks were black and still. I dropped onto the rack fully dressed and stared up into the bunk above.

In my pocket the borrowed ID pressed against my thigh, carrying the weight of a secret.

The redhead's laugh echoed in the folds of my mind. Slipping further each time I tried to hold it.

Outside the wind kicked at the siding. A man moaned in his sleep. Another whispered someone's name. It wasn't mine.

I didn't sleep.

Just waited.

Soon they would come for us. Barking and stomping, dragging us back into the drills, the shouting, the hunger.

But for now I lay still.

And in the dark I could feel it again.

The music. The warmth. The soft hand on my neck. All of it already turning to smoke.

They'd give us liberty again someday, another night to pretend we belonged to ourselves. But it would cost us more bone and more sleep before it came.

Hemphill Institute

They sent me north with a duffel and a packet of papers that carried the sea in their folds. Boot was behind me. The shouts and the whistles and the raw skin of obedience. What waited ahead was quieter but no less demanding. They said I was to learn diesel. I didn't know what that meant exactly, only that it would keep me moving until the Navy found a ship for me to stand on.

The train pulled north through the night, hugging the coast like it didn't want to let go. I sat at the window and watched the dark pass in bands of color I couldn't name. Sand and chaparral. The black spill of ocean under moonlight. We reached Los Angeles just after dawn. The sky was a pale burn and the city a blur of steel and smoke. Perman had been shipped out the day before. I didn't get to say goodbye. I never saw him again. I never learned what became of him.

Los Angeles felt swollen with the war. Every street crowded. Men in uniform shouldering past each other, all of them bound somewhere that might kill them. Women in slacks carried toolboxes. Banners hung over the sidewalks telling us to buy bonds and keep faith. There was no silence anywhere. Even the sky seemed to hum.

Hemphill Institute sat behind a fence of rusted wire on a stretch of cracked pavement. Low brick buildings stood in rows under the hard western light. The air hit us first, oil and hot metal and the faint sweetness of burnt gas. Beyond the buildings, concrete lots opened wide, with engines and trucks lined for instruction, hoods raised, panels off, their inner workings exposed. Inside, the halls were lined with engines the color of gun barrels. Each one marked by the hands that had torn it open before us. Superior. Cummins. Detroit Diesel. Cleveland. The names a litany. I didn't yet know it, but they would become a kind of prayer.

We were twenty men in all. Recruits mostly, a few merchant sailors, a couple of Marines who'd been reassigned after wrecking something valuable. They gave us bunks upstairs, two to a room. Long narrow halls ran past those rooms, beds squared away, lockers dented by hands I'd never know. At night the voices of men drifted through the vents, low laughter and muttered prayers. The mattresses were thin, the springs close enough to feel with your shoulder blades. The windows stuck when you tried to open them. Nights were hot and the air hung still. From the street below came the whine of trucks and the laughter of people not yet called to war.

The instructors were civilians pressed into service. Hard men with soft bellies, voices rasped by years of carbon and smoke. They spoke the language of machines and expected us to learn it fast. First day they handed us solvent and wire brushes and pointed to a rust-seized block on the floor. Clean it, one said. We scrubbed till the gray came back through the black, our arms shaking, the stink in our clothes. When we finished he said, Tear it down.

That was the rhythm of it. Clean. Strip. Measure. Rebuild. Again. Dry teardowns, every type they could throw at us, not a screw or gasket lost. Every bolt its own sermon. We learned the pitch of a wrench as it bit down. The scent of coolant when it ran too hot. The small cough of an injector gone bad. I started hearing those sounds in my sleep. In dreams the engines breathed slow and steady, beasts resting in the dark. Nights were short, full of camshafts in my sleep and the quiet dread of a broken valve.

Corby was my partner. A thin boy from Iowa with freckles on his neck and a stare that could find truth in anything mechanical. He handled every part like it was alive. When a gear stuck he didn't force it. Just waited. Listened. Then moved his hand the other way and it came free. Patience was his religion. We balanced each other. I was quicker, he steadier. He'd look over and say, You don't fight the machine, Pat. You learn its mood. I nodded, pretending I understood, though I didn't yet.

Sorella came from the Bronx. Italian. He slept through roll call twice and smiled his way out of punishment both times. He had the lazy grace of someone who would never rush unless fire touched him. When the instructors barked, he blinked slow and said, Huh? as though English was a second language. It wasn't. But he used it like armor.

The three of us worked the same bay most days. Sweat pooled on the concrete. Our coveralls turned the color of oil. When we got hungry we chewed the stale sandwiches the Navy called lunch and drank water that tasted of tin. There was no clock. The day ended when the lights shut off.

At night the city glowed beyond the fence. You could see the smog floating low, yellow in the streetlamps. Sometimes the girls came down from the apartments across the alley. They leaned on the fence and called to us, their voices carrying through the metal links. Powder and perfume hung around them, and a kind of promise that went no farther than the fence. We'd slip through a gap near the corner and walk them to a bar two blocks over. Cheap beer. Jukebox songs. The floor sticky underfoot. They laughed at everything we said. Corby blushed when one touched his arm. Sorella just grinned and said his usual Huh? It was a line that never failed.

There were others. Sparky was short and wiry, with a grin full of trouble and a sailor's quickness in his hands. He had worked merchant ships before the Navy got him and he knew semaphore the way other men knew dice. One afternoon in the cafeteria he came over carrying two signal flags rolled in his fist. I was sitting with a girl I had met the night before. She looked at the flags and asked him what they were.

For talking, Sparky said. With flags. Would you care for a demonstration.

She nodded.

He stepped into the open floor between the tables and raised the flags. Red and white flashing under the hard cafeteria lights. His arms cut the air with solemn purpose, letter by letter, and he spelled it clean for every man in the room.

F. U. C. K. Y. O. U.

The cafeteria broke apart. Men howled and slapped the tables and bent over their trays. The girl sat there bright with embarrassment, trying to understand what she had agreed to witness. Sparky brought the flags back to her and held them out.

Your turn, he said.

She stood. Took the flags. Set her feet just as he had set his. Then she spelled the same thing back to the whole room, slow and perfect, every letter plain as daylight.

F. U. C. K. Y. O. U.

I laughed until I could hardly breathe. Sparky bowed to her with the solemnity of an admiral's inspection.

And there was Edwards. Tall, heavy, full of noise and foolish courage. He could make a whole shop laugh until men had to lean against the benches. One night he and I were walking back from the bar with two girls we had picked up there, and Edwards began boasting that he could fart from the gate all the way to the dorm.

We bet him twenty dollars. It was one full block from the gate to the dorm, with barracks windows along one side and the open yard along the other.

Edwards started strong. Proud. Almost military in his bearing. Then halfway down his face went grave and the girls saw ruin coming before the rest of us did.

They screamed and ran, laughing so hard their voices broke. I was laughing too, bent over with it. Edwards had crapped himself and tore for the latrine at a dead man's gallop.

Morning brought him back, pale and humbled.

Twenty dollars well earned.

We were boys trying to forget that we were property. We laughed too loud and drank too fast. But the engines waited for us all the same.

One evening the others drifted off and I stayed behind. The shop was half dark, a single bulb burning over the bay. The machines stood silent, their shadows long against the wall. I wiped the grease from my hands and sat on the floor. For the first time I listened to the quiet. The orders had ceased. Laughter had gone with them. Only cooling metal ticked in the quiet, with faint air breathing through the vents. The place had the pulse of something older than the war itself. I thought then that maybe we were not only building machines. Maybe we were building men who could endure.

The weeks stacked up like crates. We rose before dawn and worked till the bones of our hands ached. Corby got pneumonia but came to class, his cough echoing off the walls. Sorella cut his palm open on a stripped bolt and wrapped it with electrical tape. I lost a thumbnail to a flywheel. None of us said much about pain. The instructors told us pain meant progress. We believed them because we had to.

Sometimes after chow we sat on the steps and smoked while the smog rolled in. The city lights shimmered behind it, ghosts moving through glass. Corby would hum low and tuneless. Sorella would talk about New York like it was a country that might not exist anymore. I mostly listened. The sound of traffic out on the boulevard mixed with the slow thrum of engines cooling in the shop, and the world went on while we sat already set apart from it. There was comfort in it, in the hours at the bench and the oil under our nails and the simple fact that none of us was alone.

I stayed late again near the end. The others asleep, the shop empty. I ran my fingers along a valve cover warm from the day's work. The metal was smooth where the grit had worn it down. I could smell the oil in the pores of my skin. I thought about home, about the cold fields of South Dakota and the sound of my father's boots on the porch. That life felt far away now. I wasn't the same boy who'd boarded that train. Something had been ground off and replaced with iron.

Graduation came with no music or ceremony. Just a clerk handing out papers that said we were fit for service. They gave us ranks and told us where to go. Corby to San Francisco. Sorella to Pearl. Me to Mare Island. The yard where ships waited to breathe.

We shook hands without saying much. The kind of goodbye that didn't need words because it had already happened.

When they left I walked to the fence again. The city spread out in haze and firelight. The machines behind me cooling slow in the dark. I rested a hand on the nearest one, feeling the last of its warmth fade into my skin.

Pride had nothing to do with it. Readiness either.

But I knew broken machinery.

I knew how to bring dead iron back to life.

LA

We were stationed at the Hemphill Institute of Technology, which was a grand name for a collection of hangars and classrooms where they taught us the inner workings of diesel engines. The place was just a row of squat, sun-blasted buildings strung along a weedy fence. The air carried scorched rubber and burnt oil. Diesel smoke blackened the eaves. Inside they taught us engines. Cylinder heads. Injection pumps. Compression ratios. The gospel of combustion. Men with oil-black hands and flat eyes and no time for jokes. Faces carved by heat and labor, hands black to the wrist, voices worn thin by years of shouting over the noise. They had no time for boys. No time for war stories or heroics. They taught because the world needed machines to run and someone to keep them running. I learned to keep my mouth shut and my tools clean. I learned that nothing mechanical forgives neglect.

On weekends they turned us loose. Liberty, they called it. But liberty is a crooked word. They did not give us anything. They only loosened the leash for a few hours. We belonged to them all the same.

I came down the steps and found Corby and Sorella by the fence, uniforms pressed sharp as razors, shoes catching the last of the daylight. They stood there grinning like sinners at the chapel door, ready to let the city swallow them whole.

A few others too. Brooks, Mendez, a big Irish kid we just called Red. We were all boys in uniform pretending to be men and maybe in a way we were. Red laughed with the cough and grind of a bad engine trying to turn over. Mendez never stopped talking unless he was asleep. Brooks walked tight and wary, every step braced for impact. We were a strange bunch, cobbled together by war and habit.

We'd catch the trolley out to Hollywood. Holly, some called it. A country all its own. A place where you could forget the shape of the world for a little while. We'd pile in and ride under the orange glow of streetlamps, the city rising around us, scenery nailed together for someone else's story. Los Angeles had teeth. It bit and didn't let go. The city moved wild inside its cage of streets.

I wasn't twenty-one yet but no one ever asked. Not here in LA. Too many sailors. Too little time. The barkeeps just poured and moved on.

The streets were a boiling mass. Thousands of us. Sailors, soldiers, Marines just back or about to ship out, all shoulder to shoulder in the night. Cabs honking. Headlights rolling slow through the fog, pale and searching. The sidewalk a river. Servicemen drifting in packs, some loud and laughing, some dead-eyed and already drunk. Women too. Plenty of them. Some girls just out to dance and some working. All of them watching you from behind their lipstick and smoke.

Vendors hollering. A man selling peanuts from a brass cart. Another pitching postcards with Rita Hayworth in a red dress. A drunk Marine asleep in a doorway with his cap over his face. Radio music bleeding from bars and windows and jukeboxes, swing tunes and some cowboy song playing down the block, a prayer no one asked for. A man with a saxophone stood on a corner, pouring loneliness into the street. We stood and listened. Corby dropped a coin in his case.

It could be beautiful. If you let the smoke and light blur together. If you didn't look too hard.

The Palladium was our first stop, most nights. Big dancefloor. Big band. You walked in and your whole body shook with the sound. Horns and drums and heels on polished floor. Brass bands playing as though the world wasn't on fire. Girls in dresses that glimmered fishscale bright, heels clacking in time. Girls spun in loose circles, all glassy laughter and wobble. Men in uniform trying to remember how to move their feet and smile at the same time.

Mendez said, You think they'll remember us?

Red leaned in and said, Only if we dance like hell.

Later we'd hit the Brown Derby or wherever the crowd bent. Places with red leather booths and waitresses with dead eyes. We drank bourbon like it was medicine, and some nights it was. We leaned on counters slick with beer and listened to lies from strangers who swore they'd just come back from Midway or New Georgia or hell itself. It wasn't always lies.

By midnight, half the city was slurring. By two, a fight had usually broken out somewhere.

You could feel it coming the way a bar gets quiet before something breaks. That hard edge in the air. Too many men wound too tight, carrying too much. Some from Guadalcanal or the Atlantic crossings. Some who hadn't seen a fight yet and were burning to prove something. Usually it was just fists. Wild punches in alleyways. Blood on white dress uniforms. MPs whistling and yelling and swinging nightsticks. Some nights it got worse. Knives. Bottles. I saw a man thrown through a plate glass window once on Sunset and no one even looked surprised.

We kept Corby close on nights like that. He didn't fight. Wouldn't. He'd step back and let it pass like weather. Same way he'd stand silent in the rain and not curse it.

One night I remember, we were walking back toward the trolley stop. The street slick with spilled beer and gasoline and the kind of neon that gets into your bones. A fight had broken out across the road. A sailor and two Marines. Corby just stopped and watched. The light on his glasses. His face unreadable.

I said, You all right?

He nodded. Then he said, Just a long way from home, is all.

That stuck with me. Still does.

Because we all were. No matter where we came from.

And there were others too. The Zoot Suiters. You couldn't miss them. Suits hung baggy and sharp, coats to the knees, trousers ballooned wide enough to catch the street wind. Shoes shined to mirrors. Hair pomaded into black waves. They walked in packs, laughing loud in English and Spanish both, and they weren't trying to look like anyone else. That's what got some boys all twisted up.

I knew a few sailors who'd had run-ins with them. Big fights out near Main Street or Chavez Ravine. They told stories about ambushes in alleys and razor blades sewn into cuffs. Most of it was talk. Some of it wasn't. The city felt under pressure, ready to boil over.

One night, out behind the Palladium, Red came up to me with that grin of his and said some guys were going out riding. Said they were rounding up some Zoot Suiters downtown. Said one of them had mouthed off to a petty officer and they weren't going to let that slide. Asked if I wanted to come along.

I said no.

He laughed. Said, Come on, what's it to you?

I said, I never had any beef with those guys. It wasn't about the clothes. It was about the men wearing them not being white, and I wasn't gonna be a part of that.

Red blinked. Said, Christ, Flynn. You sound like my old man.

I said, Maybe he had the right of it.

I wasn't any kind of saint. I'd seen what hate could do, and I wanted no part of it.

A few days later it broke wide open. Servicemen poured into the streets, released and unruly, filling every block. Packs of them. Hunting. The Zoot Suit Riots, they'd call it later. But it wasn't a riot. It was a beating with uniforms and flags on it. They dragged kids out of bars and movie houses. Ripped their suits off in the streets and burned the scraps in the gutters. Stomped them bloody on the sidewalks. The cops mostly looked the other way. Or helped.

I watched some of it from a corner near Alameda. Could hear the shouting a block away. Some of those kids couldn't have been more than sixteen. Dark hair, thin faces, scared and angry all at once. Not much different than us, really. Except they weren't wearing the right uniform. They were wearing the wrong skin.

Corby stood next to me, arms crossed.

He said, This is the kind of thing folks write about years after, pretending they didn't know better.

I nodded. Because he was right.

It went on for days. Until the papers got tired of printing it and command got tired of pretending it wasn't happening. They clamped down. Pulled liberty. Told us to stay close to base. Some apologies were issued in the vague language of men afraid of losing votes. But the damage was done. The city felt different after that. Some sacred thing had been split. You could feel it in the silences.

And Monday always came back. That dry sun over the Hemphill yard. The engines waiting. The bark of orders and the stink of oil. And you carried it with you, the music, the women, the blood, the ghosts of it all. You carried it quiet. A tattoo under your skin.

That was liberty. That's all it ever was. A few hours to remember you were human, or try to be, before they took you back and bolted you back into the big machine you'd never see all of. You paid for it in bone and sleep and blood.

And even now, when I smell diesel or hear old horns playing through static, I remember. The nights and the weight of them pressing down. The sound of boots on sidewalk and laughter too loud to last. The war waited behind everything, a second shadow.

We were boys trying to stand up inside men's lives.

But we were there for all of it. God help us, we were there.

VENICE

Sometimes the city was too much. Too filled with horns and sirens and jukeboxes and men shouting just to hear themselves over it. So Corby and I would ride the trolley west. We skipped the Derby and the Palladium and every place where the uniform worked like currency. We went to Venice. All the way to the end of the line, where the land ran out and the sea began. Venice. Where the lights were off-kilter and the people matched them.

Past the stucco sprawl and the wet-lit gas stations. Past half-finished houses and slow-turning oil pumps in the fields where jackrabbits once ran. Past neon diners with girls leaning out of upstairs windows, waving at no one in particular. We sat side by side beneath the humming wires and didn't talk. The sea air came in thin, even that far inland. A ghost of salt across the tongue. The air tasted cleaner than the base. Cleaner than the city.

Venice wasn't beautiful. Not really. The place had worn through most of its old paint. The plaster crumbled and the boardwalk swelled where the sea had crept in. The buildings leaned. The windows were fogged with decades. But it had something. A stillness in the bones.

The pier was old even then. Splintered boards and rusted bolts. An amusement park on the edge of the sea, rusted and prayer-held, defiant in the way of things built to vanish. Lights strung above us, buzzing and unsteady. The rides stood half-lit and groaning, relics in the dark. The Ferris wheel turned slow, casting long shadows that passed over the sand in sundial arcs. The air carried brine and grease and old dreams. You could hear the ocean under everything, one long breath that never ended. Beneath it the water beat against the pilings in rhythm. Unbothered. Unmoved.

We walked the pier. Didn't say much. Corby never did, and I'd grown used to letting the silence stretch. Our boots sounded hollow on the boards. Soldiers and sailors everywhere. Some were loud and some already drunk. Throwing coins at games they couldn't win. Kids laughing. Barking vendors. Lights flickering, nearly out of breath. Mostly locals beyond that. Kids with cotton candy on their hands. Women in dresses that had seen better seasons. A man throwing knives at a stump. Another selling cigarettes rolled tight in brown paper.

It was near the roller coaster when the girls found us.

Two of them. Bare-shouldered and laughing too loud. Maybe eighteen. Maybe older. One had dark hair pinned back with cheap rhinestones and eyes carrying knowledge she should never have seen. The other wore a red scarf around her neck with the confidence of a banner. She looked straight at me and smiled, carrying the tired knowledge of someone who had seen more than her years allowed.

The red-scarf girl slid her arm through Corby's like they'd done this before. He didn't even blink. Just nodded, quiet as always.

The dark-haired one came to me. Tall and a little sharp around the edges. Chipped nail polish. A laugh that caught in your chest and stayed there.

She said her name was Marie. I didn't ask if it was true.

She said, You boys from the base?

I said, Something like that.

She said, Then you owe yourselves a good night.

She took my arm and said, Let's go.

Let's go where, I said.

To where the night wants us, she said.

She led me down the pier like she already knew the way. We hit the rides first. The roller coaster screamed as it twisted above the water, the cars rattling down as though the old thing meant to throw us into the sea. Wind tearing through our clothes. Stars spinning. Marie held her hands up and let the wind catch her, her laughter rising over the waves, her head pressed to my shoulder when we came to a stop. I could feel her heart hammering against my shoulder, sharp and fast.

We played the games. Threw rings and missed. Shot targets that didn't fall. I won her a wax flower with a faint gasoline tang and she pinned it to her blouse, suddenly elegant in the carnival light. Corby won a cheap stuffed monkey at the ring toss and handed it to his girl without a word. She kissed his cheek and he turned red and didn't speak for a while. I never saw him look younger than he did just then, the boy in him briefly returned.

We ate fried dough and hot dogs and laughed too loud at nothing. The music changed as the crowd grew. Big band tunes that bled out of tinny speakers nailed to the rafters. A portable record player somewhere behind a concession stand. Girls danced near the bandstand with anyone who asked. Boys in uniform swayed like scarecrows caught in a storm, trying to remember how to move their feet and smile at the same time. One sailor tried to swing a woman twice his age. Another just leaned against a rail and watched the sea with a face made for bad news.

It was then Marie turned and said, You don't talk much.

I said, That's a lie. I talk plenty. Just not when things feel real.

She looked at me.

What do you mean?

I mean this. Tonight. The way the sky smells of salt and sawdust. The way your voice sounds in all this light. I don't want to talk and ruin it.

She stared at me for a long moment. Then smiled, and the smile wasn't like the others I'd seen that night. It didn't ask anything from me. It just was.

Later, we walked the sand beneath the pier. Driftwood and bottlecaps. Tar stuck to the soles of our shoes. The salt hit harder here, almost bitter. Wooden beams above us creaked like an old man's knees. Other sailors were scattered under there. You could hear them. Muffled voices. Soft laughter. A cry or two that wasn't pain. The whole underside of the pier turned into something secret and close, some rough service being held there with sand for a floor and the ocean for a choir. A couple lay sprawled behind one of the supports, too drunk to move or too in love to care.

Marie tugged my hand.

Let's lie down.

In the dark?

Where else?

We found a dry patch beneath the roller coaster. The timbers above us crossed overhead in dark cathedral angles. The sea came louder now, hungry against the shore.

She leaned in. Her mouth was warm and the kiss tasted of powdered sugar and vodka. Her hands were firm. My heartbeat kicked hard in my chest.

Wait, I said.

What?

Just want to look at you a minute.

She frowned.

Why?

I said, Because this is real and I want to remember something good when I go where I'm going.

She didn't ask where. Maybe she already knew.

She kissed me again and this time it wasn't sweet. It was hungry. Fierce and human. Two people trying to climb out of themselves. Her hair tangled in my fingers. My belt came undone without a word. We didn't speak except for the things you whisper in the dark, names and little lies and half a prayer.

The boards groaned above us. A lone gull cried out in the night. Somewhere in the distance a bell rang out of time. Marie's breath came short and sharp and mine followed. Other bodies shifted in the dark, close and far. The waves pressed in against the shore, listening in the dark.

Then stillness.

We lay there, our skin slick with salt and sand and sweat. The war had yet to begin for us, though we could feel it coming like a sound just below hearing. For a little while we were only bodies under the stars, stripped down to breath and skin and the quiet mercy of being alive.

She touched my face.

That's the only time I'll ask anything of you, she said.

What's that?

Don't forget this.

I won't.

I never did.

When we climbed the steps back up to the boardwalk, the Ferris wheel had gone still. Lights out. The vendors packed. The crowds gone. Just wind and litter and the long dark of morning.

Corby stood by the rail. His girl nowhere in sight. He didn't say anything. Just turned when he saw me and nodded once.

You okay? I said.

He nodded again. Looked out over the sea.

She tell you her name?

He said, No.

You ask?

He said, Didn't seem important.

We walked to the trolley in silence. The car screeched in on rusted wheels and we climbed aboard. The city passed the window, a dream unspooling. Rows of quiet houses. Empty yards. A man sweeping a sidewalk beneath a naked bulb.

When we reached the institute, the sky was just beginning to pale.

I never saw Marie again.

But sometimes when I'm near the ocean or hear a trumpet cry in a song I don't know the name of, I remember the heat of her thigh pressed against mine. The weight of her. The taste of her name in the dark. The reek of oil and frybread from the stands along the pier. Her voice saying don't forget. And I remember how much of myself I left there, under the bones of a roller coaster on a beach made of dust and wind and vanished things.

Maybe we were only trying to build one small thing worth remembering before it came. God help us if we did.

TREASURE ISLAND

The air off the bay was a cold hand on my face, carrying salt and diesel and something old, a strange kind of silence that clung to your skin. We were on a bus. The engine grumbling underfoot, its shadow a black wound on the gray asphalt, moving with us low and long. They called this place Treasure Island, a name born of some long-dead dream. It was a lie. A name for a thing that held only rusted iron and the dead lights of a fair.

Once it had been the site of the Golden Gate International Exposition. A thousand flags raised high for a future they thought they could build out of steel and light. Seventeen million people had walked those grounds once, hand in hand, eating popcorn and talking about the future. A world's fair built to honor the new Golden Gate and Bay Bridges. That was before the war. Before everything came apart. Now it was a depot and processing station. A holding pen. It housed men like us, funneled in to be sorted and assigned to ships we had not yet seen. Now it held only ghosts and young men waiting to become them.

The bus cut across the causeway, the wind carrying the groans of the Bay Bridge above us. On the island the buildings of the fair were still there, vast shells of stucco and wood. They had the look of old ribs, bleached by sun and time. We were a line of men walking in, small against what was left of it.

The bus shuddered to a stop in front of what had once been a grand hall. Its curved facade carried traces of gold paint and forgotten banners. I stepped down into the wind and sunlight and watched it move across the cracked pavement, thin and restless. Ahead of me the line of sailors moved on. Sea bags over their shoulders, eyes blank, mouths set. Nobody spoke. There was nothing to say.

Inside it was colder. The ceiling arched high above us, curved like the belly of some great overturned ship. You could hear the echo of your own boots and it made you feel smaller than you already were. The light came thin and mean through high windows painted over and filmed with dust and dead flies. The air held mildew and engine oil and the stale breath of years. A Navy clerk sat behind a folding table with a clipboard. He did not look up.

Flynn, I said.

He flipped a page.

LST-482.

That was all.

Landing Ship, Tank. Otherwise known as Large Slow Target. Built for war, not grace. Flat-bottomed and square-nosed. Made to carry men and machines onto beaches they had never seen and might not leave. The kind of ship you did not dream about. The kind they assigned you to when dreaming was done. She was not finished yet. Just a designation in an office ledger. A number spoken by men who had never stepped aboard. But already she had a number and a crew and a place in the war. Already she had me.

Every ship had its own section, a corner of the grounds where her crew gathered, a rough sketch of order drawn over the ruins. They told you where you belonged and left you to find it. There were no directions and no signs. Just wind and silence and the clatter of trucks somewhere beyond the buildings. I walked until the fairgrounds blurred into one long run of cracked concrete and pavilions stripped to their beams, murals half-painted over, windows clouded by grime and salt. Birds wheeled overhead beneath a low-lidded sky.

I came to it at last. A weathered sign hung crooked on a chain-link fence, the ship's number stenciled in black paint, flaking. Inside was a cavern the size of a hangar. The ceiling arched high above, beams blackened by age, windows fogged with dust. Fluorescent lights buzzed in crooked rows, harsh and uneven overhead. Bunks ran in long lines across the concrete floor, frame to frame, each man with barely enough room to turn over in the night. The place stank of sweat and boot polish and chow from some other morning. It was not a place you stayed. It was a place you waited.

I had put in for thirty days' leave after Hemphill. Customary. A breath between the end of one world and the beginning of another. A chance to go home. To see Mom and Dad. To breathe the air of South Dakota one more time before the ocean had me. The officer stamped it denied without looking up. Said there was no time. Said the war moved faster than permission.

So I stayed.

They gave us liberty, but it wasn't worth much when you were broke. A man without money is a man on a short leash. A few of us took the bus into Oakland at dusk, where the pavement bled tar and smoke in the heat. We worked the Campbell's Soup factory on the line. Tin and steel and the hiss of steam. Belts moving without end. Hands slick with the brine of tomatoes and beans. The floor wet with runoff and soap. The foreman never asked our names. Just pointed to the gap and you filled it.

Four dollars for a night's work. Paid in cash. I folded the bills into my boot and we rode back in the dark, windows open to let the factory stink out of our clothes. That money was how I drank. How I bought a few hours in bars where the floors stuck to your shoes and the lights stayed low. Enough to forget, for a while, the ship throwing sparks in a yard across the water and the war standing somewhere ahead, unseen and certain.

Bull was one of the first I met. He came into the barracks swinging a sea bag over one shoulder, carrying it with no effort at all. Built heavy through the shoulders, his forearms corded and scarred. When he grinned it was all teeth and no real change in the eyes. Boston accent thick as paste. He dropped his bag on the lower bunk and looked around once.

This'll do.

That was his hello.

Nicky Powers was the opposite. Short, neat, with a picture of his wife and baby taped inside his locker door. Each night before lights out he wrote letters, leaning over the page with the stillness of prayer. Sometimes you'd see him smiling faintly as he mouthed the words, trying to send them warmer that way. He said he'd worked a bakery in Pomona before the war. Said bread was easier than bullets, but the Navy didn't need bread. The Navy needed boys who could bleed.

Then there was Walker. A Wyoming man. Long and lean and silent. A cowboy with a face carved by wind. He rolled his own cigarettes and smoked them with one boot up on the rail, watching the horizon like he expected it to break. You never knew what he was thinking and he never seemed in a hurry to tell you. One night I asked what he'd done before the Navy.

Rode broncs, he said. Broke horses. Nothing I'd call honest work.

He smiled once and let it go at that.

Some evenings we sat together in the dark outside the hall, watching the lights of San Francisco blink across the bay, another country across the water. Bull told stories that got taller with each telling, about fights in South Boston and girls whose names he could not quite recall. Nicky would hum lullabies from home under his breath, the tune too soft to carry. Walker leaned against the wall and smoked, looking past the water watching some old trail only he could see.

Four months I lived in that echoing hall. Waiting. Marching. Eating from warm cans that all tasted the same. Watching the sun rise over the same barbed fence and fall behind the same warehouses. We drilled until our legs ached. We stood in line for shots and inspections and orders that never seemed to change. In the distance, across the bay, the shipyards burned with war's cathedral light. Sparks rose into the night. Torches hissed. Men moved along the scaffolds, ghosts stitching a flat-nosed brute into life. That was where LST-482 was taking shape. Welded and bolted into being. Already spoken for before she was alive.

Word finally came down. The ship was under way. Orders said we were to be transferred to Mare Island, Vallejo, to ready her for the shakedown cruise. The waiting ground had done its work.

We packed our sea bags and fell in before dawn. Each man quiet, the concrete cold under our boots, our breath white in the dark. You did not speak when the road turned. You just took the step.

Treasure Island slid away behind us, shrinking into the gray, already half remembered.

Ahead was the part of the world that would not let us come back the same.

Mare Island

They sent us north to Mare Island, a Navy Yard in Vallejo at the upper end of the Bay. The shipyards were already swollen with war. Cruisers lay in their berths, carcasses with steel skins torn open. The welders worked them with fire until the night itself was stitched with sparks. Our own vessels lay unfinished in Richmond across the water, skeletons of iron waiting for breath. And so we were housed in barracks on the island.

The war breathed through every beam and bracket of that place. Men moved with purpose but spoke little. You'd pass a welder under his hood and see the arc stutter in his mask, a captured sun, and he'd not look up. The cranes groaned. The sirens called the shifts. Somewhere across the yard, a hammer rang bright and kept on ringing.

The barracks were long low houses of wood painted dull that carried the breath of pine timber and the mildew of old nights. Rows of iron bunks stacked two high. Mattresses thin as paper, harboring their own stale damp. At night the place was loud with men turning in their sleep, coughing and cursing until the sound seemed carried in the boards. When the lights went out you'd hear the low murmur of voices, some praying, some speaking names no one else knew.

The mess hall was a short walk away, a squat bunker of concrete that seemed forever steaming with boiled potatoes and coffee so black it could have been poured straight out of the boiler. Tin trays clattered and cooks cursed like drill sergeants. The air hung with grease and soap, and it clung to you even when you walked back out into the cold. We sat elbow to elbow at the benches, men with faces raw from youth or already cut with lines, each carrying his own kind of silence.

What we lacked was work. The hours dragged. Some wrote letters until the words were worn thin. Some played cards, smoke curling in the rafters and vanishing into the dark. Some lay flat on their bunks staring at the planks above willing themselves through them by sheer force of will. Fights broke out quick and passed quicker. A wrong word, a shove in line, fists thrown before thought could catch up. And then laughter. Always the laughter afterward, young men laughing at the dark before it found them.

Sometimes I sat with Bull and Nicky and Walker on the low retaining wall near the barracks, boots on the gravel and the cigarettes burning down between our fingers. We'd watch the ships take shape across the water and say little. One morning Walker squinted at the drydock, the smoke trailing off his lip.

That's where we're headed, he said. Someplace like that, broke open and steaming.

Bull spit in the dirt. Long as it floats, I'll ride it.

Nicky looked over. If it don't, you'll sink with it. That's the Navy way.

We grinned but no one laughed.

There were elephant trains on the yard, tractor rigs pulling great trailers fitted for men. They lumbered around the base on set paths and you could climb aboard with nowhere in mind to go. We'd ride them just to watch the yard spool past. Great cranes loomed over the piers, cables drawn taut as the rigging of a gallows. The wind off the Bay was sharp and salt-laden, and at times when the fog rolled in, the world disappeared. Even the nearest ship vanished and then loomed up again, sudden and ghostly.

I remember a battleship in dry dock. Her name is gone now. Her hull split open, a hole the size of a house punched clean through her engine room. They said a Japanese torpedo had done it. You could stand on the edge of the dock and look down into her wound. Steel bent back on itself, the bones of some beast. Dark water pooled in the bilges and the sharp tang of oil rose alive from the ruin. It was not a thing you forgot. You could tell yourself it was only metal. Down there lay labor unmade and prayers unanswered. Beyond it all waited the sea, patient and unsatisfied.

At night the barracks lay under a silence deeper than the day. Outside you could hear the hammering, men working by floodlight, the sound carrying across the water. The air tasted of paint and scorched iron, fog and salt. We lay in our bunks. A hundred men breathing together in that dark room, each carrying the same waiting, the same shadow of a war not yet met.

We were shipmates without a ship, a crew in name only. But the days gathered themselves and passed all the same. The ships in Richmond grew closer to completion. Word came down in whispers and in notices tacked to the wall. Soon. Soon.

And then one morning it was there. The waiting ended. Orders read. Bags packed. We were marched out from Mare Island and across to Vallejo where the ship lay moored, paint fresh, decks alive with the scent of new steel and oil. She rose from the water gray and angular, more machine than ship, and they told us she was ours. An LST, broad and blunt-nosed, built to carry men and war to the far side of the sea.

We boarded her in silence, each man crossing the gangway as though stepping into another world. The deckplates rang beneath our boots. Below in the engine room the air lay close with paint and grease, gauges shining like eyes in the dark. Civilian engineers moved among us, men in coveralls with notebooks tucked into their pockets. They spoke in clipped voices, instructing us in the ways of the ship. Valves, Logs. Engines strange to their own heat.

When we cast off it was under a pale sun. The Bay lay calm, fog dragging low across the bridges in ragged strips. The ship moved with a heaviness, slow to answer her rudder, and you could feel in your bones she was untested. We pushed out past the headlands and down the coast, the Pacific stretching vast and indifferent, and we kept our course toward Monterey.

Days at sea on that shakedown were a kind of trial. The engineers ran us through drills, through checks and rechecks. Every gauge noted, every pressure marked. We learned the sound of her engines, a deep thrum that carried through steel and bone alike, the pulse of her heart. We stood watch, we turned wrenches, we filled the log each hour with numbers that meant the difference between life and death.

Monterey came and went, the shoreline gray and green under the fog. We made our turn and came back north, the sea rising up in long swells that lifted our bow and let it fall, over and over. At night the ship groaned and settled. We lay in our racks listening to the water strike her sides, the steady slap of water on steel reminding us what waited beyond this coast.

When we returned to Vallejo the ship was no longer just iron and rivets. She was ours. We had taken her measure and she had taken ours. The war waited ahead of us, nameless and dark, but the long waiting of Mare Island had come to its end.

But the next morning we went again. This time without the civilians. The engineers with their notebooks and their clipped voices were gone and the vessel was ours alone. The weight of her. The feel of her engines, the stubborn lag of her rudder, all of it belonged to us now and we moved about her decks with men who knew her language.

They loaded troops aboard, packs and rifles, men crowding the steel decks and filling the berths below. Along with them came cargo, jeeps and crates and ammunition boxes lashed down with chain. The ship settled lower in the water and you could feel the mass of her, the way she strained against the sea with her burden.

We drove south again toward Monterey, the gray coast sliding past. Orders barked, drills carried out. Men practiced disembarking, scrambling down nets and gangways, the decks alive with motion. In Monterey we brought her nose to the beach, the great bow doors groaning open, the ramp dropping into the surf. Out they went, men and machines, into the shallows, a practice landing but carried with the solemnity of war. The sea foamed around their legs, vehicles grinding forward into the sand, and for a moment you could almost believe the beach belonged to some far island in the Pacific and that the bullets were coming even then.

When it was finished we hauled the ramp back, the doors sealed shut, and we pulled her off the sand with engines straining. The ship shuddered and then she was free again, turning north into the swells. Night fell as we made way back toward Vallejo. The deck went dark and the men fell silent. Each carried his own thought of what it meant: men and machines loaded aboard, bow doors opening on some foreign shore, practice giving way to the real thing.

By the time we tied up again at the yard the truth had settled over us. The ship was ours. She had carried troops and cargo, she had landed them on a hostile shore in all but name, and she had carried them home again. We were no longer apprentices waiting out the hours in Mare Island's barracks. We were a crew, and the next time the doors dropped it would be for real. Out past this coast the Pacific waited.

And we knew, even if no one said it, that there would come a time when the decks ran slick and the air shook with gunfire. Then Mare Island would return to us as the last easy days we didn't know we'd had. Later, when it came, we would understand what Mare Island had already decided for us.

Monterey

From the moment we pulled from Mare Island, I belonged to her. The ship. LST-482. I slept in her steel belly and worked in her guts and her bones. She was no great beauty but a squat beast of war, squared off at the bow with doors like a barn to spill forth men and tanks and trucks onto some hostile shore. She rode low in the water. Wide of beam, ungainly as a barge, but she could nose up onto sand and spit out an army and that was her worth.

The crew would come to be a hundred and forty sailors and sixteen officers. Men from every corner, green kids and old hands both. At their head was Captain Whelan. A quiet man, lean and hard about the face, his cap set square. He seldom raised his voice yet every word carried the weight of command. From the bridge he looked down on the decks and men scurried to their posts moved by some unseen wire. He knew the ship better than any of us, and though his world was apart from mine in the engine heat or topside at the guns, his shadow lay across us all.

The berthing compartments were stacked with bunks three high. Coffin racks of steel pipe and canvas held us in rows where we breathed each other's sweat and smoke and the faint reek of oil worked into the skin. Forward was the mess deck where we choked down chow off steel trays. The galley stank of beans and coffee and grease, and the cooks cursed like devils as they banged pans in that sweltering box.

I was in the black gang. My place was aft in the engine room, where the twin diesels glowed under the lamps and roared inside their steel, giving off a heat that coated the skin and fumes that darkened the lungs. Faces streaked with sweat and soot, the ship's life beat through our hands. Above us was the steering gear and beyond that the fantail, open to the sea, where we smoked and spat and stared into the wake, a white scar trailing across the dark water.

The main deck was a plain of steel, bare save for the vehicles chained down in rows, olive drab hulks that rattled when the sea was up. Amidships rose the conning tower and wheelhouse, square and ugly, from which the officers peered and barked orders. Above it, the bridge, windswept and lonely. Higher still, the radio shack with its glowing dials and the crackle of distant voices.

Below that broad deck was the cavern, the tank deck, long as a city street and so dark the engines felt louder there. It could swallow whole platoons of men, whole companies of machines. The air there was rank with paint and fuel and sweat, and the steel walls sweated with the breath of the sea.

And forward of all. Behind those great clamshell doors, was the bow ramp, lowered by cables thick as a man's arm. It was the ship's mouth, her iron tongue, and from it would come the cargo of war.

We sailed down the coast to Monterey and dropped anchor there. For two weeks, we did amphibious warfare drills. Before every landing, the anchor was dropped a couple hundred yards out in the bay, the cable running heavy and taut into the sea. Then we drove her full ahead until her bow ground into the sand. The great ramp lowering, tanks and trucks and troops pouring out into the surf, engines churning water and sand alike.

When it came time to leave the beach, the diesels roared and strained. The ship's hull shuddered, and the anchor cable hauled her back out to sea. With that line for leverage, the engines pulled her off the sand, inch by inch, until the sea took her weight again and she floated free. Then we would back into the bay and turn her about, only to repeat the whole thing again and again.

It grew monotonous, a grind that wore the edges off a man. Diesel smoke dragged over us, salt spray stung our faces, and the ramp crashed down with a hammer blow. The same orders barked, the same men cursing, the same armor grinding ashore. Day after day the drill wore into us until it was muscle memory, until the ship herself seemed tired of it.

She was no battleship. She was made for burden, not honor, yet the Navy had studded her with guns all the same. Twin forties mounted in steel tubs, their blackened barrels jutting at the sky. Single twenties scattered along her flanks, squat and mean on their pedestal mounts, each fronted by a curved splinter shield. Fifties bolted on pintles, lean barrels ready to snarl. Enough to throw lead skyward at whatever enemy dared to come.

My station when the guns were manned was one of those twenties. An Oerlikon anti-aircraft gun. Squat, ugly, and reliable. I was the gunner. Hands on the grips, eyes through the sight, it was mine to fire. When the alarm rang I would let it scream until the barrel glowed, shells pouring out in a brass shower at my feet.

We were three to the gun. I the gunner. To my side was Wilkins, the loader, wrestling the full drums into place. Behind me crouched Ortega, the spotter. He called bearings, kept me swinging, and swapped out the barrel when it ran red-hot. Three men chained to a steel mount, bound by fear and duty, waiting for the speck in the distance that might bloom into fire and wreckage or nothing at all.

We had only one day of training. A crop duster flew above the bay dragging a canvas sleeve behind it, bucking and snapping in the wind. That was our enemy. We opened up on it, the twenty roaring, brass pouring out and piled warm around our boots. The gun jumped in my hands, cordite burning in my throat. The sleeve was riddled with holes as it trailed in tatters. It was practice enough to know what awaited us would not be practice at all.

We had liberty in town one evening. Walked the wharf with our jackets open to the salt air. The sea lions barking on the rocks. Windows glowing warm behind drawn curtains. A girl in a yellow dress passed us near the bandstand. The music was slow. I remember the way her hem moved like water. Sailors gathered in little knots, smoking and laughing while the night slipped away around them.

Nicky pointed to the beach where the last rays caught the foam.

If I die out there, he said, scatter me in water just like that. Quiet and blue and empty.

Walker lit a cigarette. That's not how it works.

Bull looked at the stars coming out.

Maybe not. But maybe.

Just around the time we found that rhythm, when the watches and the landings and the endless practice had become a second skin, orders came down. We were to embark for the Aleutian Islands, to take back Attu and Kiska from the Japanese. The words went through the ship like a note struck low, and you could feel men change before they spoke. The very names carried with them the weight of fog and rock and bitter sea. The dice games and idle talk died away, and in their place came silence, each man turning the thought over in his head. We knew then that Monterey and its beaches were behind us, and that the next time our bow doors dropped the shore would answer with fire.

PART TWO

Roll on, thou deep and dark blue ocean-roll!
Ten thousand fleets sweep over thee in vain;
Man marks the earth with ruin-his control
Stops with the shore.
- Lord Byron

THE ALEUTIANS

The convoy stretched north across the slate waters, a procession of steel and smoke. Gray hulls hunched against the swell, their wakes drawn pale across the dark Pacific. We were bound north for the Aleutians, those raw islands off Alaska where the sea never seemed at rest and the fog took sky and water and made them one. August of forty-three. The war was old already, burned into the marrow of every soul that bore it.

The sea ran black and hard as hammered iron. Spray froze on the railings until they shone with ice. Men stood at the rails in silence, their breath torn away in wisps of white. The engines drummed beneath our boots, steady as a heart too stubborn to quit. You could smell oil and brine in the air and sometimes when the fog lifted you'd glimpse the dark outline of another ship moving beside us, its silhouette drifting, a ghost without flag or nation.

At night the world was stripped of color. The sea and sky the same black. Our running lights dimmed to slits of red. The wind came down from the north with a mind to kill. I'd step out on deck to smoke and feel the cold slide through my coat and settle in my bones. The cigarette glowed and the ash blew away unseen. Out there, it seemed a man's soul could freeze solid in his chest if he stood too long thinking about what lay ahead.

Back in May the Army had taken Attu. A place of snow and stone where the wind cut men to pieces and the land itself conspired to end them. They said it was the first time in the war that American soil had been retaken, though it was no soil anyone had claimed before. Thousands lay dead upon that icebound rock. The Japanese had charged screaming out of the fog in their final hour, bayonets gleaming, and they fell by the hundreds. When it ended, the field was white and red under a hard silence. The stories drifted through the fleet, thin as smoke. Men frozen where they fell, rifles locked in their hands. Whole squads swallowed by fog. You could feel that fear settle into the ship. Some laughed it off. Others said nothing. None of us wanted to be sent there, but we were steaming north all the same.

Our target was Kiska. The last of their hold on the Aleutian chain. They called the invasion Operation Cottage to make it sound small and harmless, though it was thirty-four thousand men and over a hundred ships crossing black water to reach a desolation of rock and wind. The greatest force ever sent to that forsaken edge of the world.

The harbor was under fog when we arrived. It rolled down from the cliffs in folds, sealing the bay into a world without horizon. Landing craft jammed the water. Engines coughed and sputtered around us. Soldiers sat hunched inside them with rifles between their knees, waiting for the signal. When the ramps dropped they spilled into the surf, boots sinking in volcanic sand, expecting fire that never came. They climbed the bluffs with bayonets fixed and found nothing. The Japanese had gone. Slipped away through the blockade under the veil of weather, leaving their camps empty as homes of the dead. Pots warm. Rifles stacked. Letters pinned to walls. Pictures of wives and children staring from the gloom of dugouts.

You could hear your own footsteps in that place, each one loud as a gunshot. The silence pressed in like breath. Men spoke in whispers or not at all. It felt wrong to break that quiet, The island itself seemed to be listening. A corporal picked up a helmet and found a skull beneath it. Another man opened a footlocker and turned pale at the rank air that came out of it. The fog swallowed us whole. Even the gulls had fled.

Men still died. A battleship struck a mine and seventy sailors went down in an instant. Others vanished to booby traps, to buried mines, to their own fire in the mist. By the time it ended three hundred were dead. Not one shot fired in defense of the island, yet the ground drank its share all the same.

When they said Kiska was secured I went ashore. The tundra was bleak, the ground black and frozen beneath my boots. Smoke and rust hung in the air. The fog hung low. In the bunkers were blankets rolled neat, tools set down midwork, food left half eaten. The enemy gone as though they'd stepped out of the world. It felt haunted, that place. Empty yet not abandoned. A ghost left breathing.

I thought of Attu and the slaughter. I thought of Kiska and its silence. One demanded blood, the other absence, and both seemed satisfied.

We stayed there a week, shuttling men and cargo from ship to shore. The fog never lifted. Each day bled into the next until you could not tell one from the other. The ship grew slick with frost. Oil froze in the lines. At night I'd sit on the fantail and watch the wake vanish into ink water, the diesels beating low through the ship's bones. I thought of home, the wind moving over wheat fields, the earth green beneath a sky untouched by smoke. I could not picture it right. The cold had scoured it from me. We had come to the end of the world and found only ghosts waiting for us.

When the order came to turn south we cheered. Men laughed on deck for no reason, coats open, cigarettes burning in the wind. We were leaving that far edge behind. The fog thinned, the sky turned pale. For a few hours the sea lay smooth as poured glass.

Iron and ozone hung in the air, the taste of the whole world ready to split. But the Pacific never held its peace for long.

The wind came first. A low moan in the rigging. Then a shriek. The sea rose up, black and heaving. The skies turned the color of lead and the horizon vanished. The gale tore through us with a living fury. The wind crossed the land mean and ancient, carrying cold and the feeling that we had gone where men had no welcome.

A williwaw came down off the peaks, sudden and merciless. A blast of frozen air that flattened the sea and sent it flying in sheets. The ship heeled over till the deck stood at an angle and men pitched from their feet and flung against the iron walls, trays and tools clattering into the dark. Steel screamed in its seams. Water came over the bow in a roar. The diesels howled and the hull shuddered near to breaking.

Men prayed in the dark. Some cursed the sea, some called for their mothers. One man laughed until the sound broke in his throat. The ship bucked and moaned under us, every plate and beam complaining. I held fast to the bulkhead and thought we were done. Thought we'd roll on our beam ends and never come up. But she did. The ship clawed herself upright. Seams cried out, rivets wept, and we drove on into the heart of the storm.

Battle had faces. Storms did not. There was only black water and blind rage and the certainty of death.

Then the gale deepened and the sea rose fifty feet and more. The LST, flat-bottomed and blunt, climbed their faces and fell from their backs with a sound like the world coming apart. Each drop struck the hull with a hammer blow. The plates groaned, the bolts sang. Men were thrown from bunks. More than once the chains tore free and the bunks came down in a heap of iron and canvas and men. Lockers burst open. Knives and cups flew through the air. On the mess deck, food slid off the tables and splattered against the walls. Those who could eat did so crouched low, legs braced, bowls held tight to their chests. The rest lay sick in their racks and prayed to see another dawn.

In the engine room it was worse. The screws lifted free of the sea and the engines screamed empty, governors slamming shut, the whole ship jerking with the pain of iron. The air was hot and sharp with oil. Deck plates shuddered beneath my boots. I restarted the mains four times that watch. My hands black and slick, my lungs burning. Each time I thought the sea would come pouring in through the plates and take us all.

We rode that storm seven days. Each sunrise a smudge behind gray clouds. The men were ghosts by the end, hollow-eyed and salt-streaked, the skin raw on their hands where the steel had bit them. By then I knew it was not bravery you felt out there, only the next thing your hands had to do.

On the fourth night word came that an LCT under tow had lost its line. The cable had snapped and the sea had her. Eleven sailors were aboard that little craft, and we watched her lights swing wide and vanish in the troughs. The storm caught her broadside and rolled her near over. She came up again, smaller each time, a toy caught in the grip of the sea.

Then through the squall came another LST, black and low and fighting the weather. Her skipper backed that flat-bottomed ship through the madness until she lay abeam of the LCT, the smaller craft rising and falling wild against her side. Each wave came on with breaking force. Yet he held her there. Ropes were thrown. Nets and ladders went down the LST's side. Men who had strength watched the rise and fall of both hulls and jumped when the sea brought them close. Some caught rope or netting and were hauled up by hands reaching down through the spray. Some struck the steel and slid under. Others came aboard nearly senseless, coughing salt and trying to breathe. Men hauled from the grave.

I watched from the deck with one hand on the rail. Men went down into the dark for men they barely knew, and a holy thing moved through the work of their hands. Not one soul was lost. When the last man came aboard, the cheering rose across the ships, rough and grateful. No man there mistook what he had seen. It was a heroic act, done in black water and storm.

The empty LCT drifted in the convoy lane, loose steel in a black sea. A cruiser came on through the weather and took station. Her guns opened, and the LCT blew apart in the dark, flame rising once before the sea closed over her and cleared the hazard from the path of the ships. What had happened belonged to the deep, and to the men who had seen one vessel go back for another when the sea had already made its claim.

When at last the wind died the silence was strange and soft. The sea smoothed to long gray swells. The men moved old, slow and deliberate. We washed the salt from the decks and from our faces. We were alive and it felt stolen.

Days later the air grew warmer. The fog broke. The sky turned blue for the first time in weeks and gulls wheeled overhead. And then one morning a shout went up from the bridge and men ran to the rails.

Out of the haze rose the towers of the Golden Gate. Red against the light. The bridge stretched across the bay, red and unreal, and beyond it the hills of San Francisco lifted out of the mist. No one spoke. We just stood there, salt-streaked and silent, watching that red span draw nearer until it filled the sky.

After so much gray and storm, that sight hurt in my chest. The engines throbbed through the deck. The gulls cried overhead. We passed beneath the bridge, and sunlight burned across the ship's plates.

We had crossed into something new, beyond training and rumor, beyond every boyhood idea of war. Somewhere ahead of us, the real fire waited.

PEARL

—·—

Pearl Harbor. That was where we were bound. Out there in the middle of the Pacific, in the Hawaiian Territory, a name spoken low, remembered in smoke and in pictures of men floating in oil. The word hung over us like weather. Our ship drove west for ten days and more, loaded down with tanks, trucks and crates lashed to the deck. One hundred and fifty soldiers were penned below.

Mornings began in the heads. Men shoulder to shoulder at the sinks, steel sweating, the air raw with soap and piss and salt. I shaved with a straight razor. The blade sang in that sour light and the others watched the way men watch someone cross a line.

Why in the hell don't you use a safety razor, they said. One roll and you'll cut your throat clean open.

I told them I liked the shave a straight razor gave. They muttered and went on scraping their cheeks with their little contraptions while the ship lurched drunkenly under us.

After mess the day turned to labor. The deck gang fought rust with brush and paint. Salt rose new every hour and crawled into seams until the ship looked old and mended with tar and color. Tanks and trucks sat chained in rows, iron cattle bound for slaughter. We climbed among them, checked lashings and took up slack where the sea had worked the ropes. The ship groaned low in the water under her burden.

Below, in the black belly, the diesels hammered without let. The sound prowled through the steel with a low animal menace. Gauges ticked. Needles swayed. Each hour the log took down the ship's life in cold numbers. Fuel, coolant, temperature, ink on paper, medicine for a dying man. We worked with rags black as night and the air grew hot and close until a man could taste the iron of it. And always you thought of the sea pressing against the plates and how thin the steel was between you and the deep.

Lieutenant Wilbur Branch was our CO, young in the face, with cheeks soft from whatever life he'd led before the war. If I looked young, he looked ten years younger. All of us in the black gang were taken aback when we saw him, thinking here was a boy set above us by mistake. But he turned out a good man. He spoke plain, never barked for the sake of barking, and carried himself without arrogance. We followed his orders because he never asked what he wouldn't do himself. In time that face of his seemed less boyish and more the mark of some hidden steel.

I recall one squall when the sea rose in a wall and rain hammered so hard it stung the skin. The ship pitched. Cargo groaned in its lashings, and men scrambled on the decks, shouting against the roar. Branch stood among us, his face wet, his cap blown askew, but his voice was steady. Quiet hands. Few words. He told us where to stand, what to secure, and we did it because his calm cut through the storm, blade-clean and sure. Tanks shuddered on their chains and water foamed white across the steel, but we held our ground. When it passed, steam rose off the deck in dark, bitter wisps. Men looked at one another in silence, knowing it was him who'd kept the fear from breaking loose. From then on, none of us doubted him.

The soldiers lived below as freight one hour and men the next. They smoked and played cards and dozed on the deck plates, packs around them, rifles sheaved in racks. When they came topside for air they stood in small groups, faces browned by sun or ashen with whatever they'd left behind. I liked to go down among them. I liked to hear a man's story. I'd sit on the cold steel and pass a cigarette, and for a while the hull seemed wider and the days less hungry.

Nights were longest in the engine room. The hum never stopped. Oil and heat lived in every breath. Sometimes I thought if the engines ever went quiet, the world itself might stop with them. The sound got inside you, the rhythm of it. It became a kind of heartbeat you couldn't unhear. When I lay in my bunk I could feel it in the bones of my skull, steady and eternal, the only thing keeping us from the deep.

Afternoons were for drills. The gunners swung their twenty-millimeters, drum magazines clutched in grease-slick hands while officers barked the motions until they were burned into muscle. Signalmen ran flags, and at night flashed lamps into the black. The cooks fought with tins, kettles, powdered eggs and coffee bitter with steam and metal. In the mess we ate from dented trays, mugs clanging with each roll of the deck.

And there was poker. Nearly every night it came, as regular as the roll of the sea. The mess deck was their chapel and the cards their hymn.

Rivera the kid, Mexican, young and sharp. His slicked hair shining under the bulbs, his grin carved deep whether he won or lost. He talked fast, needling the others, never quiet, nervous in any silence.

McDaniel sat across from him. Chief of the black gang, hard-faced, with the look of a man who'd never smiled in his life. He stacked his chips in perfect towers and guarded them the way men guard rations in a famine.

Dolan was the fool of them. Broad-shouldered, blond, with a laugh that broke loose at nothing. He lost more than he won yet came back each night with the game itself the only thing that mattered. He'd slap the table, grin, and buy back in with the last of his pay, shaking his head at his own bad luck but never blaming anyone else.

Hendricks was different. Dark-eyed, soft in the face, a man who smiled through everything. Good-natured in a way you couldn't help but like. Even when broke he leaned back in his chair and laughed, never bitter, always ready to share a smoke or a dollar.

And Bennett. Smooth as varnish, with black hair combed to a shine and eyes that never blinked when the stakes climbed. He sat, a fox among mutts, quiet and graceful, his hands quick and sure. He never raised his voice, never bragged, but you saw the pride in how he stacked his winnings. The men cursed their luck and muttered about his charm but kept their seats. You don't chase out the fox. You watch and hope he eats someone else first.

Smoke filled the mess and hung there in layers. The clatter of chips echoed like bones rattling in a dead man's cup. The red lights overhead made masks of their faces, fortune and ruin passing back and forth with every deal.

I never sat with them. I did not know the game and I did not want to learn it. My money was too hard-earned, blackened with soot and sweat, to lay down on cards. I stood apart, leaning on the bulkhead, watching them take the shape of some old parable. A man could walk away from that table poorer in ways you couldn't count.

But my circle was larger than the card table. Bull and Nicky ran with me most nights and knew the rhythm of my silence. Walker came after. He was a different kind of man. Tall and rangy, the type who watched a place before stepping in. Said he used to break horses in Wyoming. You believed it when you saw how he moved, patient enough to wait out the world.

There was Cohen too. Tall, flabby, a Jewish kid with a preacher's appetite and a rusted-hinge temper. He laughed loud and held grudges like savings. We got along. But Cohen had a mean streak, small and sudden and ugly. He kept old wrongs on his tongue. And for reasons none of us could figure, he hated Nicky Powers. The two of them never spoke a word, yet Cohen would glare at him from across the mess, eyes fixed on him, bitter and accusing. Maybe it was jealousy. Nicky's good looks, his easy manner, the way men respected him without effort. Whatever it was, Cohen carried it under the skin, eating at him unseen. It soured the air when both were near. I stayed clear of it, but I kept my eye on Cohen.

We marked the days. The voyage kept its long rhythm. Then on the eighth day something happened that split the routine open.

I had finished the midnight watch. The ship breathed slow and the diesels thumped in her belly, a great animal sleeping in the dark. My last task was the ice machine. We kept ice for the mess, for the wounded when there were any, and for men roasting on the hot decks. I topped up the machine. Saw to the feed and the float and the pump. Watched the first slow bars of ice take shape in the trough. Then I went below and turned in.

Morning came hard and bright. Somebody called me to the bridge. The captain was there and another sailor, Keller, stood off by the rail. He was wiry and dark-eyed, with a pinched face and a look that never seemed far from contempt. He had the kind of stare a man uses when he has already judged you.

The captain said, Hey Pat, what happened with the ice machine?

I told him the truth. I said I topped it up before I came off duty.

Keller cut in at once. No you didn't. You're a liar.

It hit me before I could think. You're full of shit, Keller. I did my task.

He gave me a thin grin. You always were half-assed.

Better half-assed than a damned shirker.

His voice rose. You're nothing but talk, Pat.

Say that again and I'll shut your face for you.

The captain looked from one of us to the other. His own temper seemed held tight behind his eyes. Then he said, Go up to the fantail and settle it.

We went topside, the three of us. The sea ran rough and the deck moved under our boots. Wind tugged at our sleeves. Salt stung the cut of the morning. By the time we reached the fantail a knot of sailors had gathered there, drawn by the promise of trouble. Bull stood among them with his arms folded, watching close.

Keller gave it one more time for the crowd. You son of a bitch.

I stepped toward him. Don't call me that again.

You're a son of a bitch, Flynn.

Then he swung.

The blow caught me across the brow and split the skin. Blood ran hot into my eye. The whole world narrowed to the sea and the pounding in my chest. I drove both fists into his ribs and felt the body under him give. He stumbled and came back. I hit him in the face and felt my knuckles split on his teeth. Something gristly gave way and blood brightened my hands.

He went down.

Stay there, I told him.

But Keller had too much spite in him to stay down. He got back up, swaying, and came at me blind with both arms working. I hit him square under the chin and he dropped again, this time hard, rolling toward the guardrail with his legs caught awkward through the gap. There came a sound like green wood breaking. For an instant I thought the sea had him. A pair of sailors lunged and dragged him back onto the deck. He lay there limp, his face bloody and ruined.

The captain stepped in then. That's enough. He's licked. Pat, you'll pull extra duty tomorrow.

Yes sir, I said.

My hands throbbed. Blood kept slipping down beside my nose. The whole fight had taken minutes, but it felt like I had poured a year's worth of anger into it.

I pushed through the crowd and Bull met me there. He caught my arm and steered me toward the hatch, the men opening for us. His face had that shut look he wore when something serious had just happened.

Christ, Pat, he said. You laid him out good. He had it coming. But you can't answer every bastard on this tub with your fists. You do that and you'll spend the whole war bloodied up. A man has to know which fight belongs to him.

We walked the steel deck with the wind pressing hard against us. My boots left little drops behind.

He glanced over. After this, no man's calling you a liar. Not to your face. Come on. Let's get that cut cleaned up before you bleed out on the deck.

He pushed open the hatch and guided me inside, his hand heavy on my shoulder. Behind us the sea kept working at the hull and the ship went on westward with the same blind purpose as before.

Later I learned Keller had broken his leg in the fall. They transferred him to a hospital ship and he never came back.

After that the ship changed in a quiet way. Men had always carried their nerves around half hidden, with too little room and too much heat and no true privacy anywhere. The captain must have seen what such pressure could turn into. From then on, when there was space for it, gloves came out and men settled matters in a cleaner fashion. We boxed on the tank deck when the cargo was offloaded and boxed topside when it was not, stripped to our drawers beneath a blank sky while the crew formed a rough ring around us. I fought whoever stepped in. Sailor, soldier, old hand, young buck. If an officer came forward I eased off the punches, but I gave him enough to let him feel the business of it. It spared us worse things. A man could spend his anger there and leave the rest of the ship standing.

The days blurred. The sea took on that color between blue and gray that means land is near. Even the laughter on deck carried a different edge, nervous, expectant. Men stood longer at the rails. The air grew warmer, the wind softer. We were heading for a thing we'd all heard of but none had seen.

Pearl came slow over the horizon, just light at first. A place born from memory. Men gathered at the rails, silent, holding their caps. We passed the wreck of the Arizona and no one spoke. The sun glinted on the water, and the oil rose faint and iridescent, a prayer that would not die. Even the loud ones held their tongues. I could feel it in my chest, same as the others. A kind of reckoning. We had stepped into a graveyard no one had finished burying.

I wondered what we'd leave behind when our turn came.

We moored slow. Lines tossed ashore. Dock crew in khakis and boondockers. One of them said, Welcome to paradise. Another said, You're late. They laughed and took our lines and tied us down like we might float off somewhere we didn't belong.

When the engines cut, the ship went quiet in a way that rattled your bones. The black gang stood in the hush. Vibration and heat gone. Silence held. You felt it in your teeth. The world suddenly missing the hum that had carried you this far. We looked at each other as men returned from something, though we had not yet gone.

There was work to be done. But we stepped off the gangway that day into a port made sacred by fire and grief. We walked softer. We spoke lower. The war had begun here and it hadn't left. It waited just offshore, quiet and patient as ever.

THE STEWARDS

The ship groaned in its bones and every day brought the same sun through the same salt haze. Men passed each other in passageways without speaking, each with his role etched into his shoulders like rank itself. The black gang kept to their furnace. The deck crew worked the topside lines. And the stewards moved quiet through the corridors, a shadow no one wanted to name.

There were three of them. Black men assigned to the service of officers, not in the conning tower or at the helm or down in the black heat of the engine room. They carried trays, polished brass, folded linens. They lived in the same steel cage as the rest of us. They breathed the same diesel stink and heard the same hammering engines below. Fewer doors opened for them, and those doors stayed shut longer.

I got along with them. Other sailors wouldn't sit in the same room with a Black man, but I'd had my fill of those types. The stewards kept to their work and did it right, and that counted for a lot with me.

The head steward was called Snowball. I never learned his real name. Maybe I never asked. He had a round face and eyes that saw more than he ever said. He moved with a formality that seemed older than the war, older than the ship itself. A man of small order in a world without it. He laid out silverware with a priestly care, each plate set as an article of faith only he remembered. His posture was straight, his shoes always shined. He was proud of the mess, proud of the polish on the brass rails, proud that his work could hold chaos at bay for one more day. The officers liked him because he made their world clean. What carried him more than duty was a hard, private pride, the kind that would rather crack than bend.

Smith was different. A quiet man. Small in the shoulders, calm in the eyes. He never spoke more than he had to. YYou could pass him in a hallway and feel the warmth of him, steady and banked, old fire held under iron. He was the sort who made no enemies and few friends. He did what was asked of him and did it right, and when the day was done he sat apart with his thoughts, the kind of man who carried whole worlds behind his silence.

I'd bought a Gibson guitar from a pawn shop in Frisco, a sunburst thing that looked better than it sounded. I couldn't play worth a damn. I just wanted to hold something that wasn't steel or grease. Smith saw it and asked if he might try. When he took it in his hands, the air around him changed. His fingers knew where to go. The sound that came out wasn't just music; it was old rooms and old voices, somehow alive in his hands. Old songs, slow and deep, rising and falling like breath. I sold it to him months later, fifty dollars and a pack of smokes. It had never really belonged to me.

Most nights he played on the fantail after lights out. The sea was a black plain and his notes carried out over it, thin and trembling, until they vanished. The men would stop talking. You'd hear boots scuff, matches strike, a few men turning their backs to the sea and just letting the sound carry whatever they had in them. The small sound of men remembering what they'd left behind. Sometimes I'd see him out there alone with his head bowed, the guitar glinting faint in the starlight. The moment felt private, solemn, and near to prayer.

Then there was Jackson. Tall, wiry, restless. The kind of man who filled a room without trying. He had eyes that dared you to meet them and a way of standing like he was ready to fight the world. He said he came from Chicago and left it at that. He walked with the city still in him, its alleys and heat and broken glass. Danger lived in him beside a hard kind of innocence. He could laugh one moment and break you the next.

Where Snowball loved order and Smith loved music, Jackson loved the fight. It lived in him. You could see it in the way he moved, the way his shoulders rolled when he walked. He never looked for trouble but he didn't hide from it either.

It was down on the empty tank deck that we found our common ground. The cargo gone, the wide steel bay turned into a makeshift ring. Ropes strung between stanchions, men crowding close, their shouts echoing up through the hull. I'd fought plenty back home, but Jackson was different. Quick. Precise. He fought with a dancer's feet and a killer's hands. I swung hard, the kind of hits that could fell a bull, but he wasn't there when they landed. He'd slip past, tap me with a jab that felt like an insult more than a wound, and circle again.

The men yelled from the lines. Watch him dance.

He'd grin then and move faster, and I'd be chasing shadows until he caught me high on the cheek and the deck pitched away for a second. I never solved him. All the times we fought, I never learned where he would be next. He had the gift. Feet light, hands cruel, eyes steady. In a different life, Jackson might have stood in a prize ring with a robe over his shoulders and a cutman waiting in the corner. But aboard that ship, when he saw I'd taken enough, he ended it with a quick tap to the nose, just enough to start the blood. That was his bell. We'd stand there breathing hard, bloodied and grinning, and shake hands. No words. Respect didn't need them.

After that he'd nod when we passed in the corridor, and I'd nod back. That was friendship enough.

One night I went aft for a smoke. The sky low, the wake running white behind us. Jackson came out of the dark with a sandwich in his hand.

Take this, he said. It's good.

I ate it standing beside him, the mustard sharp on my tongue. The sea hissed under the screws and the stars burned cold and far away. I told him about home. The river, the fields. Hay cut at dusk and left in rows, the sweetness of it hanging in the last light. He listened without looking at me, eyes fixed on the horizon like he could see it all there. When I ran out of words he said, Folks is folks. They all got the same hunger. Then he walked off.

After that I would find him there some nights at the rail, staring into the dark. Smith would come out with the guitar and play low behind him. The notes moved through the wind and down into the sea noise, and all of it seemed to belong to the same sorrow.

But not every man aboard shared the peace of that hour.

There was a deckhand named Hayes. Arkansas hill country. He'd spit when one of the stewards passed. Thought it made him a man. One afternoon Jackson came through with a mop and bucket. Hayes was sitting on an upturned crate, chewing, his eyes fixed on Jackson with a cur's patience.

Move, Jackson said.

Hayes didn't.

I told him to let it go. But Jackson didn't move either.

You wanna wrestle? Jackson said. You wanna box?

Hayes smiled with his mouth closed.

Jackson took a step closer. Kid, I'm gonna count to three.

One. Jackson dropped the mop.

Hayes was gone before he said two. The bucket clattered. The mop water spread slow across the deck. Jackson watched him go, then looked at me and grinned. That hillbilly almost got himself hurt. I laughed till the smoke from my cigarette stung my eyes.

It was only a few days later when things broke for good. Snowball had been riding him harder than usual, sharp with his orders, and Jackson's patience had worn thin. A shout went up in the quarters. Boots pounding the deck. I came running. Snowball was on the floor and Jackson was on top of him. The two of them locked together in a tangle of limbs, sweat and rage rising off them.

Say it, Jackson roared. Say who's the boss here.

Snowball's face was red, his breath coming in ragged bursts. Around them the men stood silent, half afraid, half enthralled. Someone moved like he might step in but stopped when Jackson's eyes cut toward him.

Say it, Jackson said again.

All right, damn it, Snowball gasped. You the boss. Now get off me.

Jackson held him there another heartbeat, then rose. He brushed off his dungarees and walked away. The circle gave way for him, wide and quiet. Snowball stayed where he was, chest heaving, whatever was left of his pride scattered there on the deck with him. Nobody helped him up. I did not move either, and that sat in me heavier than the fight itself.

After that, the mess deck changed. Snowball went quiet. His orders came soft, almost apologetic. Smith said nothing, just polished the same cup over and over, head bowed. Jackson didn't gloat. He didn't need to.

That night, when the lights went red for night watch, I found Smith alone on the fantail. The guitar was in his lap but he wasn't playing. He looked out to sea, the reflection of the compass light trembling on the water.

He said without turning, Men always got to have a boss. Even when the sea don't care.

I didn't answer. There was nothing to say.

The days blurred together, all heat, steel, salt, and sweat. The stewards moved through the ship, silent as ever, though something between them had shifted. Snowball's shoes weren't as bright. Smith kept mostly to the shadows. Jackson carried himself lighter, but it wasn't joy. It was the kind of freedom that comes from winning a fight you wish you'd never had to start.

One evening I saw Jackson in the galley doorway. The light behind him was red and the air was full of steam. Snowball stood at the counter, his hands motionless on a stack of plates. For a moment they faced each other without speaking. Then Jackson nodded once and walked away. Snowball's shoulders eased. That was all the peace they'd ever get.

The ship went on through the water. The days wore down. In the engine room the diesels drummed, and fuel clung to our clothes and hair, a weight you carried even when you slept. I would pass the stewards sometimes in the narrow passageways and nod. Smith would smile faintly. Snowball would look past me. Jackson would look through me.

And there were moments of grace. One night the air fell away and the ocean lay flat and shining, taking the last of the light into itself. Smith brought his guitar to the open deck and began to play. The sound rose slow and mournful, drifting out into the dark. Men gathered without words. Some leaned on the rails. Some sat cross-legged on the steel. Even the officers paused at the hatchway. The music filled the space between us where words had no business being. Jackson stood at the edge of the light, his face turned to the sea.

When the song ended, nobody clapped. Smith laid the guitar beside him and looked down at his hands like he didn't know what they were. The waves slapped soft against the hull. The night closed in again.

I remember thinking then that war had a thousand kinds of silence. The silence before a gun went off. The silence after. The silence of men who had learned not to speak what they knew. And this, the silence between men who would have been brothers if the world had allowed it.

When I think of them now I see the three of them as they were. Snowball in his white apron, eyes sharp even when the world had dulled him. Smith with his music, his quiet smile. Jackson with his fists and his pride and the fire that never went out. They were bound to service, but they carried themselves as free men in the only way left to them.

I felt closer to those three than to half the crew that wore my color and called me brother. The sea had burned away what men said mattered. What was left was work, sweat, hunger, fear. That was what lay under every uniform, no matter the stripe.

But the world wouldn't see it that way. It never did. They will not be named in the books. When the war was over their names would vanish into the logs. The mess deck would be cleaned, the brass polished, the sheets changed. And men would go home and tell their stories, leaving others unspoken.

I remember them even now. Men before any uniform, station or color. Their voices went into the wind, and the wind carried them beyond us.

Sometimes when I wake in the small hours I think I can hear Smith's guitar again, faint in the dark, the sea playing back its own memory.

THE BLACK GANG

The engine room was my world. They called us black gang though coal was long gone. Down there no man spoke. You wrote on a pad or carved words in the air with your hands, for the roar was such that a man could set his mouth to your ear and howl and you would hear nothing. The sound lived in the steel and in your bones. It rang on years later when you tried to sleep in quiet rooms ashore.

It was hot in that belly. Heat pooled under the deckplates and crawled into your lungs with each breath. Sweat ran off your back and soaked your dungarees till the salt cut your skin raw. The air was stale and close. When the hatches shut behind you, iron took the place of sky and horizon, and the ship seemed to press its full weight inward.

Watertight integrity they called it. The Navy's sacred law. Every hatch dogged and sealed so the sea could not find its way in. But that integrity was our death warrant too. If a torpedo ever struck home in that belly there would be no escape. We were sealed inside, and men topside might live to swim or fight, but the black gang would not. We knew it. Every clang of the hatch behind us was a reminder that we were already half buried, bones laid out unseen.

The two great diesels thundered in their beds. GM twelve-cylinder engines with pistons big as your leg. They hammered without cease, shaking the very plates of the ship.

Their flywheels spun and their gears clashed and they drove the screws that pushed the vessel through the sea. We tended them with a priest's care at the altar, watching gauges and logging the temperatures, pressures, oil, and coolant.

McDaniel was the crew chief. A son of a bitch through and through. He never liked me, probably because I knew more about engines than he did, though I never said it outright. He barked orders to drown the silence he feared most, the silence that came when the engines stopped. He leaned on others for the work and took the credit, but even his cruelty seemed born of something brittle, with command the only thing keeping him from breaking.

Gund was his pet. A suck hole if ever there was. He shadowed McDaniel. Fetched tools, stood at his elbow, eager to repeat whatever order had already been given.

Whitey worked the pumps. Frail and thin as wire, hair gone all to white though he could not have been fifty. To us he was ancient, so old another watch might have put him flat on the deck. Even so, he kept the bilges dry, checked the strainers, and made his slow rounds through the engine room, watching the pressure lines with the focus of a man holding himself together by duty.

Dawson watched the gauges. A quiet man from the hills of Tennessee, eyes pale as milk glass, hands made for wrenches. He rarely spoke and never hurried. He marked every needle with a calm that seemed to slow the room. If there was trouble brewing in the pipes, Dawson saw it before it boiled.

Hendricks was the oiler. Carried his can with a kind of reverence and walked the length of the engines, feeding the moving parts their lifeblood. He laughed at things most men cursed. Once he dropped a wrench into the bilge, down into the muck of oil and water, and had to belly-crawl in the filth to get it back. Instead of swearing he just leaned his head back and laughed, loud and deep, the joke laid on the whole world.

Bennett was hand on the throttles when we needed speed. Slick hair always combed neat even in that hellpit. He stood at the levers with a little private smile, easing the diesels up like he trusted them more than he trusted men.

Croyder was the muscle. Big and broad across the shoulders, built heavy as a farm gate, an Oklahoma boy. He handled the heavy spanners and the valve wheels that took the strength of two men. When the diesels shook the deckplates he braced against it, hard as iron.

And I was there among them. Motor machinist's mate second class. I kept the records straight, knew the guts of the engines, could tear down an injector or rebuild a pump blindfolded. All of us were bound to those two great beasts penned in iron.

Storms were worse when you were shut in the belly with the diesels. On deck a man could look out and see the sky and the sea's fury rising in black walls of water, cold and merciless. But down below there was nothing to see. Only the steel around you shivering alive and the deep thunder of water smashing against the plates. The ship groaned in her seams. Bolts sang in their threads. The diesels thrashed in their beds, chained and furious, and we kept them fed, kept them breathing.

The deck bucked beneath us. You could not tell if you walked straight or crooked for there was no horizon to guide you. Tools clattered across the gratings and vanished into the bilges. A lantern broke loose and swung, its flame cutting the dark in slow arcs. Men staggered into bulkheads with curses swallowed by the roar. The air was a furnace, the heat tasting of oil and fear.

The sea outside was faceless and endless but inside it was worse. A blind brute pounding the iron belly, shaking the air from your lungs. You braced yourself at the gauges and prayed the screws held, for if they failed the sea would have us whole.

One such storm had knocked out our steering, and a crew was sent into the aft compartment to disengage the main steering and work the rudder by hand. The place was narrow as a grave and the air stank of rust and bilgewater. They called it the trick wheel, a crude crank near two feet long with a wooden handle jutting from the gears like a limb. A man braced his feet and leaned into it, turning the rudder by sheer force. When not in use it had to be disengaged, for if left in the gearing it would spin with such speed that no hand or bone could survive its strike.

I had seen men down there in storms, stripped to their undershirts and slick with sweat, bent over that crank with the full weight of the ship working through their backs. The ship shuddering, the seas slamming her stern, and them fighting that wheel against the will of the ocean. Each turn a contest with the sea itself.

One night I was sent down there to check the rudder linkage. The ship rolled under me, the air foul and close. I ducked into the compartment and did not see that the crank had not been secured. It spun so fast the eye could not see it, only the blur of air and the whine of steel screaming in its housing. At the last instant I caught the movement, the ghost of it, and shouted oh shit and tried to jump back. Too late. The crank caught me in the guts, hammering me with the force of a piston five, six times before it flung me across the room.

I hit the bulkhead and slid to the deck. The breath gone from me, the room shrinking to a narrow ring of light. The pain came in hard pulses, deep in my gut, the crank's violence still working there. I could not rise. Could not breathe. For near half an hour I lay there certain I was done. The crank kept spinning, blind and murderous, humming in the iron dark, a clock that would not run down.

At last I dragged myself forward, clawing along the deck on my belly, each movement sending fresh waves of fire through me. I hauled myself through the hatch and collapsed where the others found me.

They grabbed me up and carried me topside to the sick bay. The world tilted and blurred. Their boots rang against the deck. Red lights buzzed. The air reeked of oil and men.

Jesus Christ, Pat. What happened.

The crank. The trick wheel. Caught me in the guts. Spun loose.

God damn. It is a miracle you are breathing.

I ain't so sure.

Their voices were low, close. The sound of them passed through the steel corridors, hushed and uneasy.

You look bad, said Bennett.

I feel worse.

Did you pass out?

No. I wish I had.

How many times did it hit you?

Five. Maybe six. A swinging wrench set to my guts and left to run.

Croyder looked down. Your shirt is soaked through.

Yeah. I think I pissed blood.

You didn't. That is just oil.

Then I am ahead of the game.

My boots dragged behind me. My head lolled. The men carrying me would not look at my face. Their hands were tight on my shoulders, steadying themselves as much as me. Somewhere deep below, the engines beat with a buried violence.

We will get you there, said Dawson.

Just hang on. You better not die, said Whitey. We need a man who can read the gauges.

I smiled weakly. I am not going out like that.

They carried me through the ship's heat and shadow. The light flickered in the seams of the bulkheads and I thought I heard the engines falter for a breath. The sound dropping away terrified me more than the pain. The thought that the heartbeat of the ship might stop and take me with it.

The sick bay door swung open and the light spilled out like a verdict. They eased me inside and called for the corpsman.

Baker came at a run, sleeves rolled, his face gone hard. He looked me over in silence, his hands quick and sure, listening as though to some language only he could hear. He pressed a palm to my gut and watched my face. Lifted each arm. Took my pulse. Then stepped back, lit a cigarette from the burner, and shook his head.

No broken bones and no rupture I could feel. You are one lucky Irishman, he said.

I don't feel so damn lucky, I said.

For a week I lay in my bunk, wracked and half crippled, with bile and old blood in my mouth.

I listened to the ship move under me, her iron bones groaning, the faint hum of the engines carried through the steel. I could hear the black gang at work, the distant clang of a wrench on iron, the muffled thud of boots on deckplates. The world went on without me. And in the quiet I began to understand that the sound of those engines had entered me for good. I would carry it all my life. Even ashore the silence would never be pure again. Always that low hum in the blood, the sea beating somewhere inside.

At last the day came when I could rise. My body weak but willing. I pulled on my dungarees and went below again. They dogged the hatch shut behind me. The roar closed around me, and I was home. The heat, the stink, the iron walls pressed close. The faces of the gang turning toward me through the haze of sweat and smoke. No words passed. None were needed. I stepped to my station and laid my hands on the gauges. The ship throbbed beneath me.

And I knew I belonged there.

But it was a belonging paid for in flesh, and the engines would keep their share of me till I died.

That was the black gang. Men swallowed in steel and heat and noise, sealed away from the world above, each with his own way of bearing the weight of that buried hull around him.

Tarawa

Pearl Harbor lay around us, restless with ghosts. The air was a strange thing, half salt and half memory. It seemed the harbor itself breathed the dead. Rusted hulls jutted from the shallows, their ribs rising through the water, whale-bone pale in the gray light. Oil drifted on the tide, thin and rainbowed, always moving. The place felt haunted in the way a wound is haunted. You could feel the past pressing close.

We were moored there while the ship took on fuel and food and water and ammunition. Crates and drums and boxes of rations stacked and swallowed into her hold. Forklifts rattled on the dock. Cranes swung loads overhead. The winches groaned and the cables whined and the men shouted above the din. Diesel and rope and tar clung to everything.

We were confined to the ship. Liberty was canceled. Shore leave ended at the rail. Men stayed aboard and looked anywhere except toward the island lights. The officers kept quiet. We knew all the same. The ship felt different once she was sealed and busy, already carrying orders in her steel.

Someone said, You hear what they're saying.

About what.

Tarawa. Some Jap island. Never heard of it.

Neither have I. But they say it's bad.

The kind of bad where they don't let us off the ship.

That's the one.

Gilberts. Makin. Tarawa. Betio. These words were unknown to us and yet they carried a weight that pressed on every man's chest.

Below decks the black gang labored without pause. Pumps tested. Lines bled. Gauges checked. The engines threw heat against our faces. Topside the gunners stripped their weapons and fed them with grease, their hands black and shining. Ammunition drums stood stacked in offerings of steel. The Marines aboard cleaned their rifles, wrote letters home, sharpened knives, folded socks in hopes that might hold off what waited. Each man performing his small ceremony of denial, men already aware their names might outlive them.

The ship throbbed with motion, but a silence ran beneath it, the kind men feel before the world changes.

Seven days of silence before the word came down. We were bound for the Gilbert Islands, for Tarawa itself. Part of the Fifth Fleet in a convoy so vast it seemed the ocean itself could scarce hold it. We crawled at eight knots across the Pacific, war in no hurry to get there. We were bound for the fire.

The sea itself changed with it. Even the light seemed thinner. We steamed southwest under a hard sky and the ocean spread in every direction, gray and impenetrable. From horizon to horizon the ships lay spaced in ranks. Carriers and destroyers and transports. Black stacks streaking the heavens with smoke. A sight so large it numbed the mind.

At night we darkened Ship. Every porthole sealed, every bulb hooded. The whole convoy gone to shadow. You couldn't see your own hand before your face. Even a cigarette coal was forbidden. The sea was an absence, the world reduced to vibration.

Bull muttered, Might as well gouge my damn eyes out.

Nicky said, You ever known dark like this.

I told him, It ain't the dark I mind. It's what moves in it.

A man learned the layout of steel by feel, the rungs beneath his palms, the tilt of the deck, the rhythm of turns. You could walk from bow to stern blindfolded. The engines beat underfoot, the breath of the ship constant, and beyond her the whisper of a hundred other hulls sliding through the black. It was like drifting inside the chest of some vast animal whose heart would not stop. A silent armada bound for death.

Eighteen days. We crossed a sea cut open by war. A black smudge of ships cutting the bitter blue. Our ship was no greyhound but a barge, flat-bottomed and square-bowed, built to beach and die. It pitched and wallowed, and every shudder of the engine transmitted straight into my gut. The water beat against her hull, hard and hollow as a coffin lid. I felt each blow in my bones. Every man aboard carried that same vibration inside him, a tremor that did not stop even in sleep.

Fuel and brine thickened the air, and beneath it all lay the dread that stalked us day and night. The tanks and trucks strapped to the deck were ghosts, waiting for their turn. We ate our thin rations in silence, the deck vibrating beneath our feet. The watches fused, dawn to dusk to dawn, marked only by the slow churn and the constant spray of water over the low bow. Eyes stayed on the horizon. Waiting for that thin white line where everything would change.

We passed the equator and the heat turned savage. The air was hot and close. Salt crusted our uniforms. Men slept on the deck in the wind, shirts open, eyes glazed. Diesel, sweat and fear carried in the air. The ocean had no mercy, only patience. We crawled across it inch by inch.

On the eighteenth day, the ocean gave up a shape. A charcoal smudge that grew by the hour, resolving itself into the flat, coral-ringed geometry of Tarawa. The ramp chains groaned to life, and the sound of them was worse than any shell I'd ever heard. Tarawa. Betio. A name the world would learn in blood.

We were there. No more waiting.

We had reached that low sand-spit, and standing on the steel deck of the ship, I knew with a bone-deep certainty that the true price of the journey was about to be paid. Right where the sand met the steel.

On the morning of November twentieth, 1943, the Battle of Tarawa began in earnest. The sea was black with ships. Battleships in their ranks, iron cathedrals afloat. Their guns rose and fell and then the air was split with a concussion that shook the teeth in your head. The whole horizon strobed with fire. Shells as big as trucks dropped out of the sky and the island came apart in chunks. The island leapt. Geysers of earth and smoke and fire tore skyward, the island coming apart before our eyes.

For hours it went on. The roar of it was without pause. The sea jumped with the shock. The sky dark with cordite and soot. We stood on the deck and watched. The men said this was the softening up. The prelude. The island was nothing but smoke and ruin, and they said nothing could live under such a hammering.

But when the guns at last fell silent, the smoke thinned and you could see the silhouettes of bunkers standing. The pillboxes untouched. They'd carved their labyrinth beneath the earth, and no shell could touch them there. The bombardment was a lie, a comfort for the living.

Down in the sand and the coral they crouched unbroken, their barrels already fixed on waters empty.

The skies themselves roared. Wave upon wave of Hellcat fighters and Dauntless dive-bombers launched from our aircraft carriers came in low, their wings flashing in the sunlight, engines screaming. They dropped their bombs in long black strings and the island vanished again in fire. Great plumes rose up, palm trees lifted whole from the earth and hurled down in splinters. But when the smoke cleared you could see those same firing slits glinting like eyes in the sand. The Japs were dug too deep. They were waiting.

I stood on the portside bow with my hands on the grips of the twenty millimeter and the whole of Betio laid out before me, some ruin born from men's imagining. Wilkins was loading, Ortega spotting. The lagoon was choked with wreckage. Amtracs gutted and burning. Higgins boats split open on the reef. Marines sprawled across their decks or drifting in the shallows face down in the pale green water. Smoke blew low and black and the stench of it clung in your teeth.

The tide had run out and left the reef bare and the landing craft wallowed and stalled in the shallows. I watched the Marines climb over the gunwales and step down into the water with rifles held high. Two hundred yards of open sea between them and the sand. They waded slow through waist deep surf and the air above them was cut to ribbons by tracer fire. The bullets stitched the water and men went down thrashing, their blood feathering red through the current. No man who lived through that hour would ever sleep clean again.

The sea was filled with bodies. They rolled in the wash, their packs dragging them under. The beaches ahead were rimmed with fire. Pillboxes cracked open under iron thunder, their guns mowing the surf in long deliberate sweeps. You could hear the explosions rolling across the lagoon, shells bursting in water and men alike, deafening, a world of concussion and thunder. Men's screams torn away in the wind.

The pier jutted into the sea, a long finger of timber and concrete, every span of it holding death. Snipers crouched in the beams. Machine guns dug in at the head of it cutting swathes through the men who tried to cross. The Marines crawled forward in the wash, their rifles held up, their helmets knocking against the pilings slick with blood. Some reached the seawall and clung there like insects against a stone, pressed down by fire so fierce they could not lift their heads.

The seawall itself stood as the work of some old and malevolent hand. Coral blocks and coconut logs banded together. Behind it the island bristled with guns. You could see the pillboxes, the little slits of them spitting fire. They were buried in the sand so that only the mouths of their weapons showed and they scythed down the beach in crossing arcs. Men went down in rows. Others floundered in the tide pools behind the reef where the tide had stranded them. The reef itself glimmered with wreckage. Tractors burning in the shallows. Boats broken open. Men trapped in the surf with no cover but the bodies of the dead.

On shore the battle was madness. Marines clawing over the seawall, dragging the wounded behind them, firing into the sand where the pillboxes squatted. Satchel charges and flamethrowers spitting gouts of fire that clung to men and bunkers alike. You could see Japanese soldiers burst from their holes, their uniforms aflame, shrieking as they stumbled into the surf only to be cut down by rifles waiting.

Beyond the seawall the tanks lay half buried. Japanese light armor dug in up to the turrets. They fired across the open ground and their shells slammed shut through the air, door after door in a house of the dead. When they were hit they burned where they sat, steel coffins glowing against the sand. The bunkers were endless. Concrete mouths spitting lead. Marines fell against them and slid down in heaps while others climbed over the corpses with charges clutched to their chests.

And when night came the island burned. From the ship we saw fires flicker across the beachhead, strange lights that cast the shapes of men across the smoke. The Marines were in among the ruins, crouched in the blackness with knives and rifles and grenades. The Japanese rose from their tunnels and counterattacked in the dark. The sky above the atoll strobed with tracer fire, red and green crossing in arcs. The sound carried over the water, the screams of men locked in combat hand to hand, the blast of grenades muffled in the sand.

I could see it with the clarity of a fever dream. Muzzle flashes leaping in the night. The silhouettes of men grappling, vanishing in fire. Whole squads overrun and fighting with bayonets, stabbing in blind fury until the beach itself seemed to writhe. The wounded cried out for water, for corpsmen, for God. The island shook with violence that did not cease even with the dawn.

The battle dragged on through the next day and the day after, three days without mercy. The Marines poured ashore in endless streams, fresh waves moving through the wreckage of the first. Each hour the island took more men, swallowing them into its black sand, its trenches, its bunkers.

On the third day they came in a final charge. Screaming, rushing from their tunnels with bayonets fixed, rushing headlong into the rifles and the machine guns. A futile banzai. They were cut down in rows, bodies tumbling forward until the sand was a carpet of the dead. Not a man turned back. They came until death had counted them all.

When it was finished there were seventeen left alive. Seventeen men taken from an army of nearly five thousand. The rest lay where they had fallen, blasted to pieces or buried in the sand.

On the fourth day they let us go ashore. Me, Bull, Nicky Powers and a few others stripped naked and waded through the shallows with our clothes held above our heads. We dressed on the black sand where the dead lay strewn and bloated. Marines rolled dead in the surf, their bodies lifted and turned by the waves in a slow, broken dance. My stomach churned. Death in the air was beyond words. You breathed it in and felt it catch in your throat, there no matter how much you swallowed. There were arms and legs scattered about, severed heads locked in helmets, faces pale and swollen and unrecognizable. Rifles and packs, canteens and helmets lay among them the beach itself seeming to have vomited back the war.

We caught glimpses of the natives as we moved inland, the islanders fleeting at the edge of the ruin. Women in grass skirts drifted by the trees, breasts bare in the heat, their faces blank with fear or the old sleep of war. It set an unease moving under my skin.

Bull spat and said, Christ, you see them women? Half naked like nothing ever happened here.

Nicky shook his head. And here's the ground all tore to hell. Don't make sense.

I said, This is their home. Or it was. What is left of it. Leave them be. Anyhow, I want a keepsake off this island. A rifle, a knife, anything. A man needs proof he stood here.

Bull gave a short laugh. You and your damn souvenirs.

Nicky said, Careful what you carry, Pat. Some things follow you home.

I found a pillbox that was still somewhat whole, its roof sagged where the sea had thrown a shell and the concrete had split and slumped under the blow. It was half caved in, but there was room to crawl through. Nobody wanted to come with me, so I went down alone.

Inside was a small cathedral of ruin. Concrete cracked and scored where the shell had taken her, the sandbags about the embrasure a sodden ruin of burlap and smoke, rebar hung like the ribs of some dead thing. Light came in a thin slit and the rest sat in a kind of permanent dusk where the air moved slow. The stench was a vile wall and I could not breathe through my nose. I opened my mouth and pulled the air that way. I tasted the rot, death sitting on my tongue. It clung in my throat and would not go down.

Four bodies lay where the blast had left them: one face up with his mouth a slack circle, one curled, a thing folded away, one half under a torn oilcloth, the fourth splayed so that his jaw had gone to loose bone and the wind through the slit sighed at it. Flies worked the air in a hard bright cloud, buzzing with the thin sound of distant machinery; they walked the wounds and the hollow of the eyes and the noise filled the place until I could not hear my own breath.

One of the soldiers had a rifle slung over his shoulder where he lay. I tried to slide it free and the body would not give. Flesh had swollen and the webbing would not move. I dug a knife from my pocket and cut the strap. The .31 calibre rifle came loose and was mine.

From the dead man's belt I unhitched a short knife, a Hari-Karri. It had a round wooden handle and the long skinny blade rested inside a wooden sheath. It was a suicide knife. He never got a chance to use it. Mine now. I rummaged through the pouches and found a small satchel and some Japanese money and the usual small, useless things a man keeps when he thinks he will return.

Next to one of the bodies was a small desk, splintered and cracked from the blast, a drawer knocked halfway loose. Inside was a photo album, curled and blackened. I flipped it open. Young men posed in training camps. A suited man with his hand resting gently on his wife's shoulder. A girl with braids, smiling with all her innocence intact. She looked to be around my sister's age and the ache of it sat hard in my chest. Their parents had that same look mine wore when I boarded the train. The last photo showed the man himself, the one lying dead on the ground beside me. Young. Clean. Believing he might come home.

Then I looked down at him. His eyes had gone to glass. They held the light and gave nothing back, fixed on some far place only the dead could see. My stomach turned with a coldness that had nothing to do with fear. He was a boy in another country's uniform, carried to that shore by orders and tide, same as I had been carried. Different flags above us. The same mud under us. I crouched there with his gun in my hand and understood I was reaching into a grave. When I had cut the weapon free and took it, something of him came with me.

I said nothing aloud. I just tipped my head to the dead eyes, the nearest thing to acknowledgement I had.

I gathered what I had taken. The rifle hung heavy in my hands, the knife, the album folded against my chest. I crawled up out of that tomb and into the bright, bad light of the island.

The guys crowded me at once, wanting to see. Nicky lifted the rifle and peered down the sights. Bull yanked the suicide blade from its sheath and pressed it laughing to his belly, faking a grimace before chuckling like a boy at mischief. That reek clung to me and one of them asked how I could bear it. I said, Just don't breathe through your nose. They laughed, but inside me I was down there with that soldier, and it was plain to me how easily it could have been me or one of them. Gratitude washed through me but so did fear.

We walked that ruined island for another couple of hours. I borrowed a cigarette to a wounded Marine sitting in the sand with his leg bandaged in bloody rags. I thought to ask him how it had been in the fight, but the answer was already written everywhere in blood.

When we went back to the ship, climbing the ramp and looking once more to that blasted shore, we carried with us a new kind of respect for the Navy. For the steel decks beneath our feet and the water that lay between us and such carnage.

That night in my bunk I lay awake with my eyes open to the dark. The ship moved quiet under me, but in my ears I heard the flies, their droning rise and fall. I breathed through my mouth and the taste was there again, the rancid air of the tomb. I swallowed against it and it would not go. I thought of the photograph of the boy with his parents, of the girl with the braids, and I knew him then as I knew myself. Death had walked close beside me on that island, silent and patient, and I could feel the shadow of him lingering at the edge of the berth. I closed my eyes but there was no sleep, only the long roll of the sea and the memory of Tarawa burned into me.

Dog Days

The weeks blurred into each other after Tarawa. We moved from one scrap of coral to the next, ferrying men and machines, the endless cargo of war. At dawn we raised anchor and by dusk tied off in some other lagoon that looked no different from the last. The palms bent the same way in the wind, the beaches white and empty, the natives long gone or buried. It was a routine that dulled the mind. The roar of the engines below. The creak of the winches. The stink of diesel and sweat. Always a convoy. Always a cruiser or a battleship somewhere out there, sentinels of iron with guns scanning the horizon for shadows.

For a month or more we steamed in heat that made every breath labor. Even the sea seemed tired of us. The days slipped by like bilge through a pump. The islands lost their names and shapes. They were waypoints only, no more. The war made them all the same.

Boxing was a saving grace in those dog days. When the tank deck was empty we roped it off and laced on the gloves, and when it was full of cargo we boxed topside beneath the sun. Men circled on the steel deck, yelling wagers, and the smashing of fists on flesh became its own kind of rhythm. I fought whoever stood before me, short, tall, green sailor or grizzled petty officer. One afternoon I boxed Bull again and he split my lip open with a jab that made the men holler, and later Croyder stepped in grinning and took three rounds before stumbling to the ropes. Blood on the deck. Sweat in the eyes. For a few minutes the war felt far away.

And I had my Gibson guitar. Smith had shown me a handful of chords and though my fingers were clumsy the sound gave me solace. Before long I found other players among the crew. Russo was a city boy with a trumpet and a head full of jazz, always talking of smoky clubs and names I barely knew. Armstrong, Ellington, Goodman and Basie. When he played he bent the notes until they quivered with the life of some dance hall I had never seen. To me it was foreign talk. I liked country western songs and a few big band numbers you could tap a boot to. Harlan played a concertina with slow patience, his music plain and strong as church hymns. Fincher, a lanky machinist's mate from Kansas, built a washtub bass from scrap and a piece of line. Benson, a mess cook with a battered harmonica he carried in his pocket, could pull a tune from that harp that made the hair lift on your neck.

We sat in the shade of the empty tank deck and played for the men. Hymns, cowboy ballads, jazz runs that slid in whether I wanted them or not, and the blues Benson carried in his lungs. The crew clapped or leaned back smiling, and for a time the boredom lifted. Once we were moored beside a cruiser and they let us come aboard to play. The big-gun sailors stamped their boots and cheered. For a moment black gang, deck crew, and gunners all became men with music in them. The songs drifted into the night, thin as breath, and were gone.

Other times we sat idle. I remember one evening leaning against the rail with Walker from Wyoming and Nicky Powers, watching the wake boil white under the setting sun.

Walker squinted at the horizon and said, Back home you can watch a storm roll in for fifty miles. Out here you don't see it till it's on you.

Nicky chuckled. Out here you don't see nothin but water, cowboy. You could drown a whole state in it.

Walker shook his head. Yeah, but at least it moves. Back home it's the land that'll swallow you, slow and quiet.

I said, You two got no sense. All I see is the same damn ocean we been staring at for over a month.

Nicky laughed. That's the Navy for you. They don't pay us to admire it.

And I started singing low, a tune we all half knew. We went in the Navy to see the girls, but what did we see.

The other two picked it up at once, hollering the answer: We saw the sea.

We laughed till our sides hurt, the words carrying across the dark water, swallowed in the wake.

But even in the laughter there was something faint beneath it.

One morning word came that we were nearing the equator. We all knew what that meant. Crossing the Line. An initiation older than the ships themselves. The shellbacks grinned with a wolf's hunger. The rest of us they called pollywogs, and our day had come.

They dressed a chief named Malloy, a broad-shouldered brute, as King Neptune. His beard was rope yarn dipped in tar and his trident a piece of pipe wrapped in canvas. Mr. Branch was made Amphitrite, in lipstick and coconut shells. Gund was Davy Jones, painted black with grease, wearing a devil's grin. Others wore wigs of mop heads, bellies slick with galley lard, aprons of rags. We were hauled before Neptune's throne and sentenced.

The first ordeal was Reeves. He was the royal baby, a bosun's mate with a gut with the look of a keg, shirtless and slick with oil. In the hollow of his navel he planted a maraschino cherry. One by one we knelt and sucked it out while the court howled. When my turn came the reek of him near broke me. His laughter rattled in the steel.

Then the gauntlet. A corridor of men shoulder to shoulder, each with a knotted line or a length of hose. We crawled through on hands and knees and took the blows. Some sprinted and were hit worse. Others laughed through blood in their teeth. I kept my head down and moved steady. There was no mercy in it, only the law of tradition.

Next came the oyster, strung on cord, slick with spit and seawater. We swallowed it whole. They jerked it back up and passed it to the next man. By the time it reached me it was gray and rank. I gagged hard to keep it down. We were dunked in salt tanks, coated with garbage, paddled with boards carved with ship names and battles. Hayes, who had mouthed off last week, was held down and shaved bald but for one brow. Even Bull had to dance in his drawers while they doused him with slop.

By dusk we were filthy and welted, our throats raw. Neptune's court declared us cleansed. The pollywogs were gone. Shellbacks stood in their place, baptized in salt and foolishness. It was brutal and half-mad. The worst of it was the laughter. The way it never stopped. Men doubled over as though it were a grand joke, though nothing about it was funny. There was cruelty in it, some need to pass pain down as rite or curse. Maybe it was that or go mad another way.

That night the laughter had a strange edge to it, thin as wire. Men who could laugh while another suffered. Men who would soon have to.

Later that night Walker nursed a welt across his shoulders and muttered, Imagine what the folks back home would think of this. It's a damn circus. We laughed, sore and bruised, but the words stuck in me. Men carried their homes like relics in their pockets, something to hold even as the sea stripped everything else away.

The monotony was broken one day by the promise of beer. Four cans apiece, doled out by rotation. The captain had laid in twenty cases and locked them in the stores, a treasure more precious than ordnance. The word went out that a handful of us would be shuttled to a spit of land for liberty.

They lowered the Higgins boats. I went with Nicky and Bull and a quiet sort named Taylor. The boats rode the glass of the lagoon, wakes stitching white seams behind us. Other boats came in from the convoy, dark hulls full of men. We rode toward that little halo of sand and palms, solemn as men going to confession.

The island was no island at all. A shoal of sand, two palms leaning tired above the water. The sand burned underfoot and the shells rattled with the sound of rain. Crabs scuttled from our boots and vanished in the wash, their backs small black shields. A single white bird lifted from the palms and was gone. The ships sat out in the lagoon, gray gravestones against the sky, thin threads of smoke rising in the heat. Men spilled from the boats clutching hot cans, the air rank with beer, sweat, and diesel.

We sat in the shade and cracked the cans. The light off the tin made the beer shine, liquid brass in the sun. The first swallow slid warm down the throat and the heat answered it. Men began to talk loud and easy. There was singing, rough hymns and cowboy tunes. Fists found shoulders and slapped in friendship. Some sailors waded in, laughing in the surf. Two naked men fought waist deep in the surf, swinging slow, clumsy punches while the sea shoved at them from every side. The island turned wild with drink. A man on his knees retching while another stood laughing till he wept. Two brawlers locked together as brothers. One sitting against a palm tree and crying for no one. Friendships made and broken in an hour, quick and senseless as cans kicked into the surf.

Men's nerves were frayed, and a look or a word was enough to break them.

Taylor changed with the second can. He was a quiet man at sea, and I liked his company. But the drink let the buried part of him rise. One beer and he was the same. Two and the edge showed. Three and the temper came out mean as a knife. He started needling a man who said nothing, then another, until Bull told him to shut it. Taylor squared up, eyes gone small. Nicky got between them. The noise of men drinking rolled around us. Taylor turned and his words found me.

I never liked you, Flynn, he said. Always the smart mouth. Always the front seat. Think you're better than us. He spat the last word and the spit landed in the sand between us, a small flag. His breath stank of beer and salt and anger. The curses ran out of him like water from a cracked pipe, each one meant to cut. Men turned to watch. A man losing his temper is a kind of entertainment at sea.

The old readiness rose in me, the heat behind the eyes, that hard pull to answer. I felt Nicky's hand on my arm. I could see Taylor trembling, his words slurring, the liquor pulling the strings. If I hit him I would be hitting the bottle, not the man. So I kept my hands still. He sagged finally and sat in the sand, breathing hard. Bull spoke to him low. After a while he laughed, weak and broken, ashamed of himself.

The sun went down slow and the palms turned the color of rust. The boats came back at dusk, engines blue with smoke. We left the atoll littered with cans and prints of boots, the crabs creeping out to take back their sand. Men laughed and sang and argued on the ride home. The island slipped into the dark, fading from the world behind us.

In the morning I went to Taylor's bunk and shook him till he stirred.

Taylor, I said.

He stirred and blinked slow, his eyelids heavy as rusted hatches. Hey Pat, he croaked.

Get up, I said. Yesterday on that island you called me some terrible things. You called me a son of a bitch. I knew you were drunk, so I let it pass. But here we are sober now. You're either going to apologize for every word you said, or we will settle it up on the fantail with our fists.

He stared at me, half in the fog of sleep. I did not move. You can see the truth of a man in the stillness, when the bluff leaves him and only the fear or the courage remains.

Taylor went white. The color went out of him, slow as water from a cracked tin. Oh Christ, Pat, he said. I'm sorry. I was drunk. I don't even remember the island. I blacked out. I like you, Pat. I don't want to fight. I apologize.

I watched his eyes. Hunting for the lie. There wasn't one. Just shame, plain and bare as a wound.

All right, Taylor, I said. I believe you. But don't let it happen again. A man can't afford that kind of poison in his blood. Not out here.

He nodded quick, voice low. You're right, Pat. My drinking days are done. No lie.

I let it stand. The ship groaned around us with the day's first work and the sea pressed on against the hull, endless, without memory of the island or of what had passed there.

The days passed quiet after that. But something had shifted. The laughter came less often. Men moved slower, rationing what was left inside them. The sea pressed on against the hull, endless and indifferent.

Baker was our corpsman. A kind man. Gentle. He had patched me when my gut was torn up and he had done it with a hand steady as cold steel. He never said much but there was always that small half-smile about him, some private joke keeping him company. He moved quiet through the ship, always ready with a word of comfort or a hand to a fevered brow. He made the iron world of that vessel feel a little less cruel.

Then came the night of the scream.

I woke to it before I knew I was awake. A sound pitched so high it seemed to catch in the steel. The ship moaned in the swells. Boots on steel. Voices shouting. I ran with the others toward sick bay.

Baker was on the deck. Our corpsman. The kindest man aboard. His eyes rolled white, his mouth foaming. Three sailors and an officer fought to hold him down. He thrashed like a hooked fish, his body all muscle and terror. The sounds from his throat were ragged and wet, scraped from somewhere deep.

Jesus Christ, hold him down, someone yelled. They wrestled him till they were slick with sweat. An officer called for a straight jacket. Baker's screams broke into choking gasps. He spoke words that meant nothing. Then his body convulsed and went limp.

We stood there in the reek of sweat and fear. None of us spoke. The ship's lights burned coal-red above him.

It was only after they carried him off that the questions began. A boatswain said he'd seen Baker around the passageways at odd hours. Another swore he'd caught him once with a cabinet open, though he'd thought nothing of it. The officer ordered a search.

We ran the length of the ship, opening every medicine cabinet. One by one. Bandages and gauze and bottles rattling inside. Alcohol, sulfa, quinine, atabrine, aspirin. But where the morphine syrettes should have been there was nothing. Empty slots, empty tins. Every cabinet. Not a single syrette left on the ship.

God help us if we take casualties, someone muttered.

Only then did the truth rise, slow as tide. Baker had taken them all. Weeks or months of it. Each needle a small mercy until mercy itself ran out. What we had seen that night was the drug gone from him and his body thrown into fury by its absence.

The next day they moved him to a hospital ship. We lined the passage as he went by. His skin shone with sweat. His eyes found no one. He made a sound low and broken, a prayer for grace he no longer believed in. They led him away and the passage fell silent.

I thought on it a long while. How men bear fear. Some fold it and keep it close. Some drink it down. Some hide in laughter or ritual or fists. Baker sought the silence of the needle. I could not blame him. I had seen what war does to men. He had just reached it sooner than we had.

In the days after he was gone the talk turned hard. Some cursed him for leaving us without morphine. Others said nothing. They had seen his eyes. For myself, I carried only pity. He had simply fallen sooner than the rest of us, and war does not give every man the same shoulders to bear it.

After that, the dog days rolled on. Steady. Featureless. The same dull sky. The engines beating beneath us steady as a second heart. The slow unmaking of men who had little left but the sound of their own breathing.

Hollandia

The sea had grown weary of us.

For weeks we moved west across the Pacific, from one small atoll to the next, each no more than a breath upon the map. Kwajalein. Majuro. Eniwetok. The Marshalls were strung across the ocean, bone-white arcs of sand and palm clinging to the rim of the world. Out beyond them the sea was so vast it seemed to have no edge at all. To the charts they were nothing, but to those of us who sailed into them they were whole countries of silence. The horizon hung sharp as a blade, and beyond it lay the long blue emptiness that never ended.

The Battle of Kwajalein began on the last day of January, 1944.

We went in with the Fifth Fleet, the sea crowded with gray hulls from end to end. Carriers, destroyers, battleships, transports. A floating city of iron and smoke. The decks ran black with men. Their helmets gleamed under the hard sun, rifles slung, faces turned toward that low ring of coral on the horizon. The air was still. The ocean molten glass. A silence held over the fleet, vast and expectant, the whole world seeming to draw breath.

Then the guns spoke.

From the decks of the battleships the first salvos leapt, each flash cutting a wound in the day. The shells whistled overhead, the sound thin and vicious as it passed. They struck the island and the earth answered back. The palm groves went up in sheets of flame. Sand and smoke lifted skyward in gray spirals. Shells tore the palm groves to splinters, flame and steel sweeping the atoll clean of anything that breathed. The earth shook as though the sea itself wished to unmake the islands. For hours the bombardment went on, the sea itself trembling under the weight of it. The reek of burning fuel and cordite carried over the water until it filled the lungs. You could feel the concussion through the soles of your boots, a deep drumming in the bones that seemed to mark the heart's own rhythm.

Tarawa had been madness.

This was something colder.

The killing was clean, methodical. The Navy had learned precision. The same machine that had torn itself to pieces at Tarawa now moved with the calm precision of a clockmaker. The shells landed where they were told. The planes came and went without waste. Men killed by schedule. The island burned under the sun, and when the Marines went ashore there was almost nothing left to meet them. The Japanese fought without sound, without mercy, already resigned to death. By the time it was finished, only forty-nine of their soldiers remained alive. A handful of Korean laborers also crawled out from the rubble, blinking in the light as men dug out of a grave.

We stood along the rails and watched. The lagoon was choked with smoke and oil, and the sea itself had gone dark with it. Bits of wreckage drifted between the ships. The ships of the line stood off in the distance, gray cathedrals under a wounded sky. The air was sour with rot and salt and the burnt sweetness of fuel. That night I leaned against the railing and watched the fires burning low along the shore. The sky glowed orange and the water shimmered with reflection. Beneath that calm surface lay thousands of bodies, drifting in the shallows, pale and slack.

We stayed in the Marshalls for weeks. The guns went quiet but the work did not. We ferried men and machines across those scattered islands. Our decks were stacked with tanks, trucks, and ammunition, the cargo of death that followed us everywhere. Each day began with the same metallic dawn. The same calls over the loudspeakers, the same slow churn of propellers beneath our feet. The names of the islands bled into one another. Kwajalein to Majuro, Majuro to Eniwetok. The days lost their edges. Even the sea seemed to have grown bored with us.

At Majuro the lagoon was calm as glass, the ships of the fleet lying at anchor in perfect reflection. From shore you could see their shadows stretching deep into the green water. Ghosts tethered to the earth. We went ashore for supplies and found the island transformed. Rows of canvas huts, stacks of drums, towers of radio antennae reaching into the sky. Radios chattered through the night, messages meant for other men and other wars somewhere beyond the horizon. The reef flats flashed white under the sun, and the air shimmered with heat and diesel. The men walked with the stiff motion of machines wound too tight.

At Eniwetok the reefs gleamed white beneath the blue, and the wind came hard off the sea. We watched Marines wade ashore and vanish among the palms, their helmets bobbing in the surf like driftwood. Later they came back with their eyes gone flat, carrying more silence than they had taken with them.

At night we lay on deck and watched the stars burn in the vault of heaven.

The air was warm and salt-sweet. Somewhere far off a generator droned, its rhythm blending with the heartbeat of the ship. No one spoke much. We were too tired for talk. You could feel it among the men, the sense that the war had settled into a kind of rhythm, a terrible order that made no room for thought. The Pacific stretched around us in the shape of a clock face, and we were the hands moving toward an hour none of us wanted.

Sometimes when I looked at the men, their faces lit by the red glow of a cigarette or the reflection of the sea, I wondered how many of them still believed in the cause that had sent us here. It was victory, they said. Another island taken. Another link broken in the chain that led toward Tokyo. But I had seen what victory looked like. It wore silence. It had no face and no mercy. It was the emptiness that settled after the noise stopped.

When we passed Kwajalein again weeks later, the lagoon bore the stain of death. Bits of wreckage drifted up in the morning tide. A helmet with no head beneath it. A boot. A child's toy, maybe from one of the native villages that had once stood here before the guns. The sea keeps its secrets, but not forever.

In early April we were ordered south to Guadalcanal to take on stores before the next operation. The island was quiet now. The palms grew through the wrecks of planes and trucks, their roots wrapping the bones of the dead. Damp and mold and old blood lingered in the air, a warning unheeded. The jungle pressed close around the trails, the vines creeping over the rusted helmets and the spent shells. Native boys walked barefoot in the mud, calling for cigarettes, their faces bright with laughter that seemed almost cruel against the silence. Along the ridges the old foxholes were filling now with rainwater and vines.

Cohen came with me that day.

He was from New York, gray-eyed, round-faced, soft at the middle. He'd been on edge since Tarawa, his nerves frayed thin. We walked the track together, boots sinking into the red mud. The sun was high and hot. The air hung warm and slow. Flies rose in black clouds from the puddles and settled again.

Cohen said, The chow's no good. Nothing but slop and maggots.

He kicked at the mud and spat.

The jungle don't sleep, he said. It waits. You can hear it breathing at night. Everything green here wants you dead.

I said, What are you so damned sour about, Cohen?

He looked at me sidelong, his eyes dull as old metal.

Alive don't mean much out here, he said. Alive just means waiting your turn.

You talk like a man already dead, I told him.

Maybe I am, he said.

We came upon a wrecked emplacement where the Marines had fought years before. The logs were black with soot, the ground torn open, helmets scattered and half buried. The smell lingered, faint but not gone. Cohen stared at it for a long time.

You see, he said. That's the end of it. That's all this island gives back.

Then he turned away and walked on. I watched him go, the red light falling through the palms, red as blood, and I thought some part of him was broken past repair. Whatever it was, he carried it buried deep where no hand could reach, and it poisoned every word that left his mouth.

Later we passed two soldiers near the docks, shirts open, rifles slung over their shoulders. Their faces were burned down to tired lines, eyes washed pale by the sun. One spat and said, You boys Navy?

I said, LST.

You missed the party, he said. You should've seen it when it was hot. Bodies piled thick as driftwood. Nights loud enough to split the sky.

His friend nodded. Now it's just the heat, he said. And the memories.

We said nothing more.

That night, lying in my cot aboard ship, I thought of Cohen's words.

Maybe I am already dead.

The sound of the surf came through the open hatch. The jungle hissed in the dark. I could feel the ghosts moving out there beyond the trees.

When the holds were full, we turned west again, across the Bismarck Sea.

The next name was Hollandia.

We knew nothing of it but the maps, yet the officers spoke of it like prophecy. The Japanese held New Guinea, a gate across the Pacific. If we could break it, the way to the Philippines would be open.

The old men spoke of strategy.

We spoke of surviving the next landing.

April 22, 1944.

We came in at dawn.

The sea was flat and silver under the new sun, the mountains black against the light. The sky looked innocent, a hard blue that had no business watching what men were about to do.

Task Force 77 stretched across the horizon, the largest armada we had yet seen. Battleships and cruisers, destroyers and LSTs. The Australians were with us now. The heavy cruisers Australia and Shropshire, the infantry ship Westralia, the landers Manoora and Kanimbla. Their decks were packed with men, rifles gleaming, their khaki uniforms turned gray with salt. Our own LST rode low in the water, loaded with tanks and trucks, with soldiers penned below. The guns of the fleet opened at once, the sound a single voice that shook the world. The mountains echoed it back until it seemed the island itself was shouting. Plumes of earth rose through the jungle. The air was full of dust and thunder.

From our deck we could see them wading ashore, men bent under packs, helmets low, rifles clutched in both hands. The surf caught them at the knees and broke white against their legs. Mortar shells burst ahead of them, and the sound rolled back to us, heavy as a war drum.

A tank slid down our ramp and into the shallows, its treads throwing water high, its exhaust coughing smoke. Another followed. The sand swallowed them both and they lurched forward, snatching at the earth with their treads. The shore was alive with noise, and yet inside me there was only quiet.

A strange calm.

The calm that comes when there is nothing left to be afraid of.

By midmorning the enemy's fire had begun to falter. The surprise had been total. Our planes had struck their airfields days before, leaving their fighters lined up on the runway, wrecked and skeletal. Even so, some guns held out in the jungle, and the sound of them echoed from the hills.

We worked without pause, lowering jeeps and tanks, hauling crates until our hands went black with grease. Ammunition crates stacked on the sand in graveyard rows. The wounded came back the other way, carried on stretchers, their faces as white as salt. Blood trailed through the surf. The sea drew back what it had given.

By late afternoon the guns went quiet. The beach lay wide and bright beneath the sun. Smoke drifted low over the trees. The men moved slower now, their faces slack with exhaustion.

And then word came down the line that General MacArthur himself was coming ashore.

We crowded the rails three deep. The light was hard and golden, the heat shimmering off the bay.

Then we saw him.

He came walking through the surf, his cap set firm, that corncob pipe clenched between his teeth. The water climbed to his knees. His officers followed behind, carrying maps and radios, their boots splashing in his wake.

He stepped onto the sand as though the whole scene had been waiting on him.

The men along the beach cheered until their throats went raw. Some saluted and some just stared. For a moment it felt like victory, pure and unspoiled. I wished I'd had a camera, but part of me knew no photograph could ever hold what that moment carried, the faith of tired men who needed to believe.

That night, when the fires burned low on the hills, Bull said, Happy birthday, Pat.

Nicky grinned. Twenty-two, right?

Yeah, I said.

Cohen smoked and said nothing.

The hills glowed red in the dark, and I thought maybe those fires were candles for all the birthdays that would never be seen.

The days that followed blurred into labor.

We carried supplies along the New Guinea coast, from Humboldt Bay to small ports hidden among the mangroves. We came into bays no bigger than a finger's length on the map, where the beach was nothing but mud and mangrove roots. There were makeshift piers hammered together from whatever lumber the engineers could scavenge, and we nosed the bow in while cranes swung their loads ashore and soldiers sweated under the weight of crates and drums. The heat pressed up from the steel and down from the sky. The steel decks so hot they burned through your soles. Salt and sweat rode the air, along with the stink of vegetation rotting in the rain. The nights offered no relief. The jungle hissed and the insects came in clouds. You learned to sleep with your face under a towel, breathing through the cloth. In the morning the scuppers were full of dead beetles, their shells black and glossy in the light.

One day we carried a load of Australian troops, and I went below to their quarters. They sat cross-legged on the deck, rifles stacked beside them, their khakis streaked with mud. They grinned when they saw me. Their speech rolled fast and heavy. Half laughter, half thunder, and I could barely follow the words. One of them pointed at my cap and said something I thought was an insult until the others roared with laughter. We read them in posture and stride and the small weather of the face. They were rough, loud, fearless men. It was easy to like them.

We traded stories. They told of Kokoda and Buna and the long fighting through the jungle. I told them of the engines and the black gang below, the noise that never left your head. We shouted to hear each other, half deaf from the engines and the gunfire, and laughed like fools. For a moment the war seemed small, almost human.

Later Colombo, one of ours, arm-wrestled an Aussie on a mess table. The ship shook with the roar of it. Bets laid in every corner, the men shouting until their voices broke. When Colombo slammed the man's hand to the steel the room exploded in cheers, and for once the sound was joy, not war.

One morning the whole crew was called to the main deck. The officers stood in a line, faces hard, khakis pressed. The sun burned low over the sea. Captain Whelan stepped forward, his voice sharp.

Somebody broke the lock on the stores last night, he said. Somebody stole beer. I want the man who did it to step forward.

No one moved.

The wind rattled the rigging. The ship groaned.

He said, You think you can rob this ship? You think you can shame me and shame your crew? Step forward.

No one moved.

I looked down the line and saw Crawford near the rear. Pale. Shaking. His eyes sunk deep. The thirst had him bad. They'd found him the night before passed out cold, cans around him in a drunkard's ring, puke on his chin. The boys had covered for him. Dumped the cans. Fixed the lock. But the truth hung in the air, heavy and plain.

The captain's voice came again. If no one steps forward, every man aboard will pay. Extra duty. No liberty. And no beer. Not a drop.

The silence was iron.

He said, Bring it up. Every last can.

We hauled the crates up from storage, sweating under their weight. The Stewards helped, Jackson muttering as he worked.

This a damn shame, he said. Who the hell did this?

I said, Doesn't matter. What's done is done. We don't give a man up.

Yeah, he said, but damn, that's a lot of beer. Maybe I'll just slap him once, he said, grinning.

We laughed, but it was bitter laughter.

That afternoon we moored beside the Australian cruiser. We laid a plank between the ships and carried the cases across. The Aussies came out grinning, voices booming.

Look at the bloody Yanks, one shouted. Bringing us our milk.

Another waved his hat. Thanks for the grog, mates. Fine work.

One crate slipped, fell into the sea. The cans bobbed once and went under.

Fish get thirsty too, one of our boys called back.

The laughter that followed was hollow as the empty sea.

When it was done, the captain traded our beef for their mutton.

The Aussies roared with delight.

Good trade, Yanks, they called.

The smell hit us before the boxes were opened. Greasy. Rank. Some of it we fed to the sea, the sharks circling under the stern, their fins cutting the surface in silence. For two weeks we ate that mutton, the taste of it clinging sour in our mouths.

Crawford came to us later, eyes down, voice shaking.

I'm sorry, he said.

No one answered. We lived by a code, and it bound us more than orders ever could. But I wanted to shake him till his bones rattled. Something in the men had gone slack. The laughter had a bitter edge to it now, and even the sea seemed heavier beneath the hull.

By July the heat had turned the decks to iron and the air to glass.

The tanks stood chained to the deck, their steel flanks dull with salt. The soldiers came aboard again, silent, eyes hollow, their rifles black with grease. We turned north. The wakes stretched behind us in long white scars. Ahead lay the Marianas. Guam. Another jungle waiting to take what was left of us.

Guam

The sea ran endless and the sky above was hard and white with heat. Our ship bore down on Guam with the engines laboring in their deep rhythm. The horizon was crowded with ships, the gray-backed leviathans of the Fifth Fleet moving as one. Carriers and battleships and destroyers. Oilers and transports. A full armada crawling across the water in a single slow advance. The air pressed down on us. Heat like a fist. Down in the ship's belly tempers ran thin. Men snapped at each other for no reason. Shirts clung wet to our backs and our skin was slick with sweat that never dried. The heat soaked into the steel and turned every surface mean.

Guam rose green from the sea, distant beyond the gray water. Men spoke its name differently because it was no nameless atoll. Guam was American soil. Taken from us in the first surge of the Japanese tide and held these three years. Its return meant more than the ground it covered. Guam was a keystone set deep in the wall of the war. A harbor. A place to launch the bombers. A place to anchor the fleet. From its shores the path to the Philippines would open. From its airfields we could reach Japan.

Before we made landfall, the sky bore witness. I was topside at general quarters, hands on the twenty millimetre, when the horizon lit with fire. The carriers had loosed their wings and the Japanese rose to meet them. They called it the Battle of the

Philippine Sea but among the men it would come to be known as the Great Marianas Turkey Shoot. I remember the distant thunder. The high blue dome was smudged with smoke, dark weather gathering. Their planes came in waves. Hellcats rose to meet them and tore them from the heavens.

Contrails stitched the sky. White scars marking the dying. I saw black specks wheel and catch fire. Matches struck and snuffed out. Fuselages tumbled end over end and vanished into the sea. The sound came slow. Guns hammering in the distance. Engines groaning through their last descent. Smoke rose from the wreckage and black oil fires drifted across the swells like broken birds. Nearly six hundred enemy planes lost. Three carriers sunk. Hiyō. Taihō. Shōkaku. Their airmen gone with them. The ocean bore its dead without a word. The war had shifted, and Guam would not be theirs much longer.

Back aboard the ship, there was a ritual. Each month the stewards gathered up the stray clothes from bunks and lockers and laundry lines. Shirts. Trousers. Socks. They poured them out on the mess deck tables, loot from some petty raid. The room was low and stifling, the sour of sweat and coffee and salt hanging in the air. Benches bolted to the deck groaned under the weight of sailors leaning forward, their hands in the heaps. The men came in, carrion crows drawn to the spoil. Laughter. Claims. A shirt held aloft that fit no one. Socks flew back and forth over the tables. For a time the war went quiet and the game filled the air with noise.

Bull laughed until he coughed. Nicky leaned against the bulkhead with the look of a man ready to sleep through it. Walker called his claims in a slow Wyoming drawl. Hayes cursed in a tongue thick as pitch. Whitey sat on the floor holding up a pair of pants too short for a child. Bennett pawed through the heap with the patience of a man picking fruit.

Cohen sat apart, one bag pulled close, a pile of clothes across his knees. He grinned down at them, pleased by the theft more than the prize.

Then Jackson stepped in, the steward, eyes sweeping the room. He saw the shirts in Cohen's lap and stopped.

Say, those my shirts, he said. His voice low at first, but it carried.

Cohen didn't look up. They're mine now, boy, he said.

The mess deck went quiet. The laughter guttered and died.

What you call me, said Jackson.

Cohen grinned wider. I said they're mine, boy.

Jackson stepped forward, his whole body gone tight.

I said those are my shirts. You hand them over.

Cohen leaned back, one hand on the cloth, guarding it as gold. I already told you.

Jackson said, Give em here. His voice rising.

Jackson's fists clenched. His breath shook.

Or what, Cohen said. You gonna do something about it, steward?

They stood close now. Toe to toe.

I don't need to talk, Jackson said. I'll take what's mine.

Cohen shoved him with a shoulder. The shirts spilled to the floor.

Jackson stood tall, chest heaving.

You son of a bitch.

Cohen grabbed a mop, held it like a club. Come on then, he said.

The room held its breath. A mess hall full of men, every one of them waiting on a spark.

Jackson's voice broke open. I'm gonna fix you, he said. Then turned and ran for the hatch.

I turned to Cohen. What the hell is wrong with you? Those are his clothes. Give them back.

Cohen shrugged.

We heard Jackson returning before we saw him. Boots drumming. He came through the hatch with a Colt .45 pistol in both hands, the blued steel shining under the lights. Said nothing. Just raised the pistol he'd taken from the officer's quarters, a weapon waiting there for him all along.

The room went hollow in an instant. Men ducked. Cursed. Held their breath. Time seemed to slow and there were three of us there, life balanced on the edge of a razor.

Jackson's face was lit from within. Eyes red. Neck corded with rage. He raised the pistol and the air turned to glass.

Cohen did not move. Stood holding the mop up as though it could stop a bullet. But the fear was in him. It was in his eyes. Wide and wet. The mask slipping.

You cocksucker, Jackson screamed.

I don't know why but I felt no fear. I saw the man and the gun and the space between them and that was all. Maybe I just didn't want blood spilled over shirts. Maybe it was simpler than that.

Jackson, put the gun down, I said. You don't want to kill this man.

Move, Pat. I'm gonna kill him.

They'll hang you for this, I said. Or put you in front of a firing squad. Now hand me the damn gun.

His hands trembled. I reached out slow and he let go.

The Colt had weight in my hand. I slid the magazine free and handed it back empty.

Put this back where you got it, I said. Before they come looking.

He turned and was gone.

Goddamn it, Cohen, I said. If you'd given him his clothes, none of this would've happened.

Cohen looked down. The mop sagging.

I gathered Jackson's shirts. Walked them down to the stewards' compartment. The door stood open. Jackson sat on the bunk, elbows on knees.

I laid the shirts in his lap.

I was gonna kill that son of a bitch, he said.

Yeah. I know.

He looked up. His face was raw. I got an anger in me. Buried deep. When it comes up, God help whoever stands in front of it.

Jackson, I said. You've got to learn to walk away. You've got to master it. Or it's gonna kill you.

He nodded. A crooked smile. Yeah, Pat. I know.

Do you think they'll kick me off the ship?

I didn't answer right away.

Nah, I said. It'll blow over.

But I knew I was lying. And I think he knew it too.

We shared a look and it was final.

When I left, he didn't move. The door shut behind me and the sound echoed down the passageway. The ship moved through the night, indifferent to what men do inside her.

I could not sleep. I lay there and saw it again and again. The gun. The trigger. The breath that might have been the last. A killing over shirts. And in every version, someone died.

Two days later, I was in the engine room when word came.

Jackson is gone. Transferred out.

I read it twice. The words hit me both times.

They'd put him aboard a Higgins boat and sent him to a hospital ship. What came after, no one said. I wished I could have said goodbye. Given him a nod. Anything. But he was gone, and the chance with him.

That week the fleet closed on Guam. The bombardment began.

The sky cracked open. Battleships and cruisers offshore poured fire inland. Whole ridgelines vanished. The jungle caught fire. Smoke massed into stormclouds. The concussion came back across the water and settled in our chests.

When we ran close, the beaches were torn up and smoking. The fight was not done. We dropped our ramps. Tanks rolled forward into the surf. Soldiers came behind them in waves. We ferried them, the LST groaning like an ox under load.

The sand turned dark where they fell. Some men went down waist-deep and never rose. Mortar shells burst among them. Flesh and sand alike flew skyward.

They fought inland, into hills and caves where the enemy had burrowed deep. Some tunnels were taken with grenades. Others with fire. The flamethrowers roared and the caves lit from within. Satchel charges collapsed whole warrens and the cries were silenced.

At night the banzai charges came. Screaming. Sabres raised. They rushed down the slopes, men chasing death. Come morning the ground was littered with their dead. Rifles in hand. Faces frozen mid-charge.

We ferried the wounded back. Some had lost their legs. Some held towels to places where their faces had been. One Marine held his own guts in his hands. Another called for his mother until his voice failed. The decks ran slick with blood and seawater, the scuppers carrying it away.

Guam was liberated, they said. But liberation is a word for the living. For the dead it means nothing.

The jungle held out. Snipers in the trees. Mortars in the gullies. The air stank of powder and rot. A sweet-sick perfume of meat gone bad.

Days later, I was in the mess with a plate of spaghetti. The sauce rich and sharp. Garlic and onion. I lifted the fork as though it were a relic from another life.

Then the klaxon. General quarters. Enemy planes inbound.

Men dropped their trays and hustled topside. I ran for the gun. Wilkins fed the drum. Ortega scanned the sky. We stood sweating and waiting. Shadows moved high above. Fifteen minutes passed. Then the all clear.

Back below, the spaghetti was cold. The sauce gone to paste. I lifted the fork again.

Then the deck bucked underfoot, and a great iron blow ran through the hull. Another followed. Then the klaxon started its howl.

We ran.

When I reached the gun mount, the deck was torn open. A black smoking hole where I'd been standing minutes before. Steel curled back like peeled fruit. Smoke rising.

Mortar fire. They had our range.

Wilkins spat. Holy shit, Flynn. That's where you'd been standing.

Ortega pale. You'd be gone, Pat. Dead as a doornail.

Wilkins touched the rim and jerked his hand back. Lucky bastard. That's the Irish in you.

I knelt and touched the deck. Still hot.

Luck's all it is, I said. And it runs out for every man.

I found a piece of shrapnel lodged in the deck below. I ground it smooth and fixed it to my key ring, then called it a charm because men give names to the things that nearly kill them. It was proof enough that death had passed within a fork's length of me.

That night I could not sleep.

I lay awake and thought on it. How death was a wheel spun in the dark, coming to rest in a place you could not see. It did not choose by strength or cowardice or prayer. That thought stuck in me.

Two days later the order came. We were pulling off the beach. The ship was wounded. Deck holed. Plates sprung. They patched what they could but she wouldn't be trusted again until she was whole.

Pearl Harbor. That was the word. Back across the Pacific.

Back to where the ghosts slept in the harbor. Arizona. Oklahoma. Names held in rust.

We turned our bows eastward and the engines took up their endless labor once more, their roar filling the hull and the bones alike. The island fell astern, green and burning, the smoke of battle drifting up to the clouds. Guam was behind us. But the war was not. Not by any long stretch.

Long Road Home

Our ship crawled wounded out of war. Her seams wept salt. Her plates shuddered with each turn of the screw. The anchor chain bore stains from the beach at Guam, streaks of coral and blood dried in the links. Above deck, her rails shed rust in brittle flakes. We turned east and left the ruins behind, left the shattered palms and the black mouths of bunkers and the thousand men who'd gone down into the mud. We pointed our bow toward Pearl, toward quiet water and the world we knew. Every day we put distance between us and the fire. Though the weight of death grew lighter, it left a stain in the soul.

The sea lay quiet that first morning. So flat it looked painted, without depth, so calm you could almost hear your own pulse in it. It carried no voice and no wind. The sky mirrored its silence and for a time the line between them vanished. I stood by the rail alone and could see no wake. It had faded behind us, the last breath of a man gone cold. Somewhere below, the screws turned slow and even, carving us forward, but you wouldn't know it by the water.

There were other ships in the distance. Shapes, hulking and motionless. They moved with us but you couldn't tell how, slow and patient as the last watchers at the world's edge. Convoy lines drawn across a canvas of blue. At night they became shadows, vast and silent. I'd go up to the weather deck and watch them drift in the dark. Sometimes they came so close I could feel their mass before I saw them, immense in the black. No sound but the sea. And I thought, if we sank, they would vanish too. All of us drawn down together, swallowed by the same dark weight, the lights gone and the cries gone with them.

The mornings were glass. The air was clean and thin. The sun came up slow and bled color across the sea until it resembled the inside of an oyster. Even the diesel smoke curled softly from the stacks and drifted off, almost reverent. The men didn't talk. A chapel hush settled over us. By some accident we'd sailed into a place older than language, before the names had settled on things.

Then came the word: swim call. It was rumor at first, unbelieved. But it was true. The engines wound down. The old hull shivered to a halt. The screws fell quiet and we lay there on the water, steadied in a silence so complete it seemed unnatural.

The bow doors opened with a groan that echoed through the decks, the gates of some cathedral swinging wide. Men burst from the ship in a roaring tide, boots drumming the steel, voices breaking loose all at once. Some had stripped to their shorts before they reached the rail. Some were shirtless and sunstruck. Some went over naked, white as bone in the light before the sea took them. They ran down the ramp and off the tank deck and plunged from the rails with no order to it at all. Some dove straight and true and some cannon-balled. The sea flowered under them in white spray. Men shouted. Men laughed. That sharp bright laughter rose over the open Pacific, rescued from another life.

High above the swim, two sailors held shark duty with Springfield rifles in hand, guarding our foolish freedom from whatever moved hungry beneath the blue.

I dove in too. The heat of the sun gave way quick to the cold blue underneath. It took your breath and then gave it back. I swam out a hundred yards or so and turned to look back. The ship hung in the water as if dreamt there, blackened and battered and still.

Gangways glinted in the light. Her flag hung limp. The war looked far behind her.

Then came the dolphins. A whole pod. Gray arcs rose from the sea, carved from the water itself. They passed close off the bow. The men slapped the water and shouted. One yelled that it was a sign. Another said it was luck. I didn't know what it was. But in that moment something loosened in us. We laughed for real. The kind that makes you young again, if only for a breath.

When the whistle blew we climbed back aboard, laughing and soaked. The deck steamed with saltwater and sun. We stood barefoot and dripping while the doors closed, and the screws took up again. The sea closed behind us, wiping away our passage without a trace.

Five days out the sky began to change. At first it was just a shade in the west, a shadow you couldn't name. Then the wind picked up. The haze thickened. The other ships closed ranks, bunching together the way cattle do before a twister. Their profiles vanished and reappeared in the gray. I stood there at the rail and felt it before it came. The way you feel a storm behind your teeth.

By nightfall the world was black and moving. The first swell hit with an ancient anger and the ship climbed its black face. She crested, hung there weightless, and then dropped, slamming into the trough with a violence you felt in your spine. Water came over the bow and over the hatches. Sloshed down the scuppers like floodwater in a drowned street. I gripped a stanchion with both hands and felt her bones groan.

Down below the engine room boiled. The air tasted of oil and iron and fear. The heat bore down until a man could hardly think. We shouted to hear ourselves. Each time the ship rose and the screws cleared the water, the engines screamed themselves empty, choked once, and died. We lunged for the restart, hands slick with oil, sparks jumping in the dark. The engines had to catch. Without them the ship would swing broadside to the sea, and the sea would finish us.

No one said it. We all knew.

When they caught again the roar that followed was more than mechanical. It was primal. A calling back from the dead.

Each revolution a thread of life.

Above deck, the storm carved a different world. The sky boiled black and the sea broke into glass shards. Each ship in the convoy rose ghostly from the dark and fell away again, silent but for the wind shrieking through the rigging and the steel groaning under strain. We moved through the throat of some vast blind thing. I watched them vanish and prayed we would not be the ones who failed to reappear.

Somewhere in the dark, the stern anchor tore loose. It slammed the hull with every pitch. The sound rang through the steel, bright and brutal, hammer on rail. You could feel it through your boots. Through your bones. I thought, That one could go straight through us. When morning came and we saw the damage, holes punched clean through above the waterline, I knew God had spared us only by a hair.

In the galley the stoves had torn free. Pots lay scattered. Steam piping twisted from the bulkhead. The cook sat among the wreckage with his hands open on his knees, looking less frightened than betrayed. For the duration, we ate cold. Crackers and orange concentrate, the kind that puckered your mouth and scraped the throat. We sucked it down as penance.

Sleep came in broken pieces. The kind where your body folds inward with the fear of a hunted animal. I don't know how many days we drifted inside that storm. Four? Five? You lost count when every hour lasted a lifetime. Some men spoke of it as a test sent to strip away the unworthy. I stopped believing in tests. I thought maybe the sea wanted no bargain from us. She only wanted to take.

But it was the storm that stayed with me. Its memory sank deeper than gunfire or fear of the enemy. Long after the battles had faded. Because the sea does not hate. And that's what made it worse. I had seen men kill with fire and bullet. But nothing makes you smaller than a force that does not even see you.

Then as sudden as its coming the storm was over. Morning broke sharp and unforgiving. The light burned white upon a sea stretched flat and desolate.

I went topside and stood a long time. The other ships were there, though you could see where the storm had bitten them. Scars in the paint. Rails bent. Nets flapping in ribbons. But they moved. Slow and steady.

I looked over the deck. At the rust and the dents. The rigging torn and re-knotted. The places where paint had been stripped to raw steel. The sea had marked us. Marked me. And I thought those ships riding beside us were more than machines. They were sentinels, carrying the last remnant of a world nearly forgotten.

As we neared Oahu, the light changed. The men did too. Their shoulders loosened. Laughter came back slow and raw, a cracked hymn rising through the steel. Even the punishment from the beer, the extra duties, the double watches, was endured without complaint. The work meant we were alive.

We wrestled in the bunks. Slap fights. Horseplay. Men trying to call back the boyishness the war had pressed down in them. It didn't last, but it helped. For an hour or two.

There was a man named Habib. From Jersey, I think. Built from ship steel. He'd been a bodybuilder before the war and couldn't let it go. Made barbells out of rebar and coffee cans filled with cement. He lifted them with a fever in him, trying to press the war out through muscle and bone. His forearms were roped with veins, hard-ridged as cable.

One night I locked up with him in a wrestle. I figured I'd last a second. He threw me across a table, easy as you'd toss a sack of spuds. I flailed and shouted like a drowning man, and the crew roared. Habib let me go with a grin. His mercy, not my strength, saved me.

But not all of us knew when to quit.

There was another man. Kananowitz. We called him Banana-wits and he laughed right along with us. Good-natured. Quick with a joke. The kind of man who kept a crew from going sour.

That day the mood was high. We were slap-fighting, ribbing each other. I called him out, Hey Banana-wits, you wanna box? and he stood grinning. We danced, palms up, feet light. The kind of play you learn before you learn how to hate.

But I clipped him a bit too hard. The grin left his face. His eyes changed. I saw an old sharpness in him I had never seen before.

He came at me like it mattered. And I answered.

What followed wasn't sport.

Fists hit bone. Someone knocked into the wall. Another shouted. My knuckles struck wet flesh. I hit him harder than I meant to. Harder than he expected. And when he folded I thought I'd only ended a bout.

I was wrong.

The crew broke us apart. Blood on both our faces. His shirt stained red at the collar. I watched him limp to his bunk, a man beaten and found out.

For two days he barely spoke. Did his duty. Ate alone. Slept long. I thought it would pass.

But it didn't.

I went to him after lights out. He lay with his back to me, motionless.

Kananowitz, I said. I'm sorry. For what happened. I apologize.

He turned. His face was hard. His eyes darker than they'd ever been.

You stay the fuck away from me, he said. You son of a bitch. I don't ever want to speak to you again as long as I live.

He rolled over and gave me his back.

That was the last time we spoke. I had lost a friend, and the loss left a crack in me.

At night I thought on it. Maybe the war had made me too sharp. Too willing to strike. I'd come aboard a boy. Now I was a man, but some part of me had curled wrong. Turned inward and twisted.

A man wonders what shape the world has made of him. And sometimes he doesn't like the answer.

The days wore on. The air softened. The ocean turned calm again, smoothing over our wake until no trace of us remained. We worked our watches, cleaned the bilges, and waited for land. The laughter came easier now.

Then one morning the lookout's voice came down from the conning tower. Land off the port bow.

The words ran hot through the ship. Men scrambled topside, clambering up ladders, pressing shoulder to shoulder along the rail. I went with them. The light was gold and wet on the sea. And there it was: Diamond Head. Sharp and brown against the horizon, the ridgeline jagged as broken glass. The island lay beneath it, green and rising, palms bending in the wind. White breakers caught the shore and flung themselves to foam.

For a long time no one spoke. Then Walker said, Christ boys, we're near home.

Nicky Powers laughed. I'll drink a bar dry before I sleep.

Bull shook his head. I don't care about drink. I want a woman and I want her fast.

We all laughed then. The sound of it startled us. It was the first laughter without guilt in a long while. For a moment, we almost believed the war had ended.

As we neared the island, the smell reached us, the scent of land. Flowers, smoke and sweetness. Bougainvillea and hibiscus, salt and soil. It came on the wind carrying a memory of home. It caught in the throat and woke feelings that had been buried too long.

Then the harbor opened before us. And the laughter fell away.

There lay the wrecks. The Oklahoma, capsized and black in the shallows. The Arizona, gone beneath, her tomb sealed under the harbor's skin. Oil seeped from her, rising to the surface in slow silver threads. The sun caught it, turned it to fire. It shimmered over the water, red and gold, alive in the morning haze. We stood silent. The ship creaked beneath us. I felt the eyes of every man fixed on that sheen, that silent wound that never closed.

I thought, We are not home. Not yet.

They sent us into drydock. The hull bled rust, the paint bubbled with salt. They stripped her down to bare steel and sandblasted her clean. When she came out again she was gray and new, with nothing on her to show what had happened. But we knew. The sea had left its marks. Some you could paint over and some you carried in your chest.

We worked through the days. Drills and watches. The old rhythm came back, dull but steady. The world beyond the yard was laughter and light, but it felt far away.

Then one morning they called us to muster on deck. The captain stood waiting, white cap gleaming in the sun. Officers ranged behind him, faces set. He looked us over a long time before he spoke.

You have carried this ship through war, he said. You have worked in silence and carried your burdens. You have done your penance. You have kept this hull alive. You have shown what men are made of when there is no one left to carry the slack. Have you learned the lesson.

None of us answered. We nodded, slow and guilty. The gulls called overhead. The ship shifted in her moorings. The captain let the silence stand.

Then he turned to the executive officer.

Do you believe these men have earned weekend liberty.

The executive officer looked us over, stern as judgment, though the corner of his mouth had begun to betray him.

Yes sir, he said. I do believe they have earned it.

The captain said nothing. His eyes moved over us man by man, slow enough to make each face answer for itself. He let the pause stretch until it became cruel. Several seconds only, though they felt longer than any watch we had stood.

Then he nodded once.

So be it, he said. You have earned a weekend ashore.

The noise that followed shook the steel. A hundred men shouting at once, voices breaking, feet stomping, laughter spilling into the wind. The officers could not have stopped us if they had tried.

Then the exec stepped forward, lean and sharp, his voice polished to a hard edge.

Port side this weekend. Starboard next. You'll alternate. No fighting. No disappearing into alleys. Treat the islanders like your own kin. Break that and you'll answer to the ship, and to me.

We all nodded. You could see it in the eyes, the pact forming. Rules to keep. Rules to break. The whisper of bars and women already on the wind.

Port side was mine.

I was ready for a drink that didn't taste of iron, for a woman who didn't fade with dawn, for a night that forgot the war.

But even as I laid out my clean shirt and polished my shoes, I could smell the oil on my hands. The ghost of the storm in my ears. The sea was behind us, but I knew she would never let us go. Not really.

Honolulu

When the word came down that liberty was ours, we didn't walk. We flooded. We poured from the ship like water from a wound. Shoes shined, hair combed flat, white hats squared. The gangway shivered under the weight of our hunger. We hit the dock and the city took us whole.

The piers rang with boots and voices. Salt and tar rode the wind, with diesel clinging to us though the sea had given us up. Shore patrol stood in their whites with clubs at their sides and their eyes never resting, watching the flood of men as if the whole island might come loose under them.

I had never seen so many servicemen gathered in one place in all my life. Army, Navy, Marines. Uniforms rolled down every street, a storm tide of bodies and noise. The sidewalks swarmed with servicemen, the gutters filled with shouting and laughter. You could hardly walk without shoving men aside. The press of flesh, wool and sweat near suffocated you. Honolulu groaned under us, a city overrun.

The storefronts blazed bright but the faces behind them were tired. The islanders watched us with the wary patience of men measuring a brushfire against the wind. We spilled down the boulevards in columns loose and ragged, the order of ships and drills dissolved into the chaos of men half mad with freedom.

When the sun went down the streets vanished into darkness. Not a lamp nor a porchlight dared burn. The whole city drowned in night. You pushed your way through the throngs blind, shoulder to shoulder, groping forward in a tide of voices. The sea was still on us, and the sour sweat of months belowdecks. Somewhere in that dark a woman's laugh cut the air and was swallowed just as quick.

The bars and clubs sat under canvas awnings, doors draped in blackout cloth. You ducked inside from the pitch dark and the light hit you full in the face. Smoke and music, women painted up in rouge and red lips, the whole place buzzing. Surreal. A blackout cellar opening onto a carnival pitched too close to the grave.

They poured us imitation whiskey. Wartime rationing. It burned in the throat and tasted wrong, varnish cut with sugar. But it got you drunk faster than the real thing and that was all we asked. The price came the next morning when your skull rang from the inside. Each joint allowed you two chits, two drinks only. We drank them fast. Sometimes there was a woman to talk to. Sometimes there was music enough to make us dance until sweat ran into our eyes. Then we went back into the dark, hunting the next bar and two more drinks. Around and around.

Fights broke out everywhere between the different branches. We did not like each other too much. We called the Marines sea-going bellhops and they called us swab jockeys and together we called the Army dogfaces. You could hear the insults flying before the fists followed. Men locked up in alleys, faces bloodied, uniforms torn. Someone laughing. Someone vomiting against a wall. A woman's scream lost in the din. Everywhere bodies tangled in shadows, men and women pressed into corners, breath hot with desperation.

I drank and I danced. I talked to women I would never see again. Their perfume hung on my shirt, their sweat on my palms. The music beat in my chest and the whiskey kept me upright, carried me through the blur. The night became a wheel that spun too fast. The blackout turned the streets into veins. We were blood in the system, hot and loud and always moving. The streets slick with piss and rain and spilled drink. The city sagged beneath us but we didn't care.

We were in a narrow street when it came to blows. A Marine bumped Bull hard at the shoulder and Bull spun, Boston fire in his eyes. Words cut sharp between them, every insult sharpened by drink and pride. Then fists. The two locked together, boots slipping on the wet cobbles, the crowd swelling to see it. I pushed through and tried to drag them apart but another Marine lunged at me, his knuckles already flying. I met him square and the world narrowed to fists and breath and whiskey shaking itself out of our bones.

Then Nicky waded in. He caught one with a right cross and sent him sprawling against the wall. The three of us fighting side by side against three Marines, the night lit with curses and laughter, bodies crashing into doors and spilling trash cans into the street. Men cheered and shoved, drunk with the spectacle.

It burned hot and quick. Then just as sudden as it had sparked, the fury guttered out. Someone's nose broken and bloodied, someone's eye darkened, and laughter rose through the blood. We ended up shoulder to shoulder with those same Marines in a smoky barroom, raising drinks to each other. Somewhere in the noise one of them grabbed me and I grabbed him back, and we stood there laughing like brothers who had crawled out of the same dirt.

One night you are spilling blood on the stones and the next you are drinking with the man whose jaw you tried to break.

I lost Bull and Nicky later in the churn. One minute they were there, the next the crowd swallowed them. I drifted alone through the blackout, half drunk, the noise falling behind me. The city thinned, the shouts gone to a murmur. I found myself in a residential street, houses low and dark against the sky. The air was quiet, broken only by the chirr of insects.

I stopped on a lawn. The grass cool and soft beneath my shoes. I sat down, pulled a cigarette from my pack, lit it, and lay back. The sky was crowded with stars. My head swam. Smoke curled from my lips and the ground took me. The dark folded over and I was gone. I stared up at the stars, drunk and sinking, and the yard back home opened above me for a breath. Then the war crossed it dark before I passed out.

I woke to the rasp of a broom. The sun already burning over the rooftops. An old island woman stood on the porch of the house, sweeping, her bare feet pale against the boards. She looked at me with the tired recognition of a woman used to soldiers falling wherever liquor laid them down, the way you might look at a stray dog asleep under the porch. I pushed myself up from the grass, my head splitting like it was cleaved with an axe. My mouth was dry, the taste of that poison whiskey bitter on my tongue.

I brushed the dirt from my white trousers and straightened my cap. The woman said nothing. She just swept and watched until I staggered off down the street. Honolulu was awake now. Trucks rattled down the avenues, horns blared, vendors setting up stalls. Blackout cloth still hung over the bar doors, ragged and forlorn in the daylight. The alleys stank of piss and sour beer. In one doorway a Marine slept crumpled with his cap over his eyes, his hand curled in a fist.

I wandered aimless until I asked an old Hawaiian man for directions to the YMCA. He stood in a faded shirt and bare feet, leaning on a stick of driftwood polished by hand. His skin dark and weathered by the years. He pointed with the stick down a shaded avenue lined with palms. Two blocks, he said. Turn left at the banyan tree. Can't miss it. His voice low and worn thin as old rope. I thanked him and he only nodded, his eyes already gone back to the restless sea of uniforms undulating in the street.

The YMCA stood tall and white against the sun, its columns weathered, the windows open to the salt air. Sweat hung in the room, cut with soap and old wood. The rooms filled with the noise of men trying to remember normal life. There were soldiers writing letters, sailors washing up, a piano clattering in the corner with someone hammering out half-remembered tunes.

In the lounge I found Nicky. He sat with his cap pushed back on his head, a cigarette in his fingers, smoke curling around him in a veil. He saw me and grinned. Pat, where the hell'd you end up last night?

I dropped into the chair across from him, rubbed my temples. You wouldn't believe it if I told you. I drank my way half across the city, danced with every girl in sight. Lost track of Bull and then blacked out on some poor bastard's front lawn. Woke up to an old woman sweeping her porch, staring at me like I was a dog that'd wandered in from the road.

Nicky laughed and shook his head. Christ, Pat. You're lucky they didn't run you in. I had my own hell of a night. The last I saw of Bull he had some blonde pinned against the wall, kissing her hard enough to send tomorrow to hell.

Figures, I said. Leave it to Bull.

We got a dorm room at the Y. Three iron cots lined against the wall. The third bed was meant for Bull but we weren't so sure we'd see him again. His ghost seemed already in the room, his laughter lingering in the walls. But the bed stayed empty.

We cleaned up, the water biting cold, razors scraping until the skin was raw. Clean shirts and socks. It felt near holy after the streets.

When we came out the sun was hard overhead. The streets steamed with the heat. We walked to a diner on the corner, the windows open to the breeze, frying bacon and burnt coffee drifting out into the street. The place was full of khaki and navy blue, men bowed over their food, hungry past manners. We took a booth and ordered eggs, toast, coffee strong enough to make a man's hands shake.

On the way there we'd fallen in with Walker. He wore his hat cocked low and spoke slow, the prairie stretching out in his drawl. He slid into the booth beside us and stirred sugar into his coffee with the care of a man handling gunpowder.

I looked at him sideways.

You're starboard crew. What the hell are you doing out?

He didn't look up.

Swapped with Whitey. Two packs of smokes.

Nicky grinned.

Hell of a bargain.

Walker sipped slow.

Somebody's gotta keep an eye on you boys.

And the laughter climbed out of us, rough-edged and young.

Walker leaned back, his arm across the booth. Hell of a night, he said. I must've walked ten miles just to see what was what. Every joint packed, music spilling into the streets. I even sat in with a band for a spell, strumming their guitar till the owner chased me out.

Nicky smirked. You sober enough to remember the chords?

Walker winked. More or less. Some gal was watching me like I was the second coming. Would've taken her home too if she didn't have a Marine draped on her arm. Big son of a bitch.

We laughed, the sound rough in our throats.

Walker leaned closer then. I heard Canal Street's where all the action is. Bars, fights, women. They even got bawdy houses down there.

Nicky shook his head, pushed his plate away. Not for me. I've got a wife and kid waiting back home. I'm not looking to add shame to the war.

His words made me think of Mom and the farm and how far off a clean life had slipped.

Walker grinned. Suit yourself. What about you, Pat?

I laughed, though there wasn't much humor in it. I don't know. I don't even know what I want anymore. The war had taken the easy answers and left only the next step in front of your boots.

Hell, a man does what he has to, right? said Walker, grinning from ear to ear.

Something like that, I said.

Nicky frowned but said nothing. Walker chuckled and slapped the table with the flat of his hand. We laughed too, all three of us, though each for our own reason. The plates rattled and the waitress glared but we didn't care.

The day stretched before us, hot and loaded, a fuse waiting for flame.

Canal Street

— • —

By mid-afternoon Walker and I made our way toward Canal Street. There was no such street on any map. Canal Street was the name for the Honolulu red light district, passed down in mess halls and engine rooms, between racks, under breath. No one ever explained it. You just knew. You got to port and it was there waiting, a ghost map etched in the minds of every man who'd stood a watch under red light and dreamed of warmth. The name passed through the fleet with the hush of contraband, muttered in lines and over bunks in the dark.

You didn't need directions. You followed the smell and the noise. The heat pulled you like gravity. Some men laughed when they said it. Others didn't.

The streets had a carnival air. Saxophones wailed through canvas awnings, the brass crying out in long, wounded notes. Bars spilled their guts onto the sidewalks. Dice clattered on felt. A piano thumped like a bad heart. The air carried grease and perfume and wet concrete. Tattoo parlors blinked with weak bulbs. Serpents and anchors inked into arms by men who looked half-dead, their aprons stained with ink and blood. Pawn shops traded dog tags for pocket change and said nothing. In one glass case a mummified monkey curled behind a row of war knives with bone handles stained from hands long gone.

We passed a diner sweating on its windows. Inside, men hunched over plates and bottles. Steam rolled off the griddle. Voices low and slow, a sermon spoken backwards.

And the bars. Always the bars. Their doors hung open, music bleeding out. The women walked in pairs. Eyes hollow. Mouths painted to look alive. Their heels cracked across the boards with the snap of rigging in a hard wind. The laughter rose too fast. The smoke never lifted. Everywhere the stink of meat and powder and sweat. Uniforms dulled by salt and starch. Dogfaces and swabbies and Marines who hated both. The whole place leaned crooked. A carnival that never packed up, where the tickets were gone and only the price remained.

The bawdy houses didn't look like sin. Not at first. Paint flaking. Porch railings sagging. Windows shuttered. You might have thought they sold sewing machines. You might have walked past in daylight and known nothing. But at night something came up through the cracks, a sharp, sour smell that told the truth.

The military had given up trying to shut it down. They regulated it instead. Government-issued vice. Doctors with clipboards. Sheets changed on schedule. Girls clean and counted. You handed over your bills. Showed your tags. Waited your turn. They gave you silence and paperwork in return.

We stood in line with fifty other men. Boots shifting. Eyes sunk or shut. Cigarettes flared. No one talked much. The ones who did said dumb things just to fill the space. The soft murmur of need. Laughter that came out borrowed.

Walker leaned against the wall beside me. Concrete spotted with moss and old staples from a hundred flyers gone to wind.

You done this before.

He shifted his jaw like he was loosening something. Frisco. Back before we shipped out. Wasn't much.

You expectin more this time.

He watched the line move.

I ain't expectin nothin. But I sure as hell ain't waitin an hour for a handshake.

The line moved again. We shuffled forward. None of us left it. Not one.

Inside, the sound fell away. The hush closed around us. You could hear the city, but only the bones of it. The walls were painted green. Not fresh. A sickly color. Bleach was in the air, and beneath it a faint sweetness lingered, masking what the place refused to confess.

A woman sat behind a desk. Hair pinned tight. Face flat. She took our bills. Said nothing. The lighting was steady but soft. No shadows and no warmth.

Walker whispered.

Leave it to the Navy to turn whoring into administration.

I said, makes you wonder what else they got a form for.

We waited on a bench. The walls were thin. You could hear boots and breathing and the faint rustle of cotton. A door opened and shut. Opened and shut. Machinery. The sound of motion without life.

It was quiet. That was the worst part. It didn't feel wicked. It felt dead. Men stared at the floor like they were waiting for medicine.

We passed through rooms, each one deeper in the house's pulse. The parlor came next. A low ceiling. Amber light. A half dozen girls lined behind a rail. Silk and powder and perfume strong in the heat. Their faces didn't move. Eyes glassy. Bodies dressed and waiting, mannequins in a store window that never closed.

The madam had the look of someone's aunt after the mercy had gone out of her. She read names from a ledger. Called numbers. No one spoke. You picked. Or you were picked.

Walker gave me a look. Grinned without smiling.

Hell of an operation.

I've seen bakeries with more soul, I said.

The girl who called my name had dark hair pinned back and a nightgown the color of smoke. She didn't speak. Just walked. I followed.

The hallway bent twice. A warped floor. Doors on either side. She opened one and stepped in. I followed. She closed it behind me.

A cot and a chair. A low bulb swinging from the ceiling. The air sharp with soap and mildew. I took off my cap. Sat on the edge of the bed.

She sat beside me but didn't look at me. Her voice was low. Flat.

Three minutes, sailor.

She didn't mean it cruel. She didn't mean it at all. Somewhere a clock was ticking.

What passed between us was more absence than act. It was a transaction performed in muscle memory. My hand touched her hip. The sheets rustled. The room carried the moist heat of bodies and the faint trace of powder gone to dust. Her breath moved against me, quiet and warm in the dark. For a brief moment her eyes flicked to mine, quick as a bird's shadow, and in them was a softness she had not planned to give. Then it was gone. Maybe it never had been.

When it was over I sat and pulled on my boots. She opened the door before I finished lacing. Already looking past me.

Take care, she said.

I nodded. Walked out. The hallway swallowed me up. The bench was full again. The line never ended. It kept taking men in and sending them out quieter.

Outside, Walker leaned under a broken red lamp. Smoke curled from his lips. He didn't ask and I didn't tell.

We walked the street. The sun had fallen low but hadn't gone yet. The roofs shone gold. The harbor caught the light and held it. Bars screamed behind us. Laughter broke like plates. Women leaned from doorways with their hair pinned wrong.

We ducked into a joint that reeked of bleach and beer. Sat at a bar sticky with spilled drink. A band played a tune nobody listened to. We drank imitation whiskey in silence. When we stepped back into the street the city had turned violet. The kind of color that only comes before real dark. The kind you forget until it finds you again.

We wandered in silence, our thoughts dim, our feet carrying us on. The noise dropped off behind us. The bodies thinned. The island breathed again. We let it.

Down an alley we passed Hayes from Arkansas. Shirt unbuttoned, eyes red, laughing over dice and a pile of bills with Marines crowding him. He shouted after us but we kept walking. His voice trailed behind us, too bright after the dead quiet of that house.

Back at the Y, Nicky was sitting on his bunk. Clean shirt. Shaved. Reading a paper gone soft at the edges.

He looked up.

Guess you boys survived.

Walker dropped his cap on the mattress.

More or less.

I said, we figured you could take that third bed.

Bull never made it back. Either found better company or got himself locked up.

Don't mind if I do, Walker said.

He lay back without ceremony. Closed his eyes.

Nicky folded the paper. Looked at the wall.

Loud out there tonight.

No one answered.

The room settled. The city hummed through the plaster. Three cots, and sweat held in the air. The kind of quiet that never lasts but holds you for a while.

I lay back and looked at the ceiling and thought of the Canal Street girl. Of the hush around her, of the breath in her chest, and of all that went unsaid between us.

The laughter outside rose again. Someone shouted. A saxophone wailed somewhere, dragging sorrow through the street.

And the war waited just beyond it all. Quiet as a knife. Waiting its turn.

We woke early. The air hung close and gray. The room carried the close smell of sweat and the rust of men asleep in silence they'd only borrowed. I sat up slow. Walker lay on his back, mouth parted. Nicky already pulling on socks, neat as always.

He looked at me.

Breakfast?

Yeah.

We walked to the corner diner. The windows steamed. A fan spun above the counter without moving any air. The waitress looked through us with eyes that had already let us go. We took a booth near the back.

Toast and eggs, coffee black and bitter.

Walker came in late. Sat down without a word. Rubbed his eyes like they owed him something.

We didn't say much. The food came hot. The grease pooled on the plate and didn't move. The coffee scalded. Outside the street woke slow, the gutters wet with hose water, bottles broken in the curb. A pair of Marines stumbled past with their arms over each other's shoulders, singing a tune that had no words.

After breakfast we walked to the corner where the buses loaded. The Y stood white behind us. Palms swayed in the heat. The city pulsed, but quieter now. Hungover. Spent.

The bus was half full. Men in silence. Elbows resting on duffels. Eyes closed but not asleep. Boots scuffed. Faces blotched with drink. The kind of tired that settles behind the eyes and doesn't leave. The ride had gone quiet. Singing and laughter had gone out of us. The engine stuttered once and caught, and we rode on with the quiet of men headed for bad news.

We pulled away.

The city slid past. Blocks of paint-chipped buildings. Posters peeling from walls. A woman smoking on a fire escape, watching without watching. Children barefoot in an alley drawing chalk guns on the brick.

When the harbor came into view, a quiet passed over the bus. You could feel the shift. Men sitting straighter. Breath held.

There she was. Our ship. LST-482. Hauled up in drydock, gangways lashed, seams split open in surgery's raw light. Decks stripped bare. The bow lifted toward the sky instead of the sea, forgetting the water beneath her. Gray in the morning light, rust trails down her flanks like tears left too long to wipe clean.

We stepped down from the bus and crossed the dock.

The air was salt and iron. Home of a sort, if home could be built from bolts and war.

A petty officer marked our names on a clipboard. Didn't look up.

We climbed the gangway single file. Boots echoing on the steel. The shadow of the ship fell over us, a lid lowered back into place. The spell of liberty was gone.

Walker peeled off toward the starboard hatch. Nicky nodded once and was gone.

I stood there a moment.

Just stood.

Men moved past. Officers barking soft orders. Ropes went taut. The harbor noise came and went with the tide.

I ran my hand along the rail. The steel warm. Pitted and scraped where the paint had peeled. You could feel the weight of it. More than the metal. The memory.

I went below.

Found my rack. Threw my bag down. The light above me flickered. The hum of the engine room came faint through the bulkhead.

I lay back.

The pillow hard. The sheet scratchy. The same rack as always. But I lay in it a different man.

I closed my eyes.

And saw her face. Neither clearly nor with desire. Just the shape of her. A person used up who once had a name but now was just a task.

I saw the street. The line of men. The silence.

The saxophone crying in the distance.

I thought of Nicky. How he'd looked at the floor when Walker joked. How he never said a word when I walked in. How he cleaned his shirt as though a man could still set one small thing right.

Sleep didn't come. Not truly. Just that drift. That place between waking and regret.

Outside, the ship creaked. Somewhere above me a hatch slammed. Footsteps rang on the steel deck.

A voice shouted and was lost in the hum.

We were back.

The city gone behind us, Canal Street just a bruise fading in the dark.

Cohen

It was weekend liberty again and I was glad of it. The week had crawled like a busted mule, heat and hammer strikes ringing through steel, paint fumes sharp enough to taste. The ship was out of water, dry-docked, a carcass offered up to the sun. The wind passed strange through the hull without ocean under her. A dead thing humming.

The gangways swarmed with welders and yardmen and the air stank of primer and steel filings. Up on deck the light was hard and white, bouncing off blistered paint and stripped railings. The ship stood bare to the sky, her bones out. Scaffolds clung to her like iron barnacles. The silence of dry dock wasn't the silence of sea. It didn't move. It just hung there. Still and final.

I wanted out. I wanted noise and bodies and the burn of liquor. The stink of aftershave and perfume not poured from a Navy bottle. I wanted something human after a week of metal. I wanted, just for a night, to forget the black throat of the ship. I was halfway to the gangway when I heard the boots behind me.

Cohen.

He came without a word. Broad. Sweating. His arms swung stiff and his gait carried a hitch, a piece of him set wrong. His gut had thickened from spite, not food. Eyes black as a stove gone cold. He looked built wrong. His face held a permanent twist, the look of a man keeping poison behind his teeth. He was probably the only man aboard who called me a friend, though friendship in him meant only the absence of open hatred. I didn't ask him to come. I didn't want him near.

We walked in silence. Deck hot under our boots. The seams of the hull let off a low groan now and then, some metal ghost working the night watch. We passed buckets of paint, coils of hose, the stale stink of labor breathing up from the planks.

Nicky Powers stood at the forward edge of the deck. Ten paces off. He was leaned out over the side, peering down and hollering to the men below. Probably hull workers, torch crews patching scars in the underbelly. He was loose, laughing, waving his arms with drunken faith in a merciful world. There was no railing. Just the drop. Fifty feet to concrete. Maybe more. Gaps in the scaffold showed the dock floor below, wet and gray in spots, the concrete marked with old damp.

I could smell the weld smoke in my collar. That and the copper stink of hot metal. Nicky didn't hear us. He stood with his back turned and his boots set easy, and seeing him there brought a small warmth into me. He was familiar in a world that had made most familiar things strange, and I trusted him.

And then Cohen's voice slid out.

Hey Flynn, he said. Quiet as a man thinking out loud.

There's that son of a bitch Powers.

I hate his guts.

I'm gonna push that prick over the side.

I thought it a joke at first. His way of blowing steam. I half-smiled. My mind was already in town, lights in my eyes, the feel of a bar rail under my palm. The sunlight sparked off the hull like a signal mirror. The sky was ocean blue and clean. I was ready to forget the week.

Then Cohen stepped.

He came on in three angled strides toward Nicky, measured and certain, with the calm of a man who had saved the violence for this. Shoulders squared. Elbows back. His hand curled with the blunt purpose of a shove. One hard push would send Nicky screaming into the drop.

I moved.

I don't remember thinking. Just my legs snapping forward, boots loud on the plate. I caught him by the arm and yanked so hard he staggered. Spun him back toward me. My right hand came up fast, cocked and waiting.

Listen, I said. My voice sharp as cold iron.

You don't try that with me standing here.

Take one more step and I'll put you on the deck.

I don't care what your grudge is. But it ends here.

My fist trembled at my side. It felt borrowed from someone meaner.

Cohen stared at me. A change passed through his eyes. The rage sank into an older hardness. He looked pale. The sweat on his forehead wasn't from heat. He had the lost look of a man waking in a place he did not remember entering.

He stepped back. Silent.

I held him there.

We stood between two coils of cable, his arm half-wrenched in my grip, and I could feel it. The pulse under the skin. Something still wanting out.

You know what he said to me, Cohen muttered, low and bitter.

Back in San Diego. Before any of this.

Told the guys I was yellow.

Said I talked tough but shook like a drunk when it got loud.

Said I was a fucking coward.

I didn't answer. Just stared at him.

I didn't know if it was true. Didn't care. Not then.

Because truth wouldn't have mattered.

He wanted Nicky gone. That was enough.

Nicky kept hollering below, oblivious. His voice bright. A sound that seemed to belong to a world far from this one.

I hauled Cohen toward the fantail. Ten paces before I let go. He looked at the deck and said nothing. His mouth opened once, closed again. Whatever he meant to say had burned up in him.

Voices drifted down the gangway. Laughing voices. The kind that break easy.

I stood a while. Watched Nicky head down to the dock without ever knowing. Saw his back retreat into the maze of scaffold and shadow. His voice echoing once more before fading. A man unaware he had walked close to death.

It hit me then. If I hadn't moved.

If I'd lingered.

Lit a smoke.

Stopped to tie a boot.

Cohen would have done it.

And it would have looked like an accident.

A slip. A stumble. A bad step near the edge where the railing gave out. Men would accept it because men had seen worse accidents at sea.

I stood there tasting the knowledge of that. A hard copper taste lodged behind the teeth. A secret your bones know but your mind doesn't want.

And I started to shake.

It came on quiet. Just the fingers first. Then the wrist. Then the shoulder.

A ripple moving backward through the body.

I let my hands drop. Walked away. Slow.

I stopped by a scupper and leaned there.

Tried to spit the taste from my mouth.

Couldn't.

It was in me now. The nearness. The weight.

Some things you hold in the dark. They don't die. They lie there and grow fat on silence.

He sat beside me in the flatbed truck on the way into town. The sun high and the wind snapping our shirts. Marines hollering. Some sailor strumming a ukulele like he'd been cursed with it. Cohen sat next to me, arms crossed, his anger giving off a buried furnace heat.

He didn't speak. Neither did I.

Between us rode what he'd almost done.

But I knew this. I couldn't drink with him. Couldn't talk with him. Couldn't stay close.

A meanness lived in him. Coiled. A patient hate that watched and waited. He'd keep the grudge warm like a coal, nurse it through the night, and hold tight to whatever wrong he believed he'd suffered.

I needed him gone.

Not dead or broken. Only out of reach before that hate found somewhere else to land.

JOYCE

I found Lucky Lulu's by accident. I'd left Cohen behind at The Lotus Room, lost him in the crowd, slipped out a side door while the trumpets screamed and the bodies swayed. The night air hit hard, a wall of furnace heat. I moved fast through the alleys, past crates and garbage, past the sour drift of beer gone old. I didn't look back. There are men you don't need to fight to know how it ends.

The street beyond was darkened for war. Lamps shrouded. Windows boarded. The street felt emptied of breath. I walked until I heard music again, softer this time, the whisper of brushes on drums. A sign above the door sat dead in the blackout: LUCKY LULU'S. I went inside.

The place breathed low and slow. Smoke pooled in the rafters. Fans turned lazy circles bored by their own work. The boards underfoot were scarred by years of spilled nights. I took a stool at the end of the bar and ordered imitation rye. The glass came thin and warm. I drank slow.

That's when I saw them.

Three WACs in a corner booth. One tall and sharp, freckles scattered like rust. One round-cheeked and quick to laugh. And the third, and the whole room seemed to narrow to where she sat. Dark hair pinned low. Eyes quiet as winter fields. She had the stillness of someone who could watch a storm without blinking.

She looked at me once. Didn't turn away. Something in me swung toward her and stuck, a needle fixing to north.

After a while I stood and crossed the room. My legs felt borrowed.

Mind if I sit a minute, I said.

The tall one smirked. The round one laughed. The dark-haired one studied me a moment and said, Sure, sailor. Sit.

Her name was Joyce.

We talked. Or mostly I did. Her presence loosened the tight places in me. She listened with her chin propped on her hand, her eyes half-smiling. When she laughed it was quiet and real, the kind that slips out of a person who's forgotten how.

Where you from, sailor, she asked.

South Dakota, I said. But these days I belong to the Pacific.

She nodded once. You all talk that way?

Only the ones left standing.

And you, I asked her.

California, she said. Fresno. Born and raised. Then after a pause, Second generation.

I didn't say anything but she leaned in slightly. Japanese-American. I work intelligence. They send us the captured stuff, maps, orders, troop notes. I read what they can't.

There was an edge in her tone. Polite but practiced. A blade kept just sharp enough.

I know which side you're on, I said.

That smile again. Good. I get tired of reminding people.

Her friends rose, ready for the next bar or whatever the night wanted from them. Don't let him bore you to death, the tall one said.

He's not boring, Joyce said, and her voice held.

When they were gone I slid into her side of the booth. Our legs brushed. A small contact but enough to change the air between us.

You want to get out of here, I asked.

She smiled. You Navy boys always running.

Only when I can't stay still. Back home the winters are long and there is not much to do. You learn to talk or you go quiet for life.

She laughed soft. It stayed with me.

We left together.

The street outside breathed heat. Somewhere down the block a bakery worked late and the warm scent of it moved through the dark. The moon hung swollen above the blackout city. She took my arm. Her touch was light but sure.

We walked until we heard music again, the drums low and muffled behind canvas walls. A small club gave off a dim lantern glow. We went inside.

The place wasn't pretty. Lights low. Corners cluttered. The crowd moved as one body, swollen with music, drink, and want. We bought rum and lime and stood a moment, letting the sound find us. Then she took my hand.

Come on, she said.

We moved into the press of bodies. The music didn't shine or dazzle. It hammered, a raw rhythm built from hunger and sweat. Her back against my chest. Her hair brushed my cheek. Her body moved with a hard living need, and the last resistance in me broke. For a little while, the war fell back.

You're trouble, she said.

And you're not?

She laughed, and it rose from her, sudden and alive.

When we stepped outside, the night lay hushed. The moon cut a white path through the quiet. A jacaranda tree stood in full bloom. Purple petals drifted down like shed bruises. She looked up at me. Her lips parted to speak.

Pat.

I kissed her.

Once, then again.

There was no gentleness in it. Only need. The kind born from months of steel decks and dead-eyed mornings. Her hands gripped my shirt. Mine slipped through her hair. The world narrowed to heat and breath and the knowing that we were alive. The kiss went on with the blind pull of thirst.

I've got a place, she whispered. Friend's apartment. She's gone for the week.

How far.

Couple blocks.

We walked fast. The stairs creaked beneath us. Inside, the air was close. A quiet hint of starch and jasmine lingered in the room. On the dresser a small photo showed two women in uniform, one of them Joyce, smiling in a way that hadn't learned to flinch yet.

We undressed slowly at first, with a hush between us, and then the hush broke and there was only the pull of skin toward skin. The heat of her. The answering heat in me. We were not seeking pleasure by itself so much as the certainty of being wanted and wanting in return, of being creatures of warmth and pulse and living desire. The press of her body stripped away speech and left only breath, sweat, and the hard pull of wanting. Afterward, we lay tangled in the dimness, our breathing slowing, the ceiling fan turning above us, its blades keeping time.

For a long while neither of us spoke.

The fan turned above us. Somewhere below, a car passed and faded into the blackout streets.

Joyce lay with her face turned toward me. She had the look of a woman listening to more than the room.

You were shaking, she said.

Was I.

A little.

I looked down at my hands. They seemed ordinary there on the sheet.

Sometimes they do that after the guns.

She took one of them between both of hers.

My hands shake too, she said.

From the work.

From the rooms. From the way men stop talking when I come in. From having to be useful enough to be forgiven for being born.

The words settled between us.

Forgiven by who.

That is the part that wears you down. No one says. You just feel the debt in the air.

I watched her face in the thin light. She did not look ashamed. Only tired.

You shouldn't have to carry that.

Neither should you.

I almost said that was different, then knew it wasn't.

She moved closer.

Tell me one true thing, Pat.

What.

That you were afraid.

I was.

When.

All day. Every day. I just learned where to hide it.

She nodded and closed her eyes.

Then stay here and don't hide.

I'll stay, Joyce.

We slept with her hand over my heart and the city breathing faint beyond the window.

Dawn found us pale and slow, the city outside half-asleep. She woke first and sat on the edge of the bed with her knees drawn up. Her shoulders had gone stiff overnight.

She boiled water for coffee. We sat under a blanket on the floor with the cups warm in our hands. The light crept across the room. She stared into her cup a long time before she spoke.

There is something I should tell you, she said.

I waited.

My family. They aren't home. They haven't been since '42.

She held the cup in both hands, though the coffee had gone cold.

The government took them. Arkansas. Barbed wire. Guard towers. They called it relocation. Said it was for protection. Clean names for every dirty thing.

I said nothing.

My father had a little shop in Fresno. He worked twelve hours a day, six days a week. Sometimes more. He came home bent in the shoulders, collar dark with sweat, hands cracked from work, and he would sit at the table so tired he forgot to eat. My mother kept the house in order because order was the one thing they had not yet taken from her. Rice washed. Shirts mended. Floor swept. Bills folded beneath the sugar tin. Then most nights she went out again and worked where they needed hands. Laundry. Cleaning. Kitchen work. Anything that brought a few more dollars home.

Joyce looked toward the window.

My little brother was young enough to run the streets with a kite and believe it could lift him clear of the earth.

Her voice did not rise.

Then they came and took all of them.

The room seemed to lose air.

They did not take the Germans that way. Or the Italians. Only us. Because we were easy to find.

She looked down at her hands.

I joined the service to prove something. I read intercepted orders. I translate field reports. I do it well. But every room I walk into, I start behind the line. Same uniform. Same oath. Different face.

Her voice cracked then.

And I am tired, Pat. Tired clear through.

I moved beside her and held her. She went rigid once, then leaned into me.

I'm sorry, I said.

Don't be sorry. Remember.

I will.

The shame of it settled in me, dull and deep, that the same flag stitched on her sleeve was stitched on mine.

We stayed that way until her breathing steadied. Then she lifted her face, eyes wet and open in a way that pressed deep into me.

Stay with me, she whispered.

I'm here.

Come closer, she said.

We moved slow. Gentle. The kind of quiet that comes after a truth has been laid bare. We made love softly, as though neither of us wanted to disturb the hurt the other carried. Her hands soft along my shoulders. Mine tracing her spine. No hunger now. Only the need to hold someone who had been wronged by the world and kept walking anyway. The morning light held us. The room breathed with us.

When it was done she lay with her forehead resting against my collarbone.

Thank you, she said.

For what.

For not asking me to be anything I'm not.

You don't owe me anything, I said.

Neither do you.

We dressed and walked the beach. The sand had already taken the sun and held it. The tide came in with a slow patient draw, folding over itself in quiet lines. She held my hand as though she had known it a long while and I let her lead me up the shore with the feeling that we were trying to gather all we could from the few hours left to us. There was a clock somewhere in my head and I could feel it all through the day, ticking behind the light and the salt and the easy talk. We spoke of small things. Pie. Old records. Winter snow drifting over tin roofs. Things with no weight to them and yet they felt dearer for that, the world narrowed to what could be said before the light was gone. We walked like people borrowed back from the dead for a day.

By the time the sun began to slope west and the long gold of evening came over the water I said, I should head back soon.

She nodded.

I know.

Neither of us let go.

For a while we watched the tide move in thin bright lines over the sand.

I hate this part, I said.

Leaving?

Knowing I have to.

She looked at me then.

Do not make it pretty.

I won't.

War makes men say things at the edge of a day.

What things, I asked.

Forever. Always. After. All those big words men use when they do not own the next hour.

I looked at the water.

Then what can I say.

She was quiet a moment.

You can ask my last name.

I turned to her.

What is it.

Watanabe.

She held my eyes when she said it.

Joyce Watanabe, I said.

Again.

Joyce Watanabe.

Good.

Then she asked mine.

Flynn, I said. Patrick Flynn.

She said it back slowly, as though the name was already turning into memory.

She reached into her dress and handed me a folded slip of paper. Her number. The edges worn.

Call me if you get the chance.

I will.

No, she said. Call me if you want to hear me. Not because you pity me. Not because of what I told you.

I want to hear you.

Then I will answer.

We kissed once more. Then she walked toward the road and did not look back. That last kiss held everything we would never get to say, goodbye and a prayer folded around a wound.

I stood until the glare took her.

That night aboard ship I lay in my bunk with the paper in my hand. The dock lights flickered across the hull. I thought of her father working twelve-hour days, six days a week, believing labor could earn him a country. I thought of her mother keeping the home in order, then working most nights because dignity did not pay the bills. I thought of the boy with the kite. I thought of Joyce Watanabe saying, Remember, and I did.

The ship creaked in her dry berth. Men shifted in their sleep. Beyond the breakwater the sea waited in its endless dark.

I closed my eyes and saw her beneath the jacaranda tree, petals falling around her in slow undoing, her face lifted to the moon.

The phone number rode in my pocket through watches and moves and the churn of it all until one day it was gone.

I never saw Joyce again.

But I have never forgotten her.

THE GATHERING STORM

Pearl gave us weeks to mend, steel and bone both. The ship patched. The men fattened on beer and a few nights ashore. The dockyards burned day and night with acetylene fire, the wind alive with iron and salt and the faint ghost of things newly mended. Welders in black masks moved along the scaffolds, dark priests of the yard, sparks falling around them in showers of orange light. We slept in hammocks slung beneath the wounded spine of our ship and woke to the hiss of torches and the ring of hammers. By the time she was ready to sail she wore her scars openly, fresh cuts over old. The gray paint tacky in spots.

When the orders came down the crew grew quiet. The kind of silence a man walks into when he already knows his fate but still keeps moving. The engines warmed beneath us. The deck trembled. Lines were loosed. The harbor slid away. And we turned west once more into the wide Pacific, into that terrible blue where there was nothing but water.

The days blurred. The sea stretched endless and without memory. We island-hopped under skies too big for their own good. Eniwetok. Saipan. Tinian. The long beaches of Guam where wind carried the faint staleness of burned palms and old fuel. Down through the Solomons. Past Guadalcanal where the first dead of the Pacific seemed to walk the treelines in the corner of your eye. Then north toward Manus.

Manus rose north of New Guinea from the Admiralty Islands, a green skull crowned in jungle. The air hung wet and close. Insects thrummed at dusk with a fury that felt almost sentient. Cranes groaned over the bay. Fuel drums were stacked higher than houses. The water at the shoreline held a dark sheen that caught the light in ways I didn't trust. The place never slept. Engines. Sirens. Forklifts. The voices of tired men echoing from pontoons and quonset huts. The whole island a single machine built for one purpose.

Here the war felt close. You could feel it breathing over your shoulder.

Rumors ran through every line and ladderwell. The next great push. The Philippines. The return of MacArthur. October of forty-four and the end beginning to take shape.

We loaded the ship until she groaned. Tanks went in first. Twenty Shermans chained in rows, turrets turned inward, barrels fixed to the bulkheads, blind in the dark. The heat below had no mercy in it. Diesel and rubber clung to your skin. Chains rattled. Men cursed softly to themselves. The world down there spoke in metal and sweat.

Topside we stacked crates of ammunition. Barrels. Rations. Spare engines. Cots. The ropes strained. The deck rode low. Each swell washed the scuppers clean and left a sheen that caught the fading sun.

Then came the soldiers. The men of the Seventh Infantry Division. They filed aboard in single file, their rifles wrapped, their packs loaded with the small remnants of home, socks gone thin and old photographs softened by years. They folded themselves between tanks and crates. They slung hammocks in crooked rows and watched the ceiling like something up there might decide for them whether they lived or died. A radio played a song about somewhere far from war. No one spoke over it.

By dusk the convoy formed. Ships as far as sight allowed. Destroyers. Carriers. Transports. Hospital ships white as bones.

A whole floating nation moving into the teeth of the sea. Smoke rose from their stacks in long black ribbons. The ocean darkened beneath them. I stood at the rail and felt myself shrink beside that vast procession.

The sun bled out in red streaks. The sky closed in, dark and veined with the last of the light. Nobody said what we all felt. We were going back into the fire.

After chow I went topside. The air held damp and still. The order for blackout had come down. No lights showed from any ship. Only the pale churn of wake trailing behind us and the cold starlight hung above. I saw Jensen leaning against the rail. A thin man from Wisconsin with a long white scar from jaw to ear. No one knew how he got it. He never said.

We talked low. The sea quiet as an animal watching us.

He said he'd heard a rumor from a signalman on another ship. About the Japs. Said their pilots were loading their planes with bombs and flying straight into ships. On purpose.

Suicide runs, he said. Kamikaze.

I shook my head. Bullshit. Nobody gives up life that way. People want to live.

Jensen looked out over the flat dark water. His voice stayed calm. Billy Smith told me. Farm boy from Idaho. Straight as they come. Said a destroyer got hit off Formosa. Blew open in a yellow bloom. Men in the water flashed white and orange and then went dark.

He's wrong, I said. Has to be.

Maybe, Jensen said. But maybe not. Maybe the world's gone too far for sense now.

Lightning flickered far off without sound. A silent bloom of white on the horizon. It felt like a warning sent up from the bones of the world.

That night the ship grew quiet. The mess hall was empty but for the smell of coffee and fried salt pork. The sound of the engines thudded deep in the bones of the ship. The men moved softly in the passageways, voices low, eyes far away. On the eve of invasion, every man carries his own silence.

It settled over us, that stillness before the storm, the ship herself knew what was coming. The hush that overtakes a vessel when death hangs just beyond the horizon. The laughter had stopped. Men spoke in half sentences, afraid of what the rest might bring. We listened for answers that never arrived. The air was tense with what lay ahead. Rust coated the tongue. Even the ocean had fallen quiet, its breath held somewhere in the black beneath us.

I thought of all the faces I had known and how so many were already gone. I wondered how many more would vanish before it was over. I had no faith in luck, nor in mercy. Only in the turning of the engines and the slow grind of the world toward whatever end it had chosen for us. The truth was I no longer believed I would make it home. Somewhere deep inside, I had already made peace with dying. To live through this war seemed near to madness, a story told to make the dark less terrible.

Sleep would not come. I lay staring into the dark, the hum of the ship in my bones, the heat pressing down heavy. I made my way down into the soldiers' deck, the space set aside for the Army boys. Told myself it was to check on them, but that was a lie. I went because I needed to see faces. To know we were still men and not yet ghosts.

The air below was hot and sour. It carried the breath of men, the funk of damp canvas, cigarettes, and slow decay. The only light came from a red-shielded lantern, its glow swinging with the look of a wound that wouldn't close. Men sat shirtless on their cots, rifles propped beside them. Some cleaned their weapons in silence. Some smoked. A few wrote letters they would never mail. The glow of their cigarettes hung in the air like dying stars.

I sat with a few of them at a table. We talked about nothing. Where they were from. What they missed. One said snow. Another said the smell of rain on dry earth. A third said the sound of his mother's voice calling him in from the yard at dusk. We all went quiet after that. There are some things a man cannot speak without feeling the distance of them.

The ship rolled and the lantern swung with it, and out of the corner of my eye I caught a face half lost in shadow. A soldier sitting alone at the edge of his cot, helmet between his boots, cigarette burning low. I looked once and then again, thinking the heat and the dim light were playing tricks on me. The ship creaked. The shadows shifted. Yet that face remained, pale in the red glow.

My breath caught and held.

It was as though the years had turned in the wind and sent the past back into the room, filling the space around us. I felt the blood go cold behind my ribs. The noise of the ship faded, the cards, the talk, the scrape of boots. All of it gone. Only that face remained.

Harold Bass.

He was older now, leaner, the boy's softness burned away. The jaw sharper, the eyes hollowed by heat and hunger. But it was him. No question. The same crooked mouth. The same set of the brow. The ocean had drawn him out of the dust of my memory and set him here among the living.

For a long time I could not move. The sight of him struck me clean through, a relic unearthed from the ruins of my past.

Harold, I said at last. That you?

He looked up slow, eyes dulled by exhaustion, uncomprehending.

It's me, I said. Pat Flynn. From home. Wagner. I used to sweep the floor at your dad's garage.

He blinked. The fog lifted from his face, and for a heartbeat he wore the startled look of a man waking from a dream. Then I saw it come to him, a light behind the eyes, and his mouth opened in disbelief.

Pat Flynn. Jesus. It can't be.

He stood and gripped my arm and I felt his hand trembling. For a moment neither of us spoke. Two men staring across the gulf of years, each measuring the distance between who we'd been and who we'd become.

I'd known him long before the war. When I was a boy I swept the floor in his father's mechanic shop on Main Street. The place reeked of gasoline and iron and old rubber. The clock on the wall hadn't kept time in years.

His father was a grand old man with a belly that tested his suspenders and a moustache wide as a hand. He wore glasses that forever slid down his nose and he'd peer over them like a judge, kind but knowing. He'd retired but you'd find him there every morning, perched on a stool, coffee in one hand, telling stories of the first Model T that ever came through town.

His son Casey ran things then. Casey was near seven feet tall and always smiling, even when the shop was boiling with heat. He'd toss me a nickel when I was done sweeping and say don't spend it all in one place, kid. Harold worked in the back, head down, arms dark with oil to the elbows. He never said much to me but he wasn't cold. Just older. Already half gone to wherever men like him were meant to go.

Now here he was, sitting across from me in the dim red light of a ship halfway across the world.

We sat on his cot and lit cigarettes. The smoke curled in the dead air. We talked of home. Of the river when it froze, the brittle sound of it cracking under the moon. Of the fairgrounds in summer when the air filled the aroma of fried dough and sawdust. Of the girls who worked the counter at OMalley's and how the jukebox always skipped on the second verse. He said his sister was married now.

I told him my brother Dan was in the army, somewhere in France. Fighting the Germans. Shot one of them while the bastard was squatting to take a crap. Got his Luger for the trouble. Harold laughed, shaking his head. Said that sounded born out of a bad dream. I said war was nothing but a collection of bad dreams strung together and called history.

We talked until the hours lost their shape. The war fell away. The iron walls and the reek of oil, the thunder of the engines. All of it gone. For that brief time we were boys again, sitting on a curb in the fading light, a whole world ahead of us that had not yet turned dark.

You were at Tarawa, he said.

Yeah. Then Majuro. Kwajalein.

We were at Saipan, he said. That place never stopped burning. Lost two of my boys there. Casey too, back home. Pneumonia got him.

His voice faltered at the last word. I pictured the garage. The tools lined up. Casey cussing under his breath. The old man's laugh echoing through dust and sunlight.

I didn't know, I said.

He nodded like a man accustomed to loss.

We smoked in silence awhile. The red lantern swayed overhead. The ship hummed around us. For a moment I felt the distance between who we had been and who we were now. Two farm boys sitting on a cot in the belly of a ship that had forgotten every road but this one.

You think this ends, I asked him.

Harold looked around at the sleeping men. Maybe it ends for some. Maybe not for others.

You remember that shop, I said.

Yeah. Glenn Miller on the radio. Casey swearing at the belts. You sweeping like a kid on the run.

I laughed faintly. Needed to hear it.

He smiled. Casey was too tall for this world.

We sat quiet. And I thought how this meeting was its own strange mercy. Proof we had not yet been erased.

It got late. I stood.

Hey Harold. I better hit the rack. Big day tomorrow.

Yeah, he said. Big day.

Let's get a drink when this is done.

Sure thing. That'd be swell. We shook hands.

Goodbye, Harold.

He nodded once. The ember of his cigarette small as a star about to die.

I climbed topside. The fleet moved around us, a vast migration of steel. The sea breathed deep and slow. The wind carried the faint dryness of coming rain.

I gripped the rail. Oil stained the creases of my palms. The ship creaked beneath my boots. The night itself felt heavier with whatever waited just beyond the dark.

I prayed then. I asked for strength. For legs beneath me and for hands that would answer when dawn came and the sky broke open again.

The horizon was black and waiting. The sea went still listening. A gathering storm.

Leyte

War is a failure of the human spirit. A betrayal of love. A summoning of all the bile, hatred, greed, and lust in man's black heart. Hot steel the penance. Torn flesh the sacrifice. The screams of the dying the prayer.

***

October 20, 1944

They said deliverance had come. MacArthur would return to these islands, a prophet to his flock. The officers spoke his name like scripture and the invasion itself a sermon of redemption. Yet in the gray hush before dawn, when the air carried the scent of rain and diesel and the slow breath of the sea, there was no faith left in me. Only the old trembling that comes before judgment.

Our ship was bound for Dulag, south of Palo and north of San Pedro Bay, a narrow throat of coast hemmed by mountains and jungle. To the north the fleet's guns beat the land without mercy. To the south the horizon burned with tracers. We were the center of the storm, a steel mouth opened to deliver men and machines into the heart of ruin.

The bombardment began before the sun. The sea shuddered beneath the first salvos. The darkness strobed with the muzzle flashes of the battleships. Their shells howled overhead, their passing marked by a low vibration that sank into the bones. The shore vanished in explosions. Whole jungles leapt into the air. Cliffs collapsed in slabs, the old stone giving up its teeth. The sky turned orange and black and in that false dawn and the world itself seemed set aflame.

The cruisers joined in, their turrets spitting white fire. Destroyers darted closer to the reefs and poured their broadsides into the tree line. The concussion rolled back across the water. The breath of some buried god.

By the time the order came to advance, the horizon was a single wall of smoke. The helmsman's hands clung white to the wheel. The engines deep below roared and the ship pushed forward through drifting ash. The sea was alive with wreckage. Torn rafts. Oil drums. The burned husk of a landing craft turning slow in the swell.

The air pressed in around us. Cordite and burnt metal and salt. You could taste it when you breathed. The wind was hot as a forge. We moved through it and it clung to us.

I took my place at the twenty millimeter on the port bow. Wilkins crouched low beside me, his face blackened with soot. Ortega stood braced behind the sight rail, eyes fixed to the haze. None of us spoke. The deck trembled beneath our boots.

Ahead the shoreline began to emerge. A strip of gray sand behind the surf, veiled by the smoke of burning palms. The mountains beyond rose, ghostly. The fleet closed in behind us, the whole armada crawling toward land. Hundreds of ships, dark shapes against the sun.

We struck bottom with a grinding shock. The bow lifted once, then settled. Spray broke over us. Ramp chains screamed. Tanks below growled in their stalls, engines shaking the deck.

The ramp dropped.

The first tanks thundered down into the surf, water rising over their turrets. Men followed with rifles held high. Mortars burst in the shallows. Bullets snapped through the spray. The sea boiled with bodies. The first wave faltered but did not break.

The air tore with engines and shellfire. A blast landed short and covered us in spray and sand. I fired into the smoke at flashes and at the edges of jungle where fire lived. The gun hammered my shoulder. Tracers ripped the mist. Wilkins slammed in a fresh drum. Ortega tried to shout something toward the ridge but the noise swallowed it whole.

Somewhere in that chaos my mind drifted to Harold Bass. Whether he was one of those figures crawling through surf. Whether he was alive. The thought flickered once and was carried off by the next concussion.

Onshore a halftrack burned with furnace heat. Men staggered past it, their shadows warped in flame. A truck overturned in the surf and the driver clung to the wheel as the water rose over him. A medic crawled between the fallen, his armband gone brown. A soldier sat in the sand with both hands to his face, rocking before God or the ruin of Him.

The shore was chaos. Nothing held. The surf carried in bodies and the tide carried them back out. Planes filled the sky. Our bombers dove through smoke, bombs falling like black fruit. Each blast threw up pillars of fire and sand. The ground buckled. The noise drowned thought.

I kept firing to keep from thinking. The air stank of hot metal and oil. Casings spun at my feet and settled in the blood and salt spray.

Through the haze I saw other LSTs grounding north of us, spilling their cargoes into hell. Beyond them destroyers fired inland. The mountains flashed bright. The echo rolled out to sea, deep and terrible.

MacArthur came ashore at Palo with the third wave, his khaki dry despite the rain, his face faded as an old print. They said he promised the Philippines would rise again, but I saw the same beach he did and it was already crowded with the dead.

The landings stretched for miles. At San Jose the Seventh Infantry waded through mud and blood to reach the first ridge. At Burauen engineers blew paths through the reef with satchel charges while snipers cut them down. Inland, tanks ground through cane fields and villages, their treads crushing everything. North of Dulag the jungle burned for miles. Smoke drifted out over the bay in long black strings.

The sky was a battlefield too. Hellcats and Corsairs dove on the ridges, guns tearing up earth. Liberators dropped their loads into valleys. Shockwaves moved across the ground with a living violence, flattening trees. The air shimmered with heat.

By afternoon the beach was choked with wreckage. LVTs half submerged. Tanks burning. The sea littered with debris. Men moved ghostly through the smoke. The water was red and stinking.

That was Leyte. The great return. And it was not deliverance. It was judgment.

The chaplain came aboard at dusk, his face the color of ash. He said nothing. Medics worked below, sleeves soaked black. The wounded came in silent, eyes vacant. I helped carry one boy who looked no older than sixteen. He clutched a photograph in his hand and did not release it even after he died.

Night fell and the sea glowed faint from fires onshore. The horizon flickered. The air fouled with smoke and burnt flesh. I sat by the gun long after midnight. The metal still hot under my palms. I watched breakers roll dark and slow and knew we had not come to save anything. Only to kill and endure.

$$***$$

October 22, 1944

I lay in my bunk staring at the dark overhead, the hum of the ship moving through steel with a pulse of its own. The air carried oil and smoke and the sour rot of soaked gear. Sleep would not come. The war beat inside us with a second heart.

At dawn we returned to work. Orders came. We shuttled wounded to the hospital ships off the reef. Carried stretchers slick with blood. Men whispering for water, for home. Some stared upward with empty eyes. Some clutched photographs. Some held rosaries. Some held nothing at all.

When the last stretcher was gone, we loaded new troops. Young men. Faces untested. Uniforms stiff with starch. They looked at us with the pale wonder reserved for the lost returned.

We put them ashore at Burauen, at San Jose, again at Palo where the beach still smoked. Everywhere looked the same. Palms sheared to stumps. Sand churned to mud. Cordite and decay hung in the air.

By evening we were back at Dulag. The sky bruised red. The guns inland rumbled with sleepless thunder.

It was my turn for onshore guard duty. I slung an M1 and stepped down the ramp onto wet sand. The great steel bow doors stood open to the night, the ship's vast black mouth facing the sea. Before me the jungle crouched in silence. Frogs calling. Insects buzzing. Somewhere far off a machine gun stuttered once and fell quiet.

The line of LSTs stretched down the beach, each bow agape, each ship a hulking creature left to brood in the tide. Before each stood one sentry. Men like me. Shadow cutouts against the red sky.

The jungle held its breath. Then movement inside it. A branch snapped. I raised my rifle.

Halt. Password.

Lightning, came the reply.

A figure stepped into view. An army soldier. Uniform torn. Helmet hanging by its strap. Eyes empty with exhaustion. The stench of sweat and fear rolled off him. Beneath it came the sharp reek of urine.

Sailor, he said. You got a spare bunk in there somewhere.

You need a bed tonight. Can't sleep in the jungle.

He nodded.

You have no idea how lucky you are.

Why is that.

He looked back toward the trees.

Daytime the Japs hide, he said. Dress like the locals. Lie still. But when the sun goes down they come out. I was in my foxhole last night. Black as pitch. I heard them moving. Crawling like snakes in the brush. Whispering names. Bill. Pete. Hey. Psst. Like they knew us. They were all around me. You make one sound and they cut your fucking throat. I could not even stand to take a leak. Had to do it in my trousers. It is a nightmare.

His voice trembled.

The guy next to me never made it. The one in the hole beside mine. They found him this morning on his back, staring at the sky. His neck opened wide. Looked like death carved a grin in him.

He stared at me and I saw part of him remained out there listening.

Come on, I said. There is a bunk for you.

He followed me up the ramp. The ship's belly glowed red in the dim lights. I found him a cot and a cigarette.

Try to sleep, I said. But his words had chilled me to the bone. Never had I felt so lucky to be a sailor. My mind drifted back to the losing coin flip with Perman that had put me on this ship and not in a foxhole filled with piss in some dark jungle. I gave Perman a silent nod as I walked away.

The soldier held the cigarette with a kind of reverence.

Thanks, Sailor, he said. You saved my life.

He lay down, eyes half open, smoke drifting toward the steel overhead. I watched him awhile. Outside, rain fell soft against the hull. The sea and the guns blended into a single low breath.

I thought of what he had said, of voices whispering from the black. I wondered if in time we would all hear them.

At first light he was gone. Back into the jungle. His cot still held the print of his body.

The beach was quiet. Smoke rising from palms. Mud and gunpowder and that strange sweetness after fire hanging over everything. Men moved slow. Eyes on the shore.

Bull stood beside me. The sea flat as poured glass.

Wonder what they will have us do today, he said.

Whatever it is, it will not be good.

Maybe haul ammo. Maybe take a load of dead ones out.

Or the living, I said.

He nodded. Doesn't seem to matter anymore.

We watched the smoke drift over the water. He said waiting made a man think too much. I told him the war found you no matter where you went. He laughed once and fell quiet.

By midmorning we ferried wounded to the hospital ship. Deck stank of blood and iodine. The sea littered with wreckage. Bodies rolled in smoke. Dog tags flashing then vanishing.

The hospital ship gleamed white through haze. Her lights blurred. She looked holy from afar. But as we neared, the cries carried over the water.

Then the shout came.

Torpedo off the port bow.

At first I could not see it, only the sudden tension of the men on deck, the stillness that falls when fear arrives. Then I saw the line, a thin white streak of bubbles moving fast across the water, straight and sure. And then another beside it. They came on with terrible purpose, perfect in their aim and empty of mercy.

The next sound was the ship's alarm, shrill and merciless, cutting through the air like steel teeth. It filled the deck, the passageways, the bunks below. Then the PA cracked to life, the voice from the bridge sharp and hurried. Torpedo sighted, port side. All hands brace for impact. Repeat, brace for impact.

The alarm's wail was almost worse than what we saw. It drove through bone and thought alike, that metallic shriek that meant the world might end in seconds. Men froze where they stood, mouths open, eyes wide. The sound drowned everything except the pulse in their ears.

The sea itself seemed to draw breath.

No one moved. There was no time for it. The sight of those torpedoes coming straight for us sent me numb with fear. I could feel my heart hammering but my body would not answer. All I could do was watch them close the distance, sure in that moment that I would never draw another breath.

We stood there and watched death approach, helpless. You could feel it in your chest before it reached you, the terrible knowledge that nothing on earth could change its course. One of the gunners crossed himself. Another man muttered something about home. I remember the sound most of all, a deep rolling hum, the sea speaking in its oldest voice.

The tracks reached us. The ship trembled. For a heartbeat the world held its breath. And then the torpedoes passed beneath us, two pale shapes sliding through the green depths, leaving trails of bubbles that shimmered in veins of light. They vanished astern without a sound.

For a long moment no one spoke. Then Bull exhaled slowly, returned from whatever dark place had held him.

Jesus Christ, he said.

Another voice came from the bow. Sweet mother of God, we just got kissed by the devil himself.

One of the deckhands laughed, a sharp nervous bark. I think I just aged twenty years.

There was a low murmur of agreement, half laughter, half disbelief. A man spat over the side and said he'd never piss straight again. The sound of voices spread across the deck. A spell breaking. Fear turned to talk, talk to laughter, laughter to silence once more.

When the noise faded, joy went with it, and the ache came after. The tremor in the hands, the taste of copper in the mouth. We had laughed because we were alive and because we did not know what else to do. The sea hissed against the hull and the ship rolled on, slow and steady, with nothing on her to show what had passed.

Bull stood beside me, his cigarette trembling between two fingers. He looked out over the gray water and said, She ain't done with us yet.

Every man knew what had happened. The screws had lifted us just enough. Our flat bottom had saved us, that ugly shape made for beaches and mud. The Japanese had set their gyros for the deep-bellied destroyers and cruisers they expected. Their precision had betrayed them. And our own crude design, this clumsy graceless barge of steel, had cheated death.

Down below, the wounded stirred but did not know. Their dreams were already full of killing.

We went on toward the hospital ship. The sea slapped our hull. The white cranes swung through the mist, pale and skeletal. The wounded disappeared into her belly, given over to an indifferent god.

Destroyers peeled away hunting the submarine. Ashcans rolled. The sea lifted. A dark slick came up after, spreading slow over the water. A cheer rose from another ship. Ours stayed quiet.

We survived. Others had not.

The sun bled red behind the clouds. The war did not sleep. And somewhere out there another reckoning waited.

The smoke from Leyte drifted out to sea and lost itself in the horizon. The day's last light pooled blood red along the water. Offshore the fleet dimmed their lamps. Onshore the jungle burned in long silent curtains. It felt like the world was leaning, waiting to fall.

***

October 25, 1944
Dulag Beach

The day had worn itself thin. Routine moved through the ship like an old song. Lines coiled. Decks swabbed. Mess duty posted. Men joked about home without much spirit.

By late afternoon the cooks had set out trays slick with grease, steam fogging the overheads. Beef and onions drifted through the ship. Potatoes ladled in gray scoops. Gravy dark as ditch mud. A man muttered he would trade his soul for a cold beer. Someone else said Christmas and was cursed for it.

After chow I was in the galley with Bull, scrubbing trays. The fans rattled without purpose, stirring heat instead of moving it. Bennett leaned against the sink, drying his hands on his shirt.

You hear about them girls on New Georgia, he said.

What girls.

Red Cross. They flew two in. Said they lifted morale.

Bull snorted. I would settle for seeing any girl again. Do not even care if she is ugly.

Bennett grinned. I would take one with a glass eye long as she brought whiskey.

Think this war will ever end, I said.

Not till it burns itself out, he said. Not till there is nothing left to burn.

We worked in silence for a while. Then the speaker snapped alive.

GQ. GQ. All hands. Enemy aircraft sighted. This is not a drill.

The klaxon gave a wounded cry. We froze for a heartbeat, then dropped trays and ran. The ladder rungs burned my palms. Bull's boots clanged close behind.

Topside the world was a dying ember. The sun's last breath stained the sea copper. The air lay still in that terrible way it does before something monstrous arrives.

I strapped into my twenty millimeter mount. Ortega scanned the sky. Wilkins came running with a fresh drum.

Anything, I said.

Negative, Ortega said. But they are out there.

Along the beach the blackout began. Power posts spaced down the shore went dark one by one. Pop. Pop. Pop. The sudden quiet hit harder than the alarm itself.

And then one light stayed on.

A single bright bulb burning over five acres of ammunition. Behind it a field bivouac of one hundred fifty soldiers. And under that lone shining beacon stood a soldier.

He leaned against the pole reading a comic book, its pages glowing white in the dark. The light carved him from the black, a lone figure on a stage.

Kill the light, someone shouted. Christ almighty turn it off.

Voices rose down the line, frantic, angry, pleading.

Turn it off, you idiot.

The hell is wrong with you.

You trying to get us killed.

The shouting spread, a chain of panic. Men on other ships joined in, their voices carried by the wind.

Turn it off, asshole!

For Christ's sake kill it!

He didn't move or even look up. Just turned a page. The paper flashed white in the dark.

Lieutenant Prentiss came running with the megaphone. Thin, rawboned man. Eyes hollow as a grave.

Turn off that light, soldier. Enemy aircraft inbound. That's an order.

Another officer raised an M1 to shoot it out. He didn't get the chance.

There was a whoosh overhead. A black shape cut across the stars. A lone Japanese bomber, flying low and sure. Running dark. Running alone. He had seen the beacon. That single goddamn bulb drawing him in.

The bomb struck the dump square.

The world became noise.

The blast ripped me from my gun harness and hurled me across the deck. For an instant there was no gravity, no sound, no thought. Just white fire and heat. Wilkins spun past me midair, limbs limp, mouth open but silent. Ortega vanished in smoke.

The concussion from the explosion hit so hard that for a heartbeat our ship went airborne. Lifted clean off the sea. Suspended in an impossible stillness between water and sky, creation pausing before its own ruin. Then she fell. The sound of her striking the water cracked through the world.

The deck buckled. I hit hard, shoulder first, and felt something tear in my neck. Blood blurred my vision. Wilkins groaned somewhere behind me. My mouth was full of grit and metal.

Then the dump went up.

A chain reaction that shook the heavens. Mortars, depth charges, shells of every caliber screaming into flame. The night turned to midday, then to something brighter. The colors were wrong; reds too red, whites that hurt to look at, greens like the northern lights gone insane. The ground convulsed. You could see tents and trucks lift off the earth and vanish. Men running, not knowing where, their shadows thrown a hundred feet long before disappearing in the light.

It was a carnival from hell. A thousand Fourths of July gone mad. Rockets without joy, fire without purpose. The sound became pressure that crawled inside your head and rattled your bones.

We lay where we'd been thrown. Deaf and half blind. The world was gone to smoke and ash. The dust fell without mercy, enough to turn the air to clay. It filled the mouth and nose and settled over the eyes in a blind second skin. It was worse than anything I'd ever seen back in South Dakota, worse than any storm the plains could conjure. The island itself seemed to dissolve beneath it, swallowed whole by a moving fog of earth and ruin. Sparks drifted through it, swampfire from hell. I thought we had died. I thought this was the end of the world taking shape around us.

The comic book soldier and his light were gone. The whole bivouac, gone. Those one hundred fifty men turned to nothing. The earth where they'd stood was glass.

For two hours it raged without letup. One blast swallowed the next until all of it became a single roar without end. Shells cut through the darkness, struck steel, and went whining off. Far out on the beach men stumbled through the fire glow with their arms over their heads, their faces blackened by smoke. The island burned from its own dark heart.

Our damage control crew worked through it. Crawling through smoke and flame, torches in their hands. The bow doors had buckled, the ramp twisted. They worked as men possessed. Grease streaked their faces, their eyes reflecting the inferno. Sparks rained down but they kept hammering and welding, screaming to one another over the blasts.

When the ramp was made fast and the bow doors drawn shut, a shout went up from forward. The anchor cables tightened and sang through the rollers. The ship began to strain against the beach, dragging itself backward by the stern anchor buried deep in the coral and sand of the bay. She pulled slow, groaning and heaving. A wounded beast hauling its own weight through blood. Inch by inch we felt her slide. The hull scraped rock and the sea rose beneath her. At last she broke free and drifted into the dark water, spent but living.

We were coated in dust, our uniforms gray, hair matted, eyes rimmed with salt and dirt. Ears ringing so loud it felt like silence. No one spoke at first. Just the soft slap of water against the hull.

Bull came from across the deck, his face streaked black.

You alright, Pat?

I think so.

He looked out toward the beach, shaking his head.

Jesus. That son of a bitch.

Nicky Powers sat near the rail, rubbing his ears.

You think he's still down there, that bastard with the comic?

Bull spat. He ain't anything now.

Nicky nodded slow. Good.

We laughed then. A short, broken thing that wasn't laughter at all. My ribs hurt when I tried to breathe. I felt the crust of dried blood on my temple and thought of that light, how it burned so ordinary until it became a signal to death itself.

That night we watched the shore burn. The explosions flickered through the low clouds with the pulse of heat lightning. A strange beauty to it. We didn't talk much. A few of the men sat with their faces in their hands. Someone prayed under his breath. The sea glowed faintly, reflecting the ruin.

I thought of that soldier again. The one who wouldn't kill his light. I hated him, but part of me pitied him too. Maybe he didn't hear the orders or perhaps he just wanted a few minutes of quiet to read. Whatever it was, his small defiance had called the devil down upon us.

***

October 26, 1944

At 0900 we went ashore.

The beach was a graveyard.

Sand melted into black glass.

Craters smoking.

Shells cooking off in lazy pops.

Jeep frames twisted like wire. Helmets fused to the earth. Boots without feet. The stink of burned flesh rode the air.

Bull stopped beside the ruins of a generator.

Guess he will not need his comic now.

I did not answer.

We found the remains of the light pole. Only scorched earth. Not even a shadow left.

The war moved on, but part of us stayed there, frozen in the moment a single bulb refused to die, and called destruction onto all who saw it burn.

That night I dreamed of sky on fire.

The ship rising weightless.

The beach erased.

Names swallowed by smoke.

And somewhere beyond all of it a small foolish light still burned.

The Battle of Leyte Gulf

October 23 – 26, 1944

In those days the sea moved in short, tight breaths, the surface drawn hard with wind and ash. It heaved against the beach eager to reclaim what men had built there. Our LST lay close to shore, squat and low. Dried mud streaked her ramp and months beneath the sun had blistered her paint. We were close enough to hear the surf grind the coral. The war had come to Leyte and we were its attendants, low men watching giants battle beyond the edge of sight.

From dawn to dark we heard it. The long thunder of guns over the water. A low, ceaseless pounding that seemed to rise from the seabed and work its way up through the hull. It never stopped. You could feel it in your teeth. The hills behind the beach seemed to shudder, and even the trees leaned toward the sound listening for their own ruin.

Bull stood beside me on the deck, bare to the waist. His chest slick with sweat, a cigarette clinging at the corner of his mouth, unlit.

They're out there killing each other by the thousands, he said.

They're keeping us alive, I told him.

He squinted toward the horizon. You think they know?

Know what?

That we're back here praying they don't lose.

I reckon they do, I said. Sailors same as us.

That was the truth of it. The only thing keeping the sea from swallowing us whole were those ships out there, the carriers, the battleships, the tin cans slugging it out past the horizon. Every broadside they fired bought us another breath. Every man who died out there was buying time for the rest of us crouched on this strip of beach.

The air carried a heaviness that never lifted. Each sunrise broke red, raw as an open wound. The shore steamed in the heat. We worked through it, hauling crates, pumping bilge, checking drums. Sweat ran into our eyes, stung with salt and dust. Beyond the headland the guns would speak again and we'd stop what we were doing and listen. No one said it, but we all knew: if those ships fell, the Japanese would pour through that gap and come for us next. We'd be cornered on this strip of beach with nowhere to run but the sea.

At night the horizon burned in silence. Great sheets of white and orange light rose and faded, the sky flickering with the inner glare of a furnace. The sound came after, rolling in waves across the gulf to strike the hull and rattle the plates beneath our feet. We stood beside the dark body of the war and heard its heart labor.

Wilkins leaned on the rail, his face drawn with sleeplessness.

You figure we'd stand a chance if they got through? He said.

Bull gave a dry laugh. Against what? Battleships? Torpedoes? You got your bare hands, maybe throw your helmet at them.

Nicky said, I got a wife and kid waiting in Pomona. I ain't dying on no beach halfway around the world.

Nobody answered. We all thought the same thing and it didn't bear repeating.

Sometimes in the night, flares went up far out to sea, little suns blooming and dying. Once a destroyer passed close inshore, her decks lined with men. They looked at us as they went by, faces pale in the firelight, and we looked back. No one waved. We just watched her go. The wind carried a low moaning sound across the water that might have been her engines or might have been the sea itself mourning what was to come.

The radio sputtered and hissed for hours. Voices came broken by static. Reports of Japanese cruisers closing from the west, their formation shattered, then reformed. The words came half-garbled, but what reached us was enough. We knew the great fleets had found each other, that the sky out there was full of smoke and metal. Nicky leaned in the hatchway, listening. He said the whole Pacific was on fire. Said the old ships from Pearl were out there, the ones raised from the mud, and that they were having their vengeance.

By the third day the sea began to return what it had taken. A plank scorched black. A hatch cover with Japanese lettering visible, drifting coffin-flat on the swell. A man's cap floating crown-up, open to heaven. Once a raft drifted past with no one aboard, just a single boot and a bloodstained canteen rolling with the sea. We fished nothing in. The sea was full of ghosts. You could feel them near the ship at night, moving unseen below the waterline.

That afternoon Bull said, You think they ever know it's coming?

Not when it's that fast, I told him.

He looked out at the floating debris. Jesus, he said.

Nicky stood nearby, hands on the rail. Christ help them, he said. Then he laughed once under his breath and said, There ain't no Christ out here. Only the sea.

His voice had gone flat, stripped down to certainty.

The fourth night was the worst. The whole northern sky was on fire. You could read by the light of it. The sea burned red and gold, and the guns pounded so hard the deck shivered beneath us and the plates groaned in their welds. Some men prayed in their racks. Others played cards by lantern light and kept their faces down. The rest lay in their racks staring at the overhead. We knew we were listening to men spend their lives out there, and there was no taking any of it back.

By morning the thunder had begun to fade. The horizon smoked, and a gray haze hung low over the water. The radio crackled with reports of wrecks burning off Samar and Surigao Strait. The operators spoke in low voices, their faces pale in the glow of the console. They said the enemy had been broken. That ships burned from one end of the gulf to the other. That the sea was strewn with men and iron, and no one knew how many were gone.

We didn't cheer. We stood on deck, faces lit by a pale sun, staring at the water for some confession. Oil slicks drifted near the hull. Broken planks. Life jackets. Debris that spoke of men who would never come home.

Bull squatted by the gun mount, his hands hanging loose between his knees, sweat running down his arms in slow dark trails.

You think they'll ever say who kept em from coming here? He asked.

We know, I said.

Thank God for those boys out there, he said.

And he meant it. Every man aboard knew it. Those ships had held the line. They'd bought us moments we might never have had.

Afterward the world went quiet. The wind blew steady out of the east, carrying the taste of ash and salt and something faint. Rain on rusted metal. We ferried supplies to the beach, took on wounded, scrubbed decks that still held the weight of fear. The guns to the north were silent now, but in our heads the echoes stayed. At night I'd wake to the sound of explosions that weren't there. My hands would clench before my eyes were even open.

Days later the word filtered down through the fleet. Thirty-seven ships lost between both sides. Over fifteen thousand dead and missing. They said the water was slick with oil and bodies for miles, and that the fish would not come back for years.

I stood on deck one evening as the sun went down. The horizon was quiet now. The water lay calm and flat. I thought of those men out there, the ones who had stood between us and the dark. Their faces unknown, their voices lost in static. If the Japanese had broken through, they'd have found us waiting on this beach with rifles and little else. We'd have gone before them in minutes.

Bull came up beside me and lit a cigarette.

You think this war ever ends? He said.

Everything ends, Bull. Even this.

He let out a long breath. Not soon enough, he said.

Years later they called what we'd heard off Leyte the largest naval battle in history. To us then it had been only a noise on the horizon. And I thought how the ocean kept no tally of uniforms or flags, no allegiance to the living or the dead. To the deep it was all the same, blood and steel and memory carried down into the black where no man's name endures.

I looked out over the horizon and drew deep from my smoke. The ash glowed in the fading light. I flicked it into the ocean where it vanished without a trace. The wind came soft off the bay. The world lay still. And I knew the sea would keep me if it chose, that home was only a word we used against the silence.

Tacloban

The day's work had carried us inland to Tacloban and the briefest taste of liberty. The town lay bent on the northeast shoulder of Leyte where the land hooked toward the gulf and the shallows turned the water brown. The Sixth Army had taken it back on invasion day after two cruel years beneath the flag of a sun with too many rays. Now it stood as a soul returned from darkness, uncertain of what light might mean.

Wet earth moved on the wind, brined with salt and rot and something fouler beneath, the reek of powder and old graves unspooled too fast. November bled across the clouds. The sky looked wrung out, dark with bruises.

We stepped off the LST and into mud the color of dried blood. It clung to our boots, sucked at us with a will. The first foot down never came up easy. A man learned quick to lift slow or the ground would take him for good.

A few of us had banded together, sailors from other ships drawn to shore by the twin lures of boredom and luck. We moved in a loose column through the ooze, white uniforms fouled at the knees, laughter coming only in pieces.

Among them was Slocum. A Texan from somewhere near Abilene, storekeeper off one of the other LSTs. Looked like he'd been carved out of old wind and dry tobacco. He always had something in his mouth, plug, smoke, toothpick. And he could hit a rat at twenty feet with his spit.

He and I had palled around during idle days, trading smokes and insults and whatever black humor kept a man from slipping. Sometimes we'd lace up and box on the tank deck until one of us bled. His uppercut was mean but he left his guard wide and I always tagged him. He'd sit there grinning, lip split, calling me Irish devil like it was praise. We were friends made by fists and sweat and boredom, the kind of friendship war forges.

Slocum once told me a ship didn't float by design but by the mercy of stubborn metal and dumb luck. I liked him for that. He believed in nothing, but he behaved like belief was worth the effort.

The shore rose ahead in a tangle of timber and ruin. The docks were half reassembled out of poles and frayed rope, splintered and slapped into shape by men who needed them. The road to town churned under the wheels of trucks and the boots of the desperate. Every step felt like a losing argument with the earth. Sailors in white were stained to the knee with mud. We looked ghostly, a flotilla marching inland.

Tacloban itself was neither dead nor alive. It crouched beneath its own weight. Shellfire had written its name on the stucco. The walls wore pocks where shrapnel had kissed them, stones carrying the scars of fever. Roofs sagged in places, beams exposed in broken ribs. Wood bent in exhaustion. Windows were blown out and boarded in a dozen ways or left open as wounds. A faint, almost tender scent of ash clung to wood the fire had only tasted.

Someone had laid planks down in places, boards scavenged from crates or houses and nailed across the worst of it. They kept a man above the sludge, if only just. We followed the line, our boots creaking on the wood.

An old woman stood in a doorway, a child at her hip wrapped in something that might once have been a blanket. Her eyes had been carved by long years and the things they'd been made to witness. When she saw us, her face broke open with light.

Thank you, Americano, she called.

Thank you, GI Joe.

A boy stepped out from behind a crumbled wall, carrying a crate of Coca-Cola that had warmed in the sun. He grinned with perfect teeth.

Mabuhay, he said. Welcome, GI Joe.

Slocum spit a brown stream into the muck and said, We appreciate it, son, but we ain't no GI's. We're the goddamn Navy.

The boy laughed and nodded. Okay, okay. Mabuhay, Navy Joe. His laugh broke through the wreckage, bell-clear and strangely honest.

The sun tried to show itself through the low ceiling of cloud. Its light came yellow and sickly, a tired flame. At the center of town, the provincial capitol stood like some half-buried relic. Columns scorched but upright. A building that refused to fall. Two Filipino MPs in patched khaki waved traffic past, what little there was. A rickshaw and a truck with no windshield. A man pulling a cart full of chickens.

One sailor ahead of us stepped wrong and sank to his thighs in the mire. The mud wouldn't let go. He fought it like a drowning man, arms flailing, shouting. A crowd gathered. Americans, locals, soldiers, children. Laughter rose from the edges. He pitched forward, covered in brown to the neck, and the street let out a cheer. For a moment, human joy rose off the street, small and obscene and necessary.

We followed others to a place cobbled back together just enough to sell cold beer. The front was held up by sandbags. A wire fan spun slow over our heads. The San Miguel bottles sweated in the heat. I held mine as a holy thing.

Outside, a man sat on a crate carving a small wooden figure, the knife bright in his slow hands. Another leaned against a post, the ruin of burns scrawled across his jaw and arm.

The rain, she never stops for the war, the carver said. She makes our street a river that never learns your name.

I nodded and drank deep. The beer was cold, which meant it was holy.

I grinned. Where are the pretty girls hiding? Hard to see past the mud.

They chuckled. Dry, bone-deep sound. The carver stopped his knife.

The pretty girls are everywhere, Americano. But a few months ago, they hid. Like the rest of us.

I asked, What was it like with the Japs?

The man with the burns looked at me as if I'd asked the sea to speak.

It was a thing with no name, he said. They made you bow. Made you suffer for how you bowed. Took boys into the trees and broke them open to learn what they did not know.

The carver spoke soft. My neighbor's son stole a tin of fish. Fourteen. They made the father watch. Broke the boy's legs with a hammer. Then gave the hammer to the father and told him to finish it. When he did, they shot him. So there would be no story left to tell.

He set the knife down.

You forget the hunger. The fever. But not that. You don't forget what they make a man do. He spoke slowly, each word plain enough to cut.

The room stilled. My beer had the taste of cold iron. The laughter from the mud-bound sailor seemed very far away.

Slocum stared down at his bottle. His voice came low.

We got our own sins, he said. In Guam they lined up the Japs. They gave us knives. Said finish it. Some of the boys laughed. I didn't laugh. I didn't move neither. But I still hear it.

The carver looked at him. And then what?

Slocum shook his head. Then we got back on the boat.

He stood and said, Let's walk.

We left in silence. The rain had started again. A fine mist that made no sound. Across the street, a woman sat by a stall of salvaged trinkets, scraps of life cleaned and arranged with care. Buttons. Rusted belt buckles. Porcelain dolls missing limbs. Broken watches with their glass wiped clear. A compass with no needle.

Slocum picked up a tiny wooden carabao with one horn snapped off. I found a blackened crucifix and bought it for a peso.

Two kids watched us. Barefoot. Big-eyed. I gave them coins and they held them like secrets. Slocum tossed a quarter into the mud. The smaller boy dove. Came up grinning.

Slocum said, Buy yourself some shoes, kid.

The boy nodded, though he hadn't understood.

We walked on.

Somewhere a piano played a song without end. The sound wandered, notes drifting down through the air.

On a rise stood a church, its bell tower cracked but its body whole enough to hold a stillness. The cross on top was cracked and stood witness to the broken city.

I said, Come on. I need to talk to God.

Slocum squinted up the hill. Irish, I'm Southern Baptist. You Catholics sure like to complicate things. All that kneelin and confessin. Man can't even sneeze without tellin the priest about it.

You don't believe in confession?

We confess, he said, but only once. Saves time. And we don't pray to no statues neither. A man prays straight to God or he don't pray at all. Besides, I never trusted a religion that drinks the blood of its own savior.

I shook my head. That's just symbolism, I said.

He grinned. Symbolism's what men say when they're scared of plain talk. I'll wait down here with the living. You go up with your ghosts.

The climb was steep. Clay sucked at my shoes. Stones rolled underfoot. The slope was scattered with rubble and bones of brick. The church loomed.

Inside, the church was cool, its silence steeped in wax and timber and the tired sweetness of dying flowers. The doors had been splintered and repaired with mismatched planks. Candles burned in stubs of bottles along the pews, their light wavering on the cracked plaster walls. A few locals knelt at the front, voices low and private. I couldn't tell if they prayed in grief or thanks. Probably both.

A woman in a shawl clutched a crucifix and a man sang under his breath. Two kids slept curled on the stone, small and dust-streaked, their bare feet curled beneath them. The candles trembled each flame fearful it might be the last.

I knelt in the back. The wood bit my knees. The silence moved in. I prayed.

For my folks back in Dakota. For Dan in Europe. For Bull and Nicky, Ortega and Wilkins. All the boys who laughed when they should have cried. For the men who never made it off the beach.

For the Filipino dead. For the children buried without names, for the fathers who could not protect them, for the women who had crouched hidden in the mangroves and prayed by the light that moved upon the water.

I prayed for the sound itself, for the ringing in my ears that would not stop.

For the ghosts in the water.

I prayed for the enemy too. That one came hard.

I prayed that somewhere in the great deafness of heaven there was an ear that could listen.

I prayed for mercy. Whatever shape was left of it.

The stained-glass window above the altar had been shattered but a single piece of blue remained, and through it the daylight passed, thin and cold. It fell across the face of the plaster Christ, painting one cheek in that wounded color, heaven having remembered him only halfway.

When I rose, my knees cracked like old hinges. I dipped a hand into the font. The water was gray with ash and dust. I touched it to my forehead anyway.

Outside, wet tin and salt lay on the air. The clouds hung low. The world came back to itself, damp with mud and metal and the pulse of life. I knew the prayer had changed nothing. But for a moment I had remembered how to be human, and that felt like a kind of grace.

We found a shack that served food, a roof of corrugated tin sagging over a firepit, smoke rising through holes where the rain came in. The benches were rough planks laid across oil drums and the plates were dented tin, blackened with years of use. Two women ladled rice into bowls with the care of a ritual and nodded when I came back for more. The broth was thin and sweet with fish. The warmth was real. Slocum and I ate like men just come in from the edge of the world, heads low, spoons scraping metal.

Later we walked. The boardwalk groaned under us. Someone told a crude joke. We laughed harder than the joke deserved.

At the ramp we paused.

Slocum spit into the surf.

Guess this is where we part, Irish.

See you out there, Tex.

You will. You owe me a rematch.

We shook hands. He walked into the dark and was gone.

I stood there listening to the sea. The sound of it in the hull.

And again I saw that soldier. The one with the comic book. Lit by his own mistake. The bomb that tore the world open.

Some nights it felt like we never left that beach, just kept living in its echo.

Lingayen Gulf

January 9, 1945

We left Leyte beneath a gray lid of cloud that held close to the water. The decks were loaded down for invasion. Topside the jeeps and DUKWs were lashed in rows, their canvas covers wet from the morning mist. Below, the tank deck was packed tight with Shermans and half-tracks and crates of ammunition, the steel floors slick with oil and condensation. Soldiers from the 37th Infantry were quartered there among the machines, sitting on their packs, helmets in their laps, faces drawn and quiet. The ship's belly groaned under their weight. You could feel it through the soles of your boots. A second heartbeat.

Down below the engines beat slow and patient, their rhythm steady as a pulse in the dark. The word was Luzon. Lingayen Gulf. The last great landing.

As we pushed from the bay I stood by the rail and watched the coastline slip away. The jungle hills faded into a green smudge and then nothing. Behind us lay the wreckage of battles already fought, ahead the promise of another. I wondered what waited there. What shape the dying would take this time. The talk was that the Japs had dug in deep across the island and that they would fight like men who had already written their names in the dirt.

I tried to picture the coming days and could not. War gave no clear distance. Everything ahead was smoke. You lived from hour to hour, and even those hours were uncertain. I thought about how many of us would still be here by the next sunrise. Whether I would ever see another morning at all. Whether the sea itself would take me before the war did.

I looked across the water. From horizon to horizon, ships. More than I could count. Destroyers, transports, carriers. A vast congregation of steel. They moved in silence except for the throb of their engines and the wash of their wakes. The sea itself seemed witness to the punishment of men.

By sunrise the heat had already come. The metal of the deck shimmered white. The paint along the gun mount was blistered from days under sun. The ship groaned in its seams. You could taste salt on your lips and the dry iron of it. Men moved quiet, helmets catching the light. Every one of us knew that before this day was done, some ships among us would be burning.

At seven the klaxon screamed. General Quarters. The sound cut through the morning like a blade. We ran to our stations. I strapped in behind the twenty-millimeter. Wilkins crouched beside me, his bare arms already slick with sweat. Ortega stood off to the side, his binoculars pressed to his eyes, voice calm.

You ready, Pat? Wilkins said.

I don't think ready has anything to do with it.

Doesn't matter, Ortega said. We're all we got.

We held that moment in silence.

Then Ortega spoke again, voice sharp. Contact north by west. Multiple. Low and fast.

The radio hissed to life. Bogeys inbound. Zeros.

Far ahead, the cruisers began to fire. Their salvos rolled across the gulf, deep and slow, thunder dragged through stone. Black bursts hung above the horizon. Then the battleships joined in. The sound pressed into us, deeper than hearing. The sea trembled with it.

And then we heard them. The Zeros did not sound like our planes. Ours came with a deep-throated roar, but theirs carried a thin metallic hum, unholy in its rise and fall. When they dove, that hum turned to a scream, high and wild, metal shearing in the sky. A sound that tore through the smoke and set every nerve on fire. You heard it before you saw them. That shriek of metal and wind and dying men.

Bearing three two zero, Ortega shouted. Range closing fast.

Wilkins slammed the feed drum into place.

Ready, I said.

Then the sky broke open.

The first planes came out of the sun, small and fast and silver. I fired. The gun hammered back against my shoulder. Tracers climbed through the sky in bright beads of light. One plane broke apart mid-dive, the pieces spinning away into the smoke. Another came through untouched, its engine howling.

Then I saw it. A Zero dropped from the sun like a hawk loosed from the hand of God. Its wings were steady, its dive pure. It struck the freighter alongside us dead amidships, punched through the deck, and vanished below the waterline in a burst of fire and steel. The ship bucked once and then again, her sides torn open in ragged sheets. Flames rose from her bowels and black smoke poured from the rents in her hull. Men were running, burning, falling into the sea. The ship began to list, slow at first, then steeper, the water climbing her rails. Her screws lifted clear, turning, and then she slid under, the fire snuffed out by some vast indifferent hand. The sound of it came after, deep and endless, and the sea rolled over her, a grave closing.

My hands froze on the grips. The image burned into my mind. My stomach twisted and I wanted to scream. I had seen men die before, but not that way. Not driving themselves into the end.

And it came to me then that we were not fighting ordinary men. These were men who had stripped themselves of fear and reason. I thought of Jensen's words before the Philippines, how the Japanese would come one day meaning to die. I had laughed it off. I was a believer now.

Wilkins shouted through the noise and slammed a new drum into place. Ortega called bearings, his voice sharp and steady. I fired again.

Every gun aboard pointed to the heavens, their barrels chattering, spewing yellow fire. The tracers laced the sky in a thousand burning lines. The ships around us were the same, an unbroken wall of flame and sound. Men were shadows within smoke, silhouettes against a sun gone pale. The whole sea had turned to light and thunder.

Above it all our own fighters came screaming in. Hellcats and Corsairs diving through the smoke to meet the Zeros. The sky was chaos. Planes locked together in fatal embraces. I watched our tracers climbing into their path and wondered how many of our pilots were falling to friendly guns.

A carrier off our port bow took a hit. The explosion tore her open. You could smell the fuel burning, sharp and black. Beneath it came the sickly sweetness of flesh and paint and salt.

Wilkins shouted. Port side. Two more.

I swung the gun. Tracers carved red paths through the haze. The first plane took a hit and spiraled into the sea. The second kept coming. I fired until the gun clicked empty. The Zero exploded just beyond the bow. The wave of it washed over us.

A minesweeper was hit amidships. The explosion ripped her apart. Men were blown into the sea. Some floated face down. Others thrashed and vanished. One drifted near the burning wreckage and disappeared beneath the flames. The ship was gone in minutes. Nothing left but oil and ash on the water.

More planes came, screaming low. A destroyer ahead of us caught one across her bridge. The tower folded. She went down stern first.

For a moment I lost sense of where I was. The world twisted strange. It felt like I had stepped outside my body. And then I was back. My hands gripped the gun.

The sky was screaming again. Steel rained across the water. Ships were burning. Men leaped from the decks. Some vanished and some clung to debris.

The heat was unbearable and had turned the barrel to ember. Ortega cursed and grabbed the asbestos mitten from the hook beside the mount. He clamped his hand around the barrel and twisted hard. The metal shrieked against the housing, bright flakes of rust falling in sparks. He wrenched it free and dropped it into a barrel of water. The hiss came sharp and long and filled the space between us with a living sound. Steam rose in white ribbons. He grabbed a fresh barrel from the rack and locked it into place.

It seemed to take hours. In truth it took seconds.

Wilkins slammed another drum in.

Ortega shouted. Bearing two eight zero. Two more diving.

I said, Ready.

I fired. The casings piled around our boots, hot and clinking. They reached our calves. The brass glowed faintly. A mountain of spent fury.

Every sound sharpened until it cut the mind. The crack of the gunfire, the scream of the engines, the deep roar of ships dying. Fear lived in our hands, moving them before our thoughts could catch up.

A Corsair roared past, trailing smoke. It caught a burst and vanished into the sea. The spray hit our faces.

God help us, Ortega muttered.

Wilkins reloaded with shaking hands. We need to keep firing, I said.

He nodded. His palms bled where the metal had burned him.

Beneath the noise I heard a song. Just a scrap of it, barely there. A jukebox tune from Honolulu. A woman's voice, high and strange, drifting in from another world. It made no sense. It didn't belong. But for a moment I wasn't on that gun. I was somewhere else. The war drew back, and the song rose to fill the space it left. That was when I thought I might be losing my mind. Then the song broke off. The war snapped back around me, and I was firing my gun.

By midmorning the sky was nothing but smoke and fire. The smell was everywhere. Oil and flesh and paint. It clung to your skin.

Then, slowly, it was over. The last planes pulled away. The guns fell silent. The sea hissed.

I let go of the handles. My hands raw and shaking. Wilkins sat beside the gun, chest heaving. Ortega above, his face black with soot.

The gulf burned. Ships listed, decks on fire. Smoke climbed in a black wall. The stink of metal, oil, and death lay over the water.

I looked out and thought how small we were. The sea was merciless. I thought of those men who let go of the living world. I wondered if they prayed. If they saw the same sky.

Jesus, Wilkins said. I thought we were done for.

They came out of nowhere, Ortega said.

I didn't think we'd make it either.

Those bastards meant to take us with them, Wilkins spat.

They almost did.

We stood there a long while. The deck steamed. Brass casings gleamed. The sea rolled easy now. It was the same sea that had swallowed countless ships.

I looked across to the other mounts. Men stood bent over, hands on knees. Some leaned against the rails, faces gray. Others stared at the sky. Their guns still smoking.

I saw Bull near the bow. His face blank. Eyes fixed on the horizon. A streak of soot across his cheek. His gun drooped. Smoke curled from the muzzle.

A corpsman moved with a canteen, pressing it to trembling lips. Another knelt by a sailor, his arm blackened, the flesh peeled like paper. Someone was laughing. A soft, joyless sound.

The deck was littered. Spent shells. Torn gloves. Bits of rope. A single boot without an owner. Seagulls wheeled. The wind carried the sound of burning.

I could feel my heart again. We were alive. Though I could not say what that meant.

I thought of Honolulu. Of Joyce. The scent of her skin. But those kinds of thoughts can get a man killed. I wiped my brow and turned to the gun. The sea burned. Luzon lay beyond.

The wind came soft and the world lay still. I thought of the men who had chosen death. I knew I was not like them. I did not seek the grave. I wanted to live through this hell. But wanting it was one thing and living long enough to see it was something else.

In the weeks after Lingayen, the radio carried word of Manila, a city some of the old hands called the Pearl of the Orient. It took a month to take it back. They said the Japanese moved through the streets and butchered civilians. The Pasig River carried bodies for days.

When it cleared the city was gone. They could not begin to name the dead. The true cost of the empire's dying breath.

Some called it vengeance, some madness. From where we stood it all looked the same. Manila remained no longer a city but a wound. We carried it with us without ever setting foot there. The smoke reached even the clean decks.

We heard the numbers. None of it seemed real. Over 100,000 civilians had been slaughtered by the Japanese. Yet every man aboard knew that this was the shape of the world now. We were the living, walking among what was left of men.

The sea turned quiet again. The next invasion whispered. The next shots fired would be on Japanese soil.

Iwo Jima.

Part Three

The soul that has endured war has earned the quiet of rain.
- Anonymous

The Reprieve

Saipan – February 1945

We had come out of the Philippines not long before. Leyte. Lingayen. Manila coming over the radio in pieces. Long days of fire and rain and men turned to shadows. Convoys torn open, the sky alive with flame, the sea spitting back pieces of ships and men. We watched others go under and waited for our turn, but the sea had not yet claimed us. We came north with faces that no longer belonged to boys.

We were anchored off Saipan, the ship loaded for war once more. Her decks strained under the weight of steel and ordnance. Below, the 5th Marines were stacked in their quarters, packs beneath their heads, boots lined along the bulkhead. Some slept with rifles in their arms. Others only stared at the ceiling, their eyes pale and unreadable. The tank deck groaned with the weight of Shermans. The air held grease and metal dust. The engines ticked from the test runs.

Up top the jeeps were lashed to the rails, canvas tight, the barrels of the howitzers wrapped against the salt. The morning light came without warmth, flat and gray. Out in the bay the fleet lay still and endless. The ocean smooth as slate. The quiet was so wide it felt unnatural, a world gone under cover.

Word spread in whispers. Iwo Jima. The name carried a silence all its own. No one said it aloud for long. It was the kind of name that made men swallow and look away.

We had survived six campaigns. From the Aleutians to the Marshalls. From Tarawa to Leyte. Years of storms and hunger and men who never came back. We buried friends in the sea and watched their names fade from the logbook like they'd never lived. All that remained were the ghosts we carried in our heads, their faces rising sometimes in the hum of the engines or the rattle of a loose chain.

I was tired in a way that went deeper than the body. The mind dulls after a time. You stop believing there's an end to anything. I'd spent every bit of luck I was given, and what remained was borrowed. There's a feeling before an invasion, a waiting that creeps into your bones, and I felt it now as I walked the deck. The sound of my boots on steel echoed with the distant patience of a clock.

That morning I was topside, checking lashings, taking up the slack in the chains that bound the jeeps. The deck plates were hot beneath my boots. Sweat ran down my face and into my collar. The sky hung colorless over the bay. All around us the fleet shimmered in the haze, hundreds of ships riding at anchor, their black gun barrels turned toward the horizon.

We were standing on the edge of a thing vast and unseen.

A Navy inspection unit came aboard before noon. They climbed the ladder in pressed whites, shoes so clean they caught the light. They carried clipboards and pencils, their faces set in that quiet expression of men who'd never been near what we'd seen. They moved across the deck slow and methodical, tapping rails and testing welds while their eyes traced every line of the ship. The captain walked with them, the exec at his side. Their heads bent together in low talk. I saw the captain gesture sharply. One of the inspectors shook his head. Whatever was said, it left a shadow on the old man's face.

Fowler came up beside me. A wiry deckhand, half an ear gone from Tarawa, his coveralls streaked black. He wiped his hands on a rag and squinted toward the officers.

Look at them, he said. Clean as a church choir.

Probably wondering how we made it this far, I told him.

If they find a scratch maybe they'll call the whole thing off.

Wouldn't that be swell.

I'd even help them polish, he said. Be worth it.

He chuckled once, low in his throat, and spit over the side.

They look like undertakers, he said.

Maybe they are, I said.

He nodded and went below.

The inspectors vanished into the captain's cabin. The deck went quiet again. Only the slow pulse of the generators and the clang of a wrench somewhere deep in the hull. The sun climbed high, baking the paint, turning oil and salt in the air acrid and old. The men worked without words. There was nothing left to say.

Maybe thirty minutes passed. Then came a low groan from deep in the hull, and the ship shuddered. Hydraulics whining. Gears straining. The bow doors began to open.

It made no sense. We weren't scheduled to move.

The ramp dropped with a hollow clang that rolled through the bay. Below, engines coughed to life, light blue smoke pouring from the vents.

The Shermans rolled down the ramp one after another, steel tracks grinding. The sound filled the ship, deep and resonant, trembling through the plates beneath our boots. The Marines stood in line, faces blank, rifles hanging at their sides.

What in the hell is going on.

The jeeps followed, then the trucks. The ship rose with each ton that left her belly until she rode light in the water once more. When it was done, silence.

I found the gunnery officer near the rail. His sleeves were rolled up, his jaw set tight.

What's happening, I asked.

He didn't look at me. Captain will speak to us later, he said. That's all I know.

By afternoon the ship was hollow. Footsteps echoed through her decks with a churchlike hush. The men moved slower than before. The air had shifted, and we all felt it.

At dusk we were called topside. The sky over Saipan burned red, and the sea carried it in thin red smears. Captain Whelan stood before us with the exec beside him. The wind lifted his cap and the lines of his face looked carved from the same steel we stood on. His voice carried clear across the deck.

Men, he said. I suppose you're wondering why we've emptied the ship.

We nodded. Every man of us.

The inspection team found eight cracks across our main deck, he said. Structural. Deep. Medium seas could swamp us. We're not seaworthy.

He drew a slow breath, the light fading from his face. I know what that means. We were to take part in the Iwo Jima landings. And I know what that place will be. But the order has come down. We won't sail north.

He paused, eyes sweeping the line of men.

We're going home. San Francisco.

The silence that followed was strange and absolute. Then it broke. A laugh from somewhere aft. Another from the bow. Soon the deck was alive with shouts and laughter. Some men clapped, some cried, some only looked at the sky like they'd never seen it before.

Whelan stood and let it go on a while, a hint of a smile ghosting his face, then raised his hand.

That's enough, he said. Compose yourselves. We sail at dawn with a convoy of other damaged ships and a couple of cruiser escorts, all of us patched and limping east for home.

We're not out of the woods. Pray for calm seas. If we find rough water with the damage we've taken, she'll take on more than she can bear.

The laughter faded. The men listened. The wind came up faint and steady. The ship creaked and groaned against the current. A cable rattled somewhere forward. The sky had gone the color of rust and smoke.

You've seen what the Pacific can do, he said. Don't forget it now. Then Captain Whelan turned and walked to the bridge. His boots rang once, twice, and were gone.

No one spoke. For a while we just stood there, breathing in the warm wind. Then Fowler broke the silence.

We dodged a bullet, he said.

Hell, we dodged the whole magazine, I told him.

Bull came grinning, his face streaked with grime.

I was halfway through writing my will, he said. Guess I can tear it up.

Nicky drew a smoke from his pocket and lit it off a match cupped in his palm.

You tear that thing up every time we ship out, he said.

Bull shrugged. Maybe this time it sticks.

Wilkins leaned from the hatch. His face had that boyishness, like the war hadn't managed to take it yet.

Frisco, boys, he said. Drinks on me if I remember how whiskey tastes.

Nicky called back, You never knew.

And we all laughed. Low and long and half in disbelief.

The captain's warning hung over it all, quiet as a prayer. The sea was calm now, but no one trusted it.

I leaned on the rail, the heat trapped in the steel. The sun went down behind the ridges, bleeding through the clouds until the whole sky glowed in molten iron. The wind carried salt and an old sourness, rust and life turning together in the same breath.

I thought of Leyte. Of that night when the sky went white and the ammo dump on shore went up like a thousand suns. The shockwave had lifted the ship clean out of the water. The deck had cracked beneath our boots. A soldier had left a light burning while he read a comic book. He died for it. But it had saved us now. The same cracks that had cursed us then were the reason we'd be going home.

It is a strange world.

Men lingered on the deck, quiet now. Some kneeling, some staring east. Their faces wet with sweat and tears.

San Francisco. The word itself carried grace.

I stayed long after the others had gone below. The stars came out cold and countless. The water below moved black and slow, and the ship rose and fell in a long breathing rhythm. I thought of the 5th Marines who would soon land on that island of ash. I thought of the men who'd gone before us, their bones scattered in the deep.

Somewhere below, laughter echoed faintly, the low worn sound of men spared one more time.

I looked toward the dark horizon. Saipan's lights burned low along the shore. Beyond them lay Iwo Jima, waiting with its black sand and hidden guns, waiting now for others.

By the good grace of God the seas held. The weather stayed mild, the wind soft out of the east. The swells came slow and patient, the ocean grown weary of breaking men. The sky turned pale in the mornings and gold by dusk. Days slid into each other until time lost shape.

We stopped in Guam to take on fuel and stores. There was no liberty and no wandering the docks. The Navy wanted the ship whole again and the work done quick. Crates of rations and rope and diesel drums came aboard under the crane, swinging over the deck with the slow certainty of fate. Men hauled and stacked and cursed. Sweat darkened the backs of our shirts. The heat pressed against the steel until it hummed.

At Pearl Harbor we tied up just long enough to refuel and take on water. We stood topside and watched the harbor lights shiver across the water. No one asked to go ashore. We had stopped belonging to the land somewhere back in the Marshalls. The cranes moved slow over the docks, patient and blind, while white birds wheeled above them.

Life aboard settled into a rough kind of peace. The war had passed us by, for now. Men smiled more. The laughter in the mess was easier. Nicky ran a poker game in the corner, smooth as a preacher taking tithes, and Bull lost two weeks' pay before he knew it. Walker tried heating his coffee with a torch and blew the flame out with a curse that echoed through the passageway. Nicky said he'd just invented naval combat. Even the cook laughed at that.

We rigged the boxing ring again in the tank deck. Ropes frayed and slack, the canvas patched and sweat-stained. The light came from one bare bulb, swaying with the ship, sending the shadows along the walls in slow dark waves. The heat down there had no give, and the clang of boots on metal rang through the hold. When the gloves came out the men gathered close, bare-chested and hungry for noise, shouting in that old language of sailors who had seen too much and still had fight left in them.

I boxed often. It gave shape to the waiting. I boxed a machinist's mate named Reardon out of Ohio, a lean farm boy with hands built for old work and a quiet in him that could unnerve a man. He seldom spoke. When he did, his words came slow, weighed and measured before leaving his mouth. He fought straight and honest, hands high, wasting no punch. When the bell rang he would nod once, calm as a man splitting wood, and come at me. He could take a beating and give no sign it had reached him. When it was over he wiped the sweat from his face and said only, That'll do.

The other was a boatswain's mate named Kelley from Florida, thick-necked and sun-browned, with eyes the color of sea glass and a temper that flared quick and hot. He fought angry, every swing carrying an old wrong that had stayed with him. His breath came harsh through his nose and he would drive in close, shoulders rolling, gloves cracking like wet canvas. He never smiled, not in the ring or out. When I caught him clean he staggered back and shook his head once. He grinned without joy, the way a man does when all he has left is the fight.

But the bout that stayed with me most was with McDaniel, the black gang crew chief. He had the body of a dock piling and a voice that could grind stone. He gave the black gang no rest. Every watch he found fault. The pressure too low. The feed too slow. The gauges wrong even when they were right. I had taken his shouting and his smirk and the long nights he left us sweating in the dark of the engine room, his voice riding us hard through that furnace of steel and noise. When the gloves came on I wanted to knock him down for every hour he had made us endure.

He came at me hard, fists wild, his breath loud in his throat. I hit him square and his head snapped back. After the first round he spat blood. Said I was showing off. I told him I was just hitting what was in front of me. He came again and I caught him with a left that buckled his knees. Keep hitting like that, Flynn, and I'm going bare-knuckled, he said, blood running over his teeth. I wanted to oblige him, but I didn't need him riding my ass harder in the engine room. Sorry about that, I said. I'll tone it down. The men shouted and stomped the deck. When it ended he smiled through the blood. You hit like you mean it, he said. I nodded. I did.

That night he brought me a cigarette on the fantail. The sea moved slow beneath us, the wake shining faint with light. He smoked a while in silence. You're all right, kid, he said at last. Then he flicked the butt into the dark and walked off into the wind.

There were moments of foolishness that felt almost holy. One night old Whitey found a dented trumpet in a crate and tried to play it. The sound came out low and awful, a dying whale down in the deep, and Hendricks laughed so hard he fell against the bulkhead. Bull tried to dance, his boots slipped, and both of them went down tangled in rope and laughter. The noise rolled through the deck as music, and men came from their bunks to watch. Even the captain came by, his hands behind his back, the ghost of a smile on his face. He said nothing, only stood there a while, warmed by a memory he kept private.

Later we hung a sheet across the tank deck and set up a projector borrowed from the wardroom. The film was some old comedy, grainy and skipping, full of men falling into barrels and women fainting at nothing at all. The reel stuttered and the sound came thin through the speaker. For an hour we sat there in the flicker of it, faces lit and open, laughing until our ribs hurt. For that small piece of time, the war seemed far away.

But even in the laughter the shadow of it lingered. It lived in the quiet after, when the ship rolled and creaked and the sea whispered beneath the hull. I boxed until the skin split over my knuckles, and when the gloves came off I leaned against the rail and watched the water slide by. It went on forever, dark and endless and without memory.

Sometimes I thought back to Hollandia. The night the storm came down from the mountains and rolled over the bay with the hand of God. The wind howled through the rigging, rain so hard it stung the eyes. We had lashed the jeeps and the tanks, and the sea came for us in sheets of white, beating the steel till it rang. The deck pitched under us, alive with the force of a great animal. Chains screamed. Water tore through the scuppers. Lightning split the sky and for a heartbeat everything was clear. The men bent over their work, their faces white and their eyes wide, every soul aboard caught between prayer and defiance.

We lived through that storm by some mercy I couldn't name. If one weld had given way, one chain had snapped, the sea would have taken us whole.

At night I leaned against the rail and watched the horizon blur into the dark. The sea moved slow and black beneath the stars. The ship's steel bones groaned with their own tiredness. Somewhere deep below, the engines throbbed, a great heart keeping time.

We sailed on beneath a sky vast and empty. The convoy stretched to the edge of sight, the other ships rolling in the long swells, their wakes trailing pale ribbons of light. The sea broke against our hull in long white sighs. Sometimes, in the stillness before dawn, the world felt like it had stopped turning altogether.

Every sunrise came soft and golden. Every night a map of stars that felt older than the war, older than men. The sea had spared us, for now. And for that, we asked no questions.

One afternoon I went topside to clean the fantail. The sun lay low across the Pacific and the light came down red and wide over the water. The sea stretched away smooth as hammered metal and the ship moved through it slow, her engines low and patient, her hull cutting a long white scar behind her. Heat lifted off the deck in soft wavering sheets. Salt came to my lips, mixed with fuel and paint and the old metallic breath of work done by men in close quarters.

The ship had grown tired. You could see it where rust bled from the bolts and gathered under the seams. The hull patches told the rest, each repair laid over some old violence. The brass rails had lost their shine. The rivets were dark with grime. Even the wind crossing her decks felt used up by war.

Voices carried from near the ladder. The stewards were at work there, polishing brass cups until they caught the light and flung it back against the bulkhead. They were talking low, laughing at some small thing. Their laughter rose and fell with the motion of the sea, and I found myself listening to it as one listens to a sound from home, a human note cutting through the emptiness. I had spoken little with them since Jackson left the ship. But that afternoon I felt the need to.

The new steward was there. Richardson, they said his name was. A short man, soft in the middle, with the uneasy look of a man who never knew quite what was expected of him. Sweat ran freely down his temples and along his neck, soaking the collar of his whites. When he smiled it was quick and fleeting, his eyes darting away again as though even his smile needed permission. His handshake was weak, his palm slick and trembling, the grip of a man afraid to be measured. I could see that Snowball had chosen him himself. He would not make the same mistake twice.

Snowball stood nearby, arms folded across his chest. His uniform was spotless, the creases sharp. His shoes held a dark glass shine. He carried himself with pride in his post, and the way he watched the others told you he liked control for its own sake. Smith stood at the rail, working a rag over the metal. He moved slowly, though the place beneath his hand already shone.

How's the guitar, Smith, I said.

He looked up and grinned. You mean Sally.

I laughed. I knew you'd name that thing.

Sure did. She's been good to me. Been learning a few new tunes. She purrs like a kitten in my hands.

Yeah.

Yeah, he said. Got one about a girl waiting on a train that never comes. Heard it from an army boy down below. Sad one. I like those best. Another's an old hymn but I play it slow. Sounds adrift, too far from shore.

He smiled a little as he spoke, and the light caught in his eyes. The wind tugged at his sleeves, and the sound of the sea pressed faint against the hull. For a while we talked about music. Chords. Strings. The way a song could hold a man steady. It felt good to speak of something untouched by killing.

Then Snowball spoke, quiet at first, testing the air before he stepped into it.

So you heard about Jackson?

No, I said. What kind of trouble did he get himself in.

Snowball turned toward me. His eyes were unreadable.

Dead kind of trouble, he said.

The words struck me like one of Jackson's right hooks, sudden and absolute.

The deck went quiet. The voices faded. Only the sound of the ocean came up through the heat.

What do you mean.

Firing squad, he said.

I froze. My hands slick on the mop handle.

How. Why.

Snowball exhaled through his nose.

It was on Guadalcanal, he said. He went into a bar one night looking for a drink. They wouldn't serve him. Told him the place was for sailors, not stewards. There was a man there, a gunner's mate from another ship, half drunk and talking big. White fella. He started laughing at Jackson. Said things no decent man should ever say. Jackson told him to shut it. The man shoved him.

Snowball's voice stayed calm, but there was iron beneath it.

They went to fighting right there in the bar. Tables went over. Bottles broke. Jackson was a strong man and he fought hard, but there were too many of them. Someone hit him with a chair. He went down, and when he came up again, he had his knife in his hand. That same one he always kept in his boot. He swung it once, maybe twice. They say that boy was dead before he hit the floor.

Snowball looked off toward the horizon.

After that the place went mad. The others jumped him. Beat him till he stopped moving. MPs pulled them off before they killed him. They said when they dragged him out his hand kept hunting for the knife. His face was so torn up they could hardly tell who he was.

He went quiet for a while.

They court-martialed him on the island. The Navy wanted it quiet. Didn't take long. The man he killed was white. They said he was guilty before he ever opened his mouth. They shot him behind the barracks at dawn. Six rifles. No chaplain and no last words.

He paused. His eyes fixed on a far distance, the whole thing laid out before him.

They say he stood straight when they tied him to the post. Never flinched. Never bowed his head. Just looked at the sky till they fired.

The wind shifted and the sound of the sea filled the silence.

You stopped him once, Flynn, Snowball said. You kept him from killing Cohen. But you couldn't save Jackson. All you did was point him in a new direction. Like a hurricane changing course. You sent him walking another road that led to the same end. None of us could have changed that. The world does not make room for that kind of man.

He turned to me again. Snowball watched me close. He knew the weight I was taking on, could see it in the way my eyes had gone somewhere else. He could sense I was already blaming myself for unleashing Jackson on that poor dead sailor, carrying the blood and ruin as my own doing.

None of this is on you, Flynn, Snowball said. Don't carry that. The world does its own killing. Always has. Jackson had too much in him and nowhere for it to go. This was always the way they were going to meet him.

I said nothing. The horizon was white and wide. The sun burned low, and the sea carried a hard bronze shine.

Jackson's face came to me then. The scar on his chin. The wildness in his eyes when he was cornered. I could see him in that bar, the sweat on his face and the knife in his hand. Chaos all around him. The shouting. The blood and then the silence that followed.

I thought of him standing before those rifles. The sky pale. The ground hard. Grass and oil drifting together, carrying the same quiet promise of ending. I thought of the men who pulled the triggers, how they must have looked at him, how some of them might have closed their eyes when the order came.

Smith had gone still. The rag hung limp in his hand.

Jackson wasn't built to fold sheets or serve meals to officers, he said, shaking his head. Damn shame what happened to him.

Snowball stood at the rail, unmoving. His jaw was tight, his eyes far away.

Richardson stood by the ladder, head bowed, sweat running down his neck.

The ship rolled slow under us. I leaned on the mop handle and watched the wake draw long behind, pale and broken, a road made of dying light. The engines beat their steady rhythm far below, the sound of a heart that refused to stop.

I thought then of how one small thing could turn a life. A word spoken. A door closed. A man denied a drink because of the color of his skin. The sea does not care for justice. It remembers. Always.

Jackson was a storm that followed. Wild and inevitable. The kind that tears through and leaves the air empty and the world changed.

The sun sank deeper and the sea burned red. I finished my work though the deck was already clean, and the water in the bucket sat black and unmoving.

The ship rolled slow and steady on the long easterly run, her bow cutting through a calm sea glazed with pale light. The engines throbbed deep below, the same pulse that had carried us through fire and smoke and all manner of dying. Some things can be mended. Steel can be hammered straight. Decks repainted. Engines made to run true again. But men were harder. Some came home with damage no hand could reach. Jackson was one of those. Whatever cracked in him, he carried it clear through. As the ship rolled toward home, I knew there are some things on this earth that cannot be fixed.

THE BRIG

We came in through the Gate at dawn. The fog lay over the water, pale and drifting, parting only in slow breaths. Somewhere beyond it the Pacific stretched away in its endless gray silence, carrying with it all the things we'd left behind.

When the mist broke, the Golden Gate Bridge rose before us, immense and red and glistening with the wet of morning. The towers loomed over the mouth of the bay, their cables vanishing into cloud, humming with the wind. The span rose above us, mercy and menace held in the same red arc.

We passed beneath her slow, the ship listing slightly, her plates sprung and her seams breathing like tired lungs. The engines labored, each turn of the screw a slow heartbeat. The men stood along the rails, caps in hand, silent. The ship slid beneath the iron span with her plates sprung and scarred. Above us the bridge held its silence, vast in the morning, watching another wounded thing come home.

The fog clung to her girders, and the wind strained through the cables with a low iron moan. Then she was behind us and the bay opened wide and gray, the city waking beyond it. Smoke rose from the chimneys. The gulls wheeled and cried. The spell broke, and the world came back.

We limped into San Francisco in a ragged convoy, more funeral procession than fleet. The war had bent us near to breaking. Our main deck was split in eight places, the welds sprung and weeping rust. The bow plates warped with the bend of old bone. When the swells rolled under us, you could hear the steel cry. It was a miracle we made it home at all.

They tied us up along the pier among a dozen wounded ships. The dock carried the tang of oil and salt and the strange sweetness of burned paint. The welders crossed the decks slowly, heads lowered over their work. Torches hissed in their hands, and chalk dust followed them in pale drifts. The noise of hammers carried over the water, the heartbeat of the bay itself.

We'd be going into dry dock soon. They'd open her up, peel back her plates, and lay bare all that the war had done to her. For now she rested, creaking softly against her lines, an old horse led home and left to stand in the yard till daylight.

The days blurred together. Gray mornings. Hammer strikes. The bitter stink of cutting torches and wet iron. The ship lay still, waiting her turn for the dock. Then the list went up on the board: one day's liberty for those not on watch. I signed my name and went ashore alone. I followed the streetcar tracks into the heart of Frisco, where the fog turned to rain and the shop windows burned gold against the wet street.

Downtown was a world of noise and motion. The cable cars screamed on the rails, and the shopgirls leaned in the doorways smoking cigarettes wrapped in red lipstick. Christmas trees gone brown and slumped in the gutters. Paper stars taped to the glass, forgotten.

I went from store to store with my pockets loaded with back pay and my head still somewhere out on the water. I bought a scarf for Mom, blue with a white fringe, soft untouched by the cold. For Dad, a pipe carved from cherrywood and a pouch of tobacco that smelled like home. For my brothers, tins of pomade and a deck of cards with girls drawn on them, smiling as though they knew the joke. For my sister, a small bottle of perfume, cheap and floral and lovely. I had to smell three before I found the one that reminded me of spring before the war. I had all of it wrapped in brown paper and tied with string and tucked under my arm. Not too much. I'd be the one hauling it when my leave finally came.

The city was alive with sailors. Bluecoats and white hats and that restless laughter that belongs to men who've seen too much and plan to forget it for a while. Streetcorner bands. Newsboys yelling. A blind man selling pencils from a tray. The whole place humming with noise and life. I stepped into a bar off Market Street, drawn by the sound of music and the promise of warmth.

Inside it was dim and crowded. The windows fogged. The place breathed heat and noise, a beast fed on laughter and spilled gin. Somebody said it was a sailor's birthday and the drinks were on the house. That was all it took. Bottles clinked and laughter rose, and I let it carry me. A jukebox in the corner played a slow tune about home and rain and girls who long for love. I raised one glass and then another. The edges of the world softened. The hours lost their shape.

Men shouted over the music. One sailor climbed onto the counter and tried to dance, knocking over bottles, the barkeep shouting half in anger and half in laughter. Another showed off a raw tattoo fresh from the needle, a hula girl bent at the waist, her colors wet. A girl with a ribbon in her hair passed with a tray of drinks. Someone reached and she swatted him without spilling a drop. The crowd roared. The jukebox blared a fast number, all brass and heartbeat. Some men danced, others just swayed and drank and forgot.

I sat back and watched it all. The laughter, the music, the unspoken knowledge that every man there was burning through his own short mercy of time. The hours drained out of the day, and I made no claim on them.

By the time I left the bar, it was afternoon, the fog beginning to roll in off the bay. The streets gleamed with rain, the lights winking to life in the shop windows. I made my way to the Navy bus stop, gifts tucked under my arm, the wind sharp enough to wake the dead. There was a line a block long. Sailors packed shoulder to shoulder, smoking, jawing, stamping their feet. The buses idled, belching diesel. The whole scene looked like a slow migration back to the sea.

In one of the buses I spotted Southern. He was from the ship, an oiler from Tennessee, tall and lean, his jaw cut hard as hickory. Quiet man, but decent. We'd talked a few times on watch, mostly about home. I called his name and he turned, saw me, grinned. He slid the bus window down and waved me over.

I cut through the line to the jeers of a hundred sailors. They shouted to get back where I belonged, called me every name in the book. But I didn't care. I tossed my packages through the window and started climbing in after them, laughing at the absurdity of it all. Halfway in, halfway out, when it came. Five or six of the hardest whacks I've ever taken. Fire ran through my backside, bright and mean. Invisible hands yanked me out of the window.

I turned and there he was. A military policeman, red-faced and square-jawed, swinging that nightstick with every intention of beating the joke out of me.

What do you think you're doing, sailor.

My buddy said I could climb aboard.

You're drunk, aren't you.

Maybe. I tried to look offended but my grin betrayed me.

Come with me.

He grabbed my arm and pulled me through the crowd. Some laughed. Others shook their heads. I stumbled into the paddy wagon, hat crooked, dignity gone. Inside were a dozen men like me, worn down and drunk. The air had gone sour with whiskey and bodies. One man hummed tunelessly. Another stared at the floor, motionless. The MP slammed the door and we jolted into motion.

Through the small barred window I could see the city sliding past. The fog swallowing the towers. The lights turning the wet pavement gold. Frisco rolling away, a dream already gone. I thought about the gifts left on that bus, Mom's scarf and my sister's little bottle of perfume. My father lighting his pipe. Then the memory slipped, dulled by the sway of the wagon and the ache in my bones.

We reached the jail near the Embarcadero as the last light drained from the sky. They herded us out one by one, lined us up under a bare bulb. The floor slick with tracked rain. The sergeant behind the desk didn't even look up.

Name, rank, ship.

I gave him mine. He sighed and wrote it down.

They took my belt and cap and tie and tossed them in a bin. I stood there stripped down to my shirt, the top button undone, feeling reduced to a schoolboy caught sneaking cigarettes. Then they pointed to the holding cell. Steel bars. Cold and dark.

The cell was long and narrow, boxed in by walls the color of ash. The floor was cracked cement, slick and stained, with a rusted drain in the middle that looked like it had swallowed more than water. Along the walls stood a row of iron cots, thin as hunger, canvas stained with the memory of a thousand sorry nights.

The air was foul. Sweat and whiskey and something worse. Men slumped on bunks or paced in tight circles. One crooned to no one. Another sat in the corner, his eyes unfocused, mouth working silently.

Then a man in the far corner leaned forward and vomited into the drain. The sound was a wet heave that echoed off the concrete.

Jesus Christ, someone said.

Plug your damn nose, another barked.

The smell rose off the deck in a sour, sickening wave. Another sailor gagged, then doubled over and added to it.

Ah hell, a voice groaned. Now we're all gonna catch it.

Soon the air was alive with it, a wretched chorus of gagging and spittle and misery. A sick music filled the place, the sound of men brought low and bound to the ruin they had made of themselves.

One man slipped in it and fell, swearing. Goddamn floor's alive, he muttered.

Another laughed through his hiccups. Welcome to the Navy, boys.

A third shouted toward the bars. Hey guard, you gonna hose this pit down or just let us drown in puke. The guard never looked up from his newspaper. Shut your mouths and sleep it off, he said flatly.

Sleep, someone said. Who the hell can sleep in this stink.

I pressed my sleeve against my face and breathed through the wool. My eyes burned. My stomach clenched but held. I found a spot in the corner and sat silent, my back against the cold stone. I sobered up fast. The place had that effect on a man.

A sailor with a busted nose started a fight.

You looked at me funny, he said.

I looked at you cause you're ugly, the other replied.

The first man swung wild and caught him on the chin, only to get laid out cold for his trouble. Ten minutes later he came to, wiped the blood from his mouth, and did it again. Same outcome.

Somebody teach that fool to stay down, one voice said.

He don't learn, said another.

He rose a third time, swearing vengeance on everyone who'd ever worn blue. Two men stepped forward and dropped him clean. Then, tired of the show, they dragged his limp body to a corner and shoved him under one of the cots.

You think he's dead, someone asked.

Maybe he's lucky, came the reply.

I never saw him move again.

Nobody checked. Nobody spoke. The cell fell quiet except for the breathing. The minutes dragged. The bulb swung slow on its wire, marking time that refused to move. I thought I'd been dropped into a place reserved for men the sea didn't want. The walls seemed to lean inward. The air stank of endings. I thought of the ship and how far away it felt.

I thought of home too, but it felt small now. Out of reach.

Somewhere in that night I promised myself I'd never see another liberty like this one again.

They came deep in the night. Keys jangling. Orders barked. Boots in the corridor. We rose slow, blinking, dazed. The door opened with a clang and we filed out. Disinfectant and rain lay in the corridor.

They gave us back our belts and caps and neckties without a word. Marched us out to the waiting paddy wagon, our footsteps beating out the rhythm of a fading parade. Outside, the fog hung low and pale. Streetlamps burned soft as coals.

The wagons rolled toward the waterfront, stopping at each ship. Names called. Men stumbled out into the mist, handed over like lost property.

When mine came, the guard checked his watch.

9:55 p.m. You're lucky. Five more minutes and you'd be AWOL.

They walked me up the gangway, boots loud on steel.

This sailor was drunk and disorderly at the bus. Spent the night in the brig. He's yours now.

The watch officer nodded.

All right, sailor. Hit the rack. Captain'll see you in the morning.

The air aboard was hot with oil and scorched metal. The ship sat in her cradle, belly opened wide, torches hissing. I found my bunk. On the mattress were the packages I'd bought. Southern had kept them. I set them aside and lay down in my clothes. Sleep came fast and deep.

In the morning I was called to the captain's cabin. Coffee and pipe smoke sat in the room. Captain Whelan sat behind his desk in shirtsleeves. Light from the porthole cut across his face. He didn't look angry. Just tired.

Pat. What happened.

There was a mix-up. I told him part of it. I'd had a few. Meant no harm.

He watched me, eyes steady.

You know I could court-martial you.

Yes, sir.

But I'm not going to. You've been solid aboard this ship. You'll be confined to ship two weeks. Extra duties. Understood?

Yes, sir.

Don't make me regret it.

No, sir.

I saluted and stepped out. My head throbbed. My backside ached. But I walked away lighter.

Topside, the morning fog was lifting. Sunlight spilled through the cranes and girders, falling in bands across the dock. Light flared from the welders patching the hull. Bright against the steel.

I thought about the night before. How close a man could come to ruin without knowing he'd stepped over the line.

Then the whistle blew for muster. And I turned to go. The ship waited, scarred and steadfast. I went to my duties, grateful to still have them. Above the dock the welders' sparks floated and died in the air, small brief lights that should not have been there and were.

SAN JOSE

— • —

I earned a weekend's liberty and thought I'd ride it south. My aunt lived in San Jose with my uncle who managed the Santa Clara Hotel. They had three kids I hadn't seen in years. I remembered them small and sunburned, running barefoot through the dust, hollering wild through the corn. I figured it was time. Time to look them in the eyes and remember I had blood in the world.

At the station I stepped into a glass phone booth. The coins were slick in my hand. The train behind me huffed its slow breath and the steel underfoot vibrated with its idle hunger. I closed the door and the noise of the city fell away like a tide. The world on the other side of the glass became shape and shadow. I dropped a coin and heard it fall through some unseen chute of time.

Then her voice.

Hello?

Aunt Margaret, I said. It's me. Patrick.

There was a silence, then a sharp intake of breath. Patrick? My god. Is it really you?

It's me. I got liberty this weekend. Thought I'd come visit.

Lord have mercy, she said. You come. You come stay with us. We'll set the table. The kids'll be beside themselves. I'll have your uncle bring home a roast.

I smiled though she couldn't see it. I should be there by dinner, I said.

We'll keep it warm for you. You be careful now.

I will.

She was my father's sister. A small, square woman with strong arms and bad knees. Worked in the canneries until the chemicals ruined her hands. After that, the laundry. Steam and bleach and the slow death of skin. Her voice carried the tone of someone who'd known both love and cruelty and survived them both. When I was a boy she'd sneak me pie crusts from the cooling rack and whisper things about my father he wouldn't have told me himself. She had his eyes. That pale flint gray. When she smiled, I saw the part of him that had existed before the hardening.

Her husband was a quiet man with the worn hands of a carpenter and the silence of a man who knew the weight of waiting. He'd been too old for the war. He worked in shoes. I remembered him mending soles on the porch, tobacco burning slow in his pipe. They were the kind of people who left porch lights on. Who believed that if a man went to war, he'd come home again. That God's ledger kept the right columns.

The line went dead. I hung up and stepped back into the noise and smell and motion of the station. The booth door sighed closed behind me.

The train pulled me south through the long throat of the valley. The orchards came close, limbs slick with rain, fruit swollen and red in the morning dark. The windows rattled with the breath of the machine. Men slept in their coats, arms crossed, mouths open. I watched the country pass. Rain streaked the glass like tears turned sideways.

San Jose came up around noon. Pale sky, low roofs. Light scattered on wet pavement. The scent of turned soil and stonefruit. I had hours to kill before dinner so I walked the streets, past cafes and barbershops and hardware stores with windows gone milky from the years.

Storefronts stood open to the daylight. A woman swept the steps of a dress shop, her back bent. A man smoked with his foot on a crate. A boy on a bicycle threw a folded newspaper without looking. The town had the soft hush of places passed over by storms. A gentleness held in prayer.

There was a bar down a narrow street, its sign broken, the neon giving off a thin electric snarl. I stood outside a long time before going in.

The light in there was warm and golden. The wood dark and sweating with years of hands and spills. A jukebox in the back sang a low and mournful tune. The place had the stillness of a church that had forgotten what to pray for. A few men sat hunched over their glasses. I took a seat at the bar. The drink came wordless. The ice cracked loud in the quiet.

Across the room sat a sailor with two women. The man had a hard predatory look, all shoulders and cold patience. His hair black, his uniform immaculate. A cigarette lived in his hand. The women were dressed for someplace else. The blonde had a laugh that missed the eyes. The other one had dark curls and sharp cheekbones, with eyes that could wound a man or mend him depending on the hour. Her face hardly changed, but her eyes missed nothing.

The man raised his glass and nodded me over.

Hey sailor. Pull up a chair.

I didn't move at first. I watched the room stretch thin around us. The old songs played low. Time seemed to hold its breath. Then I took my glass and crossed the floor.

Name's Wolf, he said. USS Gallatin. You?

Flynn. LST. Frisco.

This here's Vera, he said. And the blonde's Darlene. You might as well know their names before they rob you blind.

You only get robbed if you stay the night, said Darlene.

She gave a tired smile, one she seemed to have carried too long.

We drank. We told stories we didn't care if the others believed. Wolf said he drank once with a boxer in Manila who'd lost his name in the war and only answered to Kid. Vera claimed she was raised in a funeral home and could embalm a man if given a needle and a bottle of gin. Darlene said she once danced in a gold room in Reno where the mirrors ran floor to ceiling and nobody ever saw their own reflection.

I said less. I watched them closely. Vera's hands were ringless, her nails clean. She drank slow, always with her eyes on Wolf. Darlene fidgeted. She folded her napkin in neat triangles and then tore them apart. Wolf had a scar above his eyebrow that ran like a fault line. I wondered who'd put it there.

At one point Vera asked me if I had family. I said yes. She said nothing.

I stood there pretending I was ready to leave. Said I had someplace else to be. Wolf smiled through his smoke. One more won't kill you, he said. I believed him.

Wolf lifted his hand for another round. Darlene leaned closer.

Don't go just yet, she said. The night's still figuring out what it wants to be.

We left the bar when the light outside had turned the color of rust. The air was wet and the lamps burned dull in the fog. The streets were nearly empty. Our footsteps sounded too loud.

The motel sat behind a gas station, a two-story box with peeling paint and a lobby that stank of mildew and wax. The clerk didn't look up. One key. Room upstairs. Thin walls. Two beds.

Wolf set the six-pack and the bottle on the dresser. The radio was already humming. A low, weathered voice sang of heartbreak and freight yards. He pulled a deck from his pocket and slapped it once against his palm.

Strip poker, he said. If you're not afraid of the truth.

I almost laughed. Almost.

Vera poured the drinks. Darlene lit a cigarette. The room began to drift.

Wolf dealt quick, the cards sliding across the table like bones.

Vera lost first. She sighed and took off her shoes with the weariness of a woman removing an old burden. Darlene grinned and shrugged off her coat. Wolf rolled his sleeves. I drank.

Next hand came fast. Laughter rolled through the room, then thinned away. Darlene leaned forward and brushed my hand. Her skin was warm. Her perfume hung faint and sweet as decay.

Wolf cheated. We let him. Darlene said something about fate being a crooked dealer. Vera didn't laugh.

Clothes came off slow, a performance for no one in particular. The bottle dwindled. The walls drew closer.

At some point Darlene stood. She'd lost again. Her blouse hung open. She reached back and fumbled with the clasp of her bra.

Can somebody help me? she said. Laughing a little, like she might cry if she didn't.

Vera moved to rise, but Darlene stopped her with a glance.

No. I want sailor boy.

I stood. My hands weren't steady. I touched her back, the line of her spine sharp beneath the skin. Her shoulder blades shifted under my fingers, warm as sin beneath my hand.

She turned her head slightly. Her eyes met mine and there was no seduction in them. Just a long tiredness. A look that said she had asked the same question of a hundred men and never got an answer that held.

The next hand never came.

The deck was forgotten. The beds pushed together.

The room went quiet except for the low murmur of the radio and the small sounds of people choosing not to be alone.

I don't remember much after that. Just moments. The scrape of the bed frame. The hush of her breath near my throat. Her hand in mine and then not. The rain beginning somewhere outside. The slow unravel of everything I was trying to forget.

We didn't speak.

There are nights that burn you clean. And others that leave their stain.

This was both.

I woke in the gray hush of dawn. Darlene lay beside me, curled small, her hand forgotten on my chest. The room was a ruin of bottles and clothes, stinking of whiskey, heat, and spent desire. I watched her breathe.

For a moment I almost believed in the quiet.

Then I remembered.

The house. The porch light burning. My aunt waiting. The food gone cold. The kids watching the clock. The silence of that phone ringing into the dark.

I hadn't just missed dinner. I'd disappeared. I had vanished into a night with strangers and abandoned the only people who trusted me to come.

I sat up slowly. My shirt was on the floor, soaked in sweat. Vera was gone. The bottle was empty. Wolf snored soft from the other bed. Darlene didn't stir.

I stood, dressed, washed my face in the sink. The mirror showed someone I didn't know. Neither sinner nor hero. Just a man who kept choosing the same road and pretending he didn't know where it led.

Outside, the morning was cold and pale. The fog hung low over the tracks and the puddles lay still as sheet glass. I walked to the depot and slipped aboard the first train heading north, a fare owed and my mouth shut.

The whistle sounded long and low. It knew the shape of my failure.

The train moved through the mist. The valley closed around us. Orchards stood in rows, open-palmed to the sun. A landscape

I could never seem to leave behind. I sat near the back and watched the glass blur. My own reflection pale and watchful. A ghost staring back.

I thought of the voice that never came.

I arrived in the city and the fog lay low over the bay. The gulls wheeled above the piers, white questions over the water. I walked the wharves until I found a phone booth. I stepped inside.

Dropped the coin. Waited.

It rang.

And rang.

And rang.

No answer.

I could see it. The kitchen light low. My aunt by the counter, apron bunched in her hands. My uncle sitting quiet at the table. The meat cold. The children at the window, faces lit by the streetlamp, listening.

I hung up.

Tried again.

Nothing.

I stood in the booth until the city moved around me. Until the sound of the ringing had crawled into my ribs and settled there.

The ship waited at the pier, gray and without judgment. I climbed the gangway and stood a long time at the rail. Behind me the city, ahead the sea.

The gulls called overhead, sharp and restless. Their cries followed me down into the dark of the ship.

The Waiting

While our ship limped home across the Pacific, Iwo Jima was burning. A black stone in the sea, lit from within by fire and death. Men fought on it as the earth swallowed them whole. The magazines called it victory, but the pictures told the truth. I saw one in a shop window in Vallejo, the flag going up on Mount Suribachi. Six men bent forward in the wind, the cloth caught mid-whip. Their faces hidden, the island smoldering behind them. They said it cost us more than six thousand lives for a piece of ground barely big enough to bury them.

Then came Okinawa. Eighty-two days of killing. Rain without end. The ground turned to red paste and took men to the knees. Civilians went over cliffs rather than surrender. Kamikazes burned ships and men together. More than a hundred thousand soldiers dead between both sides, and nearly as many civilians with them. Not an army only. A people. And when the news reached us, all that ruin had to fit inside one name on a chart.

Across the world, my brother was bleeding. He was with the Seventh Army in Germany. A sergeant. They were in Nuremberg when the city came down. He said the stone turned black and the old spires burned like dry kindling. Fire in the bones of the world. Ash in the air. Men screaming in stairwells. The fighting went house to house, doorway to doorway. He said the city seemed caught between dying and going on.

On the fourth day he caught a bullet high in the thigh. He said it struck from nowhere and took his leg out from under him. Crawled behind a fallen wall and laid there for hours with the rifle across his chest and one hand clamped hard to the wound. Said the blood made a lake in the rubble. They pulled him out from under what used to be a bakery. He was covered in soot and crusted red, couldn't tell where the wall ended and he began. The river ran black with fuel and bodies.

He spent a week in a field hospital before they sent him back. The letter he wrote was short. Said he was lucky. Said it was enough.

He came home with a limp and a medal and a silence I never could touch. I was proud of him. And I envied him too. He was finished with the war. I was still waiting to find out if I ever would be.

By spring our ship stood whole again at Mare Island. New plating. Fresh paint. The scars welded over but still there beneath the skin. When they lowered her back into the water, she hesitated, the sea itself seeming to remember her weight and her name.

The crew returned by degrees. Men dragging seabags up the pier, sunburnt and squinting, hungover and slow-footed. Bull came up beside me, staring at the hull like it had insulted him.

They fixed her just so we can go break her again, he said.

Wouldn't be the Navy otherwise.

We were ordered to readiness drills that spring and into the long stretch of summer. Rumors flew, maybe the Philippines again, maybe Okinawa. Some said we'd be the spearpoint for Japan itself. Nobody knew. The days blurred under the weight of routine. The paint baked. The deck scorched. The sea gleamed with quiet menace.

We ran beaching exercises off Treasure Island, loaded tanks that weren't headed anywhere, aimed the guns at sky that stayed empty. Ortega timed our drills with a stopwatch, pencil tucked behind one ear.

If this were live fire, you'd both be dead, he said.

Then you better pray hard, Wilkins told him.

Ortega grinned. I already do. You're in most of them.

Later that day Wilkins and I were greasing the breech when he muttered, You realize we been at this three years straight?

Feels longer.

Convicts get better treatment.

Convicts don't get shot at.

Yeah, but they get time served. We just keep adding to the sentence.

He spat over the rail and shook his head. You ever think the Navy forgot we're even out here?

I think about it every time I smell this grease.

If I ever make it off this boat, I'm buying a bar. No uniforms allowed.

Make it two bars. One for the living. One for the ghosts.

Wilkins gave a low laugh. Then you'll need a bigger bar.

By June, the heat had turned cruel. The deck could blister your feet through the soles. The air shimmered above the gun barrels, bending the world out of shape. Nicky leaned against the rail one afternoon, shirt stuck to his back.

Feels like God left the stove on.

Bull wiped his neck with a rag. He's cooking something, all right.

Nobody laughed.

There was talk of Operation Downfall. They said the invasion would come by winter and the first wave might not make it out of the surf. Half a million of us wouldn't come back. Ortega said the Japs would never quit. That they'd fight with their teeth if it came to that. Bull said he didn't care what they fought with as long as he wasn't there to see it.

At night we played cards in the mess. The fans only stirred the heat. The place reeked of sweat and old diesel, the air sticky with coffee and nerves. Nicky said, You think they'll ever let us go home?

Bull said, Home's a myth sailors tell themselves to keep from going nuts.

Walker shrugged. Then I believe in myths.

On weekends we got liberty when the schedule allowed. Some stayed in Vallejo, others crossed to the city. I rode with Walker most times. We hit the bars along Market, the kind that stank of beer and salt and a hundred lost paychecks. Women leaned over the counters, their hair done up, their eyes already tired.

One night we sat at the far end of a bar near the wharf. A jukebox played a jumpy tune, all brass and bounce, about a girl who never waited. Walker drummed the counter in time, watching his beer foam settle.

You ever think about girls, Flynn? Not the kind who come with drinks. The kind who might wait for you somewhere.

Sometimes.

Yeah. Me too. Only I'm starting to wonder if I made her up.

You'll find her.

Maybe. Or maybe she'll find me when I've got nothing left.

He stared past me into the mirror behind the bar. A dozen faces floated in the haze. You ever wonder what comes after?

After the war?

After all of it. The sea. The orders. The noise. You think there's a world for men like us?

I said, We'll find out.

Walker nodded. Yeah. I guess we will.

Outside, the fog kept rolling in. Ferry horns sounded from the dock, long and lonesome. Walker stood and dropped a few bills on the counter.

Let's get back before we miss the last boat, he said.

Good idea, I said. I don't feel like sleeping in the brig again.

We stayed quiet on the ride back. The wind carried rust and brine, with a faint sweetness under it, rainwater gathered on old metal. The city faded into the dark, its lights trembling across the bay, uncertain and small.

By July the rumors changed. Something big was coming. A new weapon. Strong enough to end it. Bull said it was just officer talk. Nicky said, Fairy tales don't kill two hundred thousand people. We all looked at him.

He shrugged. Heard it from a yard worker. Said a radio man told him. Said the Japs might not have a country left to invade.

We laughed it off. But a strange silence settled on the ship. The drills got quieter. Even the sea seemed to draw breath and hold it.

Then came August sixth. A clean sky. Gulls riding the wind. We were loading fresh stores when a chief came into the mess with a radio in his hand. His face was drawn tight.

They dropped a bomb, he said. One plane. One city.

We gathered around him. Hiroshima. A single bomb and a hundred thousand gone.

That's a goddamn lie, Bull said.

Nicky said, How could one bomb do that?

Bennett leaned back on the bench. Maybe it's true. Maybe they finally built something that can kill the world.

No one spoke after that. I tried to picture it. A teacher mid-word. A worker stepping toward lunch. Then light beyond imagining, bright enough to turn a body into absence and leave its shadow behind. I could not.

Three days later came Nagasaki. Another city. More fire. The news reached us low and unwanted. Reports of children burned down to bone. Smoke rising over what was left.

You think they'll quit now, Bennett asked.

Bull said, If not, there's nothing left to teach them with.

Wilkins muttered, Jesus. Two cities.

Nicky kept his eyes on the horizon. Maybe that's what the end of the world sounds like.

I thought of the faces beneath that new sun. Mothers and sons. The old and the innocent. All of them turned to ash by our hand. And a coldness took root in me.

The ship went quiet. Men smoked and stared at the water. Some prayed. Some just sat with their hands empty.

That night nobody guessed where we were headed. Nobody wanted to.

Walker said, If this ends it, what then?

Then we go home. Or try to.

And if it doesn't?

Then we keep loading tanks that ain't going anywhere.

The war was over for some. Not for others. In Europe they were sweeping rubble and counting the dead. Here we were waiting to see if we would be counted too.

A day after Nagasaki they called us to mess. The yeoman came in with a clipboard, fan blowing the paper like it didn't matter. Givens. From Kansas. His voice too soft for war. He cleared his throat.

He called out names slowly, eyes on the list, each one doubtful of reaching the door. I didn't listen at first. I figured my name wasn't on it. Men like me didn't get leave. We just got orders.

Flynn, he said. Thirty days.

I looked up from my cup.

Say that again.

You heard me.

Bull let out a low whistle. You're paroled, brother.

Nicky slapped my back. Thirty days. Try not to spend them all in one saloon.

No promises.

I held the paper like it was forged. My first leave since I enlisted. Thirty days to remember who I'd been. Or forget.

That night I walked the deck. The cranes stood skeletal against the dark. The sky was gold and then ash. Lights blinked across the city like signals sent to no one.

I thought of Dan's limp. My mother's hands. A house somewhere beyond all this iron. The war wasn't done. I could feel its hand on my shoulder. I didn't know where it ended and I began.

The wind came up and touched my face. The paper lay warm in my palm, and a small mercy eased through me.

A release.

Quiet and strange.

For the first time since I'd signed my name, I believed it might almost be over.

South Dakota

I had not seen the prairie in nearly three years. It unrolled outside the train window, half memory and half judgment. Stubble fields gold under the hard light. Windmills turning slow in the heat. Every town the same. A co-op, a grain tower, a sunburned flag hanging without wind. The train clicked through it all, stitching me back toward what I had left.

My orders were folded in my coat pocket. Thirty days' leave. I sat in that coach car and thought how strange it was. The second bomb had barely stopped ringing and already I was bound for home. The world was smoldering and here I was rattling through Nebraska like some salesman with a suitcase he couldn't give away. A boy with a satchel and the war riding home in his bones. The countryside blurred past. Nebraska. Then Dakota. I thought of all the dead boys who wouldn't see cornfields again. The ones still out there in the water or the dirt. I kept my thoughts to myself. Watched the land roll by and tried not to let my thoughts slide down into the same hole. The truth was I was praying for it to end. I'd seen enough. The idea of going back in, of hitting another beach or hauling another burned boy out of the black water. It made my chest go tight. A gear stripped smooth. I was afraid that if they sent me back again, I wouldn't come home whole. Or come home at all.

At Sioux Falls my brothers met me at the platform. Leo had grown tall. Dan limped from bullet he'd taken in Germany. We shook hands and climbed into the truck without much talk. The road home ran through fields turned green with August. Crows in the furrows. Dust on the fenceposts. Heat shimmered off the ditchwater and the engine knocked going uphill. No one said much. The land did most of the talking.

When we reached the house Mom was already out on the porch. Her hair a duller red than I remembered. Eyes catching the light just the same. She took my face in her hands and looked me over, slow and afraid, searching for the boy beneath the war. Then she kissed my cheek and went back inside, having seen enough.

The house felt smaller. The air thin and close. Leo set the table and Dan lit the stove. We ate stew and bread and passed the salt. They told stories. Leo laughed too loud. Dan smoked and talked about wiring the house. I sopped up gravy with the heel of bread and looked across the table.

Where's Flo these days?

Mom set down her fork.

She's in Yankton, she said. Living with a girlfriend. Works as a waitress in some café there.

She doing all right?

Far as I know.

She didn't say more and neither did I. The name of the town hung in the air a moment. Then Leo cracked some joke about a teacher who caught him cheating on a spelling test and we all laughed and kept on eating. I listened and watched the kerosene lamp throw its glow on the wall and tried to believe I was back in my own skin.

Dad was away with Orville, visiting kin near Chamberlain. The quiet of the house held us in its ribs. At night I took Leo's bed and he laid out a blanket on the floor. I stood a long while in the doorway looking at that old iron frame. The mattress thin as ever. The ticking worn. But it had the mercy of a grave. I lay down and let it take me. The rafters creaked above me. A screen door tapped in the wind. I don't remember closing my eyes. Sleep took me whole and without argument, and I didn't wake until morning. The dead had given me one night of their silence.

Next morning Dan and I ran wire through the walls. Bare bulbs from the ceiling. Two switches. When Dad got home and saw the work he stood in the kitchen doorway without a word. Then he said how dare you boys do anything without asking. How do you think I'm supposed to pay for electricity?

Dan reached up and pulled the chain on the bulb. It came on. Bright and cold. A soundless kind of triumph. Dad looked up at it, his face opened by wonder. Then he grinned.

Boy that works pretty damn well.

We laughed and he flicked it off and on again just to watch it go.

That evening I went into town. The Sawdust Trail hadn't changed. Boots on the floorboards. A jukebox wheezing out a cowboy song. I saw Earl Haskins and Hank Talbert at a back table, cards between them. I didn't wave. I wanted something quieter.

So I walked down to Mama Kale's.

The windows were fogged from the stove. A few men at the counter hunched over empty glasses. The floorboards creaked underfoot, remembering every footstep ever made. The kind of place where the past sat right beside you.

The barmaid stood behind the bar with a towel over her shoulder. Brown hair pinned up loose. A flush on her cheeks from the heat. She brought me a beer before I'd even spoken.

You're a Kubal, aren't you, I said.

She smiled. That's right. Blanche.

I thought so. You went to school here, didn't you?

Sure did. You're Flynn, right? Pat Flynn. You were a few grades ahead.

I nodded. Guess I remember you now.

I remember you too, she said. You used to sit near the back. Always stared out the window like you were somewhere else already.

I probably was.

She didn't ask more. Just wiped down the bar. There was a quiet between us that wasn't unfriendly. A few stools down, her sister was drying glasses. A younger girl. Pale blue eyes and a stillness to her. Quiet in herself, standing apart from the room. She seemed sealed under glass, living inside the hush.

That your sister?

That's Dot. Short for Dorothy.

Nice to meet you, Dot.

Dorothy glanced up and gave the faintest smile before turning back to the glass in her hand. Her name seemed to move through the room, but she gave it no claim. It passed the way most things did then, quick and unkept.

Two more came in. Vernon and Cal. Grain man and corn man. They saw me and made their way over.

Pat Flynn, Vernon said. Didn't think you'd come back whole.

Mostly whole, I said.

You kill any Japs?

Blanche looked up hard.

Enough to know better than to talk about it, I said.

The silence after that sat long. Then Blanche set another beer in front of me. No charge. Just a look that said nothing and everything.

You glad to be home, she asked.

It feels smaller somehow.

She nodded. It's not the place that changes. It's us.

Her voice was soft but held shape. I thought to ask if she'd walk with me after closing. Maybe just to the bridge and back. But before I could speak, Cal raised a shot and shouted Here's to the hero come home. And the glass was in my hand. And the fire of it took the words from my throat.

By the time I looked up, Blanche had moved off. Dorothy stood where she had been, folding a towel, watching me like she'd been watching the whole time.

I stepped out into the night. The lamps along Main burned low. Cicadas screeched in the trees. I walked past the feed store and the shuttered five-and-dime and thought how strange it was to be alive in the town I once thought I'd never see again.

***

V-J Day
August 14, 1945

The sun beat down with a will to flatten the earth. I'd spent the day cutting back the fenceline. Thistles, weeds, grass to a man's thigh. The scythe blistered my hands and the flies clung to my face in black specks. By sundown I'd washed at the pump and put on a clean shirt and walked into town with the taste of iron in my mouth.

Humpy's was a low room with yellow bulbs and scarred boards, smoke pooling under the ceiling, the bar rail sticky with years. I took a stool and nursed a beer. The beer sweated on the wood and left a ring like a brand. The radio crackled from behind the bar. A voice found its signal. The war is over, it said. Japan has surrendered.

The room did not react at first. Then a chair scraped back. Then a cheer. Then the noise came up all at once.

Over the racket a man bellowed, Free rounds for all servicemen. I lifted my hand and heads turned. A cheer went up fast and hot. Men were on me at once. Slaps on the back that stung and meant something. Glasses pressed into my hands faster than I could set them down. Beer. Whiskey. More beer. A man I barely knew tipped a shot to my mouth with the solemn care of a priest offering sacrament. To the Navy, he said. Another shoved a mug at me and shouted, To the boys who didn't make it. The barkeep waved off my coins. Put your money away, sailor. A stranger hugged me hard and laughed with the wild relief of a man reprieved. Somebody yelled for another round and nobody paid. I tried to keep count and lost it. The numbers went under in the burn of my throat and the roar of voices. Thirty became a blur.

We spilled out onto Main Street. Horns leaned on themselves. The church bell started up and would not quit. Flags hung from windows in the yellow light. A boy ran past with a pot and spoon and beat the night to pieces. At Tom Wagner's they were pouring shots into paper cups and passing them through the door. At Joe Schultz's a row of beers stood waiting on the bar with no names to them. Back at Humpy's an old pool shark shook my hand and slipped a silver flask into my pocket and told me to keep it for luck. Every door stood open. Every barkeep waved me in. My shoulders ached from all the clapping and I did not mind.

I pushed through the crowd into Tom Wagner's pool hall. The clack of balls rose and fell in small thunder. Chalk dust hung in the lamplight above the green felt. Men called my name and pressed more drinks into my hands. One more for the road, they said, though none of us was going anywhere. I lifted a glass and the liquor ran through me and set the room shining.

That was where I saw her. Helen Nedved. The first girl I ever kissed. She stood in the doorway of Wagner's with one hand on the frame and the streetlamp caught in her hair. Smoke drifted above the tables. The cue balls rolled and knocked softly together and came to rest.

Pat Flynn, she said. Back from the dead.

Close enough, I said.

She put her hands to my face and kissed my cheek and for a second the years fell away. We drank outside with the others and then inside when the crowd shifted. She told me she was working at Buche's store now. I told her I had thirty days and a train waiting somewhere beyond them. She said that could wait. The count kept on somewhere behind my eyes and for once I let it.

We walked to the curb. The streets were glazed with light and dust. An old man sat on his step and wept quiet. Voices drifted from the open doors.

Helen slipped a set of keys from her purse. Let's get out of here, she said.

I grinned, the silver flask in my hand. Lead the way.

She had a little Ford coupe with sunburned paint and a clouded headlamp. The bench seat had split down the middle. She turned the key and the engine caught after a cough. We drove out toward the dam with the windows down. Gravel ticked under the fenders, and the town fell away behind us in the warm night.

The night hummed with crickets and frogs. Moths flared in the headlamps and vanished. The grass along the road brushed our legs when we stepped out and left burrs clinging to our socks. We passed the flask between us. The metal turned warm in our hands. Down in the dark the water lay black and swallowed the moon.

We did not say much at first. Then she asked, What did you think when you heard it?

That someone had given me back hours I did not deserve.

Then spend them, she said.

On what?

On being here. Right now.

I looked out at the black water. I still can't believe the Japanese surrendered, I said. Those two bombs must have carried a wicked force to make a whole nation lay down.

She kept her eyes on the dark. Japan is a long way from Wagner, she said. Let's enjoy tonight.

She told me her mother still cooked for an army that never came and I told her a little of the sea and left out the rest. She asked if I dreamed. I said not when I could help it. She touched my sleeve like she meant to smooth something that could not be smoothed.

We sat on the concrete lip where the spillway began. The timbers held the day's heat and the sound below was a low iron murmur. She leaned her head against my shoulder and I felt the small shift of her breath. Somewhere out in the fields a dog barked, lonely and far off.

You came back, she said.

For a little while.

A little while can be enough, she said.

The world seemed a long way off. For a time there was only the two of us and the dark plain and the moon riding over it.

Helen rose a little unsteady from the drink and took me by the hand.

Where are we going, I said.

You'll see, she said, and she was grinning.

She led me to the car and opened the door and we climbed into the back. The seat was low and sunken and the leather split and curled with age. It gave beneath us and the springs complained softly. The roof sagged above our heads and the glass was dim with old dust and the wet of our breath. Her leg touched mine and stayed there. She pulled the door shut and the dark closed around us.

We turned toward each other. Her hair had fallen across her face and she let it stay. The air in that little space was warm and close. She looked at me with a steadiness that made the rest of the world seem small. I touched her cheek, then her throat, then the narrow bones of her shoulders. She came to me and I kissed her. We moved slowly there in the dark, with the whiskey on us and the long night behind us and the war at our backs. The seat creaked beneath us. The windows fogged. The world beyond us lost its claim, and time answered only to the living warmth of her body against mine.

Afterward we lay against the back seat and let our breathing settle. We shared a cigarette, the ember brightening and dimming between us. Then we heard a car coming up the road and we scrambled to dress, laughing under our breath, hands catching at buttons.

Oh hell, we better move, I said, laughing as I pulled my trousers on.

Helen laughed too as she buttoned her blouse and fixed her hair. We climbed into the front seat.

She started the engine and the coupe idled low. We drove back into town through streets gone hollow with sleep. The east had begun to pale. A milk truck passed us, the bottles chiming in their metal racks.

This has been quite a night.

She glanced over at me. Do you mean me or the Japs surrendering?

Both, I said.

She smiled. Good answer.

We laughed then, quiet and tired.

You all right, she said.

I am, I said. You?

I will be.

After a while she said, How many days you got left?

Enough to count and not enough to waste.

She nodded. You know where to find me.

She let me out at the curb across from my folks' place. We sat a moment with the engine ticking. Dawn had thinned the world to gray.

Thank you for the night, I said.

Thank you for coming back, she said. She touched my hand once and let it go. Get some sleep, sailor.

I'll try.

She leaned in and kissed me, quick and sure, then eased the car away. I watched the taillight fade and felt a knot ease loose in me, slow and soundless.

I stood there a moment and brushed myself off. The street was the same as it had always been. The war was over, they said. It felt no different, just called by cleaner words. I walked back toward the house that had raised me, the gravel snapping under my feet, and carried in me a kind of tired joy. It would not last. Nothing does. But for one night the world had given us back to ourselves and I took what it offered with both hands.

The Last Week

South Dakota, Autumn 1945

The days peeled away, and time grew thinner underneath.

I helped Dad mend the fence out back, the two of us in work shirts and leather gloves, hammering bent nails straight and digging the postholes deeper where the frost had buckled them loose. We drew the clothesline taut and stacked cordwood by the shed, splitting each log till the axe head sang. Mom handed us lemonade in old jelly jars, beads of water tracing down the sides in thin windowpane trails. She scolded us for tracking in dirt and muttered about ruined linoleum. I raked leaves with Dan and we burned them in a smoldering pile, the smoke climbing through the trees in search of heaven.

The four of us boys played football in the yard, shirts versus skins. Tackles were rough and laughter came easy. We cursed and bled and threw elbows, and when Mom yelled out the window to quit killing each other, we played harder. Orville asked questions about the ship. About the guns. About what it felt like to be shot at and whether the dead were really dead or just looked that way. He was curious and quiet and older than he should've been. He sat beside me on the porch with his knees drawn up and asked if I thought he'd end up in it too. I told him maybe, but not yet. He nodded once, already packing the thought away.

Nights I went to the bar. Same old corner stool. Mama Kale behind it, sharp-eyed and built solid as a coal stove in a dress. She called me sweetheart and poured doubles and winked at me as though I was fifteen again, stealing sips when nobody looked. I got drunk more nights than not. I told lies to strangers and danced with girls I didn't remember by morning. I laughed too loud and picked up the tab once just to feel important.

Then came the night in the alley.

A young girl lingered by the jukebox, cheeks rouged too bright beneath peroxide hair. Beside her stood a red-eyed man whose voice scraped when he spoke. He grabbed her wrist and when she pulled away, he shoved her down hard. The glass shattered when she hit the floor and no one moved. Just the record skipping.

I stood up slow. He turned with the look of a man waiting to be stopped and already certain no one would.

I followed him out back. The alley was lit by a single yellow bulb and stank of piss and grease. He was fumbling for a cigarette when I stepped out.

Hey, I said.

He turned. Grinned.

What are you, a hero?

No, I said.

And I hit him.

Right across the jaw. His head snapped and he staggered into the wall. His swing glanced off my cheekbone. I closed the space and drove my fist into his stomach. One hit took his breath. The next folded him. He grabbed my coat and I slammed him against the dumpster and hit him again. His lip burst and he dropped.

He rolled onto his knees and spat blood into the alley. I stood over him, breathing hard, knuckles raw, heart drumming in my chest.

You might think you're tough pushing women, you son of a bitch.

But you're not so tough now, are you?

He didn't answer. Just staggered up and limped down the alley without a word, shoulders caved in.

Mama Kale stood in the doorway, smoke curling from her lip.

You didn't have to do that.

I know.

She nodded.

But I'm glad you did.

I saw Helen again. Once in town, walking with a friend. She waved without stopping. Another time she met me after work and we drove past the grain elevators out to the river. She brought a blanket and a half pint of whiskey in her coat pocket.

We sat in the dark and watched the water move.

That went fast, she said, handing me the bottle without looking.

It always does, I said.

You know what you'll do when this is done?

Drink less, I guess. Sleep more.

That all?

I shrugged. Maybe find a job where nobody's shooting at you.

That'd be a start.

She looked out at the current, then back at me.

You ever think about just not going back?

To what?

To the whole goddamn thing.

Sometimes. But that's not how it works.

Yeah, she said. It never is.

We passed the bottle and didn't speak for a long time. The air carried damp leaves and river mud. The stars were out and even the river sounded far away.

I didn't kiss her. I wanted to. But it felt like stealing.

When she dropped me off she said don't disappear.

I said I'd try not to.

The days thinned away. I counted them as bullets in a chamber. Each night I lay in bed with the ship on my mind. She was afloat beyond me, fresh paint over old steel. I wondered if I was being carried back to her, and if this time she would carry me under.

Then came the knock.

It was morning. The sun warming the eastern windows. Mom stood at the stove with a wooden spoon, the aroma of toast and scrambled eggs soft in the air. Dad sat at the table in his undershirt, newspaper folded beside his plate, coffee cooling in a chipped white mug. Dan sat quiet at the table, one hand cupped round his coffee, letting the heat climb into him. Orville and I passed butter and jelly as though breakfast itself needed hiding.

Leo came barreling in half-dressed and dripping from the pump outside, knocking into chairs and laughing at something only he knew. He snatched toast off my plate and dodged a swat from Orville, talking about some kid who tried to jump a ditch and wrecked his bike. The kitchen filled with his noise until it seemed there was hardly room for the rest of us.

Then came the knock. One knock. Hard and final.

Everything went quiet. Even Leo froze mid-chew.

I rose and opened the door.

The mailman stood there, a square-jawed man in a brown coat with a leather satchel over one shoulder and his cap pulled low against the morning light. He held a yellow envelope in his hand, the ink faded, the edges creased like old worry.

Letter for Patrick Flynn.

Which one? I said. Dad was behind me now, dish towel over his shoulder.

The one in the service.

That's me.

I signed. The envelope was thin. I held it like it might bleed. I didn't open it right away. Just turned it over once. Twice. The kitchen behind me had gone quiet. Chairs stood back from the table. Forks hovered above plates. I broke the seal and unfolded the paper and read.

Well? Dan said.

Orders, I said. Report to the Navy office in Sioux Falls. They'll issue new station papers.

Where to? Dad asked.

It doesn't say.

You leavin soon? Orville asked.

Couple days. Maybe less.

Dad folded his arms. Looked at me hard.

Think they'll send you overseas?

I don't know.

He didn't answer. Just breathed slow through his nose.

Mom turned from the stove. Her eyes met mine but she said nothing. The eggs in the pan had started to brown at the edges.

Dan drove me to Sioux Falls the next morning. The fields lay gold and stubbled under the pale sky. The wind through the windows carried harvest dust and the smell of cut hay.

The Navy office was on a quiet street in Sioux Falls, with the flag out front and U.S. Navy painted on the glass. Inside, typewriters clacked behind a half wall. A sailor sat at the desk with his sleeves rolled and a pencil tucked behind his ear.

He looked up.

Name, rate, and service number.

Flynn, Patrick. Motor Machinist's Mate Second Class.

He pulled a card from a file box and checked it against the paper in front of him.

LST four-eighty-two.

Yes.

He took an envelope from a tray and slid it across the desk.

Orders.

I opened it there.

Upon expiration of present leave, report to Great Lakes Naval Training Station, Great Lakes, Illinois.

I read it again.

Chicago.

Outside, the wind shook the trees. Leaves skittered across the hood. Dan looked at me.

Well?

Chicago.

He nodded.

At least you're stateside.

For now.

We sat a while. I folded the orders into my jacket pocket.

Let's get a cup of coffee, I said.

We drove out into the wind.

That night I packed.

The house was quiet in that way old houses get, listening. I folded my things slow. Sea bag open on the floor. My socks. My dungarees. My blues. The shaving kit. Each piece anchored in its place.

While I packed, my mind went to the ship.

To Bull and Nicky. My best pals on board. The ones who knew how to find laughter even in the dark. I could still hear Bull's cackle echoing through the tank deck, Nicky with that sly grin like he'd seen it all twice already.

To Wilkins and Lopez. My gun crew. Wilkins steady as stone, never missed a feed. Lopez sharp-eyed and quiet, already pointing skyward before the alarm even rang.

Then Walker. Moved saddle-born, loose and sure. Could hum a hymn in a boiler room and make it feel holy.

To Cohen. Haunted and proud. He carried a silence inside him that felt older than the sea itself. I hoped the darkness that clung to him might lift someday, that he'd find a place where the war couldn't follow. Some quiet street with trees and a good woman who'd never ask him what he'd seen.

And the black gang. My brothers below decks.

We lived and worked in a steel tomb below the waterline, deafened by the roar of engines that never slept. Oil on our skin. Salt in our blood. Every bolt mattered, every gauge, every bearing and valve. We moved through that hot dark belly by memory. We knew each other's footsteps. We spoke in hand signals and looks. One torpedo and we'd never have made it out. And we all knew it.

McDaniel and Gund ruled that space as tyrants, hard-eyed and joyless, their word law in the roar and heat. They were sons of bitches, both of them. But the kind of sons of bitches a war machine needs, cold, fast, brutal. Even so, I often thought how neither of them was half the man that Captain Whelan was. Whelan was fair. He didn't shout. Didn't need to. You knew what he expected the second he looked at you. He walked the deck as though the ship lived through him, her weight in his shoulders, her fate bound to his own.

I saw their faces. In gun light. In red lamp. Bare-chested. Grinning. The sea behind them. The war in their mouths. I saw the ones we lost too. In silence.

Jackson came last. Wild-eyed and laughing. Then gone.

I saw the battles. Tarawa. Guam. Leyte. Water turned to flame. Sky full of smoke. The dead drifting where men once shouted. All of it still in me.

Then Joyce came into my thoughts. A tide returning.

Her face in the soft light of morning. Her voice low and certain. The way she had looked at me when I left Honolulu, already knowing we would never meet again. I thought of her walking that beach alone, with the morning light on her and the whole ocean between us. Honolulu seemed a dream now. The ship. The crew. The war. The laughter. The sorrow. They were ghosts, every one of them, and I was the one who lived to remember.

That night she came to me in a dream. Stepped from the sea. Her dress soaked and clinging. She kissed me and her mouth was salt and memory. She touched my face and didn't speak.

I woke cold. Alone.

The next morning, Mom sat on the couch. Hands folded. Dad stood by the door, coat on. My sea bag beside him.

You got everything? Mom said.

I think so.

She stepped forward and fixed my collar.

Don't let them make you mean.

I nodded. She kissed my cheek.

Dad opened the door. The porch was slick with dew. The sky was pale.

I guess you'll be fine, he said. Just don't be stupid.

I'll try.

He reached into his coat and handed me a folded five.

For the bus.

Thanks.

You'll write?

Yeah.

He clapped my shoulder.

Go on then.

I walked down the steps with the bag heavy in my hand. Morning lay pale over the yard. I turned toward the road and went.

CHICAGO

They sent me to Great Lakes when the war let go of us. North of Chicago, pressed up near the lake's edge, the base sprawled in low geometry across a land of wind and water. Brick barracks and admin halls in long square rows. Gravel paths stitched with bootprints. Steel fences humming in the breeze, old wire strung for ghosts. You could hear the gulls and the distant labor of diesel engines out on the lake. The mornings came gray and fast, and the sky stayed close to the earth.

I arrived just after daybreak. There was frost in the grass and smoke rising from chimneys in long ribbons. My gear had already come in from California, shipped ahead in crates and canvas bags, tagged with my name and number, proof the world wasn't done with me yet. I signed for everything in silence and stacked it on the floor of the cold barracks room that would be mine.

The surroundings were new but not unfamiliar. A different kind of order. I fell into it like I'd been waiting for it. They gave me shore patrol. I wore the brassard through those streets, finding sailors in gutters, in alleys, in booth seats, their bodies gone loose and foolish with drink. Haul them out of the trouble they'd poured themselves into. I did it by the book. Tapped them on the shoulder. Got them to their feet. Called it in.

I'd spent half the war drunk and the other half trying to forget I had been. I knew every trick they pulled and every lie they told.

And I let most of it slide. A man could drink too much and still be decent.

My commanding officer was a man named Lieutenant Harrow. Long-faced and bitter-eyed, with the look of a man who had already heard the bad news and hated hearing it again. He spoke low and clipped and never smiled, afraid perhaps that laughter would open a crack in him no doctor could mend. His uniform was always squared away, plain and exact. Pressed and sober and regulation-bound. The knuckle on his middle finger jutted sideways, crooked from an old violence. I figured it came from the war, but he never offered and I never pressed.

He gave me my patrol assignments without looking up from his desk. Just slid the clipboard toward me, already signed.

You know what to do out there, Flynn. Try not to make it worse.

I nodded.

It wasn't long before I fell in with two fellows, Lewis and Clarke. No one could say their names together without smirking, least of all them. They leaned into it. Told folks we were on a government expedition, looking for rivers and landmarks. Trouble too, when it could be found.

Lewis was small and quick, always moving. His voice had the grind of gravel under a truck tire, and his teeth were stained by years of smoke and Navy coffee. He talked fast and never stopped moving his hands, a man held upright by nerves and talk.

Clarke was built broad across the shoulders, made for carrying weight. Slow in his movements and slower in his speech. He had the look of every barn-raised boy you ever met, all jaw and good teeth and honest eyes. He laughed with his whole chest, untouched by whatever the world had tried to take from him. You got the sense he'd seen plenty and learned how not to let it stick.

We drank hard and often, down on the Loop, the three of us spinning from bar to bar. We'd come in loud, make a circle round the room, spot the girls, judge the crowd. Lewis always found someone to argue with. Clarke always found someone to carry home. And I just drank.

When we weren't drinking, we were at the Pepsi Center. Ten stories tall and lit bright against the Chicago dark. It was the single finest building I'd ever set foot in. Built for us and only for us. Uniforms and dog tags and tired eyes. And it was all free. Every floor. Every amenity. Free, as though your name had been written down long ago and marked for rest.

Food stacked high on platters. Meat cooked to the bone. Hot bread wrapped in cloth. Butter soft as cream. You could eat until the world went quiet. Showers that steamed long as you needed. Clean beds. Lush carpets underfoot. Barbers who didn't ask questions. Pepsi stacked cold in every corner, a strange blessing in a world gone dry.

But it was the girls that kept us coming back. They bussed them in from all over. Evanston. Joliet. Cicero. Towns I'd never see again. They came in laughing, eyes wide, their perfume sweetening the stale air. Young and soft and good-hearted. They wanted the music, the eyes on them, the bright unnamed thing the night promised.

We danced with them under the vaulted ceilings. The floors were slick from wax and sweat and the scrape of soles. The music was loud and sweet and old. We told lies and war stories and listened to their dreams.

Sometimes we got lucky. I did, a few times. The details are gone now. So are the names. What's left is the memory of a girl's voice in the dark, her fingers at my collar, the click of heels on marble as she walked away. The feel of silk buttons under my hands.

One night we got it in our heads to see how the other half drank. We'd had our fill of servicemen joints. Lewis said he wanted to see how silk ties got drunk. Clarke just nodded. So we cleaned up best we could and took a cab to Clark Street.

McGovern's sat there like it had always sat there. A red-brick vault with windows high and tinted. Brass handles and a man in a black coat who gave us a long look before he opened the door. Inside it was quiet. Carpet soft and dark. Lights set deep in the ceiling. Glass didn't clink and nobody raised their voice. Everything was measured and padded.

The bar stretched long and clean. Polished wood. Gold trim. Glass shelves gleaming. The bartender wore a white coat, cuffs starched, shoes polished to a mirror shine.

We took three stools near the middle. Before we could speak, the bartender slid three shots across the bar.

Compliments of the gentlemen, he said.

We looked down the line. Three men sat at the far end. All suits. All dark. Shoes polished to black glass. Watches that didn't tick. Hair slicked back with the shine of oil on marble. They had the look of men who never explained themselves. They raised their glasses toward us. We raised ours back.

We drank. Another round came. Then another. Then one of them rose and walked toward us, hands in his pockets.

You boys Navy?

We are, I said.

Good men, he said. That's good. He pulled a hundred-dollar bill from his coat and set it down. The bill lay crisp and flat, untouched by sweat, dirt, or honest handling. I picked it up. Felt the weight.

If you boys want more drinks, you take it from that. Compliments of us.

We nodded.

He tapped the bar with his fingers.

We're stepping into the back room. You enjoy yourselves.

Then he turned and disappeared behind the curtain. The others followed.

We didn't move. We nursed our shots slow. The air carried old leather and cologne, with a blade of sharpness under it all. The kind of scent you didn't forget but couldn't name. Jazz played low through a speaker somewhere, warped and tinny, a half-drowned memory. The light above us flickered now and then but never fully died.

Lewis leaned in.

You boys ever feel like maybe we walked into the wrong damn bar?

Clarke watched the curtain breathe faintly in the draft.

They ain't Army, he said.

No, I said. They ain't.

Lewis took a pull.

They ain't bankers either.

We looked again. One seat had a hat resting on it. The kind of hat a man kept with him even in the grave.

One of those men is wearing a watch that could pay off my mother's house, Lewis said.

And I'm sure the other one had a knife under his coat, Clarke said.

Nobody spoke for a moment.

Then Clarke said it plain.

Those guys are gangsters.

Lewis stared into his glass.

Well hell. We came looking for classy dames and found the Chicago mob.

I looked at the bill and saw it for what it was. Bait.

Then we leave the mob's money right where it is, I said.

We drank slower after that. Sat straighter. Talked quieter. Boys who'd wandered into the wrong chapel.

After a while they came back. Same as before. The man saw the folded bill. He looked at it. Then at me.

I picked it up and held it out.

Here's your money. We didn't need it.

He studied me a moment. Then he nodded.

Out of curiosity, I said, what would've happened if we'd walked out with it?

He smiled. A gold tooth caught the light.

You'd have never made it out the door, sailor.

Then he put one hand on my shoulder.

Have a good night, gentlemen.

He walked away.

We left. The street outside was wet. The wind off the lake carried the tang of iron and pavement and the last bit of autumn dying slow beneath the concrete. We didn't speak. We walked until our shoes ached and didn't look back. I kept glancing at windows, half-expecting to see him there, reflected.

I never saw them again. But I've thought about that hundred more than I ever thought about the girls.

That bill had been a door, and I thank God I never stepped through it.

The days blurred. The city pressed in with its brickwork and smoke and left me restless. Jackson came to mind more than I liked to admit. He never spoke much of home, but one night Cicero came out with old bitterness on it. I didn't know why it stayed with me, but it did. So I boarded the train. Thought maybe I'd see the kind of place that could forge a man like that. Drink a whiskey for him. Say his name to the walls.

Cicero was quiet. Rain on the sidewalk and neon blinking in the puddles. I walked until I found a bar with its windows lit and its door cracked open, waiting for me. I went inside. Ordered a whiskey and a beer. The bartender said nothing. Poured the drinks and left me alone.

I sat and drank. Thought about Jackson. About the night I took the pistol from him, his hands trembling with the look of a man already dead and trying to come back.

There was a woman under the mirror at the end of the bar. She had the look of someone waiting on a train that would never come. Italian maybe. Her drink was clear and cold. She turned the glass in slow circles. Once she looked at me. Then again. At last she pushed her glass away and came over.

You look sad, sailor.

Just thinking about an old friend. He's from around here.

Was he Navy like you?

Yes.

Is he overseas?

Yeah. Still over there.

But I wasn't thinking of oceans. I saw him under Guadalcanal sky. A cross made of sticks. His name carved by hand. Rain falling on the dirt.

She nodded.

I'm sorry. You look like you could use some company. Mind if I sit?

That would be nice.

Her name was Elena. She moved with the care of a woman raised in quiet houses, her hands always measured, her eyes steady and full of thought. Her hair fell smooth to her shoulders, black as burnt sugar. Her voice carried a tenderness in it, the hush before a hymn. We spoke across the grain of the bar and the silence of half-empty glasses, and when the lights began to lower, we were still talking.

It's late. You got somewhere to go? she asked.

Not really.

I've got a couch. My parents are home. They won't ask.

You sure?

She nodded.

We walked beneath the streetlamps. Her house was small and square. Inside was a world of its own. Crucifixes. Pictures of the

Virgin. A photo of a boy in uniform and a folded flag. The room held the grief, dry and weightless.

Mom and Dad are sleeping, she whispered.

Okay.

She set a blanket on the couch and smoothed it out.

You'll be fine here.

Thank you.

She leaned in and kissed my cheek.

Sleep well, Pat.

Then she turned off the light and went upstairs. I lay on the couch in the dark. Pipes ticked. A door creaked. Her voice hushed. Then nothing.

Later I heard the steps. Bare feet on wood. She stood at the bottom, backlit in a quiet dream. The robe hung loose. Her hair fell across her chest.

She came forward and crouched. One hand to my cheek. The other to my chest. Her eyes wide.

Shhh, she said.

I reached out. Found the edge of her robe. She pressed close. The blanket fell across us. Her breath warmed my neck.

She kissed me with the ache of a memory nearly lost, then returned all at once.

Her robe came open. Her skin smooth. We moved in whispers and breath, in touches and pauses. I held her with careful hands. She moved slow. Careful. Her fingers trembled along my ribs. We lay beneath the blanket, two creatures lost to time, the old clock ticking in the hallway, the house deep in its sleep. Between us passed an old language no voice could carry.

Then the creak of another door above.

Elena?

She froze. A man's voice. Then the rail.

What in God's name is going on down there?

Nothing, Papa. We were just talking.

Talking my ass. Get upstairs.

He looked at me.

You. Five minutes to get out. Or I'll make you wish you were never born.

Elena touched my arm.

I'm sorry, Pat. You have to go.

She kissed me once. Then turned and darted up the stairs, her robe trailing like a shadow. At the top, her father loomed. She stepped in front of him and held out both hands.

Please, Papa. He's leaving.

I dressed fast. No words. Just the rasp of fabric. I didn't look back. The door latched behind me, ending a thing I had barely allowed myself to believe.

The street outside was slick with rain. I walked a block, maybe two, before I sat on the curb and buttoned my shirt with shaking fingers. The wind cut through the last warmth she had left in me, small as it was.

A bus came slow around the bend. I stepped out and flagged it down. The driver gave me the tired look of a man paid to haul whatever the night delivered.

How do I get back to Great Lakes?

He jerked his thumb.

Climb aboard, sailor.

By the time I reached the base the sky had gone from black to iron gray. That dead hour when the world forgets its name. I found my bunk and dropped onto it, boots and all. The barracks was dark. Pipes ticked. Somewhere a locker slammed. Then nothing.

Sleep came cold and shallow. Just a few hours before the boots hit the floor and the same old orders came grinding down, steel on steel.

Points

The war was over. The Japanese had surrendered and on September second, nineteen forty-five, it became official. The guns silenced. The flags flown. The old men on the radios called it peace and said the world had been saved. But I didn't feel saved. I felt hollow. Three years gone. I'd lived each one like it might be my last. Woke each morning with a kind of borrowed breath. And now I was still here. The same lungs. The same bones. But something had been spent.

Every day ran the same. Up before the light. Muster. Shore patrol. Small duties. Long silences. Orders barked by men just as tired as I was. The boots always wet from the lake air. The chow lukewarm and starchy. I slept when I could, ate what was there. Forward was the only direction left.

I was eight points short of discharge. Might as well have been a million. Every man on that base talked points with the panic of sailors counting lifeboats on a sinking ship. They'd come up with the system to send us home, but not all at once. You needed points. Combat ribbons. Time in. Children. Wounds. Medals. I had some of it, but not enough. I marked my days with a chalkline in my mind and hoped the war would keep forgetting me.

The mornings repeated themselves. Mess hall steam and metal trays. Grey sky over the lake. The wind came off the water cold and sour, carrying the old mineral breath of the lake. Recruits fresh from boot camp passed with their voices loud and their packs high and their collars stiff with starch. I watched them sometimes, a man seeing ghosts walk backward into life.

One afternoon I was downtown with Lewis and Clarke. We'd done some shopping, soap, boot polish, a handful of postcards I'd never send. The sky was low and pale and the storefronts hung with dusty flags from the surrender celebrations. We stepped into a bar with windows fogged and a ceiling yellow from a thousand cigarettes. The floor sticky. The light weak. Some Benny Goodman tune bleeding out of a box that skipped. One drink apiece. Then we crossed the street to a little diner we knew.

Long red booths and old chrome. The place stank of fried lard and griddle scrapings burned black. A woman behind the counter looked poured into that spot back in 1932 and left to harden there. Hair of steel wool. Skin of tree bark. The kind of woman who could flip a pancake with one hand and throw a drunk sailor through the door with the other.

We slid into a booth. The table wobbled. A newspaper lay folded on the seat, waiting there with the patience of bad news. I picked it up without thinking. The Chicago Tribune. The ink carried grease and rain.

Clarke scratched his ear and said he was starving. Lewis tapped a coin on the table, trying to wake some buried part of himself.

The waitress came with a pad and no smile.

Burger, said Clarke.

Eggs, said Lewis.

Coffee. Whatever's hot, I said.

She nodded. Moved off.

I opened the paper. Just habit. The front page was full of Truman and Tokyo. I flipped through. Page three. Down in the corner, printed with no ceremony.

POINT SYSTEM SHOCKER: NAVY'S NEW RULE – 10 POINTS FOR THE HOME ALLOTMENT

I blinked. Read it again. Then a third time.

My hands started shaking.

Holy Christ, I said.

Lewis looked up.

What is it.

I slid the paper across. Pointed.

He read it slow. Then passed it to Clarke.

Well I'll be damned, Clarke said.

I sent half my pay home since I enlisted, I said. Every month. Every check. To Mom and Dad in South Dakota.

That's ten points right there, Lewis said.

I sat back. The booth seemed to lean under me. The room had tipped, and I stayed upright only because worse things had taught me how.

You were eight short, Clarke said.

Yeah.

Then you're two over.

I just nodded.

The waitress brought the plates and we sat there as though food had become a foreign thing. The burger landed in front of me, and the smell nearly stopped my breath. I picked it up and bit down. It was not only meat and grease and salt. It was memory. The first real meal after a long sickness. The coffee was black and burnt and scalded the roof of my mouth, and I drank it anyway. I wanted the pain. I needed proof I had not vanished. My mind kept seesawing between disbelief and joy. Am I really going home. Did I read it right. Was this real. I felt the floor beneath me waiting to give way, but it never did.

Across the booth, Clarke was watching me.

You all right, Flynn.

I nodded. Couldn't talk yet.

Lewis leaned forward.

You look like you seen a ghost.

I shook my head.

No, I said. Maybe it's the end of one life and the beginning of a new one.

They didn't press. Just kept eating. But they watched me different now. I wiped my hands on the napkin and looked down at the burger. Took another bite. It soaked through the bread and into my palms and I didn't care. I needed it. I needed to feel the weight of that food in my gut, like an anchor. Proof I remained.

The Tribune sat on the table, folded neat between the salt and the ketchup bottle. I kept glancing at it, certain some higher hand would reach down and reclaim it. But the paper remained. Black letters on gray paper. Silent and grave.

We ate in silence. The sounds of forks and the low hum of the fan above us. The woman behind the counter filled sugar jars and hummed a tune with no shape to it. A car passed outside and I flinched.

You ever think we'd make it to this, I asked.

Clarke set his fork down.

Not this way. Not with the world going on as though none of it had happened.

Lewis said nothing. He stared out the window, already seeing the train tracks running west.

And I sat there between them, chewing slow, trying to gather myself piece by piece. Trying to believe there was an end to all of it, and beyond that end, a road home.

When we got back to base I didn't wait. I broke from Lewis and Clarke before we even cleared the gate and made for admin. The corridors were half-lit, the air sharp with ammonia and the stale papery breath of old offices. Sailors passed with clipboards in hand, pale and quiet, their shoulders sagging from all the useless waiting. Outside, sunlight came through the blinds in long hard strips across the waxed tile.

I turned the corner and there was Harrow's door. Same brass plate. Same chipped paint. Same air of finality. He was at his desk, just as he always was. That square-jawed bastard who looked carved out of boilerplate. A man who kept exactly five inches of clean space on his desk and let the rest go to hell. The kind of man who looked like he'd been born in uniform and raised by filing cabinets.

I didn't knock.

Sir.

He looked up slow. Blinked once.

Flynn.

I stepped in and held out the folded clipping. The ink had smudged where I'd been squeezing it too tight.

Read this, I said.

He took it slow, distrust already in his hands. Squinted at the print.

Chicago Tribune, he muttered. Jesus Christ.

He read the headline. Then the body. Then again.

Where'd you get this.

Diner in town. Dated today.

He grunted.

You know how many rumors I hear in a week. Dozens. Sailors reading every scrap of print with a gambler's faith, waiting for the golden ticket to turn up.

This isn't a rumor, sir.

He drummed his fingers on the desk.

Navy don't confirm policy in a goddamn newspaper. Could be a leak. Could be nothing.

Says ten points for family allotments. That's me. I sent half my pay home since forty-two.

He looked at me, his face gone hard.

I'll have to make some calls. Could take a day. Could take two.

That's it, he said. I'll get back to you.

Sir.

Dismissed.

I stepped back. Turned. The door latched shut behind me with the final click of a file drawer locking. I stood in the hallway and listened. Nothing but the hum of the overheads and some clerk's typewriter pecking at the silence. My hand still held the ghost of that paper. My mouth tasted of steel.

I walked out stiff, my shoulders locked and my fists in my pockets. A goddamn newspaper. That's what it came down to. Not Wilkins dragging a wounded Marine across the tank deck. Not the blackout nights praying the Jap torpedoes would miss us. Ink on pulp in some far-off office. Three years at sea and the weight of it came to rest on a headline and a phone call.

Outside, the light was thin and cold. The flag above the admin building moved in slow folds. I could hear the wind coming off the lake, steady and low, a voice just out of reach. I stood there a long time and watched it ripple the puddles on the blacktop. My anger cooled and settled low in me, almost prayer.

That night I did not sleep. The pipes ticked. Some poor kid down the row coughed half the night. I lay with my boots on, hands under my head. The mattress was hard as steel. The air held wet wool, rust, and boredom. Sometime past two, a train whistle blew, and it seemed to know my name.

***

Next morning I was out on perimeter patrol when Harrow's clerk found me. The sky was a pale slate and the lake wind came in sharp off the water, carrying the odor of old raw iron that never left the air. My boots left prints in the frost along the gravel path that ringed the administrative buildings. The clerk came trotting up like a man late to his own burial. Thin and stoop-shouldered, his teeth yellow dice, his breath sour from tobacco.

Harrow wants you, he said.

That was all.

I nodded. Turned. My shadow stretched long and pale against the cinderblock wall as I walked back toward admin. My heart thudded slow and deep, buried somewhere below my ribs, waiting to rise. I reached the door and paused. The brass handle was cold. Inside, the fluorescent lights hummed with a hive's low menace.

I stepped in.

The room was quiet. Harrow sat behind his desk, carved down to uniform and bone. His cap hung on a peg, rigid with its own little authority. The desk was half order, half wreck. Paperwork. Ink-stamped forms drying in the dull light.

Enter, he said.

I stepped forward. Parade rest.

You wanted to see me, sir.

He glanced up. A faint light moved in his eyes, low and stubborn.

That article you brought me. It's confirmed. Navy's making a push to reduce personnel. Ten points awarded for home allotments. Applies retroactively.

His words landed with the force of hammer blows.

You were eight short, he said.

Yes sir.

You're not anymore.

He flipped a folder open.

You're two over. It's done. You're going home.

I said nothing. The floor felt lower. My spine locked. My eyes burned.

You'll process out in a couple weeks. Paperwork, transport, the usual mess. You're on the list.

He turned the folder toward me.

Sign here.

I stepped forward and took the pen. My name came out slow, dredged from deep water. Each letter curled tight as wire.

He slid the folder back.

That's all, Flynn.

Thank you, sir.

He said nothing.

I turned and left. The door clicked shut behind me with the finality of a safe locking. The hallway outside was colorless. The vents exhaled the faint scent of brass and polish, long since faded. I stood a moment. Breathing like I'd forgotten how.

I walked the long corridor past the bulletin boards and the men waiting for shots and for forms and for their lives to begin again. I passed them all and didn't say a word.

I walked out into the morning sun. It had burned off the frost and left the walk wet and shining. A bird lifted from the wire at that exact moment, timed by a hand I could not see. A breeze stirred the flag high above the admin roof. I stood and watched it, the cloth rippling soft against the wind with the look of a prayer half-remembered.

I was going home.

***

Back at the barracks I sat on my bunk. Reached for paper. Wrote slow.

Dear Folks,

I've got news. Good news. The war's over. And I'm coming home.

The points came through. Ten more for the money I sent home all these years. It's official. Two points over. Discharge pending.

I don't know what to say except I made it. I'm alive. I'm proud. I'm tired. And I love you.

Your son,

Pat

I folded it careful and carried it to the mailroom with the reverence men usually save for prayer. The day had the color of old steel. The lake wind cut clean through it. I lit a cigarette and watched the clouds roll in.

Later I found Lewis and Clarke behind the canteen, tossing pebbles at a trash can lid. Like boys again.

Well, Clarke said.

It's real, I said.

They stood. Slapped my back. Clarke hugged me. I let him.

You lucky son of a gun, Lewis said.

I grinned. It felt strange in my face.

So what now, Clarke asked.

Now I wait. Now I try to remember what peace feels like.

We sat on crates. The sun dipped. The wind came up. I told them stories I'd never told.

I told them how it was. The life we led out there. How some men made you laugh when you thought you couldn't. How others stood steady when the world tilted and the sky came down. I spoke of friendships forged in heat and steel and hours without sleep. How men endured. Through quiet. Through cussing. Through cards and old songs and what they never said aloud.

I told them about the work. The guns and the grit. How we watched the sky and waited for shadows to fall. How men ran boats through surf and smoke and brought soldiers ashore with a courage older than orders. How every landing asked its question. Every survival gave its answer.

I told them about the engine room. That furnace under the sea. How we worked in the roar and the dark. Breathing oil. Breathing fear. The floor hot under our boots. The steel sweating.

The knowledge always there that a single hit could turn the whole place to fire and silence. But we kept it running. We kept her alive.

There were hard men on that ship. Bastards, some of them. Mean and sharp-edged. But they did their job. Others led without needing to shout. Men who stood in the open when the wind picked up. Who bore the weight without letting it show.

I spoke it low and plain. The truth stood on its own. They listened as men hearing of a ship that had passed out of the world.

The stories slowed. The sky dimmed. Lights came on in the barracks like fireflies behind glass.

Clarke said it quiet.

You didn't come back the same, Flynn.

No.

But you came back.

Yeah. I did.

And I let myself believe maybe that was enough.

THREE DAYS, THREE NIGHTS

It took a week to process me. Physicals and paperwork. Fingerprints and signatures. One last set of shots in the shoulder that left it sore for days. The lines bent back on themselves in cattle-chute turns. Ahead of me, men shuffled forward with dull eyes, clutching their orders. Some cracked jokes. Some looked near tears. All of us emptied by the war and trying to fill the space with the thought of going home.

When the day came, I folded my dungarees for the last time and laid them on the cot. Ran a palm down the rough blue cloth, saying goodbye to a skin I had once worn. I left the barracks slow. Lewis and Clarke met me outside the gates. We stood a long while in the morning light. The trees at the edge of the base stood gold-tipped, bright with the false promise of grace.

You take care of yourself, Lewis said.

You too.

Clarke shook my hand and pulled me in close. You earned it, Pat. Every damn mile.

I nodded. Didn't trust my voice.

And that was it. I entered the base a sailor. I left it a civilian. The map of my life stopped at the gate and left the rest blank.

I rode the train downtown. The city rose around me in glass and smoke and brick. I had fifteen hundred dollars in my pocket. Back pay, hazard bonus, unused leave. It felt as if a fortune had been pressed into my hands. For a kid who grew up with empty cupboards and thrift store coats, it might as well have been gold.

I stepped off the platform into a cold wind. The sky was pewter and low and the streets were already crowding with cars. I walked without knowing where I was going. Just wanted the wind in my coat and my boots on dry land. I passed a bakery, a shoeshine stand, a flower shop with buckets of tired roses. Then I stopped outside a men's clothier. The window was dressed with mannequins in gray wool and sharp black shoes. I went in.

The clerk was a short man with shiny hair and a measuring tape draped round his neck, solemn as a physician. You looking for something special?

Yeah. I just got discharged. Want to look like someone who didn't sleep beside an engine for three years.

He smiled. We can help with that.

He fitted me for a charcoal suit. Single-breasted, soft shoulders, the lapels cut wide in the movie-star fashion. A white shirt so crisp it crackled. A narrow tie the color of old wine. I tried it on before a tall mirror and hardly recognized the man looking back. Clean face, short hair, eyes that had seen too much. I looked as if I might pass for a man who had never heard the scream of a diving Zero or held a dying man's hand in the dark.

The clerk nodded. You clean up well, mister.

Thanks.

I asked where a man might stay if he wanted a room with some class to it. He pointed me down to Dearborn Street.

There's the Dearborn Hotel. Real swank. Not cheap.

That's fine.

I checked in and paid for three nights up front. The man at the counter called me sir. I was shown to a room with a velvet chair, a tall bed, and windows that looked east across the rooftops. I stood there a while with my palms on the glass. Wondering what came next.

That night I went to dinner in the hotel dining room. Ordered steak. Ate it slow with a whiskey on the side. Every bite a prayer. Afterwards I wandered into the lounge. Dark wood, leather seats, a piano played low in the corner. I bought a round for the bar. Hats were tipped. Glasses lifted. Thank you, mister. Much obliged.

Then I saw her.

She sat quiet at the end of the bar, sipping a clear, cold drink. Her hair was dark and pinned, her eyes soft in the candlelight. She looked my way. I smiled and raised a hand. She smiled back. Small. Shy. But it held.

I walked over.

Mind if I buy you a drink?

Not at all.

She offered her name. Irene.

I'm Pat, I said. Just got out.

Out of the service?

Yeah.

Navy?

Yes ma'am.

She sipped her drink. Thank you for that.

We sat and talked. She said she'd just come from California. Honeymoon. Her husband was stationed there.

Army?

Paymaster, she said, almost apologetically. A desk job. Ledgers and payrolls. I don't think he ever left the states.

And you're headed?

To New Jersey. That's home now.

You don't sound sure.

I'm not.

She looked down at her glass. Traced the rim with her finger.

He's a good man. Safe. Predictable. The kind of man mothers hope their daughters marry. But I don't know. He doesn't see me, not really. He sees a housewife, future mother, someone to wear his name.

She looked at me then.

What about you?

What about me?

What comes next?

I shook my head. I joined up at nineteen. I been swabbing decks, loading guns, babysitting diesel engines. Only thing I know how to do is work hard and stay alive.

That's something, she said. That's everything.

We talked until the bar thinned. The piano stopped. The lights dimmed. I offered her a nightcap.

She hesitated. Looked off toward the dark windows.

I don't want to be that kind of woman, she said.

You're not.

She nodded. Okay.

In the room we stood a long time by the window, neither of us speaking. The street below shimmered with rainlight and passing cars, headlights soft flares in the dusk. I could see her reflection in the glass beside mine. Pale and lovely. Uncertain. Her hands clasped at her stomach, trying to keep herself from coming apart.

I reached for her hand. She didn't pull away.

She turned to me. I waited. She leaned in and kissed me once. Soft and unsure. I tasted gin on her lips, and beneath it, the sorrow she had carried too long.

She pulled away. Her voice barely above a whisper.

He's kind. He loves me.

I know.

So do I, maybe. But this feels more real.

I didn't answer. I closed the curtains.

I stood there in the half-dark, waiting. I wasn't going to reach for her, not unless she met me in the wanting of it. After a moment she stepped toward me, quiet as breath, and her arms found mine.

We lived a whole life in those next three days, three nights.

We slept in late and rose slow. Her bare feet padded across the carpet and I watched her from the bed as she pulled the curtains back again. Morning laid itself across her shoulders. We ate toast and soft eggs in the nook by the window, her legs curled in the chair, her hair wet from the shower. I buttered the toast for both of us, and she laughed when I cracked the yolk with the edge of my fork, careful as a man disarming a shell.

You eat as if you're starving, she said.

I thought of ships and islands and men eating from tins in the rain.

I guess I brought some of it home.

She reached across the table and touched my wrist.

We showered together and made love again with the water running cold and the tiles slick beneath our feet. It wasn't hunger by then. It had slowed into tenderness, two people trying to memorize one another by touch alone.

We talked in whispers when the sun went down. We drank too much and kissed until our mouths were numb. She wore my undershirt and danced through the silence, smoking with the window open, ashes falling like prayers.

In the dim quiet of the room, she lay against me with her head on my chest. The window was open a hair, the air cold and gray. I could hear traffic out on Dearborn and a bell ringing faint from somewhere farther off. Irene traced her finger down my side, over the scar by my hip.

That one?

Appendix, I said.

She smiled. Bored surgeon on duty?

I nodded. You could say that.

She kissed it. Still a scar. Still earned.

What was it like? she said.

The war?

Yes.

I looked up at the ceiling and took a breath.

Loud. Hot. Endless. Sometimes beautiful in ways I wish it weren't. Mostly it was waiting. Waiting to be hit. Waiting to hit back.

She was quiet a long time.

I used to imagine it from the movies, she said. Brave men. Clear missions. You save a village and everyone claps.

It's not like that.

No.

She rested her cheek where her hand had been. Her hair carried the clean bite of the hotel shampoo. Her breath was slow, and I could feel the weight of the thing pressing on her.

What is it? I said.

She didn't answer right away. I felt her chest rise and fall.

It's all laid out, she said.

What is?

My life. The name. Mrs. Sinclair. The house with the shutters and the goddamn fence. The roast on Sundays. Four or five kids. A husband who'll be gone more than he's home.

She looked up at me.

The rest of my life is already decided and I haven't even started it yet.

You love him?

She didn't blink.

He's good. He's... steady. He wants to provide. He'll make a good father. But I don't know if he sees me. Not really. I think he sees what he's supposed to have. What his parents want. What the Army thinks he deserves. And I was there. I said yes. But I don't know if I ever really meant it.

She rolled onto her back.

There's already a town waiting. Neighbors I haven't met. Potlucks and ladies' clubs. A whole life scheduled and polite.

Maybe I'll find another army wife and we can drink wine while our husbands count rations and rotate through the Pacific.

Sounds lonely.

It is. I know it is.

What about you? she asked. What now, Pat? You go back to the ranch? Join the family business?

I smiled. There is no ranch. And we never had a business. I joined up before I could vote. I know diesel and saltwater and how to keep a ship moving. I can spot a kamikaze at five hundred yards and shoot till the barrel's too hot to hold. That's what I know.

She touched my cheek.

You're not scared though. That's what I like.

I shrugged. I'm scared plenty.

Not of life, you're not. You just take it as it comes. There's honesty in that. I've never had that.

She turned her head.

I don't know what this makes me, Pat.

I didn't say anything.

I'm scared of being forgotten, she said. Of becoming somebody's wife and nothing more.

She reached for my hand and brought it to her lips.

You're not what I expected, she said.

What did you expect?

I don't know. A sailor with a story. Maybe a lie or two and a little charm.

And instead?

Someone who means what he says. Someone whose hands don't shake and whose heart won't harden. You're rough and honest. I admire that.

It won't get me far.

She looked at me hard.

It might. Not with everyone. But maybe with someone like me, if I wasn't already spoken for.

Irene.

I know. I know.

We said nothing for a while. Just the low hum of the hotel and the faint whir of a fan from the hallway. Somewhere in the building someone laughed too loud, and the walls swallowed it.

We made love again, slow and quiet. Afterwards she cried and didn't know why. And I didn't try to fix it. I just held her. And she held me.

The last morning came in quiet shades. Pale gold through the curtains. She stood at the window in one of my shirts. I sat at the edge of the bed, lacing my boots.

I don't want this to end, she said.

You have a husband, Irene.

She turned to me.

I want to be with you, Pat. I could come with you. South Dakota. I'll buy a coat. I'll learn how to live in snow.

I stood and walked to her. Took her hands.

You can't. That's not your life.

It could be.

No. What we had was good. Better than good. But it's not meant to follow us. We'd only ruin it.

She blinked fast. Her hands were cold in mine.

You're right, she said. You're right.

We held each other for a long time and said nothing. The city hummed beyond the window, indifferent.

I kissed her cheek. Her tears caught on my lips.

Goodbye, Irene.

She touched my face.

Goodbye, Pat.

We packed in silence. Her hand lingered on the bedspread, wanting to fold those three days inside it and carry them away. We rode the elevator without a word. In the lobby we stood as strangers beneath the high chandelier.

Then she turned and walked out into the light. I didn't watch her go.

The doors spun closed behind her and I stood there a long while.

She would've made a good wife. In another life. A better one.

But not this one.

Not mine.

Irene and I came together through those days and nights with a need that carried little shame while it lasted. We burned hot inside that borrowed time, and then the world took us back.

The lobby doors closed behind me and the noise of the city came rushing back, a low and endless tide. The street gleamed with rain, the gutters alive with silver run-off. I stood a while on the curb with my bag in one hand and the weight of three years in the other. A cab came grinding up from the corner, paint dull, chrome streaked with grime. I raised my hand.

The driver rolled his window down, smoke drifting out.

Where to?

Where's the nearest Catholic church?

He squinted through the glass. That'd be Saint Pat's. Not too far. Get in.

I climbed inside. The seat leather was cracked and cold. He shifted into gear and the cab lurched forward. We rolled through the streets, past shuttered stores and corner bars still open from the night before. Streetcars rattled along their tracks, hissing through puddles. The city felt tired, its lights burning with an old exhaustion. The driver hummed under his breath, tuneless and low, and the meter clicked in time with the wheels.

He slowed at a corner and pointed with his chin. There she is.

Saint Patrick's rose out of the gray, a fortress of God. The stone dark and wet, the twin spires cutting into the clouded sky. Gargoyles crouched on the ledges, faces warped with age and rain. The doors were oak and iron-bound, black from years of weather.

The stone steps were worn smooth by the weight of men with sins on their backs. The doors groaned when I pulled them open. I stepped inside and the hush lay over everything. Cold and complete.

Inside was silence. A cathedral silence that swallowed even thought. Light filtered through the stained glass in high slanted beams, fractured into colors that bled across the floor. Dust floated in the air, the ghosts of prayers long spoken. The pews stood empty. The only sound was my footsteps spreading faintly across the cold stone floor.

Christ hung above the altar. The statue was enormous, carved from pale stone. Its ribs stood sharp beneath the surface, and its eyes sat deep in shadow. His arms stretched wide to take in the whole sorrow of the world. I stood before him and could not meet his gaze. There was life in that stone. An eternal mercy beneath the marble. He saw the sorrow I carried on my back. And he did not look away.

You see me, I whispered. You see it all.

I took a seat in a pew and kneeled. I tried to pray but the words would not come. Only the ache in my chest and the sting in my throat.

A priest crossed the far aisle, his robe brushing the floor. I raised a hand.

Father.

He turned, startled. His face was pale and lined, the eyes wary at first, then softening when he saw my uniform coat and the duffel at my side.

Yes, son?

I just got discharged. I've got a train to catch. But I need to confess. I need to leave some things behind.

He nodded once. Come.

We walked together toward the confessionals along the side wall. The wood was dark, the corners polished by the touch of a thousand penitents. I stepped inside and drew the curtain closed behind me. The little screen slid open and I could see his profile through the lattice, faint in the candlelight.

Forgive me, Father, for I have sinned.

And then the words poured out like floodwater. The war. The killing. The drinking. The fighting. The women with names long forgotten. The way I held Irene and pretended we were clean. The loneliness that had turned to anger, and the anger that had turned to sin. The nights on watch when the drums of those engines rolled and I cursed God just loud enough for Him to hear. The faces of men lost beneath the waves. How I thought that God Himself had forgotten us.

He said nothing while I spoke. Only the creak of the booth, the faint sound of his breathing. When the words were gone I sat there in the silence, empty.

At length he spoke.

You have carried a great burden, he said. The world asks much of its soldiers. And sin follows service in its shadow. But confession is not for judgment. It is for mercy.

Say fifty Hail Marys, he said. One hundred Our Fathers. Reflect and go in peace.

The panel slid shut.

And I thought, what a strange mercy it was. The old Catholic way. A ledger in heaven, kept neat and clean by recitations. Words could not scrub a man's hands of all he'd done.

Maybe they could. Maybe they couldn't. I wanted to believe they could.

But I said them anyway.

I stepped out into the church again. The air felt lighter now, though the world outside had not changed. I walked down the aisle toward the doors. Christ watched from His cross. The light had shifted and His face was half in shadow, half in gold. I thought I saw a sadness there, deep and human, for the life that had grown around the sin.

Outside, the wind cut sharp. The street was filling with life again. Newsboys calling, streetcars clanging, coal smoke riding the air. I stood on the steps and drew in a breath deep enough to hurt. I felt a knot loosen deep in me, old and hard-pulled. Somewhere in me I could still feel her hand. Light as breath. Placed in mine and taken back just as quiet. I was trying to shed the Navy, the years of noise and oil and death, like a snake sheds its skin. To step out of it clean and bare and new. I didn't know if it could be done. But I wanted to believe.

I started down the steps. The stone slick. My sea bag pulled at me, but each step came a little lighter. The prayers burned through me, old timber catching at last. I let them climb as smoke and ash and be gone.

HOME

I left Chicago in the morning with a suitcase in my hand and the sea bag riding hard against my shoulder. Navy blues and pea coat. The Hari-Kari knife. A photo album. Japanese propaganda folded away, absolved by distance and dust. Relics of a life I was already walking away from.

The streetcars rattled and steam rose off the grates where last night's rain hid. I walked to the station, and the doorman watched me pass with the solemn look of a man seeing off the dead. In the window glass I caught a face I half knew. The suit was new. The shoes were stiff. So was the man inside them.

The station was iron and light. Pigeons moved in the rafters like slow thoughts. Men in uniform, factory hands with tin pails, a woman with a child old in the eyes. The board clicked its letters and the clock held all the hours at once. I bought a ticket west and took a window seat to watch the city fall behind me.

When the train started the steel sang. Brick fell to pasture and smoke to light. I set my suitcase at my feet and folded the papers that set me free and put them in my coat for fear they might lift and fly if I let them go. The car held the faint traces of coal and hot metal and coffee. I leaned my temple to the glass and let the cold through.

The country opened and I let it work through me. Water stood in the furrows and the crows lifted out of the stubble and pinned themselves to the sky. I thought of the years gone to ash. Of the names I could say that would not answer. The rails beat their steady song, a hammer taking the bend out of iron. I prayed as a man counting debts, asking only that some part of me be heard. The train carved through the land and in its rhythm I heard the truth. That I had not been chosen. Only carried. By grit. By noise. By the hand that does not shake.

At Sioux Falls I stepped down to the platform. The light there had a softer edge. The streets lay slick from rain, the air touched with the dry whisper of grain. I found a bus bound for Wagner and rode south through the low country. The road ran between fields still damp from last night's storm. Cottonwoods bent over the fences and cattle stood dark against the water. I let the hum of the wheels settle through me and felt each turn of the road loosen the tightness in my chest.

By dusk I was home. The bus hissed to a stop at the corner near the feed store and I stepped out with my bag in hand. The town lay quiet in the evening. I heard the small sounds of ordinary life. A door closing somewhere. A man calling his dog home. A screen door clacking on its spring. I stood a moment with the breeze on my face, and something in me felt newly made. The windows glowed and warm bread moved on the air from somewhere close.

I walked home past storefront glass holding the dimming daylight like water, past the churchyard with stones leaning into warmth. A farm truck rolled by and the driver lifted two fingers from the wheel and did not slow. Dust rose and hung and then was gone. Our house sat low in the lot, tar paper gone dull as old bark, the stovepipe a black finger against the sky.

My mom opened the door before my hand found the latch. She seemed smaller. Her hair was fine now, the red giving way to gray, dawn coming through smoke. She set her palm against my cheek, testing the living warmth of me. My dad stood behind her with his hat in his hands and his eyes lowered, solemn as a man in church. We did not spend many words. The ones we did spend were simple and stayed where they were put.

We sat at the table and Mom moved about the stove. She said I looked thin. I told her the Navy preferred us that way. She set bread on a plate with ham and pickles and told me to eat, her voice carrying all the years I had been gone. Dad asked if the papers were in order and I said they were. He nodded and said we will get the roof right before the first snow. That was his way of saying welcome home.

Dan came into the house with his sleeves rolled. We shook hands and slapped each other's shoulders. He said the tar paper had done its time and we ought to put siding on the house while summer held. I told him I'd missed the place, and he said it had missed me too though it'd never say so. We laughed as men who'd shared too much silence. We counted what we had and what we could borrow and we shook hands on it.

That evening Mom spoke of the others. Florence had gone to California, drawn by the promise of warmth and work that never ended. She wrote once from Bakersfield and said the air there shimmered with the hard glare of heat off tin. Orville was thinking on the Navy and I said he would do fine so long as he kept his feet and his head in the same place. Leo was still at home and half grown and went looking for trouble like it owed him money. Dad said Leo was a quick study in the wrong subjects and Mom put a hand on his arm and smiled, tired and proud.

The next day, after the wood siding had been delivered and laid out along the grass, bright with promise, we chalked our lines and raised the first boards. Work has a way of sending the mind off to better country. The hammer spoke and the wood answered and fresh cut pine rose around us and stayed. We worked with little to say. The sun climbed and shadows moved across the yard and the house began to look like it could hold against the weather.

I was on the ladder when I saw her. The hammer in my hand hung quiet a moment.

I'd passed her once in the noise behind a barlight and now she stood in daylight and I felt the old picture click into place.

The house across the street was young and unweathered, raised on the bones of the Kruger place that had burned in 1934, the year of dust and hunger. The fire took it quick and left only the foundation, black and stubborn as a scar. For a decade the ground lay empty, nettles and rain doing the slow work of erasing memory. Now this new house stood in its stead, fresh timber gleaming, windows unblinking in the sun. A young woman stepped out with a pail, her hair the color of chestnut bark, her eyes the color of sky after rain. She looked across and I looked back and felt the hard weather inside me begin to pass.

Who is that, I said.

Dan set a nail and drew the head flush with the wood. The Kubal girl, he said. Dorothy. Bought that little place.

I knew the name. The Kubals farmed out past the river where the Bohemians kept their old tongue and their saints and their ways. I had seen her once at Mama Kale's, back when I was home on leave. She worked there with her sister Blanche, carrying beer to men who could not stop their hands. Seventeen then and the world already showing its teeth. Dan said her husband had been killed somewhere in Europe while she was with child. He said she bought the house before the frost because a widow needs a roof of her own. I watched her lift the pail and go inside and felt an old lock turn open in me.

Days went on. We kept at the siding and I kept finding my eyes drawn across the road. I saw her hang shirts that snapped in the little wind. Saw her carry the baby on her hip and speak soft in the old tongue to settle it. One noon she raised a hand and I raised mine and that was how it began.

The next time I crossed over. She met me at the step with a cloth in her hand, a look that was neither shy nor bold but steady. Her voice was low. Not many words. Each one set true. We spoke about the boards and the price of flour and how the nights had turned kind. She smiled once, and light seemed to enter a place long closed.

I asked the baby's name, and she said Virginia. I said the name back to her, and she nodded as if I had passed a test I did not know I had taken. She said the child slept better now. I said the nights were easier for me too. She regarded me a moment, then looked away. We let the quiet stand between us without shame.

Later that week she spoke of her husband Virgil. She said he had been a sniper and that he was killed in Germany in February 1945. She said it in a voice worn smooth from saying. He never saw the baby. I bought the house before winter. Needed a roof that was mine. No plea in it and no bitterness, but her eyes betrayed the hidden sadness. It was truth set down where it belonged. I told her I was sorry and she answered there was nothing to be sorry for and I knew she was right.

I began to help when help would not shame her. A loose tread on the porch made right. A hinge set straight on the bedroom door. A sack of coal carried to the bin. Sometimes she paid me with coffee in a blue cup and sometimes not at all and both felt proper. In the evenings we sat on the steps and watched the sky go to violet over the wheat lots beyond the last houses. She hummed a low tune in the Bohemian way and the sound of it worked on me like water over stone.

The baby learned my face and reached for me when I came. Dot said the child knew good from bad. It was her small joke, and I carried it warm in my pocket. I began to sleep the whole of the night. The mornings came gentle. Roosters and milk wagons and women talking soft. It seemed to me the soul is a room that can be aired out if a man will open the windows and wait.

One Sunday, Mom watched from the window and said that girl is a strong one. I told her Dot's name and she said bring her by with the baby if she will. The next week Dot crossed with Virginia in her arms. Mom set out bread and jam and bent close to the child. Such eyes, she said, her voice gone gentle. Dot thanked her quietly, and I heard the truth of it. Dad came in from the yard and set his hat on the chair and nodded at Dot and said you've done well with the place. It was the highest praise he had. Dot said there is much to mend and he said there always will be and she smiled. In that small kitchen their words fit together like boards cut square.

I learned more of her people. The Kubal place was big as a parish. Twelve children born to the same house and the fields around it rich with corn and soybeans. They kept cattle for milk and pigs for meat and hens for eggs and the land for everything else. She spoke of it not with pride so much as reverence, the soil holding equal claim with their mother in the making of them. She told me how June set the wheat moving in the fields, long-backed and restless under the wind. On feast days the men danced until dust climbed around them and the sun made it shine with a borrowed gold. Her words were simple and they carried the weight of things that last.

Orville came by one evening and said he had signed his papers. He stood in the yard with his shoulders set and his eyes bright and young. Mom saw to the small things. Dad set his hand on the boy's shoulder. Keep your head, he said. Your feet will know the rest. Orville looked at me and said I am following in your wake. I told him a wake only shows where you have been and you still have to steer where you are going. He grinned the way boys do when they are not afraid enough.

Leo came late, slick with engine grease, the dust of the plains trailing behind him. He had been racing a friend's car out past the grain elevator. He told it bigger than it had been. Mom shook her head and smiled against herself and Dad said a boy made of gasoline will one day learn the cost of fire. Leo laughed and said not tonight. He ruffled Virginia's hair and the child took hold of his finger and would not let go.

We kept working. Some days the old darkness came to sit with me and I did not send it off. I let it sit until it tired and left. I worked. I ate. I sat with Dot and held Virginia. Slowly the darkness came less often, with less authority when it did. I'd known men better than me who never made it off the beach. I never asked why. I only listened for the answer and it never came. A man does not win such things. He outlasts them.

One evening Dorothy said stay to supper. Bread and beans and a small piece of chicken. The lamp burned low and Virginia slept in the next room. Dot told me her husband Virgil had liked storms and would stand in the yard and let the rain take him. She smiled at the window, waiting for the prairie to answer. I told her the sea had a thousand voices and none spoke comfort. She said that sounded true and then we were quiet. After a time she reached her hand across the table and set it lightly on mine. It was warm and sure. There was no claim in it. Only mercy.

By late summer the siding was done and the house held its line against the weather. My parents slept easier and Dad said the place looked proper at last. I kept a habit of crossing the road. Sometimes I brought a coil of wire or a loaf or nothing. Sometimes I found her at the line and we talked little and worked much and it was worth more than talk.

The first night I stayed over, the wind in the eaves carried a note of forgiveness. The light dimmed to an amber hush and Virginia slept between us. Her small breaths rose and fell with the rhythm of a world begun anew. I lay awake a long time listening to the night breathe through the house and the small flex of boards cooling, and in that stillness I felt the peace of the living settle into me at last.

A day later Dot stood with Mom in our kitchen. They spoke of peaches to can and shoes the child would need, handling the state of the world in the same practical voice they might have used for weather or seed. Dad brought in a small box of nails for Dot and said a house eats more iron than a man thinks and she laughed and thanked him. It seemed to me then that the war had begun to loosen its grip through small trades of kindness moving back and forth across the road.

One night I walked home under a sky laid thick with stars. At the gate I turned. Dot stood in her doorway with the lamp behind her and Virginia against her shoulder. The light made a kind of crown around them. Wind moved in the cottonwoods, breath in the chest of a sleeping thing. I thought of all that had been taken and all that might yet be given and felt something in me come level and hold.

I knew then I had crossed back into the country of the living. The war had emptied much from me, and life answered with small mercies given in ordinary ways.

I crossed the road in the morning and Dorothy met me halfway and we spoke of things no ledger would record. She said Virginia needed shoes and I said I would see to it and she said she knew I would and there was no more to say.

The days slipped one into another. The work went on. Seasons turned slow and sure, and life began to take its shape again.

Months later, Dan and I found work at Marty Mission hauling lumber and digging foundations for the new schoolhouse. The days were long and clean and the pay small, but it kept food on the table and the mind at ease. Dot and I grew closer with each passing week. Some evenings I'd walk over after supper, and we'd sit on her porch with the baby between us, watching the light fade from the fields. Lilac and dust moved through the air. Above the water tower, the stars burned clear, and Virginia murmured in her sleep, lost in some gentler world. I had known women before but never peace, and peace was what I found with Dorothy. I fell in love for the first time in my life.

One evening I stayed after she'd put the baby down. The house was quiet, the light dim and flickering with its own tired pulse, and the crickets calling in the dark beyond the open door. She sat across from me at the table, her hands folded, her eyes soft with the kind of knowing that doesn't need to be spoken. I asked her to marry me. The words came plain and quiet, without ceremony. She looked at me for a long moment and then smiled in that slow way of hers, the kind that started in the eyes. She said yes like she had known it all along. She kissed me once, soft and sure, and in that moment the long wandering of my life came to rest.

We were married on July eighth, nineteen forty-six. The morning was bright and clear, the church bells carrying over the town. I was so broke I had to borrow twenty-five dollars from the bank to pay the priest. Dorothy wore a white dress she'd sewn herself and carried a handful of wildflowers tied with string. Virginia wore new shoes and wouldn't stop staring at her mother as though she knew the world was changing.

My mom cried softly and said she hadn't seen a prettier bride. Dad stood stiff as a fencepost and said little, but I caught him wiping his eyes when he thought no one saw. Dan slapped my back and said you've done all right for yourself, and Orville raised a jar and said to the end of all wars. Leo laughed and said to the start of new ones. The church rang with their voices, bright as the morning itself.

After the ceremony we drove out to her father's farm for the reception. The Kubal place sat wide under the sun, the barns painted red and the fields alive with the hum of bees. The yard had filled with family. Cousins stood in clusters near the fence, uncles talked under the trees, and the oilcloth tables sagged beneath roast pork, bread, and pies steaming in the warm air. A fiddle played from the porch, and the sound carried out across the fields. The men drank beer from jars and the women laughed until they cried. The dust rose golden around their feet as they danced. Dot's father stood at the gate and shook my hand with both of his. He said take care of my girl and I said I would.

When it was done we loaded Virginia and her high chair into the back of my old Model T coupe. The road home was quiet, washed with the clean scent of rain and cut hay. The stars were coming out one by one. We crossed the edge of town and turned up the lane. The house sat in darkness, with a single window lit against the night. I pulled the car into the driveway and shut off the engine. The world fell quiet. Dot reached for my hand. Virginia stirred and sighed in her sleep. I sat there a long time listening to the crickets in the grass and the wind singing through the trees.

And in that quiet, the old hold gave way. The war, at last, unhooked its claw from my chest. The shadow that had walked beside me stepped off into the dark. I was home.

Epilogue

The Funeral
Wisconsin. November 2005

The church was vast, its shadows ancient. Candles guttered in their sconces. The air held wax and incense, breath clinging to stone. Outside, the sky had gone black with storm, and rain drummed against the stained glass windows. Thunder moved across the heavens with the weight of old grief.

The priest's voice carried from the altar and fell again, words of dust and return and the promise of heaven. Beyond the rail, the casket lay draped in white and silence. I sat with my family in the front pew and watched the light filter through the colored glass, blue and red and gold upon the marble floor. It shifted across the coffin like some unbidden benediction.

Grief came slowly, pressing the breath from me. I understood then that I stood alone in the world. That the line had ended. The house I came from was gone, if not in wood then in the heart. My father gone and no one left to call me son. I watched the light bend across the marble and felt nothing at all. Drowning in air.

And beneath that numbness lay something deeper still. A kind of final silence. The sorrow that settles into the bones and makes its home there. For when a man loses his father, he loses the last light on the road behind him. There is no one left to carry the map of who you were. No witness to your beginning.

And now he was gone. My father. My guide. The man I had measured myself against. The one I thought unmovable, unshakable. A hero to his country. The man in the doorway of every room I came from.

I sat there with that knowledge heavy as iron. The sky beyond the windows breaking open with rain and thunder and the grief of all things mortal.

When the service was finished, we stood in the hush that follows sorrow, a silence made holy by the dead. My father lay before us. The church air held the echo of the priest's last word, and then even that was gone. The pallbearers bent their knees and the coffin lifted from its stand. It settled onto the wheels with a wooden groan that filled the nave and lingered. One of the bearers slipped, the wheel caught the edge of the rug, and for a moment the whole church seemed to hold its breath. Outside, the storm pressed hard against the walls and the gutters sang with water. We turned and followed. The organ gave one last thunder behind us and then it too was gone.

Behind the sanctuary, the school hallway stretched long and narrow, lit by fluorescent bulbs that buzzed faintly in the stillness. The walls bore the bright work of children's hands, crayon drawings of animals and saints, a construction paper cross bordered in green. We went slowly down that corridor toward the hearse that waited outside. The wheels of the coffin rattled on the tiles. Our footsteps fell in measured time.

Halfway down, the bell rang, a sudden shriek of metal that cut the silence clean in two. Doors opened and children poured into the hallway, their voices a rising tumult, their bodies small and quick as they ran. They streamed around us in a river of noise and color. Their shoes slapped the tile. Their laughter rang wild and high, reckless against the hush we carried like a flag folded in silence.

They did not look. They ran past the coffin as though it was a shadow. Some brushed against it with their shoulders, not knowing, not caring. They spilled out through the doors and into the yard where the rain fell in silver sheets. Their cries mingled with the storm and were carried off into the day.

I stood watching them go and the weight of it came down on me. For in that box lay my father and my hero. He'd gone to war with boyhood clinging to him like a coat not yet outgrown, had stood in the Pacific barely grown, and seen death on the water and lived. To the world he was a sailor who had answered his country's call. To me he was more.

It came to me then that this was how the world had always gone. The old borne out in reverence. The young set loose into the world, sparks from a flame. That in their running was not disrespect but continuity, a sacred trespass. Since the silence took him, grief had filled the room in me. Then a gentleness came and stood beside it. Stormlight spilled through the door, and for a moment I saw my father as a child instead of the man laid in the casket. Running with the others. His arms out. His hair soaked. Vanishing into the storm with joy on his face. And I understood that grief too must give way. That love does not end with the grave.

Still the world turned. Grief could not stop it. Life and death walk the same road, yielding to each other in silence.

A boy listened. A man remembered. And a son did not let his father be forgotten.

ACKNOWLEDGEMENTS

With deepest gratitude to all the men and women, past and present, who have served in uniform.

Their time, courage, blood, and sacrifice have helped preserve the freedoms too easily taken for granted. This book honors them, their families, and all who have carried the cost of service in defense of freedom and democracy.

ABOUT THE AUTHOR

PJ Flynn is the author of Saw the Sea, a World War II novel about youth, survival, and memory aboard an American landing ship in the Pacific. He has lived in Australia since 2001 and leads a quiet, private life.

For publisher inquiries, rights inquiries, reader messages, personal correspondence, or any matter related to Saw the Sea, please contact:
author.pjflynn@gmail.com

If you enjoyed reading Saw the Sea, please consider leaving a review on Amazon or wherever you purchased the book. It would be greatly appreciated and would help other readers discover the novel.

Thank you for reading!